THE LATE BLOOMERS' CLUB

Also by Louise Miller

The City Baker's Guide to Country Living

THE
LATE
BLOOMERS'
CLUB

A NOVEL

LOUISE MILLER

PAMELA DORMAN BOOKS / VIKING

VIKING
An imprint of Penguin Random House LLC
375 Hudson Street
New York, New York 10014
penguin.com

A Pamela Dorman Book/Viking

ISBN 9781101981238 (hardcover)
ISBN 9781101981252 (e-book)

Printed in the United States of America
1   3   5   7   9   10   8   6   4   2

Set in Berling LT Std
Designed by Cassandra Garruzzo

For my sisters,
Brenda and Lisa

THE LATE BLOOMERS' CLUB

PROLOGUE

❧

Freckles would have smelled the change in Peggy Johnson before her car slammed into the town's oldest white oak, but the window on his side had been rolled all the way down and the air out on Pudding Hill Road was thick with the scent of the fresh cow manure the farmer had spread over his kale field just that morning.

Peggy had woken up before dawn like she did every day. She drank a single cup of black coffee at the kitchen table while she read the paper, then she tied an apron around her waist to protect her housedress from grease stains and got to work mixing the batter for a 1-2-3-4 cake. Once the last traces of flour had disappeared into the thick paste of sugar, butter, eggs, and vanilla, Peggy released the beaters from the body of the hand mixer. She held them steady for Freckles.

"There you go, now," she said as he licked the beaters clean.

By the time the cake layers came out of the oven, the sun had burned off the morning fog. Peggy pulled on her hiking boots, their leather cracked and worn, and loaded up the backseat of her car with cakes she had decorated the night before. Four in all, three layers apiece, each frosted with yellow buttercream, pink flowers piped along the edges. Peggy tucked a couple of bunched-up blankets around the boxes to encourage them to stay in place.

"We'll drop these off, then stop at the White Market for more sugar," Peggy said, opening the back door for the dog. "I bet the butcher set aside a few stew bones for you." She reached down and scratched behind his black, velvety ear, which made his back leg kick. "When we get back, I'll take you down to the pond to cool off. Feels like it's going to be a hot one."

Freckles settled on the backseat as Peggy rolled the windows down. They drove up Pudding Hill, the dog stretching his neck out as far as he could, enjoying the warmth of the sun on his cold nose, and the rich scent of mown grass. His ears flapped back as the car picked up speed, and his tags tinkled like the mobile made out of mismatched pieces of tarnished silver that Peggy had hung on the eaves of the back porch. Freckles was dreaming of rolling in the manure-caked field when he heard a gasp. He pulled his head back in to find Peggy slumped over her steering wheel as the car picked up speed. Freckles stood, sniffing the air around Peggy. With a crunch, the car struck the wide trunk of the old oak that marked the property line of the farm. Freckles's thick black body crashed against the back of the driver's seat, then ricocheted back, slamming against the cake boxes before sliding onto the floor.

When he came to, the scents of blood and sugar mixed with gas and butter flooded his snout. The chime of the open door echoed across the field, punctuated by the sound of falling chunks of shattered glass. Freckles pulled himself up, placed his two front paws on the leather seat, and sniffed the back of Peggy's head. She was leaning back, one leg hanging strangely out the open door, her clean dress now covered in bits of soft yellow cake, and her snowy hair streaked with frosting. From across the field the farmer shouted. Freckles climbed over the seat, his body stiff. He leaned over, whining as he licked Peggy's face. He nudged his head under her hand lying splayed on the seat—a surefire way to get Peggy to pet him no matter how tired or busy she was—but it remained still.

The howl of a siren rose and fell in the distance. The farmer was approaching, his gait shifting from a walk to a hobbled sprint. Freckles's hackles stiffened and rose to attention as he pawed at Peggy's still body, pressing the pads of his feet into the familiar softness of her belly.

"Mrs. Johnson," the farmer cried, now a few steps away.

Freckles slid into the backseat, slipping on a greasy cake box.

The sirens grew louder. The farmer was at Peggy's side, frantically shouting her name. An ambulance turned off the state road onto the dirt and stopped abruptly. Two men leapt out, running toward the car.

Freckles slipped out the open window, keeping his body low. He took one step into the woods that lined the road, then another. Behind him, he heard the rumble of men's voices, followed by the sound of car tires kicking up rocks.

Freckles stepped deeper into the woods.

And then suddenly, he was running.

CHAPTER ONE

❧

Some people dream of diner life, others are born into it. It was my dad's vision to own a little breakfast-and-lunch place. He bought the original Worcester Lunch Car Company diner #723 the year I was born and lovingly restored it to its original glory. Sparkly aqua Formica counters and tables were paired with ox-blood Naugahyde stools and benches. Buffalo china cups and plates stamped with the Miss Guthrie logo were special ordered. He polished the hand-stamped chrome backsplash that lined the wall separating the counter from the kitchen until it gleamed. He even managed to find replacement tiles for the black-and-white, basket-weave-patterned floor. It was my mom's idea to add on the dining room out back, and then to extend our hours to include dinner so we could serve enough customers to actually make a living. Together my parents created a successful business and a place for themselves in the heart of the community of Guthrie, Vermont.

I was born into it.

As a baby, I was placed in a high chair next to the stack of Styrofoam take-out containers so my mom could work the hostess stand. When I was steady enough to sit on a stool, I spent my days at the counter drawing pictures with crayons on the back of paper place mats. During my middle-school years I ate cereal in a little two-seater booth in the back, cramming for math tests and finishing assigned reading before the regional bus honked its horn outside. When I turned twelve, my dad finally relented and allowed me to work the cash register on weekends and school vacations. I took over my mom's hostess shift when I was thirteen, the year she started treatment for breast cancer, and have been behind the counter ever since.

Every day at the diner was pretty much the same, until Peggy the cake lady died.

It was the first week of August, the Wednesday after the Coventry County Fair. July had been a brutal month of sticky heat that had the folks of Guthrie escaping to the glacial waters of Lake Willoughby every chance they could get. But when August arrived it brought with it the kind of dry, sunny days and crisp nights that made everyone's heart ache with the desire to stop time. The corn was tall and heavy. Glossy red and purple heirloom tomatoes were piled high on the farmer's market tables. The late summer days were the ones we all lived for, the reason we endured the long, snowy winters and the damp, muddy springs.

I arrived early that morning as I always do, before the bread man delivered his plastic pallets of English muffins and loaves of sliced sandwich bread. I got there even before Charlie, the breakfast cook, who sleepily pushed through the back door and into the kitchen to heat up the griddle and crack the first flats of eggs. I propped the door open behind me so the fresh air could chase away the lingering scent of last night's dinner special. That hour before anything begins is my favorite time of day in the Miss Guthrie Diner. Don't get me wrong—I love the hustle of a busy breakfast shift when every Naugahyde stool is filled and the line for one of the booths stretches out the door. But there is a magic to that hour when it's just me, wiping down the counter, placing napkin-wrapped cutlery and paper place mats at every seat. There's a stillness that reminds me of being in the woods, where everything feels right in the world.

The quiet lasts only an hour, of course, usually less. On that day it had taken just five minutes from the moment I had switched on the dining room lights and turned the window sign to OPEN for the counter to fill with regulars. Some came in pairs—mostly guys who drove to work together. But the majority of regulars arrived alone, reading the *Coventry County Record* while eating their French toast, knowing if they wanted company they could find it. Mom always said it was our job to take care of the morning people of Guthrie, and to make sure the people who served the town—the school bus driver and the folks who plowed the roads—had a good start to their day. She saw the diner as a kind of utility, as necessary as the dump and the post office, and I liked carrying on my mom's spirit of community service and passing it on to the regulars. I kept the coffee fresh, handed out free blueberry muffins, and smiled graciously at the old men who considered a crisp dollar bill a generous tip.

"In the window," Charlie called from the kitchen behind me, his voice rough.

I took a look at him. "Late night?" His beard was more scraggly than usual, his hair was a wiry mess, and the skin under his eyes was puffed like dumplings.

"Filled in at the Bear Cub."

The Bear Cub, in neighboring Shelby, is the closest thing we have to a gay bar in the Northeast Kingdom. It's the sister bar to the Black Bear Tavern here in town. I think when my dad hired Charlie, he had a daydream that Charlie and I might hit it off someday, get married, take over the family business. Dad was never crazy about Sean, my first boyfriend, who eventually became my husband, but he loved Charlie like a long-lost son.

"Meet anyone new?"

Charlie gave me a look that said *Have I ever met anyone new at the Bear Cub?* and nudged the platters of food in the window toward me. I grabbed the two plates—one Hungry Man's Breakfast and one egg-white omelet—and carried them to the end of the counter.

"Here you go, gentlemen," I said, placing the plates down in front of the two customers.

"You know what those places can do to a town, Chris," Burt Grant was saying. He was the owner of the Guthrie Hammer and Nail, the town's only hardware store. "Think about what a place like that could do to my business. To all of the businesses—not just mine."

I reached under the counter for the bottle of ketchup I knew Burt would ask for. I tried my best not to eavesdrop on conversations at the diner, but inevitably I would hear a sentence or two. I figured people wouldn't talk about something out in public if it were truly private, although you'd be surprised. I know more than I thought I ever would about skin tags after one of the regulars had to have hers surgically removed.

"Anything else I can get you?" I asked.

"That's the town bylaw, Grant. My hands are tied," said Chris Franklin, one of the town selectmen. He smiled up at me. "That will do, sweetheart."

I had grown up in the diner, so I didn't mind being called "sweetheart" by regulars like Chris who had known me since I was in pigtails—they said it with affection. Most of the folks around my parents' age saw me as a forty-two-year-old kid. But I wasn't crazy about being called "sweetie" or "honey" by the guys closer to my age. And by a stranger it was a different matter altogether.

"Everything going well, Burt?" I asked. Burt was only a little older than me, but the new creases in his forehead made him look more like his dad every day. I considered giving him Chris's Hungry Man. He looked like he needed the nourishment.

"Can't complain," he said, but he wasn't convincing.

"Nora, in the window," Charlie called.

The bell on the door tinkled, and Fern, the Miss Guthrie's most senior waitress and my oldest friend, rushed in the door. "Sorry, sorry," she called as she pushed her way into the kitchen, trying simultaneously to take off her jacket and pull back her frizzy blond hair into a bun.

"Just one last refill, Nora, if you don't mind?" Sheriff Granby asked as I walked by, nudging his ceramic cup toward the edge of the counter. After I served a couple of plates of poached eggs, I returned to the sheriff with a glass pot of coffee.

"Can I pack you up anything for later?" The sheriff and his wife had just split, and he had been taking most of his morning and evening meals at the diner ever since. I figured no one was making him lunch.

Granby looked up from the paper. "You're an angel. Have any of that shepherd's pie left over from last night?"

"Let me check."

I pushed through the swinging door that separated the counter from the kitchen. Charlie was scrubbing the grill with an iron brush. "Shepherd's?" I asked. Charlie and I had developed our own language over the years, mastering the art of saying the most with the least amount of words.

"Fridge, top right."

Next to the reach-in refrigerator, the back door was open, the still-cool morning air rushing in and cutting through the heat of the kitchen. I pushed plastic containers of coleslaw and pickles out of the way until I spotted the pie plate and pulled it out. Out of the corner of my eye I caught something moving in the backyard. The morning fog had lingered, softening the shape of the Dumpster, the crab apple tree, and the picnic table that I kept for the staff smoke breaks. I heard a rustle of movement through dried leaves. I squinted and pressed my nose to the screen, touching it with my tongue. Between the table and the trees I caught the flick of a white-tipped tail. A snout emerged from behind the table, and then a torso. It was a large dog, jet black with white feet and a white stripe running down his snout. His head would easily come up to my hip. He looked like a Border collie whose kibble was sprinkled with Miracle-Gro.

"Hey, Charlie," I called over my shoulder. "Come here. Doesn't that look like Peggy Johnson's dog, Freckles?"

"Peggy the cake lady?" Charlie wiped his tortoiseshell glasses on his apron and peered out. "Nah. Freckles is brown. And curly. And fat."

"That was Freckles number three. I'm talking about Freckles the fourth."

Peggy delivered her cakes herself and she was usually accompanied by a dog or two. I had only seen the newest Freckles a couple of times when I walked by her car parked in the White Market parking lot.

The dog sniffed the ground under the table, looking for scraps. He nosed a green crab apple on the ground and licked it.

"That dog doesn't even have freckles," Charlie said.

I narrowed my eyes at him and pressed the pie plate into his chest. "Pack that up for Granby. No charge."

Over at the dish station, I grabbed some crumbled scraps of bacon and a soggy slice of toast and stuffed them into my apron. I pushed the screen door slowly, trying not to make a sound. Peggy Johnson's place was miles from town, over on Hunger Mountain Road. She had been my family's next-door neighbor for as long as I could remember, until we had to sell the place. If this was Freckles the fourth, he was far from home. Peggy loved her dogs and they were her constant companions—it was unusual to see one not by her side. Maybe he had got caught up chasing a rabbit and lost his way? It had been a banner year for rabbits. The door slipped from my fingers and snapped shut behind me, squeaking and slamming. The dog's head shot up and he took two steps back.

"Hey there, sweetie. It's okay." I dropped down into a squat and held out the toast in one hand, tossing bits of bacon with the other.

"Come here, now, Freckles. Are you Freckles? Aren't you a good boy?" The dog raised his muzzle in the air, sniffing in a circular motion. He took one step toward me, leaned down and inhaled the bacon on the ground, backed up, then quickly slipped behind the picnic table. With two fingers I eased my phone from my apron, careful not to get grease all over the lens, and snapped a few photos before he disappeared into the woods. I had only captured his tail and a bit of curly fringe that trimmed his back legs.

"Hey, Nora." Fern popped her head out the screen door. "A bus full of antiquers just pulled in."

"I'll be right there." I stood, emptying my pockets of bread scraps and bacon and tossing them toward the trees, then wiped my hands on my apron. I glanced one more time into the woods, but Freckles was nowhere to be seen.

From over Charlie's shoulder I peeked through the window into the dining room at the line of tourists gathered at the door. "It's going to be a busy one."

Fern's hand appeared in the window, fingers heavy with rings, waving a chit. Charlie took it wordlessly from her and turned up the grill. The shepherd's pie lay untouched on his prep table.

"Granby change his mind?" I asked, pulling my hair back into a fresh ponytail.

"Got a call. Didn't even finish his eggs."

Two more tickets appeared in the window. I pushed through the swinging door, grabbed a stack of plastic-coated menus, and got to work.

The Victoria Hotel hasn't been a hotel since the 1950s. In its heyday, at the turn of the last century, it was a magnet for the guests who flocked to the northern mountain towns in search of fresh air and what were thought to be the healing waters of nearby Lake Willoughby. The hotel closed after the owner was arrested for hiring someone to give very thorough massages, and sat empty and decaying until one of the developers in the White family bought it and turned it into apartments.

I moved in a couple of years ago, after my marriage crumbled. I had always assumed I'd grow old in the little farmhouse I had lived in my whole life—but there was a lien on the estate to pay off the nursing home we put my father in once his dementia progressed, and neither I nor my sister, Kit, had the money to settle the debt. In the end it came down to selling the diner or the house—and since the diner had been my one and only career, and the farmhouse we had grown up in was built for a family and not a single woman, the decision seemed clear. We sold the house and paid off the nursing home. I gave Kit everything that was left, including the proceeds of the sale of all the antique furniture our mom had loved, dad's baseball card collection, and everything in the barn, with the agreement that the diner would be mine. The decision suited us both—Kit had the money to fund her next art project and I got to keep the diner that was both my home and my livelihood. But I did everything I could to avoid driving down Hunger Mountain Road. I didn't want to see what the new owners had done to my mother's kitchen garden.

My apartment was nice enough: there was a kitchenette that I used only to boil water for tea, a bathroom with a porcelain tub, a small bedroom, and a living room with floor-to-ceiling, curved windows, their original opalescent glass still in place. That time of year, in the early evening, the room took on a rosy hue that reminded me of the inner petals of pink peonies. I liked the fact that you could tell what month it was by the color and angle of the light.

I had just changed from my work uniform—knee-length

black skirt, light blue Miss Guthrie T-shirt, short white socks under an ugly pair of black sneakers—and into my favorite pair of denim overalls when I heard a knock at the door.

"It's open," I called, assuming it was one of the neighbors. Someone always needed something: a smoke detector battery replaced or help changing their cat's litter box. As the youngest tenant of the Victoria Hotel, it fell on me to take care of these little tasks when my neighbors' sons or daughters weren't around to help.

"Hey." Sean LaPlante, cabinetmaker, know-it-all, Guthrie's newest town council member, and my ex-husband, walked into the living room like he was surveying his estate and immediately began to pace the parameter, opening windows. "How can you breathe in here?"

The first thing I did when Sean and I split was drive the two hours to the Macy's in Burlington to buy a bottle of perfume. It smelled heavy, like church—vetiver and myrrh. The second thing I did was plant petunias in my flower boxes. Lavender-scented laundry detergent came next, followed by tangerine dish soap. Sean was scent sensitive—anything with fragrance gave him a migraine—and I had been living a hypoallergenic, unscented existence up until the divorce. Afterward, whenever I found myself ruminating over some dumb thing he said or did, I spritzed myself. It always made me feel a little better.

"You should have called first," I said, snuffing out the stick of nag champa I had burning on the mantel. "What's up?"

It wasn't that unusual for Sean to drop by. We had had a cordial split, and it had been coming on for years. Sean and I had been together since we first kissed while slow dancing to "Lady in Red" at our freshman semiformal, and had gotten married at twenty. We were already growing apart when we were hit by ten years of endless stress—his mom's depression, my father's Alzheimer's, his dad losing the furniture business, which also meant Sean losing his job, me putting my dad in the nursing home, his brother's son dying in a motorcycle accident. And then there were my infertility problems. I asked him for a separation the morning after my dad's funeral. I think he was relieved—he packed his things and moved out the next day.

Sean banged on one of the windows with his palm, then lifted and lowered it until it moved smoothly. Satisfied that I had proper ventilation, he flopped down on the couch. "Did you hear about Mrs. Johnson?"

"Peggy?" My stomach dropped a couple inches. The image of Freckles, alone in the trees behind the diner, filled my mind. "What about her?"

"There was an accident, Nora. She died."

"Oh, that's awful," I said. Peggy Johnson, Peggy the cake lady, was a fixture in Guthrie. She was like everyone's third grandmother. Peggy was an excellent baker, and if there was an occasion to celebrate, it would include one of Peggy's creations. Baby showers, birthday parties, ribbon-cutting ceremonies, wedding anniversaries—it was unusual for more than a week to go by between slices of one of Peggy's cakes. "What happened?"

"Her car hit that big white oak over on Pudding Hill. Word is she had a heart attack while driving. Didn't feel a thing."

"Poor lady." I tucked my arms into the bib of my overalls and hugged my waist. "She'll be missed."

"I'm going to miss her lemon chiffon. God, she was good. Remember our wedding cake?"

Our wedding cake had been a simple one—just two tiers, a

tender vanilla sponge so soft you could slice it with a spoon, filled with whipped cream and fresh strawberries from the farmer's market. It was the best cake I had ever tasted.

Sean stretched his arm across the back of the couch, making it impossible for me to sit without touching him. He always took up too much room. I grabbed one of the wooden stools from the kitchen and sat down. "I'm so sorry to hear about Mrs. Johnson, Sean, I really am, but why stop by? You could have just called." I cared about Peggy as much as the next Guthrie resident, but it's not like we were so close that I needed to be consoled in person. I was quickly growing annoyed that Sean was in my apartment.

Sean leaned forward, his brown curls falling into his face. He was my age, but he still looked boyish and he knew it. "Here's the thing. I was having a beer over at the Black Bear, and I overheard Granby talking with—what's the name of that guy who works in town records?"

"She lets you go out drinking?" The *she* I was referring to was the new girlfriend, the one he had hooked up with two weeks after we split.

"You know the guy—one of the Burke cousins?"

"You really should know this, now that you are a council member. Jason Burke, he graduated with our class." Our graduation class was only seventy-five students, but Sean has a selective memory. Like how he didn't remember we were only separated and not yet divorced when he hooked up with Margot—his intern—a petite woman from New York City. She had left a lucrative career in PR to learn how to make furniture the old way, before power tools. *She* always smelled like Obsession by Calvin Klein, but apparently that didn't trigger Sean's migraines.

"He did? Wait, did he play baseball?"

"You overheard Granby and Jason Burke . . ."

Sean looked smug. Like most residents of Guthrie, he loved to know the dirt. "Do you have anything to drink?"

"Don't you need to get home?"

"I have time. Beer? Wine? Whiskey?"

"Isn't she waiting for a lesson on mortise joints from the master craftsman?"

"Nora," Sean said in a deflated tone.

My ability to take the wind out of Sean's sails was as much a part of why our marriage failed as anything Sean ever did. I felt bad, but I couldn't help myself. Yes, it was my idea to separate, and yes, I had given up my right to have an opinion about what he was doing with his time and with whom, but *two weeks*. As soon as they were seen picking out eggplants together in the White Market I started getting pitying looks from the customers at the diner.

I let my voice soften. "What did you overhear?"

"Mrs. Johnson had a will."

"I would hope so. She has a lot of land. I'm glad she—I don't know." I stood and went into the kitchen to open a bottle of cold beer and split it into two glasses. I had been about to say that I was glad she had made her wishes known since she didn't have a spouse to rely on to take care of things. Peggy had never married. I think it's why she liked to bake so much—it gave her a chance to get out and be a part of other people's families and celebrations. "Did it mention who would inherit Freckles? I think I saw him behind the diner. He must have been in the car with Peggy. Now he's out wandering around alone."

"Not that I know of."

"What about the funeral? I hope she made arrangements. Remember last year when Gert Brown passed, and that cousin from California insisted on having her cremated and shipped to him?"

"First time Gert left Vermont."

A shiver ran through me. "I wonder who she left it to? I don't think I ever saw her with family. Maybe she donated her estate to the dog warden? I hope it's not summer people. It's too pretty a house to let sit nine months out of the year. Who did she spend Christmas with anyway?"

Sean drank the beer in one swallow. "You."

"Now, you of all people know I work Christmas morning." Sean hated that I served breakfast Christmas morning and pushed me to close the diner every year, but then where would the plow drivers and the loggers without family go? I couldn't leave them out in the cold. Besides, we did pretty good business that day. The waitresses never complained about the tips.

"No, you, Nora. Granby and Burke were saying they thought Peggy had mentioned she was leaving her estate to you."

"What? That doesn't make any sense." I rocked back and forth from heel to toe, staring down at my worn-out pair of red Keds. My right big toe was poking through a hole in the canvas. "She was our neighbor, but we barely spent any time with her. Why would she leave us anything?" Peggy and my family had had a friendly, wave across the yard, drop off a box of fudge at Christmas, trade stalks of rhubarb for some apples kind of relationship, but not a close one. She always kept to herself.

Sean shrugged. "Don't know. Guess she didn't have anyone else to give it to?"

I felt a wave of sadness wash over me. If I had known that we meant that much to her, or that she had so few people in her life, I would have had her over to play crazy eights or something. Peggy was kind. I hated the thought that she didn't have people.

Sean stood up and wrapped his arm around my shoulder. "I see what you are doing there. She wasn't your responsibility."

"I should have been more neighborly." I let myself lean into Sean for just a second. I've always liked his soft, wood-shavings scent. Sean had been my only sweetheart. The boy I lost my virginity to. His body was as familiar to me as the oxblood Naugahyde that covered the stools along the diner counter. I may not have been married to him anymore, but that didn't make me know him any less, or feel any less comfortable around him. When I felt him toy with the strap of my overalls, I twisted out of his embrace. "Well, thanks for telling me. I would rather know before the peanut gallery arrives tomorrow."

"Anytime. You should probably give Kit a call."

"Kit? Why?"

"It's half hers. At least that's what I heard. Peggy left her estate to you and Kit. If it's true, you'll have some decisions to make."

"Right." I took a deep breath. Calling my little sister required mental preparation. Kit, a filmmaker, screenwriter, and actress by trade, thrived on drama, on set and off. My phone calls with her were usually followed by several glasses of wine and a nap.

"How long has it been?"

Kit hadn't been home since our dad's funeral. It would be two years in September. "It's been awhile."

"She must have been home for the holidays," Sean said, "right?"

"Right," I lied. Without Dad to make her feel guilty, and without the traditions that the house held—the balsam fir in the front hall by the staircase, the stockings that mom had embroidered hanging over the fireplace—there wasn't anything pulling Kit to come home. I didn't want Sean to know I had spent the past couple of Christmas afternoons in the back of the Miss Guthrie, long after the door had been locked and the basket-weave tile floor had been swept, watching *Miracle on 34th Street* alone in the kitchen on the little television we kept in back, eating pistachio nuts until my fingertips were red with dye and my belly ached. It was bad enough that I had to imagine him pulling my chair at the LaPlante table out for the intern, as if it had never been anyone else's.

Sean looked around the apartment as if seeing it for the first time. "You doing okay here, Nora? All the lights working? Water pressure good?"

The bathroom faucet leaked steadily, and one of the windows in my bedroom had been painted shut, but the last thing I wanted was to ask Sean LaPlante for help. I put my hand on his elbow and led him to the door. "Nothing the landlord can't fix."

"Need help hanging any pictures? It looks like you just moved in. Why don't you put up some of your paintings?"

Sean was talking about the paintings I did when we were younger, back when I thought I would still have the chance to go to art school, even if it was just a low-residency program. When I moved from our family house into this apartment, my old canvases and paints—untouched and collecting dust after years of neglect—I left behind. That was just something else that Sean wouldn't understand. I decided to spare myself the conversation.

"'Night, Sean."

Sean kissed the top of my head, like he used to. "Let me know if you need anything."

The next day was my day off. I'll sometimes go into the diner for breakfast even when I'm not working—I've never been much of a cook and it seemed silly to stock a refrigerator full of food for just one person when I owned a restaurant—but I wasn't prepared to respond to all the questions about Peggy so I stayed home. And besides, if anything important came up, Fern would fill me in. Peggy's lawyer had called early in the morning and confirmed everything Sean had overheard. He also let me know that Peggy had expressed that she didn't want a funeral or a graveside service, just to be buried quietly next to her parents in the town cemetery, and that all arrangements had already been made with the hospital and the funeral home. I put him in touch with Jack Hickey, our family lawyer, who said he would meet with the estate attorney and get back to me in a week or so. But I didn't need things to be official to make a trip to the feed store while I was running errands, to pick up a fifty-pound bag of dog kibble. Inheritance or no inheritance, Freckles needed to be fed.

I drove up Pudding Hill, kicking up rocks, a dark, rich field covered in rows of lettuce sprouts to my left, scruffy pine woods to my right, trying to gather my memories of Peggy. She never came into the diner except to drop off a cake. She was always friendly, but a little shy. She wasn't in the habit of pausing to share a bit of gossip, even though I'm sure she heard plenty. Most of my memories of Peggy were of her off in the distance, hanging laundry on the clothesline in her backyard or on her porch calling out to one of her dogs. I stopped when I came to the white oak, wincing at the bald patches where the fender had torn off the bark. It was the oldest tree in Guthrie, said to be here over a century. I hoped that the accident hadn't done too much damage. The grass beneath the tree looked scorched, and the leftover bits of windshield glinted in the sun. It was just a few minutes away from her place. She had been so close to home.

Peggy lived at the end of Hunger Mountain Road, past the little farmhouse where Kit and I grew up, in a small, dark red Victorian surrounded by a post-and-rail fence recently repainted a glossy white. I pulled into her driveway that led straight up to her front steps, opening and closing my car door quietly, not wanting to startle Freckles if he was close by. I walked around the exterior of the house, looking for signs of the dog, but the house was surrounded by a thicket of vines and sharp-bladed grasses, which made walking nearly impossible. It looked as if no one had mowed since Peggy had broken her leg some years back. I set the bag of kibble on the front porch, then picked up the mail in the mailbox at the end of her walkway. Not sure what I would find, I braced myself for chaos and turned the doorknob of the front door, but when I stepped inside I was greeted by a well-kept home. The floors had recently been swept. A woven wool blanket was folded squarely and draped over a leather armchair in the sitting room. A fluffy, fleece-lined dog bed lay next to the wood-burning stove. In the kitchen there wasn't a single dirty dish, and the sink itself was wiped down and clean. The walls were lined ceiling to floor with metal cake molds in every shape and size you could imagine—lambs and trucks, rainbows and hearts. I recognized Minnie Mouse and SpongeBob Square-Pants. Two vanilla sheet cakes sat on wire cooling racks on the kitchen counter. I opened the refrigerator. It was crammed with pounds of butter and dozens of eggs. Tubs of sour cream were nestled between cartons of pasteurized egg whites. I made a mental note to come by and empty the fridge before the perishables spoiled. Maybe the food pantry could make good use of its contents.

It really was a cozy home. Braided rugs in dark maroons and rich purples covered the wooden floors. The bright afternoon sun poured in the living room, filtered only by the lacy curtains that hung from all the windows. The room was as warm as a greenhouse. I opened the two windows that faced front and watched the curtains drift in the breeze. Small ceramic statuettes of dogs of every stripe stood in a straight row on the mantel above the fireplace. The walls were hidden behind bookcases stuffed with oversized books—collections of photographs, exhibition catalogs, books about English gardens. Poetry volumes with cracked and broken spines. Travel guides from Burma and Belize. In between the books there were notebooks, some leather bound, a few black-and-marble composition books, and photo albums as well. And of course there was a large selection of cookbooks, classics like *The Boston Cooking-School Cook Book* sitting alongside plastic-bound collections from church groups and the Guthrie Garden Club.

Upstairs, I found a tiny bedroom, the bed made up with an old quilt in the hens-and-chicks pattern, the nightstand and dresser both covered in lace doilies. A pretty flannel nightgown was folded under her pillow, light pink roses on white cotton. There was a jug of water by the bed with an upside-down glass over the top to keep the dust out. They were such intimate things, and I felt shy seeing them. Several library books were stacked on the nightstand as well, a few novels, a book of poems, and a guide to the wildflowers of Vermont. I sat down on the edge of the bed and flipped through the drawings.

The wall facing the bed was covered in old family photos. It was the classic Vermont farmhouse, untouched in some ways by time. I pulled open one of the dresser drawers. The scent of cedar filled my nostrils. Wool sweaters were wrapped in paper, awaiting winter. There was a large trunk at the foot of her bed covered by a thick, bright red blanket.

I made my way back downstairs, opening doors until I came to the one that led to the small, attached barn. I stepped into the cool, dark room expecting to find the usual collection of yard tools and summer lawn chairs, and walked straight into something large and crinkly. It felt like a plastic garbage bag. I waded through the room, waist deep in stuff, pushing aside bags and boxes with my feet and hands until I reached the door that faced the driveway and pushed it open to let in the light. A long workbench hugged the back wall under a pegboard that was bursting with tools, the outline of each tool traced in paint. But that was where the organization ended. The barn was crammed floor to ceiling with—everything. I pushed aside the heavy-duty clear plastic bags, like the one I had walked into, that littered the floor, filled to bursting with soda and beer cans, bubble wrap, corks, and bottle caps, all separated by type and brand. The shelf below the pegboard was lined with rusted coffee cans. I dipped my fingers in each can—they contained nails, bits of wire, coils of silver solder, and drill bits in varying sizes. There were stacks and stacks of plastic bins. I opened one to find it stuffed with remnants of old silk ribbon. There were gallon-sized milk jugs overflowing with pennies and a garbage can full of broken shards of ceramics, all white with a blue toile pattern. There was even a bag full of bags. Every inch of space was spoken for. It looked like an abandoned recycling center, only the room gave the distinct feeling that everything was being saved, not discarded. It didn't seem possible that the person who kept such a tidy house had such a chaotic barn. It felt like I had stepped into the handiwork of two different brains.

Back in the kitchen, I rinsed out Freckles's dog bowls, filled one with fresh water and one with kibble, and set them out on the front porch. It was tempting to leave the back door open for the dog, but I didn't want to be responsible if squirrels or raccoons, or even a bear, decided the little farmhouse would make a nice place to hibernate.

I was sitting in my car about to turn on the ignition when I heard a deep *woof* off in the distance. It sounded like it had come from behind Peggy's house. I kicked off my sneakers, pulled on the pair of hiking boots I always kept in the backseat of my car, tucked my jeans into my socks, and rolled down my shirtsleeves.

The east side of the house wasn't too overgrown—cornflowers and yarrow instead of vines. Once I turned the corner, a rough-looking path appeared before me—not an actual clearing, but the grass looked as if it had been stomped down on repeatedly, perhaps by deer. I followed the trampled-down grass into the trees behind the cabin. Maples and oaks, a few tall spruce mixed in—a typical northern New England forest. Another deep *woof* sounded through the trees, followed by the crunch of paws on leaf litter.

"Freckles," I called, whistling a couple of notes for good measure. I picked up my pace, hoping to at least catch sight of him so I'd know he was okay. Maybe he would recognize my scent from the other day behind the diner? I wished that I had a pocketful of bacon.

I was at least a mile away from the homestead when my foot caught a slick spot on the ground and suddenly I was in the air and then on my back. "Crap," I said, gently testing my legs and arms to make sure nothing was broken. I had landed on a bed of something lumpy and damp, and the wet seeped through my jeans. The air smelled faintly like red wine that had been left too long on the counter. Above me, craggy branches were covered in hairy leaves and hung with russet-colored fruit the size of Ping-Pong balls. Among the fruit, suspended high up on one of the branches, something glinted, a flash of bright yellow. I hoisted myself up to standing and leaned my head back, squinting into the treetops. It looked like a yellow warbler—not a real one, but a good likeness, fashioned out of some sort of metal. I pulled out my phone and snapped a picture of the bright yellow bird against the green leaves. As I walked, the little brown fruit gave way to knobby-looking apples and tiny, bright green quince. Another warbler in one tree, a pair in the next, their sharp, black beaks pointing in the same direction. It felt like they were ushering me forward, inviting me in. The trees were taller than any fruit tree I had ever seen, and had grown wild and close together. It looked as if no one had been cultivating the trees or harvesting their fruit for years. If not for the sculptures, I would have felt that I had stepped into another time, when food was foraged instead of grown.

When the last warbler was a quarter mile behind me, I stopped to take stock. I had always felt comfortable alone in the woods, but I wasn't the best orienteer. I still had a couple of hours before sunset, but the woods swallowed the light long before the fields did. I must have walked for an hour at least, which meant I had the same amount of walking ahead of me. *Just another couple of steps*, I murmured to myself as I ducked under a thick, low branch. There, in the distance, stood a horse. A magnificent bright orange horse in mid gallop. I walked quickly toward it, my ankles rolling as I slipped on the pulpy ground. As I drew closer I saw that the horse's hair seemed to have a stripy pattern. A few steps more and I recognized the familiar blue-traced white letters. This horse was fashioned out of cans of Moxie. Hundreds of them, their lids and bottoms sawed off, the remaining flat planes molded and shaped into the perfect likeness of a carriage horse. The blue and white lettering on the cans was positioned erratically, adding the illusion of texture to its flank. Its mane and tail were made out of a bright blue fishing line. I ran my fingers through its hair, admiring the silkiness of it, which still lingered despite the wind and rain. "Did Peggy make this?" I asked the trees, and wondered what other secrets Peggy had left behind. I longed to keep going farther in. A breeze kicked up and I shivered, my wet clothes cold against my skin. I wiped off the juicy bits of fruit that clung to me, took a couple more photographs of the horse, and reluctantly turned back toward home.

———————

Jack Hickey and I sat in a corner booth late one afternoon, legal pads, copies of birth certificates and death certificates, Peggy's last will and testament, the deed to the Johnson land, and a map spread across the Formica table.

"Now you see here, Nora," Jack said, tapping on a copy of Peggy's will, "I'm as surprised as you are. But it looks like you and your sister are Ms. Johnson's heirs."

"What does that look like, exactly?"

"Two hundred acres, the house, some cleared farmland, and a good amount of old-growth forest. She didn't have any savings to speak of—or an account with the bank, for that matter. I wouldn't be surprised if you find cash stashed somewhere in the house. She has to have done something with all of that cake money. Might want to keep an eye on the place until you've had a chance to go through it thoroughly. Of course, this will all have to go through probate."

I smoothed out the white paper straw wrapper and rolled it into a tight spiral. "How long will probate take?"

"Well, that all depends."

"Would it be all right if I went ahead and took care of the house?" I was worried about the house sitting vacant, uncared for. If it was to be mine, even for a short amount of time, I needed to think about how I was going to heat the place so the pipes wouldn't burst during the first deep freeze. And I needed to make sure teenagers didn't catch wind that there was an empty shelter available for late night parties.

"Of course, go right ahead." Mr. Hickey cleared his throat. "There is one matter you should be aware of."

Mr. Hickey had been my dad's lawyer, and he had handled

selling our house and the transfer of the diner into my name, but he tended to still treat me like a little girl who couldn't handle all the information. I wished he would come into the diner on a Sunday morning during peak color and see me juggle a rush of hungry tourists while taking in vegetable deliveries and keeping everyone's coffee cups filled. "Go ahead, Jack."

"Well, it looks like Peggy was in the process of selling the place. One of them big-everything stores. They claim they had an agreement, but haven't provided the documentation."

A big-box store in Guthrie. That would certainly be a story above the fold in the *Coventry County Record*.

"That seems, I don't know . . . odd, don't you think? Peggy selling her home?" I couldn't imagine her packing up all of her cake pans and life-sized horse sculpture and relocating to a fifty-five-plus community in Florida. "Where would she go?"

"Hard to say. But she needed money for something. She's sold off several parcels of land over the last couple of years. This patch of forest." Jack circled the northeast corner of forestland on the map. "And this little patch of pasture she sold to one of the sheep farmers." Mr. Hickey shuffled through some papers. "From the looks of it, she owed an awful lot of back taxes. Those don't disappear, even when you die." Mr. Hickey gathered up his papers. "There'll be a lien on the estate."

It didn't surprise me that Peggy owed back taxes. Even if she sold a cake a day, the cost of butter alone meant that she couldn't have made much of a profit. But a lien took the option of keeping the house and land off the table. It had never really been on—I couldn't afford to pay out Kit's half of the inheritance, never mind paying the government as well.

"The property isn't zoned for commercial building, but I

heard a rumble that Ms. Johnson had already approached the town council about it. It'll come up during the town meeting, you can bet on that." Mr. Hickey stood, buttoned his suit jacket. "It could be a significant amount of money, Nora. Something for you and your sister to consider. Have you talked to Kitty?"

I stood, smoothing down the waitress apron I still had on, long after my shift had ended, its pockets heavy with loose change. The little bell over the front door rang and the door swung open, but instead of the scent of car exhaust that usually blew in, the air smelled sweetly of orange blossoms. I heard the thump of something heavy being dropped to the ground, and before I could turn around, two purple-sleeved arms wrapped around my waist like tentacles, and suddenly I was being lifted off the ground. For a short person she had strength.

I looked down at Mr. Hickey. "I did talk to Kitty."

Kit put me down, spun me around, and kissed me on both cheeks. "We're home! What's for supper?"

I looked over Kit's red curly head to find a tall, slight-looking man with a mop of thick brown hair sticking out from under a worn silk top hat. It looked as if his nose had been broken at least twice. When my gaze returned to my sister, she was all smiles.

"That's Max," Kit said, as if that explained everything. It didn't surprise me that Kit hadn't come alone—she was always surrounded by new and ever-changing groups of friends who came and went like strays.

Max waved and gave me a slightly apologetic smile. I liked him immediately.

"Good to see you, Nora borealis." Kit grabbed my hands,

holding me at arm's length, then pulling me in close for a hug. Even when we danced as kids she always had to lead.

"Go find an empty booth for you and your friend," I said, trying to sound unfazed at her surprise arrival, as well as her surprise guest, but a smile teased at the edge of my mouth. "I'll go see what Charlie has lined up for specials."

"Let me turn on some lights," I said as I entered my apartment a few steps ahead of Kit and Max. "Here is the living room, and the kitchen." I waved my hand vaguely around the apartment from the center of the living room. With the addition of my boisterous sister and her towering friend, it suddenly felt tiny. "Just put your things anywhere, I guess."

Max carefully placed his army-issue duffle bag and Kit's woven Indian-print bag against the wall and took a seat on my green velvet sofa.

I busied myself in the kitchenette, pulling out olives and a couple of wedges of cheese that Tom Carrigan had given me as a thank-you for comping his lunch when he lost his wallet.

Kit followed me, nudging me over so she could reach into the refrigerator and pull out a bottle of white wine. "God, your fridge is empty. What do you eat?" Kit tore off the metal wrapper and began to open and close every drawer in the kitchen.

"You should have let me know you were coming. I would have gone to the store. Besides, you can't possibly be hungry. You just ate two entrées at the diner." I took the bottle out of her hand and twisted the tip of the wine opener into the cork.

"They were *small* entrées. And I had to finish them. You know how offended Charlie gets if you don't eat every bite."

"Right, so you're not hungry."

"But I'm snacky."

I pushed a plate of cheese and crackers into her hand. "Put this out on the coffee table."

I watched as Kit settled herself on the couch next to Max. She rested her head on his shoulder and took his long-fingered hand into hers. "Wine, please, sister," she called. "Stat."

Here's the thing about my little sister: we're pretty sure that one of us was switched at birth. And I look exactly like my dad, so I know it wasn't me. Over the years there were a fair amount of milkman jokes. Where my mom and I were quiet and bookish, you could always hear Kit from two rooms away. Where my dad and I were nice but reserved, Kit was friendly, really friendly, like a Labrador puppy. She was all movement and energy and enthusiasm. I loved her dearly. And she could be completely exhausting.

"The place looks great, Nora. It's super cute. Do you like your neighbors?"

Most of my neighbors were widows and widowers who found the apartments easier to keep up than the homes they had grown old in. The hall outside my apartment door had the distinct odor of Pond's and Aspercreme.

"It's fine," I said, handing them each a glass of wine. "Quiet. I'm sorry there isn't much space." I looked apologetically over at Max, whose knees were practically up to his chin.

"Nonsense. This is like a palace. Max and I just spent the last three months living in the back of his Vanagon while we were on the road scouting locations."

Max nodded and reached for the bowl of olives. "It was cool. It has a sink and a refrigerator and a bed and everything."

"Locations?" I asked. "Are you working on something?" Kit is a filmmaker. Or at least she was the last time we spoke. She has also been a trapeze artist, a novelist, and the lead singer in an all-girls Kiss cover band, so anything was possible.

"I'll tell you all about it tomorrow." Kit swallowed the wine in two long gulps, then scooched down, laying her head on Max's thigh. Max reached for the blanket I had thrown over the back of the couch and pulled it over my sister, tucking her in. "For now all I want to do is sleep. It was such a long drive from LA."

Max brushed the curls out of Kit's face. I turned away, feeling a little embarrassed. I knew Kitty was an adult, with adult relationships, but I still always saw her as my little sister.

"It's good to see you, Nora," Kit said sleepily.

"Well, the couch folds out. Let me get you some bedding. I'll be out the door early, so you'll have the place to yourself tomorrow."

I walked over to my bedroom, where I kept the extra linen, and pulled out sheets, blankets, and a couple of towels. When I returned, Max was lying on the couch, with Kit stretched out on top of him, snoring gently against his chest. "I'll just leave these here," I said, placing the linens on the chair, and switched off the reading light.

CHAPTER TWO

✻

Guthrie Front Porch Forum

<u>Missing Dog</u>

User: MissGuthrieDiner

Hey, everyone. Peggy (Peggy the cake lady) Johnson's dog Freckles has been missing since Peggy's accident on Wednesday, August 2. Freckles is a Border collie mix (mixed with something BIG), around 100 pounds. He is black with white feet. The tip of his tail is also white, and he has a white stripe running down his muzzle. People who have met Freckles say he is a gentle dog and friendly. If you see him, please contact Nora Huckleberry at the Miss Guthrie Diner. 802-228-0424.

The afternoon light spilled across the empty Formica counter and made the embedded gold and silver flecks glint. The sugar shakers that stood guard looked as if they were lit from within. I framed the jars with my smartphone camera, taking pictures from several angles, trying to capture the light. No one paid me any mind. Charlie had long since stopped commenting on my taking pictures, even when it was in the middle of a lunch rush. I get an occasional odd glance from a customer, but the regulars will offer to move their coffee cups or rearrange the empty creamers on the counter if they catch my gaze lingering on the remnants of their breakfast.

I had just slipped the phone back into my apron when the door opened, the little bell chiming the arrival of Kit and Max.

"Hey, big sis." Kit leaned over the counter and kissed me on both cheeks. "We're starving."

Max smiled from behind her.

I waved my arm, Vanna-style, at the empty front booths. We were in our lull between lunch and dinner. "You must be. It's late—you haven't eaten at all?"

Charlie, through the window, snorted. "Tell her to get her order in in the next five minutes or Sam will make her breakfast."

Sam was one of our part-timers. He was a decent line cook, but no one could top Charlie behind the grill.

"Pancakes, please," Kit called from across the room, settling into one of the booths across from the counter. "With extra blueberries. And hash browns, extra crispy!"

I brought over two waters and handed Max a menu. He had sat beside Kit, instead of across.

"Could I just have a salad?"

"Are you sure?" I glanced at him worriedly.

Kit tore the paper wrapper off a straw and stuck it in her water glass. "He doesn't eat any animal products. Not even honey."

"Let me see what Charlie can do."

Charlie grilled a mountain of vegetables, which he served with rice and black beans left over from last night's burrito special, but not before raising his eyebrows, his way of saying *Let me guess, next you are going to expect me to cook tofu?* I shrugged and nodded my head in affirmation. He made Kit's pancakes "nana-style," which meant they were stacked tall, cut into perfect wedges, and topped with butter and maple syrup, so that the butter and syrup had a chance to melt down the layers before they reached the table. It was something the regulars knew to ask for.

Once I had them fed and watered, I slipped into the booth, sighing, my back and feet grateful for the relief.

Max had taken off his sweater. He was wearing an old V-neck T-shirt, the neck stretched, revealing a black and white tattoo of a woman on his chest. She looked vaguely familiar. "Did you both sleep all right?" I asked, sipping the diet soda that fueled most of my days.

"Yes, thank you," said Max.

"So, we are going to sell, right? Did Mr. Hickey say what the place was worth?" Kit asked as she forked a wedge of pancake into her mouth.

I looked around my shoulder to make sure the dining room was still empty. "Slow down, Kit. Mrs. Johnson hasn't been in the grave for a week yet. These things take time."

Kit glanced at Max. "How much time?"

I shrugged. "I don't know. The estate has to go through probate. I'm sure they want to make sure that no one wants to contest the will. There are back taxes that need to be paid. Mr. Hickey just said a real estate developer claimed to have come to an agreement with Peggy about the property, but they haven't shown him any documentation. It's not like we have a formal offer." I took a long sip of the soda, looking out the window, and thought about the sculptures I had found. There were more of them in the woods, I was sure of it. I wanted a chance to discover what else Peggy Johnson had left behind. "And besides, we need to be thoughtful about who we sell the land to, when we do."

"But we're going to sell the land to the highest bidder, right?" Kit took the saltshaker out of its metal holder and started furiously salting her hash browns.

"Kit, we can't make a decision that will affect the whole town just because someone is offering a lot of money—"

"God forbid something changes around here," Kit said under her breath. She stopped salting. "When you say a lot, exactly what are we talking about?"

I leaned my head back onto the booth. "Do you want to let me in on what's going on?"

Kit glanced over at Max. "We need the money."

"I picked up on that. Don't you have money left over from the house?" I turned my attention from Kit to Max's tattoos. The face of the woman on his chest rose and fell as he ate his breakfast.

"I invested it."

I took a deep breath. It wasn't just that we had sold the house. We had to get rid of all of Dad's Chuck Berry memorabilia. And Mom's collection of antique spinning wheels. All the spare diner parts that Dad had acquired while he worked on the renovation. And I had to find a new home for the small herd of dairy goats I had raised, a hobby I had kept up since the year I won a blue ribbon in 4-H. If we had sold our childhood home so Kit could "invest" in fire-eating classes, I was going to batter and deep-fry her.

"In what?" I tried to keep my tone light, and failed.

Kit winced. "Jesus, Nora. Could you at least hear me out before you decide it's a bad idea?"

"Kitten," Max said, reaching for her arm.

Kit brushed his hand away. "No, I told you she'd be like this."

"Like what?" I crossed my arms.

"Like *this*," she said, folding her arms to match mine, staring me down. "I don't want to talk to you about it if you're going to be all judgy."

I unfolded my arms. "I'm not being like anything." I closed my eyes and took a long sip of the soda, trying to channel my mom's calm demeanor. "Kit, it was your money, you had every right to do whatever you wanted with it," I said.

Kit snorted. To anyone else it would have sounded like I was telling the truth, but Kit knew me better than anyone else.

"Tell her, please," Max said gently. Kit looked up at Max. She took a deep breath. "We're making a movie. A feature."

Max smiled. "It's really good. Your sister is an amazing screen-writer. And director."

Kit sat up straight, beaming. "And Max is an incredible cine-matographer. And animator! I can't wait for you to see his work." Kit grabbed his arm. "Did you bring copies of the shorts?"

"They're on my hard drive."

"You have to watch them. They're breathtaking." Kit reached her arms across the table and made little grippy motions with her hands. I reluctantly put my arms on the table. She grabbed my hands and squeezed.

"Nora, we have this incredible opportunity. One of the orga-nizers of Premiere Festival saw a short we made, and after read-ing our script, she invited us to show the feature at next year's festival, as a part of their Celebration of Indies theme."

"It's huge," Max said.

"It's huge," Kit agreed. "It's a once-in-a-lifetime opportunity.

Producers come to the festival. *Distributors.* Not to mention all the A-list actors and, like, every entertainment reporter in the world. It could be our big break." Kit bounced on the Naugahyde seat, not able to contain her energy. "But we ran into a little trouble while we were shooting."

"Our camera and computer were stolen," Max said.

"We need funds to get new equipment," Kit said, pushing past the theft.

"And lights," said Max.

"And there is postproduction—"

"And travel expenses—"

"We've already maxed out our credit cards." Kit looked a little sheepish. She squeezed my hand again. "And we sort of got behind in our rent and have been living in the Vanagon."

I pulled my hands back. "You're *homeless?*"

The bell above the door tinkled. Fern walked in, singing an old Billie Holiday song.

"I wouldn't describe us as homeless, exactly," Kit said before pushing Max out of the booth. "We're just temporarily without an address. Like gypsies." She sprang up and wrapped her arms around Fern. "Third Degree Fern!" she squealed.

"I know it's not my place . . . but maybe you could just call the developer guy? See what he has to say?" Max gave me a sheepish grin. "I'm sorry. I'm not into crossing the family line, but this is an amazing opportunity. The festival scout was super encouraging. And your sister is brilliant." Max studied the swirly pattern of the Formica table. "Also . . . would it be okay if we stayed another night? Or two? It's really great to have access to a shower."

I looked from him to my little sister. Kit had sat Fern down on one of the stools at the counter and was pinning her hair in a complicated up-do with glittery hair clips. "I'll pick up some soy milk on my way home."

A man wearing a smart, navy blue suit sat in the corner booth, and by his tasseled loafers alone I knew he must be the representative from HG, the corporation that wanted to build a superstore in Guthrie. His classic men's haircut somehow looked extra polished, like it had been styled in a salon and not in a barbershop. I watched him from behind the register. I thought I might catch him wiping off the seat or something—he looked so out of place on the Naugahyde bench, his suit sleeves pressing against the tin rim of the table. Instead, he looked thoughtfully at the menu, waited patiently, and smiled at Fern when she asked if she could take his order.

Our meeting was scheduled for 3:00 P.M. I had offered to meet him someplace neutral, but he had insisted on coming to us. It was 1:30. He must have needed lunch.

"He's kind of cute," Fern said to me as she leaned over to hang her order in the kitchen window. "If you don't mind those ears."

Charlie poked his head out the kitchen window to check him out. "He looks ex-*pen*-sive," Charlie said, doing his best Nina Garcia. Charlie, Fern, and I were faithful *Project Runway* fans. We got together every week and critiqued the designs while eating nachos and drinking Fern's famous margaritas.

I peeked over at the HG rep. The sun was pouring through the window beside him, lighting him from behind, making his protruding ears glow pink. "I don't know. Those are perfectly nice-looking ears."

"See if you can sit next to him during your meeting. He smells really good."

I elbowed Fern in the ribs. "And I smell like ketchup and Windex. No, thank you." Someone had neglected to screw on the top of a squeeze bottle, and ketchup had spilled on me and on the stack of lunch menus. I had spent all of my free time that morning trying to clean them. "Besides, he's here looking for land, not a date."

"You never know," Fern said, grabbing two plates of grilled cheese and fries for a table in the back. "I've met men under stranger circumstances."

Charlie snorted loudly enough for us to hear him in the dining room. Fern had met men under *every* circumstance. At the grocery store. While bowling. At the redemption center. At the sheepdog-herding trials. While getting her eyebrows waxed. There was something about Fern that was magical. She was like Kit in that way.

The man looked over at me and smiled briefly before returning his attention to his neatly folded copy of the *Coventry County Record*.

Kit and Max tumbled in like bear cubs shortly before three and covered the counter with their tossed-off jackets and backpacks. Kit walked behind the counter, poured herself and Max cups of coffee, and helped herself to the last couple of cider donuts in the glass-lidded cake stand that sat on the counter.

"We made the cutest little stop-motion animation today," Kit said, her mouth full of donut. Max pulled out a small, red video camera and flipped open the screen.

"I thought you said you needed a camera?" I said, pointing to the screen, where a wedge of cheese was dancing the tango with a stack of green grapes.

"This is basically a toy," Max said, shrugging. "We use it to film a location we want to remember—"

"Or to do a spur-of-the-moment interview." Kit took the camera out of Max's hands, pushed a couple of buttons, and aimed the lens at me. "So tell me, Nora Huckleberry, what do you think the role of the American diner is in society today?" Kit said in a stentorian voice. "Community gathering place or—"

I held up a menu to cover my face and stepped out of Kit's frame. "No comment."

When I glanced over at the corner table, it was empty. I untied my apron, folded it carefully so the loose change wouldn't spill out onto the floor, and stuffed it beside the register. "Are you ready for this meeting? Just remember, we aren't making a decision today, we are just on a fact-finding mission."

"Dollar amounts are facts," Kit said, raising her coffee cup up to Max. They clinked drinks.

"Kitty," I warned. Kit tended to be an act-first, apologize-later kind of person. I needed to keep her in check. "And keep that thing turned off," I said, pointing to the camera. "We don't want to freak him out."

Fern came out from the kitchen with her hair down, her handbag slung over her shoulder. "All right, sisters. I'll see you tomorrow."

I walked out from behind the counter and looked into the empty dining room. "Has Liz come in yet?" Liz was my night waitress.

"Not yet. She called—something about the starter in her car?

She said she can catch a ride from her husband, but she'll be a bit late."

I looked at the clock over the counter. It was the original, an electric number with an advertisement for Dr Pepper in the center. It was time for our meeting. "You can't stay till she gets here, can you?"

"Sorry, sweetie, but I have to pick up the kids. Charlie can—"

Fern was interrupted by the sound of a man clearing his throat. "Mrs. LaPlante?"

I turned to face him and smiled. "Hi, yes, sorry—it's Ms. Ms. Huckleberry. If you don't mind." I hadn't gotten around to changing my name back since the divorce. It wasn't the LaPlante that bothered me, it was the title. Every time I heard Mrs. it made me feel a tiny bit like a failure.

"Ms. Huckleberry."

The man held out his hand to me and I shook it. He had a practiced grip—not too firm to seem aggressive, but not limp, either. He leaned toward me a fraction of an inch as he shook my hand, and I could smell the cologne he was wearing. Fern was right, he did smell good. Like leather and peat fire and top-shelf whiskey. It was what I imagined a tavern in Ireland would smell like. I had always wanted to see the Cliffs of Moher.

"Elliot Danforth. Great to meet you. And is this Katherine?" He smiled over at my sister.

Kit swiveled on her stool and slid off. "Kit Huckleberry. Excellent to meet you." The thousand thin silver bracelets she wore on both arms clinked as she shook his hand.

He held up a briefcase and pointed it toward an empty booth. Kit and I slid in, leaving Max at the counter. "Shall we get started?"

Elliot Danforth went into his pitch—about what benefits HG would bring to the town of Guthrie—the jobs, the tax revenue, the spending dollars of shoppers from neighboring towns. Kit peppered him with questions, trying to steer him in the direction of time frame, but he wouldn't take the bait.

"Of course, we hope to make this a satisfying offer for you both, Ms. Huckleberry," he said, his voice trailing off.

"Sounds great. Where do we sign?" Kit asked.

"Kit, he hasn't even made the offer," I said, annoyed that she was acting so impulsively, which is to say, acting exactly like herself. "Maybe it won't be to our liking," I said slowly, giving Kit a hard look.

"First things first," Elliot said, smiling warmly, like he knew we were in his pocket. "We've already had the land surveyed. There are some zoning issues, but that is not unusual. I plan to approach the zoning board at the next town meeting. Do you usually attend?"

I nodded. "We close for dinner on town meeting day every month so the whole staff can attend."

A flash of surprise crossed Elliot's face before he returned to his pitch. "We are looking at several other properties in the neighboring communities." He looked at me then, his expression neutral. "But I think Guthrie and HG could form an excellent partnership."

Elliot reached into his suit jacket pocket and retrieved an envelope. He took out a folded piece of paper and slid it across the table. "This was the offer we made to Ms. Johnson."

The bell over the door rang, and an older couple walked in. They waved at us as they took a couple of seats at the counter. Charlie sighed loudly as he wrapped one of the deep-pocketed waitress aprons around his waist and pulled out an order pad and a pen.

Beside me Kit made a small gasping sound. *"It's to my liking,"* she whispered as she held it open for me to see.

It was a lot of money. Potentially a life-changing amount of money, depending on what kind of life you wanted. It was certainly enough to pay off Peggy's debts and to give both Kit and me a new start in life. I thought about how nice it would feel to have some money in the bank for when the next inevitable diner emergency came up. Charlie had just mentioned that the convection oven was acting up again. And a few of the tiles around the men's bathroom sink had come loose and revealed signs of a leaky pipe. It was only a matter of time before the whole floor would need to be redone.

The phone rang, interrupting my thoughts. Charlie handed the couple two menus and grabbed the receiver.

"I know you will want to talk it over. It's a big decision."

"Is this an offer for the whole property, or just the farmland?" I hadn't had the chance to walk deeper into the woods, beyond the Moxie horse, to see if there were any more treasures hiding in the forest.

"That's for the entire property. I can have the surveyor send you over a copy of his notes."

I wondered if the surveyor had come across the horse sculpture. What would a stranger have thought of it?

"Would we be able to remove anything from the property?"

Elliot looked surprised. "We expect the house and barn to stay intact, and any valuable lumber to remain, but of course you may empty the contents of any building on the property."

Kit elbowed me in the ribs. I didn't meet her eye.

Charlie waved the phone receiver in the air. "Hey, Nora, that was Erika. Freckles has been spotted over at the Sugar Maple. She's headed over there right now."

"Thank goodness." I scooted out of the booth. Erika was Guthrie's dog warden, and had been helping me track Freckles down. "I gotta go." I looked at Kit. "Will you hold down the fort? The dinner crowd is going to start filtering in soon. Just stay until Liz gets here."

Kit held up her braceleted arms. "Nora, you remember what happened the last time you asked me to cover—"

"Don't worry, we'll take care of things here," Max interrupted from his seat at the counter.

"I'm staying at the Sugar Maple," Elliot said, standing. "Can I give you a lift?"

"I'm fine on my own, thanks," I said over my shoulder, rushing into the kitchen to grab my jacket and purse.

Margaret Hurley, the owner of the Sugar Maple Inn, stood on the front step, her silver bun bright against the green front door, her gray silk blouse buttoned all the way to her neck despite the heat. Salty, the inn's Irish wolfhound mix, was lying at her feet. Erika was beside her, wearing her official county-issued khaki shirt and pants, complete with a patch on the arm that featured the silhouette of a black Lab stark against a green mountain range. I jogged up the stone walkway to join them.

"It was Freckles, I'm sure of it," Margaret said to me, skipping the formal greeting and getting straight to business. "This one wouldn't stop barking at the back door, so I went over to look. He was by the apple trees. Never seen a dog eat crab apples whole like that before. He took them right off the branch."

"Peggy has fruit trees behind her house. He must be used to eating them."

"And he must be starving. How long has he been missing, Nora?" Erika asked.

"It's been over a week since the accident." I looked past Margaret and Erika. From the front of the inn you couldn't see the crab apple trees at all. "Do you think he's still there? Could we check?"

"Easiest to go through the kitchen. This way."

We followed Margaret through the foyer of the inn, past the sitting room and the dining room and into the kitchen. The scent of mushrooms, caramelizing onions, and brown butter filled the air. Alfred, the Sugar Maple's head chef, was bent over a large stockpot that sat steaming on a cast-iron range.

"Great to see you, ladies," he said, saluting Erika and me with a wooden spoon. "Nora, tell Charlie I'm planning on kicking his butt at poker on Friday."

"Will do." I liked Alfred. He and Charlie were best friends. Alfred liked to sit at the counter on his days off and critique every plate that Charlie sent out to customers. Alfred always found a new way to push his buttons. I'm pretty sure Charlie had a little crush on him. He always did fall for the scruffy, teddy-bear type.

Margaret led us to the back of the kitchen, where three rocking chairs faced a glassed-in porch with a stunning view of a wide lawn that led into a small stand of crab apple trees.

No dog.

"I called to him, and whistled the way I remembered Peggy did, that low whistle like a hermit thrush." Margaret looked a little embarrassed, but she repeated the mournful, flutelike call. "His ears pricked, but when he saw me he spooked and ran." She shrugged. "He might be over by the sugarhouse. Livvy said she put some of Salty's kibble out for him in the yard."

Salty licked his muzzle as he looked longingly toward the trees, as if he had sacrificed the rarest kibble in the world.

Erika raised the pair of binoculars that hung around her neck and peered out into the little orchard. "Let's go see if we can spot him."

"Erika, do you mind if I meet you out there?"

"Of course not," she said, letting herself out the back door.

Margaret and I watched Erika walk out across the lawn, up into the crab apple trees.

"Shame about Peggy. She was a kind person. We did altar guild together, years ago. She had a way with the flowers."

"Did you know her well?"

Margaret scratched behind one of Salty's ears. "Not really, if I'm being honest. We were friendly, mind you. But she was the type to keep to herself." Margaret smiled up at me. "I've always been the type to keep to myself as well. Takes one to know one." Margaret gestured toward one of the rocking chairs that faced the windows. I sat in one and let myself rock back. "Something on your mind?"

"I'm just trying to figure out why she left her place to me and my sister. It's such a big gift."

Margaret sat on the edge of the rocker beside me, keeping her feet firmly planted on the ground. She took a moment, choosing her words carefully. "You know, before Olivia came along, I was thinking about selling the inn."

"Really?" I had heard rumblings about the White family looking to buy the Sugar Maple, but I had assumed it was just gossip.

People loved to talk about the rivalry between Margaret and Jane White. "I can't imagine Guthrie without the Sugar Maple."

Margaret nodded. "Well, I can tell you I'm glad I didn't sell. But when I was considering it and talking to buyers, the most important thing to me was that the Sugar Maple would stay the same. Now, I know a new owner would make changes"— Margaret looked around the kitchen, shaking her head at imaginary renovations—"but I wanted to find someone who understood Guthrie, who would keep the community in mind when they made their choices."

"You heard about the offer from HG."

"Your husband was—"

"Ex," I said, out of habit. Sean and I had been together for so long, I knew it was going to take the town some time to get used to the idea that we really were no longer together, no matter how many times they saw him with the intern at their stand at the farmer's market. She had started a side business making little puzzle boxes out of scrap wood.

"Of course. Sorry, dear."

Margaret gave me a sympathetic smile. I wasn't sure if she was sorry for her mistake or sorry I was divorced.

"Sean was saying something about it over dinner the other night. Sarah mentioned it to me."

"You don't think I should sell Peggy's place to HG."

"It's not my place to tell you what to do, although of course I have my opinions. But I imagine when Peggy decided who to leave her land to, she was thinking about who would make the best decisions about it, for everyone." Margaret reached over and patted my hand. "She loved your parents, like we all did. And she knew that you all struggled. We were heartbroken when you had to sell your place. Maybe she wanted to give you and your sister a second chance out on Hunger Mountain."

Salty, who had been lying at our feet, his tail dangerously close to the blades of the rocking chairs, stood up lazily and walked over to the back door.

"And it looks like she made the right decision. Here you are, looking for her dog." Margaret stood. "I'll keep this one inside so he doesn't scare Freckles away. Of course, you're welcome to look anywhere you like."

She made a clicking sound with her tongue. Salty turned and followed her into the office.

I went out the back door and followed Erika's path up the lawn. I found her kneeling under a tree, using the low branches for cover, her binoculars trained on the tree line that framed the farm. We walked together in silence, looking from side to side, trying to spot any sign of Freckles, until we reached the sugarhouse Margaret had mentioned. On the little porch were two green-and-white-speckled bowls, one with a trace of water at the bottom, the other empty save for a few scattered pieces of kibble.

I sat down on the steps, suddenly tired, and looked down the carriage trail that led into the sugar bush. "It's hard to believe that a month from now those maples will start turning."

Erika ran her fingers through her short blond hair, making it stand on end. "There's something about that humid spell we had, too. I may be superstitious, but it feels like we could be in for an early snowfall."

At just the mention of winter I could feel the months of shoveling snow and salting the sidewalks in front of the diner pressing down on me. It was never too far away. "I hate the thought of him alone out here."

"I do, too." She scanned the area again through her binoculars, peering into the trees. "I'm afraid he's in survival mode, Nora. It might make it harder to catch him."

This immediately brought to mind an image of Freckles in a camo dog coat, stocking up on bottled water and cans of wet dog food. "What do you mean?"

Erika sat beside me. "Some dogs, when they experience a trauma—it's like a switch has been flipped. They go from happy house pet to feral wolf. He's focused purely on survival. That means protecting himself from anyone not in his pack."

"Which is basically everyone, now that Peggy is gone. Could we use some of Peggy's clothes or bedding to lure him?" Peggy's house had a wonderful butter scent to it. Surely that would be a comfort to him.

"Even the dog's owners can be seen as the enemy. I don't mean to sound discouraging. The dogs usually do snap out of it once they are back home."

I thought of Peggy's empty house. Even if we did find Freckles, he wouldn't have a family to help him snap back. For a moment I wondered if the humane thing would be to let him go—but then I pictured him cold and hungry, out in the dark woods full of predators.

"I'm sure we'll find him," Erika continued. "It just means we might have to trap him. And it might take some time until he comes round again."

I stood, shoving my hands into the pockets of my black trousers. I still had on what I considered one of my dressier outfits from the meeting. I picked off the couple of burrs stuck to the hem of my blouse. "I'll update the Front Porch Forum. Someone will find him."

Erika hopped up. "I'll let you know if I hear anything."

I walked around to the parking area in front of the inn where I had left my car, not wanting to bother Margaret when we didn't have any news. I paused for a moment to take in the view. From this high up in the mountains, you could see the patchwork plots of farmland and the church steeples that marked the townships. I had just opened the driver's side door when a Mercedes two-seater pulled into the space to the left of me. Elliot Danforth gracefully unfolded himself from the little car, and walked around the front, leaning on his hood.

"Ms. Huckleberry," he said, smiling. "Did you have any luck?"

I threw my purse onto the passenger seat and turned to face him, keeping the door solidly between us. "No, not yet."

"How long has your dog been missing?" He looked sympathetic, but I found myself questioning how sincere he was.

"He's not mine. It's Ms. Johnson's dog, Freckles. He escaped in the accident, when Peggy passed away."

"That's nice of you to look."

I shrugged. "Someone needs to. He's all alone out there. You can't just inherit someone's everything and not take care of her dog." I found myself becoming angry and had no idea why. "Peggy trusted us to take care of what she cared for. That has to mean something."

"Yes, of course," he said stiffly. Elliot looked uncomfortable.

A wave of embarrassment washed over me. It wasn't Elliot

Danforth's fault that Freckles was missing. And here I was, being terse to a stranger for no reason. "Listen, Mr. Danforth—"

"Elliot."

"Elliot. Listen . . . I'm not sure where Peggy left things with you, but we don't want to rush into anything."

"Your sister gave a different impression." Elliot put his hands in his jacket pockets. It looked like he was trying not to appear hot in his buttoned-up oxford and tie, but his face had a shine to it.

"What did Kit say?"

"She asked how long it would take after you signed the contract to receive the check."

I sighed. Of course she did.

"The answer is no time at all, by the way," he offered.

I took a deep breath. "Look, Kit can be impulsive," I said carefully, "but you need to know we will be making this decision together, and I'm not one to rush into anything. Especially something like this."

"Do you have reservations?"

He said this calmly, as if he were asking me if I had dinner plans, as if I weren't the one thing that stood between him and his big-box goals.

"Of course I have reservations."

He took a few steps toward me, stopping when my car door blocked his path, and absently fiddled with his side-view mirror. "Can I ask what they are? Was it the offer?"

Why is it that people from the city think that money can solve all problems? I can't tell you how many times I've had tourists up from Boston or New York be incredibly rude, and then leave a giant tip, as if to wipe the slate clean. Let me tell you, all is not forgiven. And I'll remember your face when you come back in for dinner, after you've discovered we are the only place still serving food in Guthrie after 8:30 P.M. "We're not just making a decision for our bank accounts, we're making a decision that could affect the whole town, even the surrounding towns."

"Your sister implied that you aren't in a position to keep the land. If that's the case, someone's going to buy it."

I was going to strangle Kit when I got back to my apartment.

"Yes, but if we sold the land to a young farmer, it means one more farm in town. If I sell to you, it means—"

"It means change."

"Yes, exactly. It means change."

Elliot cocked his head to the side. "Is change always a bad thing?"

"I'm the wrong person to ask," I said and climbed into my car. "Look, you should know—if I were making this decision on my own, my answer would be no."

Elliot rested an arm on my car door, and bent down so I could easily see his face. "I respect your thoughtfulness. And your honesty. I want to say take all the time you need." His cell phone pinged loudly. He flinched. "It's just that it can take months, years sometimes, to get the right permissions and permits before we even break ground."

"When do they want a decision by?"

"Officially, yesterday. But I think I can stall them until around the first of October." Elliot Danforth's expression did look apologetic then. The tips of his ears burned red. "That will give the lawyers time with the contracts. Nothing gets done between

Thanksgiving and the New Year. They like to have these matters wrapped up before then."

That gave us less than two months. I'm sure two months felt like an eternity to Kit, but to me it seemed like a blip—certainly not enough time to weigh the needs and wants of the whole community.

"I'll be looking at other properties, of course, so there is a risk in waiting."

I wished suddenly that Peggy had left the land to anyone else.

"There's a risk no matter what I do," I mumbled. No matter what decision we made, if it was anything other than the impossible—keeping Peggy's place exactly how it was—there were going to be consequences.

Elliot rubbed his cheeks unconsciously. His voice lost some of its smoothness. "Look, I know this isn't easy. I don't mean to imply that it is. If it's the community you're concerned about—could I ask you, before you make any final decisions, to hear what the community has to say? Sometimes people will surprise you."

"Guthrie isn't known for its surprises."

"What is Guthrie known for?" He sounded genuinely interested. For the first time I saw him as a person, not a corporate representative.

"Well. For its magnificent leaf peeping. For the Sugar Maple's blue-ribbon apple pie—just try to get a dining-room reservation in October. We hold the world record for lit jack-o'-lanterns—you should try to stay in town for that, if you can. It's pretty spectacular. I don't know. Our library was voted best small-town library in the country a couple of years back. It probably doesn't seem like much, but—"

"It sounds like a special place," he said quietly.

"It is. To us, anyway."

With that, I tugged at my car door so Elliot would let go. He moved toward the back of his car so I wouldn't drive over his toes. I turned away, taking one last glance over toward the crab apples in the hope of spotting Freckles before heading into town.

When I got back to the diner, dinner was in full swing. It was a different crowd in the evening. High school kids filled the booths before play rehearsal or after football practice. Young couples came with their kids, knowing that the waitress would supply them with crayons and a place mat with pictures to color and word-search puzzles to solve, and that no one would pay any mind if a kid started crying. Liz, my night manager, waved hello when she saw me walk in, and nodded toward the kitchen window, through which I could see Kit arguing with Sam, the night cook. Max sat at the counter, drinking a cup of black coffee. I cleared a couple of dirty plates and grabbed a clean rag.

"What's that about?" I asked in a low whisper.

Max smiled. "Sam caught her filming him, and he wants her to erase it. She's insisting that it's her art and that he should withhold judgment until he sees it."

"Can she do that?" I asked as I wiped at the smattering of sugar granules that always seemed to coat the counter, no matter how many times I cleaned it.

"If she released it, she'd have to get him to sign a consent form first." He shrugged. "I've been at the other end of this argument. Personally, I think you have to respect a person's right to stay out of the viewfinder. The world is full of people who actually want to be filmed. Might as well focus your attention on them." Max took a sip of his coffee. "But those are never the people Kit is interested in filming."

"That sounds like my little sister."

"What does?" Kit asked as she made her way down the counter, a grilled cheese in hand. "Are you guys talking about me?" She sounded pleased.

"What else would we be talking about?" I punched Kit lightly in the bicep. "Did you patch things up with Sam? It took me two years of terrible line cooks to find him. Don't mess things up."

"Me, ruin the equilibrium of the Miss Guthrie Diner?" Kit held her hands up in mock horror, twisting her face into Janet Leigh's right before she is stabbed in the shower in *Psycho*.

Max, catching the reference, sang the violin shriek of the score while making exaggerated stabbing motions.

"That reminds me," Kit said, "I convinced projectionist guy—"

"Stan Wilkerson," I interjected. Kit never bothered to learn people's names, even when we were kids. It was always *droopy-suspenders guy* or *hot grocery-bagger guy* or *world's saddest baby*.

Kit rolled her eyes. "I convinced *Stan Wilkerson* to show *Road House* at the Nickelodeon next week, when he told me that the distributor had accidentally sent *The Cook, the Thief, His Wife and Her Lover* instead of *Babette's Feast*."

I shuddered, thinking of how the elderly women who made up the bulk of the Nickelodeon's customer base would have responded to *that* feast scene. "Isn't *Road House* a Patrick Swayze movie?" Kit had eclectic tastes, but I thought that was stretching it even for her.

"*It's quarter to three,*" Max began to croon.

"*There's no one in the place, 'cept you and me,*" Kit joined in.

"*So set 'em up, Joe, I've got a little story I think you should know,*" they sang in unison.

"It's this amazing film noir, starring Richard Widmark," said Max.

"And Ida Lupino," Kit added excitedly, "who plays a tragic cabaret singer at a bar-slash-bowling-alley."

"And the owner, Jefty, is in love with her—"

"Jefty!" Kit shouted.

"But she loves his best friend."

"And she sings this absolutely heartbreaking rendition of 'One for My Baby.'"

Max stood. "Before she starts playing, she lights a cigarette." Max acts out the action, putting two of his fingers to his lips, flicking the thumb of his other hand on an imaginary lighter, and taking a long, deep drag. "And instead of putting it in an ashtray, she balances it precariously on the edge of the piano."

"And she just lets it burn as she plays," Kit added. "Like she couldn't give a single fuck. It's so badass. You have to see it."

If someone were to ask me what was the one thing that Kit and I had in common, no question it was the movies. Both of our parents were film geeks. While other kids were watching Saturday morning cartoons, our mom sat us in front of the entire Frank Capra canon. When our peers were playing with Barbies, Kit and I were acting out scenes from Katharine Hepburn and Spencer Tracy movies. (I always played the Spencer Tracy role, at Kit's insistence—she was a director even then.) John Hughes and Steven Spielberg were our surrogate parents. By the time we were in high school we could sing all the lyrics from every Judy Garland film and none of the lyrics of any pop song on the radio.

"Count me in," I said, making a mental note to pick up some popcorn kernels on the way home. A movie wasn't a movie without popcorn.

The bell over the door chimed, and with a burst of cool air, Walt, who runs the Guthrie recycling center, ambled in.

"Hey, Walt," Kit said and leaned over the counter to kiss his cheek. "How are you doing? Are the recyclers of Guthrie sorting their plastics like you told them to?"

"I heard you were in town, Katherine." He took Kit's hand in his. "Nice to see you've finally come home."

"Can I get you anything, Walt? Charlie made that split pea soup you like." I pulled out my order pad and a pencil.

"Wasn't here for dinner, though I'll have to take some of that to go. The missus will be happy." Walt pulled a folded piece of notebook paper out of his jacket pocket. "Mary wanted me to ask about our great-granddaughter's first birthday cake."

I looked at him blankly. "I'm not sure what you mean."

Walt unfolded the paper. "Mary ordered a cake for Masie's birthday from Peggy. We figured since you inherited Peggy's estate, then you must be taking over her business."

I had never really thought of Peggy baking cakes as a business before. I thought it was just Peggy, being . . . Peggy the cake lady. The woman who likes to bake cakes. But of course I knew that she charged for the cakes. And I didn't remember her ever having another job. It suddenly struck me how easy it is to think you know a person without really knowing them at all.

"The party is on Saturday." Walt read from the paper. "Vanilla sheet cake, with a drawing of a clown holding a bunch of balloons. *Happy 1st Birthday Masie* to be written in green icing. My daughter says green is Masie's favorite color. Don't know how you would come to know the favorite color of a one-year-old." Walt shrugged. "Will it be ready by eight on Saturday morning? If that's too early, Mary could swing by here and pick it up after her Garden Club meeting."

I looked at Kit. She held up her hands in surrender. Neither of us had inherited our mother's talent in the kitchen. I couldn't even manage to bake the Jiffy mix muffins when Charlie was busy. The one time I tried they came out like pasty, artificial-blueberry-flavored hockey pucks. Charlie wouldn't let me near the oven for a week. "Walt, I'm so sorry, but—"

"We'll have it for you by eight," Max interjected.

"But—" Kit and I said.

"By eight. No problem," Max repeated. He pointed to Walt's piece of paper. "Do you mind if we keep that?"

"Sure."

"Thanks, Walt," I said, handing him the brown paper bag with the soup. "You can settle up on this when you pay for the cake."

Walt tipped his scally cap and shuffled out the door.

Kit and I both stared at Max.

"Max, it's kind of you to say yes, but I don't think you realize—" I started.

"You know how I am in the kitchen," Kit said at the same time. "What were you thinking?" Kit turned to me. "Wasn't there a bakery over in Barton? Maybe they could—"

"They closed a couple of years ago."

"What about the place where you get your desserts?"

Max looked shocked. "You don't make your desserts? What kind of diner doesn't make its own desserts? What about that 'Homemade Desserts' sign?" He pointed to the painted sign that hung behind the counter.

My cheeks burned. "When my mom hung the sign, we did have homemade desserts." I looked at Kit. "My shipment from them just arrived yesterday. They have a five-hundred-dollar minimum."

Kit chewed the end of one braid. "There isn't any place a person can get a cake?"

"Peggy filled a niche. I mean, there's Price Chopper, but they use shortening and—"

Max swallowed the last sip of coffee in his cup. "I'll make it."

We both stared at him again.

"I used to be a baker."

The braid fell from Kit's lips. "You used to be a *what*?"

Max shrugged. "When I was in my twenties, I lived at a Zen center in California. I was in charge of baking. It's been awhile . . . but it's not like the technology has changed or anything."

"You are a man of mystery," Kit said with admiration. "What other secret lives have you had?"

I had more practical matters on my mind. "What do you need?" I asked.

"People like what they are used to. I'll need her recipe. First step is finding Peggy's cookbook."

I grabbed my car keys. "Let's get to Peggy's, then."

CHAPTER THREE

❧✻❧

We drove slowly down the long dirt road, the darkness swallowing the fields I knew lay beside us. It was a clear, moonless night. The sky above us was thick with stars. With Kit and Max in the car, it felt like we were driving home, not to Peggy's empty house.

"That's where we grew up," Kit said to Max, pointing at our old place. I kept my eyes trained ahead. The new owners had chopped down the willow tree that I used to read under when it was too hot to be inside. The windows were dark, the driveway empty. Summer people had bought the place, but they couldn't even be bothered to be here in the summer.

I pulled up to Peggy's little red house—looking lonely without the lights on—and turned off the engine.

"All right, here we are," I said, trying to sound more cheerful than I felt, but I couldn't shake the sadness of wondering what it was like out here at night for Peggy, all by herself. Plenty of the old-timers liked their solitude, I reminded myself.

The sound of peepers and cicadas rose up from the field. A bright yellow pinpoint of light flashed and faded.

"Lightning bugs," said Max. He and Kit sprang from the car. I watched Kit capture one with cupped hands, show it to Max, then let it fly away.

Max climbed up the stairs to the front porch in two long steps. "Cool place."

Kit peered in the window. "I remember this house so well, but not the inside. Were we ever invited in?"

"Not that I recall," I said, noticing that the bowls of kibble and water I left out for Freckles sat untouched on the porch. I pushed open the door.

The house had held on to its vanilla sweetness, but it was chilly. Inside, it was pitch dark.

"Do you think her spirit is still here?" Kit asked from behind me. "Do you think she'll haunt the place because she left things unfinished?" She put her hand on my shoulder. "We're here for you, Peggy! Anything you need. Just give us a sign."

"Kit, can you wait until I find a light before you start a séance?" I moved farther into the kitchen, my left hand on the wall, searching for a light switch.

"I'm just saying—Peggy hasn't been gone for too long. I'm planning on sticking around in spirit form for as long as I can."

"Nah," Max said, teasing. "You're going to be reincarnated as a bodhisattva. But if it ends up ghosts are real, you can haunt me all you like. Ow," Max said.

"You okay?" Kit asked.

"Just hit my shin on the edge of something. Nothing supernatural."

"I don't think Peggy is going to haunt her cottage over an undecorated sheet cake," I said, finally finding the string to the overhead kitchen light. A field mouse stood perfectly still, staring at us before scurrying underneath the refrigerator. "And if she does, according to Max it will be finished by Saturday, and then she can rest in peace."

"I wouldn't be so sure of that," Max said, holding up a red-vinyl-covered book.

"Did you find her recipe book?"

"Not exactly." He turned the pages. "Saturday—W&M—vw/rb, gl Happy 1st Birthday Masie," he read.

"What does 'vw/rb' mean?" I asked, peering over to see what he was reading. It was a datebook. Peggy's tiny, precise letters filled the Saturday square in pencil.

"That's the cake flavor—vanilla with . . . raspberry, maybe?"

"Walt didn't mention any filling," I said, squinting down at the book. I needed reading glasses.

Kit elbowed me. "Nora, what if this code refers to something other than cakes? What if she were a spy?"

"Who hid her information in between the layers of cake and frosting."

"And her old Border collies were trained assassins," Kit said, laughter already rising up from her belly.

"Who were working as double agents—"

"Peggy's. Accident. Was. No—" Kit had to gasp for breath.

"It was Freckles!" I choked out, laughing so hard tears ran down my cheeks. "It was Freckles. We have to capture him!"

"Was there some pot smoking I missed out on?" Max asked, but he looked amused.

"It's a game Kit and I used to play when we were little," I explained.

"We called it *What If*," Kit said, wiping her eyes.

"We tried to top the other in silly ideas," I added.

"It usually ended with one of us peeing our pants."

"I see," Max said, smiling.

I reached for the datebook. "Anyway," I said, feeling a little embarrassed, "this must be some sort of shorthand. I'll call Walt and confirm the filling, just to be safe." I closed the book and tossed it onto the counter.

"Wait," Max said. "You're missing the big picture. Look."

Max lay the book on the counter so we all could see it, and slowly began to turn the pages.

Sunday—FF—12cc—s/o.
Tuesday—CSF—c/c 10"r w/wt Good Luck Father Gene.
Thursday—Rotary Club—3L hbc—no coconut. No writing.

Max turned the pages faster. Day after day, week after week, filled with Peggy's clear handwriting. I started to feel a little queasy.

"How far into the future is she booked?"

Max kept flipping. "Things start to slow down in March."

I leaned back against the kitchen counter. I didn't know how long Max would stick around, because I didn't know how long Kit would be able to stay in Guthrie. She was a restless person. Only her lack of resources would hold her in place.

"That's a lot of cakes," was all I could manage.

"Let's just worry about Saturday's cake, and maybe next week's, for now," Max offered, reading the worried look on my face. "We need to find that recipe book."

Max and I dug through all the pine cabinets and drawers of the kitchen and pantry, and looked between the worn copies of *Betty Crocker* and *The Joy of Cooking*. I even checked the refrigerator, remembering my father and the odd places he would put things when the Alzheimer's started to progress. You never know.

"I found it!" Kit called from upstairs, stomping quickly down the narrow staircase. "It was in her room, bedside table, next to a pad of paper. She was making a grocery list."

In Kit's hands was an old biscuit tin with an illustration of a bouquet of English wildflowers barely visible on the lid. She pulled off the top. Inside were greasy index cards, their corners rounded and soft from being touched. A berry-stained 4x6 index card with a recipe in Peggy's now-familiar handwriting slipped to the floor.

1-2-3-4 Cake
4 eggs, separated
1 cup milk
3 cups cake flour (sift and then measure)
4 teaspoons baking powder
½ teaspoon salt
1 cup (2 sticks) unsweetened butter, softened
2 cups sugar
1 teaspoon vanilla

"It's just a list of ingredients," I said, flipping through the cards. "All of these 'recipes.' None of them have instructions. How are you supposed to know what to do?"

Max took the stack of cards from my hands. "That's all I need."

I looked at him doubtfully.

Max sat down at the kitchen table, pulled a clean sheet of paper from the pad Kit had brought downstairs, and began writing down ingredients. "I'll make a list, then check to see what

Peggy already has here in the kitchen. I'm guessing she might have some big flour and sugar bins in the basement. Otherwise she would have needed to go to the market a couple of times a week."

"The fridge is packed solid," I said, patting the door. It was covered in magnets in the shape of woodland creatures. "You shouldn't need much in the way of butter and eggs."

I left Max scribbling away in the kitchen, and went in search of the thermostat. It felt as if the chill of the woods was seeping into the house. Kit must have had the same thought—I found her in the living room, building a fire in the fireplace.

"We'll have to stay here until that burns out," I said. "We don't want any accidents."

Kit balled up some newspaper and placed it under her perfect teepee of kindling. "Nora, I was just thinking." Kit pulled a Zippo lighter from her back pocket, popped it open with a flick of her thumb, and sparked a flame.

I had wondered when this was coming. "Let me guess: you and Max would like to stay here?"

"No. I mean, yes, we'd love to stay here. I know we're driving you nuts."

"You're not driving me nuts," I said, knowing it sounded a little forced.

Kit rolled her eyes. "You do realize that everything you feel gets shouted out through your expressions, right? I've seriously never met a person with a worse poker face than you. It's not a big deal. It's a small place, and if we clear out, you'd have the space to paint again."

"I don't need space to paint."

"Yeah, you do. You can't paint in that tiny bedroom. The fumes will kill you."

"You sound like Sean."

"How is Sean?"

"Who's Sean?" Max called from the kitchen.

"Nobody," I said.

"Nora's husband," Kit said at the same time.

"*Ex*," I said, shooting Kit a look. Kit and Sean were like Abbott and Costello when they got together. And the joke was always on me. They loved nothing more than to make me squirm.

"Did I mention a tarot card reader told me that you and Sean are karmically linked? I don't think this divorce is going to last."

"Okay. You're right. I take it back. You *are* driving me crazy." Seriously, Kit woke up each day talking and continued until she passed out, usually in the early hours of the morning.

"Don't think I didn't notice you trying to change the subject. Where have you been painting? Did you get a studio somewhere?"

"In Guthrie? Last time I checked, the town wasn't teeming with unused loft space. And besides, it doesn't matter. I don't paint anymore."

"That's the dumbest thing I have ever heard in my entire life. Nora, what's the point of—*everything*—if you aren't doing your work?"

"I don't have any 'work' other than running the diner. So you and Max can stay with me. The Realtor is going to start showing the place." Following our lawyer's advice, we had just put Peggy's property on the market.

"But that's not what I was thinking." Kit stood and leaned her head out the door. "Hey, Max, come here."

Max came in holding the box of recipes. "She was a pretty creative baker, I have to say—"

Kit linked her arm in his. "Max, look around. Do you see what I see?"

I followed Max's gaze as he took in the sitting room, the leather chair, the braided rug, the dog figurines. He took his time, really looking at the space closely.

"You're a genius," he said finally.

"Right?" Kit replied, reaching up to kiss him on the cheek. "It's perfect. It's better than the original."

"This room is great. So is the kitchen," Max said, nodding. "I bet the light is gorgeous in here in the morning."

"Wait till you see upstairs," Kit said, grabbing his hand. The two of them disappeared up the staircase.

"Look at this rocking chair," Kit cheered from the top of the steps.

"A claw-foot tub. Unbelievable," Max exclaimed.

They returned downstairs, beaming, transformed.

"All right, what on earth is going on?" I asked, tired of being on the outside.

"We can film here. It's absolutely perfect. That's why we *can't* stay here—it will be much easier if we leave everything set up—the lights, the cameras, the microphones."

"Just taping down the extension cords can take hours," Max explained, as if this cleared everything up.

"But how can this house be in your movie—haven't you already shot most of it?"

"We had shot a lot." Kit stuck a fingernail into her mouth and started chewing. "*Most* might be an exaggeration."

I looked at Max.

"We lost almost everything when the equipment was stolen."

"What about your actors?"

"She has a point," Max said, looking at Kit.

"Simone is already committed to something else." Kit looked sheepish. Based on the stunned look on Max's face, this was news to him.

"And Annie?" he asked in a careful tone.

"We can recast them both. Right from here!" Kit grabbed a notebook and started scribbling. "There's still a local theater here, right, Nora?"

"There's the Guthrie Players, if that's what you mean. And there are the folks at Bread and Puppet. There are usually a fair number of resident artists over there. Most of them are puppet makers, but it is a theater. Some of them might be actors."

Max raked his fingers through his thick brown hair over and over again. It looked as if he had just woken up. "We have about four months."

My head whipped from Max to Kit and back again. "Wait a minute. Four months? I thought the festival wasn't until August."

"They want to see a rough cut in January," Max explained evenly. "Kit, recasting sets us back months."

Kit wrapped her arms around Max's waist and looked up at him, her face doelike. "We could still use those long shots that were saved on your laptop, and the exteriors. If we cast the right people, I know we can do it." Kit snuggled her face into his chest and said into his sweater, "What do you think?"

Max's expression softened. "I think you should have told me about Simone. But fine. You're right. It's a great location. If we can find the right people for the script."

"*When* we find the right people," Kit corrected, and leaned up to kiss him.

I moved to the fireplace, threw on another log, then adjusted it with the poker. The fire finally began to give off some heat. I pulled the leather chair a bit closer and settled into it, covering myself with the woven blanket. The powdery scent of rose perfume surrounded me. When Max went back into the kitchen, Kit plopped down on the couch and sighed.

"He's very forgiving of your chaotic ways," I said, stretching my toes toward the fire. "You're lucky." In the beginning of the end, Sean and I hadn't been able to get through a shopping trip at White's without a power struggle over which brand of converted rice had the most flavor.

"It's not chaos, it's my creative process."

"How long have you been together, anyway?" I asked. Kit and I hadn't had any time alone together since she and Max arrived, and I hadn't had the chance to grill her for the details.

"How long have I been together with who?" Kit asked, lying down in front of the fire.

"Max. Isn't he your boyfriend?"

Kit barked out a laugh. "We're not in junior high, Nora. We're creative partners. He's my cinematographer."

I had heard noises the other night that didn't sound like two people creating much of anything, unless someone had forgotten the birth control. "But you seem so . . . together."

"We are, kinda. I don't know."

"Um, you live together, you spend all of your time together. Are either of you seeing anyone else?"

"Nora, don't be such a fuddy-duddy. Just because two people hang out doesn't mean they have to run and get married."

I bristled. "And what's so wrong with getting married?"

"How's it working out for you?" Kit asked. The words weren't out of her mouth for a second before she sucked in a breath. "Oh, Nora. I didn't mean it that way. It's just—you and Sean were so young, and I hate to see you so unhappy."

"Who said I'm unhappy?"

"Oh, honey," Kit said. "No one has to say it."

Is there anything worse than receiving pity from your little sister?

I stood, feeling the familiar knot in the back of my neck that can only be brought on by Kit. "It's fine if you want to film here, but I don't want you to do anything to mess up the house."

"It's not an action film. We're not going to set it on fire."

"No nailing things into the walls, no scratching up the floor. And you have to keep it clean, in case we get any potential buyers who want to see the place."

"We wouldn't have to worry about potential buyers *or* the house if we just sold to big-box guy."

"Kit," I said, my voice tight, "can you try to see my point of view here? I'm just asking you to keep the house tidy."

"I'm not planning on harming the house, Nora. I'm just saying—if HG buys us out, you know they're probably going to bulldoze the place for a parking lot or something."

"And that doesn't bother you?" I hated the thought of Peggy's house being leveled, like she was never even here. As though her life could be turned over like a compost heap. "I care because I care about the town. I care about Peggy's neighbors—"

"You hate the neighbors. They're summer people."

"—and how all of this will affect them."

Kit rolled on her back and looked up at me. "Nora, don't be like that."

Nora, don't be like that was how most of Kit's and my worst arguments began. "Be like what?"

"Like Nora, patron saint of Guthrie."

I threw the blanket off and stood. "That's enough, Kit. I'm just being pragmatic. I don't think we should sell to HG. There are other options. We could sell this house to someone else, someone local. A summer person, even. We could break the land apart and sell it bit by bit, like Mr. Hickey said Peggy was already doing."

"That would take forever. We don't have that kind of time."

"Selling to HG would *change* things forever. And I would be the one who would have to live with the consequences after you run off to Tauranga or wherever you end up next." That was the one thing I was certain of. Kit would leave, and she would leave a mess behind her. She always did.

Max walked into the room, white, floury handprints on his black jeans. "I found Peggy's stash of baking ingredients in a closet. She's pretty well stocked up. It probably makes sense to bake the cakes here, don't you think?"

I watched Max take in Kit lying on the couch with her eyes closed tight, arms knotted across her chest, then he turned his gaze to me. "Since the cake molds are here and everything." He shrugged. "I think we have the best chance of making them taste like Peggy's if I bake them in her oven. Baking is funny that way. Ovens, ingredients, humidity—even time of day can all have an effect on the finished product."

I let out my breath. "That makes sense," I replied, even though it felt as if nothing did.

❧✻❧

Guthrie Front Porch Forum

<u>Town Meeting Announcement</u>

User: ToG

A town meeting will be held Wednesday, August 23, at 6 p.m., at the town hall.

Refreshments provided by Girl Scout Troop 235. Please bring small bills.

To be discussed:

Article 1: Coventry County Fair—Rebecca Goodwin has started a petition to ban the Mrs. Coventry County pageant. A vote will be taken.

Article 2: HG Corporation—HG Corporation has expressed an interest in opening a shopping area in Guthrie that would be anchored by the store HG, and is actively looking at properties to purchase. Elliot Danforth will give a talk on why the company thinks HG would be of benefit to the town. There will be plenty of time for Q&A, as we expect people will have many questions.

Article 3: Zoning—HG Corporation has asked about the possibility of rezoning the land owned by Nora Huckleberry LaPlante and Katherine Huckleberry, formally the property of Peggy Johnson. This will be a discussion only. A vote will be taken at a future town meeting.

Freckles Sighting

User: JaneWhite

I believe I spotted Mrs. Johnson's missing dog, Freckles, behind the market, eating old donuts near the dumpster. Two of my nephews tried to catch him, but had no luck. He's fast for a dog that large. Mrs. Johnson was a dear friend from the altar guild. We at the White Market are all praying for the safe return of Freckles.

User: SarahT

I saw him there, too! His fur was covered in powdered sugar. I thought he might be rabid or something. Does anyone know if his shots are up-to-date?

User: GuthrieVet

I can confirm that Freckles has up-to-date vaccinations. He isn't rabid.

User: GuthriePD/DW

Thanks, everybody, these tips really help a lot! Keep them coming—Erika

Did You Place a Cake Order with Peggy the Cake Lady?

User: MissGuthrieDiner

Hi, everyone. We are trying to fulfill all of Peggy Johnson's cake orders, but are having a difficult time deciphering her order book. If you have an outstanding cake order, please call Nora Huckleberry at the Miss Guthrie Diner. 802-228-0424.

Please note: We will not be taking new cake orders at this time. Thank you for your understanding.

Open Auditions for Film
User: KitCatB

Do you have a passion for acting? Have you always dreamed of breaking into the cutting-edge world of indie film?

Baker's Dozen Productions is holding auditions for 2 female leads, and an open casting call for extras. E-mail bkrsdzpro@gmail.com for a time slot. Auditions will take place on August 19 from 10–2 at the grange hall. Please bring head shot and resume.

I overslept the next morning. Kit's Saint Nora comment kept turning over in my head. It was Kit's go-to insult. And the way she kept bringing up painting! She acted like I had some deep personality flaw because I wasn't *following my bliss*. When did I have time for bliss? Our mother was diagnosed with breast cancer when I was thirteen and Kit was only six. I spent my teenage years being a mom to Kit and helping out at the diner. Before she was sick, Mom had done everything. She hired and managed the front-of-the-house staff at the diner. She did payroll. Thanks to her, the bills both at the Miss Guthrie and at home were always paid on time and the checkbooks were in perfect balance. Plus she kept the house and took care of us kids. Dad had his own role in our family. He was good at fixing things, and knowing all the names of plants and birds that you might run into in the woods. And he was an excellent bread baker—we used to serve homemade bread at the diner until Dad was forced to retire. But his main job was making us giggle at the dinner table, telling stories about his childhood and making Mom blush. When the chemo made Mom too sick to get out of bed, I began to take over everything she did. And after she died, I shouldered some of the things my grief-stricken father did, too. By the time Kit left for college I was already married to Sean and running the Miss Guthrie. Kit managed to forget all of this whenever she was comparing my life to hers.

When I arrived at the diner at 5:30 the following morning, Charlie was already in the kitchen frying onions and red peppers for the hash browns, listening to the oldies station, and attempting to reach a Frankie Valli high note in his painfully off-key tenor. He nodded at me when he saw me walk in.

"All right?"

"Yeah," I said, pulling off my jean jacket and hanging it on one of the pegs near the time clock. "Just slept through my alarm."

There were several messages scrawled on a pad of paper by the telephone. I scanned for signs of Freckles, but they were all calls about cakes. I shoved the pad in my purse so I would remember to bring it to Max.

I fell into the familiar rhythm of opening the diner: setting out place mats, coffee cups, and silverware; making up little dishes of shelf-stable creamers and placing them on all the tables; refilling the sugar shakers and stuffing blue and pink packets of sugar substitute into their holders; filling up ice water pitchers; writing Charlie's special—today was an omelet with heirloom tomatoes, goat cheese, and basil—on the neon specials board. Last was filling the giant urns with coffee. We'd go through three before the morning settled down.

At six o'clock I turned on the houselights and flipped the little sign in the window to OPEN. I poured myself a big cup of coffee and topped it off with four creamers. I was only on my third sip when the bell rang. Sheriff Granby took his usual seat at the end of the counter, near the register. I liked to think he was protecting the cash from thieves.

I poured Granby a cup of coffee and placed it in front of him. "How's things? Are you keeping the peace?" I asked, pulling out my order pad.

"Bit of a tussle down at the Black Bear last night, but nothing serious."

"Surprised it was there and not the Greasy Pole." The Black Bear was someplace you could take your grandmother for lunch, and your girlfriend for a couple of beers. The Greasy Pole was the bar where the loggers spent their free time. They could be a rough bunch.

"Between two brothers. Family thing."

The bell rang again. Burt Grant from the hardware store came in, followed by my ex-husband. I wondered if they were having breakfast together, but they took seats at different ends of the counter.

"What can I get you, sheriff?"

"That special, if you don't mind, Nora. And a muffin if it's blueberry."

I smiled at him as I grabbed a couple of menus. "You got it."

I served Burt a cup of coffee, gave Sean a stern look, and headed into the kitchen. No one needs to see their ex-husband before the sun has come up.

The muffins were still warm in their tins. I picked one out and turned it upside down, trying to determine what kind of fruit flecked the surface. "Charlie, what are these?"

"Box said berry."

I split one open and sniffed. Inside, the pale surface was flecked with blue, red, and pink bits of some fruitlike substance. It smelled like a combination of Crunch Berries cereal and Starburst. I placed the muffin down on a bright blue plate, pulled out my smartphone, and snapped a couple of pictures.

"You better get out there," Charlie said, peering out the kitchen window and into the dining room. "The natives are getting restless."

"One special," I said over my shoulder.

When I returned, every seat at the counter was taken by someone I knew. It's not uncommon for the town manager, the presidents of the Rotary Club and Kiwanis, and several of the volunteer fire department all to be eating eggs at my counter at the same time. The citizens of Guthrie may be under the impression that decisions get made at the monthly town meeting, but I know for a fact that everything from the school budgets to how much sand to order for the winter to the dates of next year's Coventry County Fair was hashed out first over buttered toast and hot coffee. But the stools were not usually full this early, before I had a chance to finish my side work.

I filled up a coffeepot and poured my way down the counter. When I arrived in front of Sean I held the coffeepot back, eyebrows raised.

"What? Nora, don't tease a man like that." He pushed his empty cup toward me. "Please may I have some coffee?"

"What's going on here?" I asked in a low tone, smiling over Sean's head at Jeff Rutland, who owned the feed store in neighboring Lyndonville.

Sean shrugged. "I'm just here for pancakes."

"What, she doesn't get up in the morning and make you breakfast?" I flipped over the coffee cup of the fireman who was sitting next to him and filled it. "What can I get you, Jack?"

Sean stood, walked around the counter, and filled his cup directly from the urn. "There are rumors flying around about what you're going to do with Peggy's land," he said into my ear. I waved him off like he was a fly. "I'll take the Truck Stop, eggs scrambled. Banana pancakes, sausage," he said as he slid back onto his seat.

The bell over the door kept chiming, and by 6:30 all the booths in the front of the restaurant were taken. Fern wasn't scheduled to come in until seven. I could barely manage to keep everyone's coffee cup full.

"Is it true you're selling Peggy's land to a big-box store, Nora?" Burt Grant asked when I served him his Belgian waffle.

I handed him a little jar of pure maple syrup instead of the imitation kind in apology. Burt and his hardware store had the most to lose if a business like HG moved in. "We did have a meeting with them, Burt. Peggy was in talks with them about selling when she passed."

"I heard they want to clear-cut the whole hundred-plus acres of woods behind her house," said my elderly neighbor Pat. "Sell the trees, then pave the whole thing over."

"Will they hire local?" asked John LeFerrier, whose family owned one of the logging companies. "We could use the work."

"Good hardwood up in that orchard," Walt commented. "I remember fruit picking behind the Johnsons' when I was a boy. Shouldn't be clear-cut—some of those trees could catch a good price to someone like Betsy Caleb over in Danville."

Sean nodded in agreement. "She got a lathe last spring. Did you see the bowls she was selling at the farmer's market?" Nods all around the room. "Of course, I'd love to get my hands on some of that wood myself," Sean added, winking at me. "Could I still get a family discount, Nora?"

Some of the men in the diner laughed, and I felt the blood rise to my cheeks. "I'm pretty sure there was a 'no discount' clause written into our divorce papers," I said, slapping down his bill in front of him. "That includes breakfast."

Charlie high-fived me through the window before handing me a plate of cinnamon French toast. He never liked Sean much.

"Sheriff over in Littleton said traffic increased three hundred percent when their box store moved in," Granby said. "Needed to hire four more deputies just to keep up with the influx."

"That a good thing or a bad thing?" someone asked.

Granby shrugged. "I don't know. I like keeping the force small. I know all the deputies and their families. I can count on them."

I wondered if his force was feeling more like family since his wife left him. I put a cider donut on a plate and placed it in front of him.

"But it would mean more jobs," one of the furniture makers said. "Some good jobs, too. I'd like to work for the town. Good pay. Insurance. A pension."

The crowd mumbled in agreement. Who wouldn't want that kind of security? So many of the citizens of Guthrie relied on the tourists for their living—leaf peepers in the fall, skiers in the winter, folks from Boston and New York and Montreal in the summer; it was a life full of ups and downs and leaps of faith. A winter without snow or a wet summer could mean trouble. I know I couldn't keep the diner open if my only customers were the folks of Guthrie and the neighboring towns.

"And more tax money would give us the funds to make some upgrades. The shelter is badly in need of a new roof," Erika offered.

Burt stood up and cleared his throat. "But those kinds of developments kill downtowns, Nora. Who's going to come to the Hammer and Nail when they can get their ice melt and garden shears for pennies on the dollar? Plus all of their groceries?" Burt put his hand on the shoulder of John Harrington, who owned Guthrie Books. "And pick up the latest Nora Roberts at the same time?"

John looked up at me. I gave him a donut, too.

"I know you all have concerns," I said, holding up my hands. "Mr. Danforth of HG will be at the town meeting next week to answer all of your questions."

"But you'll have the final say," Burt said.

"Me and Kit," I said, not wanting to bear the burden alone.

The door bell rang, and in walked Fern, her frizzy blond hair woven into a perfect French braid. She laughed as she took in the crowd. "Don't you all know better than to come in before my shift starts? Nora is a terrible waitress."

The mood immediately lifted, as it always does when Fern arrives. "My savior," I whispered as she breezed past me.

"My two girls spent the whole ride to school explaining to me why I am the most horrible, unfair mother in the entire state of Vermont, so I appreciate the compliment." In a matter of seconds, Fern appeared with her apron on, menus in hand, ready to seat the parties waiting at the door. One by one the morning regulars paid their bills and filtered out the door. "Do me a favor and bus those tables while I take these orders?" she asked as she ushered another group of tourists into the back dining room.

I grabbed a black plastic bus bucket and made my way around the room picking up plates and cups, throwing ripped-open sugar packets and wrinkled straw wrappers in the bin, and dropping piles of change and dollar bills into my apron. When I got to the last table, the one in the corner, underneath a clean napkin I found a little bird the size of a saltshaker. It had been fashioned out of twist ties. A folded five-dollar bill was tucked under one of its wings. It looked like a miniature model of one of the warblers in the woods behind Peggy's house. I whipped around, scanning the diner. Most of the regulars had cleared out, and the counter and dining room were filling with people from neighboring towns and travelers passing through.

"Did you see who was sitting here?" I asked Fern as she walked by.

"In that ruckus?" Fern shook her head. "Why, did they stiff you?"

"Nope," I said, pocketing the songbird. "They left a good tip."

"So what are you thinking of doing, Nor?" Charlie had come out from the kitchen and was refilling his giant steel tumbler with coffee. "Are you considering selling out?"

Fern threw an ice cube at Charlie's back. "Easy for you to say, Charlie. You have a steady job."

"And a second job," Charlie said, a little offended. He had been on his own since he was a teenager and was proud of making his way all this time.

"My point exactly. Dan hasn't had steady work since the LaPlante factory closed down."

"Since when do you care about Dan?" Charlie said. I shot him a warning look.

Fern plopped a stack of menus on the counter. "Since Dan hasn't paid child support in nine months."

"Jesus, Ferny, why didn't you say something? Do you need extra shifts?" I could move some of the part-timers around. And the leaf peepers would be coming in soon.

"What she needs is a wealthy husband," Charlie said, ducking to avoid being hit by the barrage of wet, crumpled paper napkins Fern threw his way.

"Amen to that," she said, laughing. "One of those nice ski instructors who come up for the winter."

"Someone to warm up your bed?"

"Wood's not getting any cheaper."

I took the bus bucket of dishes in back and stacked them in neat piles for the dishwasher. When I came back out into the dining room, Charlie and Fern were huddled together, looking at something on one of their phones. I peered over their shoulders. They were looking at Charlie's dating app.

"Here he is," Charlie said, tapping on the screen. "Do you think he's worth traveling all the way to Burlington for?"

"He's pretty cute," Fern said, grabbing a couple of menus and smiling at the couple who had just walked in the door. "Dining room in back all right? This way."

I caught Fern on her way to grab a water pitcher. "Seriously, honey. Do you need anything? I had no idea about Dan."

Fern pinched my cheeks. "You are the sweetest. No, I'm fine. It's been a little slow, but it always is this time of year, with the summer people gone and school starting up. I was just making a point. People need jobs. I don't know if a company as big as HG is the answer, but something needs to be."

"Do you think I should consider it?"

Fern shrugged. "Something has to change. It can't hurt to hear what he has to say."

"I guess not," I said, because this was fundamentally true— seasons changed, people grew older, businesses came and went. Change was inevitable. But that didn't mean that I welcomed it. Sure, life in Guthrie was a little predictable. There wasn't much opportunity to meet new people or to try new things. But I liked our little village how it was. And a change like HG moving in— it could make things worse for a lot of people, not better. Did I want to be the person who gambled the town of Guthrie and lost? Peggy had been willing to. "I said I'd stay open-minded until the town has its say. But honestly, I don't think I could do it."

"That's going to be one heck of a town meeting," Fern said over her shoulder.

I was sure she was right.

We had a late lunch rush, which kept me at work into the early evening, but I drove straight from the diner to Peggy's house, my pants pockets crammed with dog biscuits, hoping that the light would last long enough for me to walk far into the woods. My mind raced with questions. Was Peggy the artist, or was it a friend or a love who had made the sculptures? Was the little bird a gift Peggy had given someone, or was it a present made for me? And who had left it? Questions led to more questions. All I knew was I needed to get back into the woods.

I left the diner prepared for walking, trading my squishy black waitressing sneakers, skirt, and T-shirt for a sturdy pair of my mother's Wellingtons, jeans, and a bright white T-shirt. I didn't want any foraging bears to mistake me for one of their own. The Vanagon was parked in the driveway, but I decided not to stop in the house until I returned from my walk. I was still angry with Kit, and wasn't ready to share the sculptures with her, or anyone. They felt like a treasure. If Kit knew about them, the woods would be filled with lights and cameras and a troupe of dancers and probably a brass band. She had a way of claiming things if she liked them, even if they were someone else's—vintage dresses, new books, the occasional crush.

My wanting to keep the sculptures to myself for a little longer wasn't just about my kid sister. I had grown more private since my divorce. I had stayed at home to take care of my dad after Mom died, so when Sean and I married, he moved in with us. I had had the naive thought that being married meant I would have someone to share the work of living with, but with Sean it just seemed like I had one more person's socks to match. And my dad—even when he couldn't remember that library books don't belong in the refrigerator, he managed to remember, and bring up, the arguments he overheard between Sean and me, usually loudly and someplace public.

The first night alone in my family's farmhouse I spent sitting at the round kitchen table my grandfather made, drinking coffee, too afraid to go to bed. I thought I would never get used to the silence or the solitude. But now it was something I cherished. I liked having time when no one knew where I was. I could go walking alone for hours. Out in the woods, or along one of the long, twisting dirt roads that cut through the mountains, I felt more like myself and at the same time like no one, just a tiny part in something much greater. Those moments felt deeply private. I felt the same way when I first found the sculptures— like I had stumbled upon something magical. They felt hopeful. I wasn't ready to break the spell.

I walked quickly through the orchard, dropping a biscuit onto the ground every so often. I followed the flock of warblers through the trees until I reached the orange-and-blue horse, his tail and mane waving in the breeze as if he had reached full gallop and would soon be a dot in the distance.

With my back to the horse, I looked deeper into the woods. A few yards away there was a murky kettle pond with water that was thick and dark like hot chocolate. Light glinted by the edge of the pond. The wind picked up and I heard a faint sound of tinkling, like ice cubes rattling in a glass. *I knew it*, I said into the trees. There, perched on the bank, as if it were hunting for to-night's dinner, was a snowy egret made almost entirely of crystal chandelier pieces, its long legs and beak made out of those old glass Christmas ornaments shaped like icicles. The raking after-noon light hit the crystal pieces and beamed tiny rainbows onto the surrounding trees. The crystal moved like feathers in the breeze. I snapped a couple of pictures before I walked briskly onward. Off in the distance I spotted a patch of bright blue. It took everything I had not to break into a run.

I found three more sculptures before the sun started to set. A doe made of flattened Pepsi cans, in the style of the galloping horse. A cat and a pair of kittens fashioned out of tiny pinecones and perched in a tree. The last was a pair of sheep whose coats were constructed out of thousands of light gray computer key-board letters that had been arranged thoughtfully, so that the letters and characters added shadow and texture. Their eyes were black typewriter keys. *There could be hundreds more sculp-tures in the woods*, I thought as I raced the fading light.

The night air held the promise of autumn. In a few months these woods would become impassable until after mud season. In the distance, I heard a high-pitched howl followed by *yip yip yip*. Freckles? Or a coyote, most likely. There had been com-plaints about a couple of them getting into some chicken pens. I was certain Freckles had slept on Peggy's couch or on her bed his whole life. He was no match for a coyote or a wolf. Then there was hunting season to keep in mind. Bow-and-arrow sea-son would begin in just six weeks, followed by rifle. And next would be the weather. It wasn't unheard of to get a decent snow-fall in mid-October.

I walked faster, my hands shoved deep into my jean pockets, the skin of my arms bumpy from the chill of the night woods, until I reached the orchard and then the warm light of Peggy's porch.

"Kitty, I'm here," I called as I kicked off my boots. Max opened the door that separated the mudroom from the kitchen.

"You're just in time," he said, smiling. He was wearing a lace-trimmed green chiffon apron over his skinny black jeans and white T-shirt. "Come on in."

The kitchen was warm and smelled of butter and vanilla and something smoky like scotch. On the kitchen counter there had been an explosion of powdered sugar. Unraveling pastry bags half filled with pink, yellow, and blue icing leaked onto the countertop and spilled onto the floor. There was an open bottle of Glenfiddich next to a carton of buttermilk. Max gestured toward one of the kitchen chairs and I slid onto it.

"First things first," he said as he poured me a juice glass full of scotch. He refilled his own, and held up the glass. "To Peggy."

"To Peggy," I said as we clinked drinks. I took a sip and let the scotch burn its way down my throat. "Where's Kit?" Kit would never miss out on a celebration, especially one that included whiskey and cake.

"She drove down to the printer in Littleton to make copies of the scenes she wants to use for the auditions." The auditions for Kit's movie were scheduled to begin the following weekend. Ever since Kit decided to shoot the film in Guthrie, I had barely caught a glimpse of her. She stayed up all night, rewriting dialogue or creating storyboard images of scenes inside Peggy's house, then rearranging the furniture at Peggy's to match her drawings. The only room in Peggy's house that had kept its original configuration was the kitchen, which Max had taken over and forbidden Kit to enter unless invited.

Max placed a clean fork on top of a folded, checkered cloth napkin next to my right hand.

"Are you ready?" he asked. His voice held excitement and pride. "Ta-da!"

Max presented me with a round cake on a tarnished silver platter. Creamy white waves of frosting swirled over the layers. The surface of the cake was decorated with dozens of tiny balloons in bright primary colors.

"I thought I should practice the balloons," Max said, a little shyly. "It's been awhile."

"We get to eat this?" I asked, using my index finger to swipe up a chunk of frosting that had landed on the plate. Its buttery texture melted on my tongue, and a round, butterscotch flavor lingered.

Max bowed and presented me with a long knife. "If you would do the honors, madam."

I had cut into countless cakes, pies, and puddings at the diner, but this felt different. Special. Important somehow. I took the knife and with gentle, deliberate strokes cut two large pieces. Max held out a plate. I lifted one of the cake slices with the knife and my fingers and slid it carefully onto the plate, bits of the moist crumb sticking to the blade. Max placed the slice in front of me. When I scooped up the second slice with the knife, he shook his head, and reached for the scotch bottle. He held up his glass and said, "Bon appetit."

The cake had the finest crumb and a warm yellow hue, like

the color of a chick's first feathers. The layers were thick and even. Holding them together were ruby red preserves, studded with chunks of whole raspberries. I pushed a fork into my slice, and with no effort cut a tiny wedge. I could feel Max watching me, but I couldn't make myself rush. It was the first homemade thing I could remember anyone making me since my mother had passed. I took my first bite. The buttery softness of the cake, the sharp tang of the lumpy preserves, and the creamy sweetness of the frosting were perfectly balanced. With less ceremony, I took another bite, and then another. The preserves tasted like summer, the frosting like childhood, the cake like a promise.

"How is it? Is it close to what you remembered?" Max asked. I had forgotten for a moment that he was there.

"Just like Peggy's."

Max smiled in a satisfied way and took a long sip of the scotch.

"I forgot you don't eat animal products. Does it bother you to bake with them?"

"I'm not into imposing my own choices on others. It's cool. I've had some great vegan cakes." He looked at me sideways. "But if I'm speaking strictly as a baker, nothing beats eggs and butter and sour cream."

I ate the piece I had cut for him, and then half of a third slice. I switched to milk but Max kept drinking scotch, which didn't seem to be rushing to his head the way it had to mine.

"I've filled Walt's sheet cake and given it a crumb coat. I'll finish decorating it tonight."

"You've given the cake a what?" I ran an index finger over my plate, coating it with just enough frosting that the crumbs left on the plate would stick to it.

"A crumb coat," Max said, picking up the abandoned half-slice of cake and dropping it onto my plate. "You put a thin layer of frosting on the cake and let it set to hold in the crumbs, so when you go to frost the final layer everything looks smooth and clean."

"So a crumb coat is like Spanx for cakes," I offered, looking down at my cake-bloated belly. I pushed aside the last piece of cake.

Max laughed. "More like a pair of stockings."

"We could all use a little smoothing over to look good." I ran my hands over my face.

"I don't know." Max reached his arm across the table for the saltshaker. "I've always been attracted to people's imperfections."

I laughed. "Like what?"

"Like Charlie's eyebrows, how they don't grow in one direction. Or the scar on Fern's forehead."

"Her dad dropped her when she was a baby."

"Or the way that developer's ears stick out—"

"And they are always burning red," I offered.

"Yes, exactly. And your sister's teeth. I fell in love with her the minute I saw her overbite. And the way those two little teeth on the bottom lean toward each other."

You're in love with my sister, I wanted to say. Instead I asked, "Doesn't that just mean someone couldn't afford an orthodontist?"

"It means they're human." Max shrugged. "I'm more interested in what a person thinks and feels anyway, but if we have to look like *something*, which we do, I'd rather look at someone whose face shows they've lived a little. That they've struggled a little. The people who look super smooth, they look . . ."

"Creepy."

Max laughed. "Sometimes. I always wonder what they're trying to hide. We're all suffering. I guess I just relate to people who
are willing to share more of themselves. A lot of pain in the
world could be alleviated if we could all admit when we're having a hard time."

"I'm having a hard time," I said. The words were out of my
mouth before I realized how much I meant them.

"I am, too," Max said, in a voice that conveyed that he was
totally okay with having a hard time, and I was grateful for both
his honesty and his comfort with it. He would make an excellent
brother-in-law. I hoped Kit would make this one stick.

"Do you think I could drop the cake off at the diner tomorrow? I don't know how Peggy managed to store anything. There
isn't an inch of space in the fridge." Max lifted his arms over his
head and stretched side to side, like he was in a yoga class. His
T-shirt rose up over his pale belly, revealing lines of black ink.

"Sure, anytime. There's tons of space in the walk-in." I grabbed
our dirty plates and brought them over to the sink. Peggy didn't
have a dishwasher, just an old enamel, two-basin sink with a
built-in drainer. I plugged up the basin to the left, squirted it
with soap, and ran the hot water. "I can't thank you enough for
baking these cakes," I said over the sound of the water running.
"I'd hate to disappoint so many people."

"You wouldn't disappoint them." Max appeared beside me.
He moved the faucet to his side of the sink and adjusted the
water temperature. I handed him a sudsy plate.

"I really wasn't exaggerating about my lack of skills in the
kitchen," I said, trying to get the sponge into the crevices of
the hand-mixer beaters.

"Nonsense." Max took the beaters out of my hand and shook them vigorously back and forth under the soapy water. "You're an artist, right?"

"I'm, um, no." I was a business owner. I was a sister. I was a friend. I was a divorcée. I was a gardener. I was a finder of lost dogs. "Where did you get that idea?"

"Kit showed me some of the pictures on your phone."

I felt simultaneously horrified and pleased. The pictures were private. Not in a sexy way. They were just pictures of things I found beautiful. I had the suspicion that they said something about me that I wasn't aware of, and that I may not want to reveal. But this wasn't something that Kit or Max, who seemed to live so freely, would understand. I kept washing the dishes. "They're just snapshots."

"Not snapshots. They're so . . . deeply observed. I love that one of the half-eaten donut on the plate—you made me really *see* it."

I peeked up at him to see if he was teasing me, but he looked quite serious. The picture he was talking about was of a honey-glazed donut left on a pink Fiestaware plate. The light was hitting the glaze in a way that made me feel tender toward it.

"Baking asks the same thing. If you pay attention to the ingredients, to the process—to the *textures*, just like you do in your photography—then everything comes out perfectly. I think you could be an excellent cake baker." He smiled down at me. "You might take to it," he said, poking me in the arm.

"I doubt it."

"You never know. You might fall in love with it."

"I don't really have that much free time, with the diner, and looking for Freckles—"

"I can see it now." Max held his hands up in the air as if he were praying to an ancient god. "After one bite of your cakes, the fine people of Guthrie will crown you 'Nora the cake lady'!" Max held his hands to his mouth and made the whirring sound of a crowd cheering. "Nora! Nora! Nora!"

"Stop it. You're making fun of me."

"I'm not. I'm serious."

I felt a prickle of irritation bite at the edge of my mood. "Nora the cake lady" sounded close to Saint Nora and it bothered me that Kit could have given Max an impression of me that wasn't true. "What makes you think I want to be Nora the cake lady?" I asked, wishing that the words sounded as breezy as they had in my head.

"Why not? It's an honorable thing to do. Being a part of your neighbors' celebrations. Making people happy." Max shrugged. "I loved being a baker. It was the only job I ever had where I felt satisfied at the end of every day." He waved toward the disaster of ingredients that covered every flat surface of the kitchen. "Pay attention, follow the directions, use good ingredients, practice technique, share with friends, and voila! Happiness abounds!"

I laughed and handed him the soapy mixing bowl I had been scrubbing.

"And besides, if you do become Nora the cake lady, I'd be grateful for the help. If Kit casts her actresses as fast as she thinks she will, we could start shooting in the next couple of weeks."

"Oh." Max, without any obligation to me, or my sister, or the town, had offered to give us so much of his time and talent. I should have thought to offer to help from the beginning. "How many cakes are there?"

Max stepped away from the sink and returned with Peggy's

red leather datebook. "Sixty-seven. We've confirmed almost all of them," he said, flipping the pages, "all except for one, but it's a strange one."

"Strange how?" I grabbed a dish towel hanging on a peg and wiped my hands.

Max leaned against the counter, opening the book to this week. "Look." His finger pointed to an entry on Friday, August 11. It read *Friday—LC—bsc/mi.*

"That's tomorrow. They haven't called? I've posted notices on the Front Porch Forum several times, and I hung a sign up by the cash register. Must be an old-timer who isn't online." LC. The first name that came to mind was Linda Cohen, the hairdresser who owned Locks by Linda over in St. Johnsbury. I made a mental note to call her when I got home.

"And look." Max flipped the page over and pointed to the following Friday, and then the next. *Friday—LC—bsc/mi.* "Same initials, same cake. It must be a standing order, every week."

"That *is* strange. Who would want the same cake every week? Maybe it's a church or something, and not a person. Someplace that has a weekly meeting." I turned the initials over in my head. "And no one has called?"

"Not yet. I'll wait until I get confirmation before I bake one. But if we don't hear, I thought maybe we could make one sometime and then run it as a special at the diner. What do you think?" Max shrugged. "'Homemade Desserts' and all," he teased.

"Not nice," I said, plucking the datebook out of his hands. "Have you figured out what cake it is?" Max had become an expert in deciphering Peggy's codes and matching the orders up to her recipes. He had had a 100 percent success rate to date.

Max stood up straight. "I think so. And I'm dying to try it." He reached for Peggy's recipe tin and flipped through until he found the card he was looking for. It was greasy and worn and covered in little brown flecks. "Burnt sugar cake with maple icing." Max sighed. "That sounds delicious."

I leaned against the sink and smiled. "That's an old one. You don't see those cakes around much anymore, except occasionally at a bake sale. Mom always baked it in a Bundt pan. It was our dad's favorite."

"Then you'll have to help me make it. I've never had one. You can be the official taster, and I can teach you the basics of Cake Baking 101."

My mom wouldn't even let me in the kitchen when she was baking. She said I'd make her bread dough sag in the middle if I got too close. "I'm not making any promises," I said. "But I'll try."

"That's all a man can ask," Max said, tipping an invisible hat.

CHAPTER FOUR

❧❧

I came home from work the next day, my arms full of groceries from White's, to find Kit on my living room rug surrounded by sheets of paper, some stacked in piles, some sprawled across the floor. Industrial-sounding music was blaring from the stereo. The couch had been pushed against the windows, and she was leaning against it, eyeglasses propped up on her head, wrestling with a dull three-hole punch I hadn't seen since my mother was alive. There were tiny paper circles everywhere, as though ticker tape had been released from the ceiling in celebration. Only Kit did not look to be in a celebratory mood.

"Would you believe the copy store doesn't bind things? What's the point of a copy store if it doesn't *bind*?" Kit jammed a too-thick pile of paper into the hole punch and squeezed with both hands.

"Um, to copy things?" I dropped the grocery bags in front of the stereo so I could turn down the volume. I kept turning until my temples stopped throbbing.

Kit looked up at me, her face stony. She held up a brass paper fastener. "Those fasteners that no one has seen since *His Girl Friday* were the only option they could offer to hold the script pages together." She tossed the fastener on the ground and returned to punching. "This is going to take me all night."

I picked up one of the copies of the script. *Side Work—*

screenplay by Kit Huckleberry was typed in the center in big bold letters. "*Side Work.*" I flipped to a random page. "Is it about a person with several jobs?"

"In a way," she said as she snatched it out of my hands.

"Ow." One of the sheets sliced my index finger. I popped it into my mouth to catch the blood.

Kit's face softened. "Sorry, I didn't mean to be so grabby. It's just that it's not finished yet. I'm not ready for anyone to read it."

"Then why the copies?" I waved my uninjured hand at the papers littering the floor.

Kit gathered the fastened scripts closer to her. "These full scripts are just for Max and me. I'm putting together packets of a couple of scenes for the callbacks." Kit waved a stack of thinner packets. "I'm not ready for feedback. I'll probably have to do rewrites, depending on who we cast and what they can handle."

"Isn't there something I could do to help?" Suddenly we were five and twelve again, and Kit wouldn't let me have a role in the tap dance number she was putting on for the Cabin Fever Reliever. Despite being the little sister, she was always the director and I was always in charge of craft services.

"Nope. We're fine. I just need some privacy during this part of the process." Kit returned her attention to the task at hand.

I picked up the groceries and stepped over Kit's legs to reach the kitchen. The sink was full of dirty dishes. I felt my shoulders creep up toward my ears. There were toast crumbs all over the counter. A half-full jelly jar sat open with a butter-slicked knife stuck in it. It was funny—I could look at people's half-eaten food all day long, but there was something about food-crusted plates in my own home that made my skin crawl.

"Kit," I said, my voice tight.

"I know, I'm sorry, I'll get to it in a minute," she said, chewing the words out around a red pen cap. She drew large sweeping strokes of the pen across one of the pages of the script.

I placed one of my mom's old Dutch ovens on the stove top, filled the pot halfway with water, tossed in a cup of rice and a pound of diced chicken thighs, and turned the flame on high.

"What are you doing?" Kit asked.

"Cooking," I said, stirring the pot with a wooden spoon.

"You don't cook," she said, and turned her attention back to her packets.

"It's for Freckles." He had been eating God knows what. His stomach must be upset. I had read online that the best thing for a sick dog was chicken and rice. I planned on setting it out on Peggy's porch, and waiting to see if Freckles came around.

I wordlessly tiptoed over the stacks of papers and pushed into my bedroom. There I found Max, shirtless in black jeans, sitting cross-legged on my bed, eyes closed, palms open and resting on his thighs.

"Oh," I said, unable to not look at him. His chest and upper arms were covered in tattoos. They all seemed to be of Hollywood film stars of the thirties and forties. "Um, is that Barbara Stanwyck?" I said, trying and totally failing to sound nonchalant.

Max peered up at me and smiled. "It is. Good eye." He untangled his legs and slid off the bed, then turned around slowly, like a model on the Home Shopping Network. "Stanwyck, Bacall," he lifted his arm, "Lupino, Bergman." He looked over his shoulder and twisted his arm to point. "And back here we have Rogers,

Lake, Harlow, and of course, Jean Arthur." Max turned back to face me. "I regret having put her on my back. She's my favorite and I never get to see her."

I nodded my head as if I thought this was something I, too, would regret, but really I was just trying to look casual, like it was perfectly normal to be talking to a half-dressed man in my bedroom. The truth was, I hadn't been alone in my bedroom chatting with a half-dressed man since Sean left. And I had known Sean since we were playing four square at recess, so there was never a feeling of unease around him. Even though I was clear about the fact that I never wanted to kiss Sean LaPlante again, I couldn't imagine kissing anyone else. Well, I could *imagine* it, but I wasn't entirely sure I knew *how* to kiss someone else. It felt a lot like being a forty-two-year-old virgin.

"She's so spunky," he continued, unfazed by my obvious discomfort.

I pointed at my nightstand. "I was just coming in to grab my book."

"Sorry to invade your space. I haven't had a chance to meditate in weeks." Max stepped to the side, so I had just enough room to squeeze by him. When I stole a glance I was eye to eye with Myrna Loy. I grabbed the paperback and darted for the door.

"No trouble. Take your time. I'm headed out anyway."

"Anything fun?" he asked as he pulled the T-shirt on.

"To the tavern with Fern," I lied. I would text her as soon as I got to the car. I needed a drink. "You two have a fun night," I said, backing out of the room.

Max's eyebrows shot up as if in question, but his lips parted, revealing his white teeth, and he gave me a smile that could light up a theater marquee. "Burnt sugar cake. I'm getting psyched. We need to make a plan. Don't forget."

"Burnt sugar cake. Maple icing."

I told Kit to turn the pot off in a half hour, and then bolted out the door.

The Guthrie town hall is a converted Gothic church building, complete with a functioning belfry. The bell was rung only on special occasions—Guthrie Day, midnight of the New Year, and the day that the sap starts running, to announce the beginning of sugaring season. A white sign that read GUTHRIE TOWN HALL in black painted letters hung over the large wooden door. The building always looked fresh, since the town manager hired teenagers to paint one side of the white clapboard building every summer, which gave it a complete paint job every four years. Rounded windows punctuated the walls, filling the hall with light and air.

After too many nights spent in my tiny apartment, which Kit and Max had turned into the Baker's Dozen Productions head-quarters, I was happy to attend the town meeting. By 5:30 the parking lot of the town hall was filled to capacity. Cars were parked along the side of the road for what looked like miles. I hadn't seen this many cars since the Coventry County Fair had featured a western swing band as its big Saturday night head-liner.

I parked the car on the shoulder and climbed out, Kit and Max trailing a few steps behind me. "If we don't get a move on, we'll have to stand in the back."

"Why do we have to go, again?"

"Because I said I would keep an open mind."

Kit snorted. She raised her eyebrows at me. "Does that mean you'll consider his offer?"

"No."

"Then let's get out of here. There's a rockabilly band playing over in Lyndonville. We could go dancing."

Max slung an arm over Kit's shoulder. "Town meeting—of course we have to go." Max, who had grown up in Chicago, had never been to a town meeting before and was excited about the idea of doing something so small-town New England.

"I made a vow twenty years ago never to go to another town meeting."

"Kit, you can't still be mad about that." I walked backward so I could explain. "Max, one of her photography exhibits was shut down by the town."

"They were completely tasteful."

"Kit, they were nudes."

"The human body is nothing to be ashamed of!"

"Of your friends. Your *fifteen-year-old* friends. They were basically illegal."

Max barked out a laugh so loud that the people walking in front of us turned around to make sure he was okay.

"Provincial, puritanical, dirty minded," Kit muttered underneath her breath.

"Anyway, it would be rude to Elliot to just not show up. I told him we would listen to what the community has to say."

"Since when did Mr. Danforth become Elliot?"

When *had* Mr. Danforth become Elliot in my mind?

"Elliot. Mr. Danforth. Big-box guy. Whatever. We go, and we hear the arguments against HG, we see how the town votes on the zoning laws."

"And if the town is all for it, will you reconsider?"

We had almost reached the front of the building. There were over a dozen people, men and women, teenagers and grandparents, walking in a circle, holding up signs that said NO TO HG and KEEP GUTHRIE SMALL and DOWN WITH THE CORPORATE MAN. That last one was held by the president of the food co-op. A young girl handed us a flyer.

"This is super important. Be sure to tell HG that we don't want their corporate blood money in our community," she said with a slight lisp. It looked like she had just gotten her braces.

"Thanks, honey," I said, saying hello to the protestors. They were all customers at the diner. I waved the flyer at Kit. "Sure, if the town is all for it, I'm in."

Rows of gray folding chairs had been set up all the way to the back of the hall, and almost every chair was filled, including the ones up in the balcony. I pushed my way through the crowd, pausing to say hello to the folks I made eye contact with, patting the shoulders of some of the regulars. The room was hot and smelled like sweat and floor wax. I couldn't get out of my jean jacket fast enough.

"Hey, Nora, over here." Fern stood and waved at me from a row about halfway down.

"Kettle corn," I mouthed, pointing toward the table where the Girl Scouts were set up. There was a long line.

Fern held up two fingers in response.

While waiting I watched Elliot Danforth chat with the town manager. His brow was glistening with sweat and his tie looked like it was choking him.

"Good turnout," I said to Fern, handing her a baggie of kettle corn. I don't know what the sash-wearing scouts of Troop 235 added to their popcorn other than sugar and salt, but it was addictive. If you listened closely, you could hear the steady crunching underneath the din of conversation. It was one of the main reasons most of the town showed up for town meetings.

"That poor man," Fern said, pointing at Elliot. "He doesn't stand a chance." She craned her neck. "Where's your sister and the hunky philosopher?"

"Someplace close to an exit, I'm guessing."

The town manager, Ed Dascomb, climbed the few steps up to the stage. He tapped the mic to get everyone's attention. "Is this thing on?"

The microphone popped to life. The sounds of conversation subsided into the low muffle of whispered gossip.

"Yes. Well, then. I never thought this many people would have an opinion about the Mrs. Coventry County pageant."

The crowd rumbled with appreciative laughter, all except Rebecca Goodwin, the head librarian and force behind the movement to abolish the pageant, who looked at the town manager as if he were eating a pile of spareribs over an overdue library book.

"Since there are a lot more of you than usual, let me go over the rules of the town meeting before we get started. Now, we here in Guthrie follow *Robert's Rules of Order.* We will only be discussing the warned articles. If you have an issue with your neighbor—yes, I'm looking at you, Ben Smith—then you need to go through the proper channels and get it on the agenda for the next meeting. Once the discussion has been opened, come up to the mic in the center aisle and ask your questions. Once we have voted on a motion we won't discuss the matter further.

If things don't go your way, you need to go through the official appeal channels. See Mrs. Fairbanks at the end of the meeting to pick up the paperwork. Agreed?" The town manager cast his eye over the crowd, giving a few warning looks to members of the audience. "Remember, folks—listen carefully, be courteous, respect your neighbor." He glanced over at Elliot. "And keep your sense of humor. All right, without further ado, let's bring up tonight's moderator, the newest member of the town council, Sean LaPlante."

Sean walked up onstage. He looked sharper than he ever did when we were married. For one thing, he was wearing a new suit, not the one he wore to our wedding and every funeral since. His hair and beard were trimmed, and he was wearing new hipster glasses. I craned my head to look up the aisle to the front row. There was Sean's girlfriend. She was wearing leather pants. She probably didn't even sweat in them.

"Thanks, Mr. Dascomb. Okay, folks. The meeting will come to order. Just one more thing before we get started—you there, in the back. Please, for everyone's privacy, no filming allowed. We don't need town business put up on YouTube."

"Sorry, Sean," Kit said, flipping closed the camera. "Hi, brother!"

Sean held his hands to his eyes. "Is that you, Kit? I heard you were back in town."

The town manager coughed loudly from his seat on the stage.

Sean cleared his throat. "I'm sure everyone in town is happy to welcome Kit Huckleberry back"—a polite smattering of applause rose up from the crowd—"but let's get to business. Mrs. Goodwin, you have the floor."

Rebecca Goodwin smoothed her sundress as she approached the mic. "Thank you, Mr. Moderator."

Sean looked puffed up. I caught him smiling down at the intern. I looked at Fern and rolled my eyes. She handed me a plastic bottle with the Guthrie Flying Squirrels logo and I twisted off the cap. By the citrusy, boozy smell I guessed it was filled up with a couple of Fern's famous margaritas. I took a swig and handed it back.

"I'll keep this short, since I know most of you are here to discuss the Johnson farm. The Mrs. Coventry County pageant is outdated and sexist. It objectifies women. And it discriminates against women who aren't married, and women who aren't heterosexual. I move to get rid of the pageant and replace it with something that would be more inspiring to the younger generation of Guthrie women."

"Thanks, Mrs. Goodwin," said Sean. "Does anyone have any questions?"

Melissa, who ran the apple pie contest at the fair, was first in line. "Mrs. Coventry County carries many responsibilities over the course of the year of her reign, including serving as hostess during the fair and awarding the ribbons for all the contests. Who do you see stepping in to perform these roles?"

Rebecca shrugged. "I'm sure we could find some volunteers to greet fairgoers and hand out ribbons. I mean, you're a volunteer, aren't you, Melissa?"

Melissa gave Rebecca a chilly look but returned to her seat.

Jane White, a former Mrs. Coventry County, cleared her thoat before speaking. "Yes, Mrs. Goodwin. Isn't it true"—Jane slowly pulled a piece of folded paper from the pocket of her seersucker skirt—"that the Mrs. Coventry County contestants are limited to married women over eighteen living with their husbands in Coventry County, and are judged"—Jane put on the reading glasses that were hanging by a chain around her neck—"and I quote, 'on *general appearance, poise, outgoing personality, and spirit of volunteerism*'?"

Rebecca looked up at the ceiling. "Yes, and a baked good."

"Would you consider an outgoing personality and a spirit of volunteerism a bad influence on the impressionable young female minds of Guthrie?"

Rebecca took off her reading glasses. "Look, everyone knows it's both a popularity contest and a beauty contest. It's archaic."

Sean stepped carefully toward Rebecca. "Any more questions, folks? No?" Sean scanned the room. I knew he just wanted to linger in the moment. He loved this kind of attention. "All right, let's take a vote. Those in favor of putting an end to the Mrs. Coventry County pageant, say aye."

"Aye," Fern and I said in unison. I heard Kit's voice in the back of the room, and Max's as well, even though technically they didn't have the right to vote.

"Those opposed, say nay."

"Nay," said most of the room. Like I had told Elliot, Guthrie wasn't a town that loved change. From the look on Elliot Danforth's face, I guessed he was experiencing that firsthand.

"Well, that wasn't a surprise," Fern said, taking another long sip from her water bottle.

"Motion denied. The Mrs. Coventry County pageant will continue. Thank you for participating in our democracy, Rebecca. We appreciate your civic engagement." Many of the townspeople clapped in a friendly way as Rebecca climbed down the stairs. Rebecca was well loved in the town. She was a generous waiver of overdue library fees and kept the DVD shelf stocked with the latest movies.

Sean held a piece of paper in his hand and moved it closer, then farther away, searching for the distance at which he could read it. I wondered if he avoided getting bifocals because he didn't want to remind the intern that he was eighteen years her senior. "Now, we won't be voting on article two. Tonight is an opportunity for HG spokesman Elliot Danforth to make a presentation, and for us to ask questions, of which I am sure there are many. Come on up here, Mr. Danforth."

A low murmur rose up from the crowd. I felt a little bad for Elliot, having to try to convince a group of people who wrote formal letters of complaint when I took silver-dollar pancakes off the menu that this wouldn't change the character of the whole town.

Elliot buttoned his suit jacket as he walked up the steps. He smiled at Sean and took the mic out of the stand. "Thanks, Mr. Moderator. And thank you all for attending this meeting. I'm impressed with Guthrie's level of commitment. As some of you already know, I work for the HG Corporation. Tonight I hope to share with you HG's vision, clear up any misconceptions about HG's impact on a town like Guthrie, and answer any questions you may have."

Up there on the stage, mic in hand, Elliot Danforth looked natural. It was the most comfortable I had seen him. I wondered if I would look odd outside of Guthrie. I wondered how Kit seemed to fit everywhere she went.

"HG helps people around the world save money and live better anytime and anywhere—in retail stores, online, and through their mobile devices. Each week, more than two hundred million customers and members visit our more than ten thousand stores in twenty-five countries and our e-commerce sites in ten countries. With fiscal year 2015 sales of approximately $460 billion, HG employs more than two million associates worldwide. HG continues to be a leader in sustainability, corporate philanthropy, and employment opportunity."

Elliot walked across the stage in long, confident strides as he talked. It was like watching a motivational speaker on PBS.

"From a consumer standpoint, HG has more choices, and choices that are close to home so you don't have to drive far. We offer lower prices on brand-name products that you love, as well as our own line of products at competitive prices."

This speech was lighting him up from within. "A typical HG store creates three hundred new jobs in the community. Good jobs with career opportunities. Many of the store managers started out as hourly associates and worked their way up. And we offer medical, dental, and 401(k) plans to our full-time employees."

"Of which there are two per store," Fern said into my ear. "They're famous for hiring mostly part-timers."

"Of course, there is the direct impact of sales tax revenue and purchases from local suppliers," he said. "Tax revenues that will go toward better roads, better schools, better services for the elderly and those who need a helping hand."

Fern leaned back in her chair. "That man could sell a slaughterhouse to a vegetarian."

"Right?" I said. He wasn't just charismatic. He was on fire. He could be a cult leader. He made it seem like all of Guthrie's problems could be solved with the opening of this single store on Peggy Johnson's cow pasture. Only Guthrie didn't really have any problems, did it? Sure, unemployment went up after Sean's family furniture business shut down, but everyone in town tried to pitch in and offer some work to those who were laid off. I hired two of the young sanders to work the dishwasher on the weekends. I looked at the crowd. A few of the people were leaning forward, listening. Could he actually change their minds?

"At the store level, a store manager has a budget and the ability to make small donations to Little League teams and neighborhood groups," Elliot said, gesturing with his hands at the group of Girl Scouts gathered behind the kettle corn table and smiling at the troop's leaders.

"He just got the mom vote," Fern laughed. "I'm glad I don't have to deal with him. He could convince me to sell my farm and I don't even have one."

"Thanks, Fern," I mumbled, shoving a handful of kettle corn into my mouth, suddenly grateful that Elliot hadn't come on this strong in his pitch to Kit and me.

Sean walked across the stage, placed a hand on Elliot's shoulder, and took the mic from his hand. "Thank you, Mr. Danforth. Why don't we pause to hear from the community? Looks like we have a good amount of questions already. Let's get right to it."

I turned around in my seat. The questions and comments line stretched the length of the room, then snaked around the back. I caught Kit's eyes for a moment. She looked like she was burning from within. This was not going to be a short meeting.

"Mr. Grant, you have the floor." Sean placed the microphone back in the stand and walked off the stage.

Burt Grant had swapped his usual blue work shirt and painter's pants for a pair of dress slacks and a shirt and tie. He looked miserable. I peeked over at Fern. She and Burt had gone on a couple of dates.

"Mr. Danforth, I'm a small-business owner here in Guthrie. My family has run the Guthrie Hammer and Nail since World War Two. Isn't it true that a store like HG wipes out small businesses and guts downtowns?"

So we weren't going to waste time. Elliot looked as if he had been asked about his favorite baseball team, or how he felt about mac and cheese. He smiled and nodded his head as if to say *I hear you*.

"Consumers from Guthrie and neighboring towns will gain tremendous benefits from access to an HG store," he said. "HG boasts average prices that are fifteen percent lower than those of our competitors." He scanned the crowd, taking its temperature. "That does mean competition for businesses whose focus overlaps that of HG."

"And those would be?" Burt asked, his voice tense.

"Drugstores, florists, and stores specializing in apparel, sporting goods, jewelry, cards, and gifts."

"And hardware stores."

"HG does carry a large selection of tools and building and repair supplies, as well as items for the lawn and garden." Elliot had enough common sense to look sheepish when he added, "We advise small businesses to grow in sectors that HG doesn't cover."

"Like what?" Burt asked, unable to mask the anger in his

voice. A low murmur rose from the crowd. "You sell clothing. You sell televisions. Hell, you even sell groceries."

"In some stores," Elliot said.

"Are you planning on selling groceries in the Guthrie store?"

Elliot's face had lost the quality that made him an individual human. It was like he had become a branch of HG himself. "Considering the population density to market availability I would say yes, if we are given the proper permits."

Burt Grant turned away from the microphone, disgusted. He gave me a stern look as he marched down the aisle of the hall. The big wooden door to the outside creaked open and shut.

Sean gave Elliot a level look. "Marshall Brown, you have the floor."

Traffic patterns were discussed. Questions were raised about whether adding an HG would affect homeowners' and farmers' property values, and whether that would mean they would have to pay more taxes. Someone from the White family asked about crime rates of the towns that HG had moved into, adding that they didn't want to attract an "unsavory element" to Guthrie, which made Fern and me giggle into our shirtsleeves, because Jane White had once said that the diner attracted an unsavory element to the town. We had joked that Jane would probably ask the same question if an order of Franciscan monks came to the town meeting to inquire about building a church. There were some questions asked that were decidedly pro-HG, and Elliot's cheerful demeanor was restored as he described how many local tradesmen would be hired for the interior and exterior build-out, the current price they were offering for lumber, and the corporation's commitment to sourcing products from local companies whenever possible.

Sean cleared his throat and took off his reading glasses. "I'm sorry, ma'am," he said as he squinted down at the person at the front of the question line. "I don't think I know your name."

Every head in the town hall turned toward the microphone. Fern leaned forward, then way back. "I can't see. Nora, stand up and take a peek."

Unable to contain my curiosity, I stood up. A tall woman with a mane of hair the color of horse chestnuts stood at the microphone. She wore one of those tight, stretchy shirts that are supposed to be for doing yoga but women mostly shop in, and a pair of well-worn hiking boots. "No need to apologize, Mr. Moderator. My name is Oona Avery. I'm the new science teacher at the high school."

Sean blushed. He actually blushed! Several people stood up to get a look at the newcomer. A new teacher in town was usually pretty big news in Guthrie, and we hadn't had anyone new move to town since Livvy Rawlings, the pastry chef over at the Sugar Maple, had arrived a couple of years back. Not a few of the loggers in the audience took off their baseball caps and combed their hair back with their fingers.

"Well, welcome, Ms. Avery." Sean made a sweeping gesture with his arm as if he were giving Oona the whole town. "You have the floor."

She beamed up at him, then set her eyes on Elliot. "Mr. Danforth, could you speak to the pollution that the building and running of a store like HG would create? I am specifically interested in how you plan to deal with the water runoff after you remove all of those trees."

Elliot took a deep breath and smiled at Oona before replying. "Of course, the engineers could—and will—speak to this with more accuracy. Traditionally we place a box vault for storm water management underneath the building."

"But a box vault wouldn't prevent pollutants from getting into the groundwater. Many properties still rely on wells for some of their water. Wouldn't planting native species and rain gardens be a more effective, environmentally friendly solution?"

"All options will be considered by our team of engineers to ensure—"

"And what about the orchard?" This did not come from Oona, or the microphone.

Sean looked unequipped to handle any Guthrie resident who wasn't following the rules of town meetings.

A pair of sneakers squeaked across the recently waxed town hall floor.

"Who is it?" Fern asked.

Dotty McCracken walked by us, ignoring the line, her white braid bouncing off her back. She didn't stop until she was standing next to Oona Avery. "I said, what about the orchard?"

"Mrs. McCracken, I'm sorry, but Oona has the floor."

Oona looked bemused. "That's okay—I give the floor to— what's your name?"

Dotty held out her hand. "Dotty McCracken. Nice to meet you, dear." Dotty turned to the mic. "I'm sorry to interrupt, but Ms. Avery talking about pollution rattled my memory. Peggy's family had an orchard on her land. My Henry and I used to steal away up there from time to time." Judging by the sweet smile on Dotty's face, it was a fond recollection.

"I wish my marriage had had half the romance the McCrackens' did." Fern sighed, and rested her head on my shoulder.

"You and me both."

"And what has this to do with the environmental impact?" Elliot asked. An edge of impatience had crept into his voice. I felt the whole room turn away from him. Dotty McCracken was one of the most beloved citizens of Guthrie. It was like Elliot had taken a phone call in a movie theater right when the couple finally kissed.

"I don't know about the environmental impact, but there are varieties of apples up in those woods that no one has seen in decades. That seems like an important part of the environment to me."

"Amen," said Oona, placing a hand on Dotty's shoulder.

"I remember that orchard," some old-timer called, and the room broke into dozens of conversations about apples that tasted like pears and the best way to blett a medlar.

Sean tapped on the mic. "Folks, folks. There are rules to town meetings for a reason." But the crowd was lost in collective memories of stolen kisses and late afternoons gathering fruit, and of the taste of turnovers that would make a man weep. Sean looked over at the town manager. "All right, folks, I'm calling it. Meeting is adjourned. Please see Mrs. Fairbanks if you want to get your issue on the warning for next meeting."

Elliot cleared his throat. "What about the vote on changing the zoning?"

Sean looked out over the crowd picking up empty popcorn containers and draping sweaters over their arms. Some of the high school kids were already folding up the vacated chairs and stacking them in the back. "Next time," Sean replied, slapping Elliot on the shoulder.

"Well, that's that," I said to Fern as I pulled on my jean jacket.

"What do you mean?"

I pointed over at Sean, who was chatting up the science teacher. "This is the classic 'make it look like you are postponing something when you have absolutely no intention of ever doing it' town meeting move. Sean pulled it off well, considering it's his first time."

"Like the time they never voted on legalizing pot," Fern said, "but the charges against Sally Banforth were mysteriously dropped."

"Exactly. It's clever, really. If the town never takes a vote on the zoning laws, they know HG will eventually move on."

"And no one has to be pissed off at their neighbors for voting a different way than they did. It really is brilliant," Fern agreed.

"Guthrie town council. Keeping the peace."

"What does that mean for you, Nora?"

Fern offered me the dregs of her kettle corn. "It means I won't have to listen to the old-timers telling me what to do," I said. "At least for a little while." I looked at the thinning crowd. Kit and Max were nowhere to be seen. "And it means I won't be the one to disappoint my sister, which will be a nice change of pace."

"I'm sure you'll find other buyers," said Fern.

"We have time."

Kit and Max waved Fern and me over to their booth at the Black Bear Tavern. The bar was packed with people still in a sociable mood after the town meeting. The pair had slipped out the back of the town hall the moment Sean had officially closed the meeting, and had texted me to meet them at the bar.

"This place is classic," Max said, his arms stretched the

length of the booth. Kit was pressed against his side, doing something on her phone. "Have you seen that stuffed bear over by the bar?"

"We've seen it," Kit and I said at the same time. Even Kit, the most enthusiastic person on the planet, seemed to be growing a little tired of Max's delight in all things Vermont. I think she was worried that he would ask if they could stay.

The waitress brought over a pitcher of beer and four frosted glasses. Fern waved her away when she started to pour. "Sally, you know I can't have you waiting on me." Fern and I always had a hard time being waited on by our own customers. It was like seeing your high school teacher on the elliptical at the gym. It just didn't feel right.

"*You* poured *me* coffee twelve hours ago."

Fern pulled the glasses closer to her. "Can't do it. Go away."

Sally laughed. "Fine. Holler at me when you want to order food."

Fern poured the beer and raised her glass. "Here's to Rebecca Goodwin. May her attempt to get rid of the Mrs. Coventry County pageant inspire the young women of Guthrie for years to come."

We held up our glasses and clinked. "Hear, hear."

The door opened and a cheer rose from the crowd of drinkers over by the empty stage. When I looked over, they were slapping Sean on the back.

"Well done, councilman," someone shouted. A few people whistled.

"I don't see the intern," Fern said. "Do you think it has something to do with the new science teacher?"

Max clapped his hands on the table. "I thought there was something going on there, too."

Kit rolled her eyes at me and returned to her phone.

"Can we not speculate about my ex-husband's sex life?" I pleaded, taking a long sip of my beer.

Fern surveyed Sean over her shoulder. "She'd be a better match than the intern."

"And she's pretty foxy, in a saving-the-planet-with-science kind of way." This was from Max.

Fern nodded. "What he said. Exactly. Sean always needed someone to boss him around. Nora was too—"

"You guys," I said, not wanting to hear the end of that sentence. "Can we talk about the meeting?"

"Yes," Kit said, tossing her phone onto the seat beside her. "Let's talk about the meeting."

This was a surprise. I assumed she and Max had spent the whole meeting whispering to each other, not actually paying attention.

Kit poured us all another round. "Big-box boy just got the Guthrie slapdown, am I right?"

"Yes," Fern and I agreed.

"So I have a proposal to make." Kit looked up at Max. He put his arm around her. "Actually, more of a favor to ask."

Max smiled down at her and gave her shoulder a little squeeze. It was obvious they had discussed whatever was coming next.

Kit took a deep breath. "Nora, I would like to ask you for a loan. As soon as Peggy's place is sold you would get the money back, plus interest."

I should have seen this coming. Kit moved a lot faster than

the town of Guthrie, or me. But the question still caught me off guard. Asking for things just wasn't something we did in our family. Both Mom and Dad were raised by Depression-era parents, and they knew better than to ask for anything extra. Mom thought anything worth doing you should do yourself. That was before she was sick, of course, but even when she was at her weakest, she wouldn't ask for more than a glass of water, and then she would apologize for having to put you through the trouble. I had learned to anticipate what she needed before she knew herself. Dad was easier to ask—at least he wouldn't make you feel guilty the way Mom sometimes did—but he never followed through with any of the promises he made, so it was better not to get your hopes up. I couldn't remember the last time I had asked anyone who didn't work for me for help. It was one of the things that Sean complained about. That I didn't need anything from him. That I didn't need him.

"How big a loan?" It was obvious that neither she nor Max had any cash to speak of. They checked out books and movies from the library, crashed on my couch, and ate at my house or at the diner free of charge. I had a small nest egg—three thousand dollars saved in a coffee can at the back of my freezer, tip money from the hour I covered the counter in the mornings. I didn't have any plans for it. I could spare at least half.

"Twenty-five thousand."

"What?"

"Fifty thousand would be more realistic," Max countered, looking at Kit instead of me.

"Fifty thousand," Kit said, meeting my gaze. "I know it sounds like a lot of money, Nora, but before you say anything—"

"It doesn't just sound like a lot of money, Kit. It *is*—"

"Even if we shoot the bulk of *Side Work* for free in Peggy's house, doing all the camera work ourselves, making movies even on a micro budget like ours—"

"You have to have a good camera," Max said. "It doesn't matter how good the script is, or the acting. If it doesn't look professional no one will take it seriously. Same goes for sound."

"And we have to pay the actors. And postproduction. Getting a decent sound person and editor—"

"Especially with the turnaround time we need."

I held up my hands. "Okay, you guys, I get it. But the diner just isn't that profitable. I had to replace the refrigeration last year, and the insurance rates keep going up. I might even have to raise my prices. I just don't have that kind of money saved. I'm sorry."

Kit looked down at her hands. "You could borrow it," she said quietly.

"Kit." If losing the family homestead had drilled anything into me—into us—I thought, it was to avoid debt at any cost. Dad had taken on piles of credit card debt when Mom was dying and had fallen behind on the mortgage. It was one of the reasons we had to sell the house.

"It would be temporary—just until we settle Peggy's estate. The money can go straight to the bank, I won't even touch it."

"It's not that simple, Kit. There's already a lien against Peggy's estate—she owed a bunch of back taxes. And with the HG deal hanging on town approval, no bank is going to give us money with that collateral."

"No one is going to give *us* money," Kit said. "But they would give *you* money."

"Why? Peggy's land belongs to both of us. I'm in the same boat you are."

"But you have the diner."

Fern met my eyes before she emptied the remains of the pitcher of beer into my glass and slid out of the booth, taking the pitcher with her to the bar.

The Miss Guthrie. It was all that was left of our parents. Would they have gambled it even for a moment to help Kit follow her dream? Our pragmatic mother—no way. She would say that any dream worth chasing was worth waiting for, and if they didn't have the funds it meant that this wasn't the opportunity for them, and that the right one would come along when they were ready. But our dad . . . he might have said yes.

And then there was the question of what would happen to me if I lost the diner.

"Kitty," I said quietly. "You have to realize what you are asking. If anything went wrong—it's all I have."

"This movie is my big shot, Nora. It's the break I've been dreaming about. This kind of opportunity doesn't come around more than once."

It wasn't the first time that Kit had asked me to put her dreams in front of my needs, but this was different. The diner was the reason I got out of bed in the morning. It was my role in the community. It was the last place left that I could call home. Running it was the only thing I knew how to do, and being the owner was who I was. If I lost the diner, I would lose my identity, my purpose. The Miss Guthrie wasn't just my job; it was my whole life.

I looked up at Kit. Her face was an illustration from a storybook, a vision of hope, all possibility. A flash of envy washed over me at her ability to dream big. But envy was quickly replaced by the love I had for the woman in front of me—the little sister I used to know, the sister who would crawl into my bed on the nights when our mom, fading in front of us, couldn't mask the pain. The sister who looked to me for milk money, to sign permission slips, to French braid her hair, who trusted me to figure out the best way to make the maximum amount of glitter stick to her fairy costume. The sister who saw me as someone who would lift her up, not hold her back.

"I'll think about it. We can ask the bank. But if the payments are more than I think I can handle—I don't want you to get your hopes up."

Kit pushed Max out of the booth, hopped into the space Fern had left, threw her arms around me, and kissed my cheek. "Thanks, sis. It won't be for long, I promise. Peggy's place will sell in a snap. We'll find some nice goat farmer. And we'll give you a producer credit!"

I looked over at Max. He held up his hand in prayer and bowed his head. *Thank you*, he mouthed.

I bowed back, thinking we needed all the prayers we could get.

Fern offered to drive Max and Kit back to the apartment after I said I wanted to stop by the diner and work on payroll. Really I just needed a little space, some time away from talk of movies and money. I drove the back roads for a while with the windows rolled down, letting the chorus of peepers drown out my racing thoughts. Eventually I found myself leaning into the familiar twists of Pudding Hill Road, each lift and curve a memory held in my body. I slowed down to turn onto Hunger

Mountain, and pulled up in front of our old house. The new owners had had it painted a colonial blue that made it look suburban. The barn was still white, though, and the roof had been replaced. Mom's garden had been turned over, and grass seed planted. They had to be paying someone to come by and mow—the lawn was trim and tidy, not a rangy daisy or cornflower in sight. The windows were dark, the driveway where Kit and I learned to ride bikes was empty. One of the carpenters had told me they had removed several walls inside and turned it into an open floor plan. I had liked the cozy little rooms. There had been a tiny room on the west side that Dad used as his "study." It was a warm, dusty space just big enough to fit an antique secretary and two comfy chairs that our cats used to sleep on during the day. Dad had hung shelves on the walls and stuffed them full of paperback books. It was my go-to place in the afternoons, where I would snuggle up with Susan, the calico, and get lost in a story. Now it was probably a walk-in closet. I pressed the gas and kept driving.

When I reached Peggy's house, I was surprised to find the Mercedes two-seater parked in front. I pulled in behind it, turning off the engine but keeping my headlights on.

Elliot gracefully stepped out of his car and walked up to my open window. "Ms. Huckleberry," he said warmly, his hand held up in a frozen wave.

"Hi," I said, searching my mind for the memory of an appointment, but coming up empty.

"Hi." His self-assured expression dropped for a moment and he looked uncertain. He put his hands in his pants pockets.

"I thought you might have skipped town by now," I said.

He laughed, and I was surprised to hear that it sounded genuine, without anger. "And miss tomorrow's reaction pieces in the *Coventry County Record*? Never."

"They will probably print at least three editions," I offered. "It's best to wait for the last printing or you won't get the full story."

A deep hoot sounded from the woods behind Peggy's barn.

"*Who cooks for you?*" he said as if he were almost singing.

"I'm sorry?" I was completely confused.

"Did you hear that? The call?" He smiled. "I think it's a barred owl. Listen. It sounds like it's asking *Who cooks for you?*"

We waited in silence for several minutes, but the bird never made another peep.

Elliot cupped his hands to his mouth. "*Whoo whoo foo yooooo.*" Nothing.

He stared at Peggy's barn. He looked prepared to wait all night.

"Um, I don't want to sound impolite, but could I ask what you're doing here?"

"Oh. I stopped by the diner, but you weren't there. I thought I might find you here."

"Did you need something?" I was never this direct, but it was getting late. *Invite him in for a cup of tea, Nora,* I could hear my mother admonishing me from the grave. But I had had a strange day. And I didn't like him here, on Peggy's land, looking at it through the filter of money. All I wanted was to clear my head, then get home and into a hot bath.

"Actually, I have something for you," he offered, popping open his trunk with a press of a button on his keys. I opened my car door and stepped out—it seemed impolite to receive a gift through an open window.

Elliot walked over and pulled out what looked like an extra-fat sawed-off shotgun.

"I'm not sure what you've heard about Vermont women, but giving me the gift of firearms isn't going to sway my opinion."

Elliot chuckled. With a steady arm, he pointed the gun toward Peggy's herb garden, aimed, and pulled the trigger. With a loud pop, a giant orange net shot at least fifty feet into the garden, attached to the gun by a long orange line, and landed softly on a shaggy, overgrown sage bush. He turned to me, his smile bright, looking like a kid who had just made his three-pointer.

"I thought it might help. With Freckles," he clarified. He tugged on the line where it was attached to the gun. The net closed itself around the bottom of the plant. "It's a little harder with a moving object, of course."

He looked quite comfortable with the net gun in his hands—not something I would have guessed that first day we met in the diner.

Elliot tugged at the line again. The sage shook and several leaves fell off the plant. "See?"

"That herb does look good and trapped," I said, rubbing my arms. The night had grown cool. "I'm not sure I could even catch a shrub, though, to be honest."

"I thought I could go out with you." The way he said it sounded a little like he was asking me out to the movies, and from the way his eyes avoided mine I could tell he heard it the same way. "I mean, next time you get a tip. About the dog." Elliot walked toward the garden, his leather-soled shoes slipping on the damp grass. "My dad is a hunter," he said loudly as he freed the net from the sage bush, winding the line loosely around his arm as he walked back to me. "He uses one of these to retrieve ducks that land in the lake. His last Labrador didn't like the water," he added. When he reached me he said, "I learned from him. I'm originally from Maine."

He had a New England accent, but I would have guessed from the tempo that he was from Massachusetts.

I watched him as he lay the net gun on the ground. He spread the net on the grass and tugged at the end of the line, making sure it was secure. He had a calm, steady way about him that I found appealing. I realized then that I wanted to trust him. He was friendly and polite and he didn't know anyone in town so I imagined he might be a little lonely. But the very nature of what brought Elliot into my life made everything he did seem suspicious to me. I didn't want to be taken advantage of, or lulled into believing a glossed-over version of what a complex like HG's might do to a town like Guthrie. But Freckles was alone somewhere and neither Erika nor I had had any luck in getting within ten feet of him. I needed help.

"Aren't you planning on leaving?" I asked.

"Why would I leave?"

"Because of tonight—I think it was pretty obvious what the majority of the town thinks."

"What do you think?"

I took a deep breath. "I don't think I—I just can't do it. I'm sorry. It would be too big a change for the town."

Elliot folded the net neatly, making sure the weights attached to the corners lined up evenly, and tucked it back into the canister of the gun. He stood, fumbling with the gun's nylon carrying case. "Would you still accept my help?"

"I suppose so. If you're staying," I said.

Elliot rocked back and forth on his heels. "I'll be here for a little longer, I think. The Sugar Maple is quite comfortable. Great food. Have you had dinner there?"

"Chef Alfred is amazing."

"You need to come by and try his gazpacho. He adds pickled corn. I've never tasted anything like it." Elliot nervously zipped and unzipped the carrying case of the net gun. "They have room for me for the month, at least. It's a good home base for my search." Elliot smiled. "And besides, I heard there is a spectacular display of carved jack-o'-lanterns that I shouldn't miss."

"That's not for another couple of months," I pointed out. "Surely you'll have closed a deal with someone by then."

"If I still want to have a job, yes. But until then." He held up the net gun, as if it were a trophy.

"The tips could come in at any hour. You'll have to let me know when it's appropriate to call."

Elliot smiled, tucked the net gun under his arm, and fished a business card out of his jacket pocket. "Call anytime. I turn off the ringer when I'm sleeping."

I took the card and stuffed it into the pocket of my jeans without looking, and got back into my car. "Thanks," I said through the open window, and turned the key in the ignition.

"Wait, your gun."

"Keep it," I said, but it came out wrong, a little harsh. "I mean, bring it with you. When we hear about Freckles."

"I'll look forward to it."

"Okay, then," I said, feeling shy all of a sudden. I rolled up the window and pulled away, leaving Elliot Danforth and his net gun in complete darkness, and confused by the sudden hope that Erika would call with a Freckles sighting so I could take him up on his offer.

Chapter Five

❧

Saturday mornings were always busy at the diner, so I scheduled four waitresses—better to have one of the high school girls standing around flirting with the dishwasher during a slow period than to be short staffed when a bus full of tourists came in. It's officially my day off, but I usually spend an hour or two getting caught up on paperwork or doing inventory or paying bills—all the little things I'm sure my dad never imagined when he was thinking of opening a restaurant. I tried to stay out of everyone's hair—the Saturday crew had their own flow and they didn't need me telling them the most efficient way to set up the coffee station, even if my way is the best.

The Saturday after the town meeting I spent decorating the diner for the upcoming Corn and Tomato Festival. It was Guthrie's annual festival celebrating the riches of summer. It was my favorite Guthrie holiday—I had loved it since I was a child, mostly because it was an excuse to eat as much buttery, salted sweet corn as humanly possible without my mom fussing at me. The highlight of the festival was the annual tug-of-war against the neighboring town of Rowan. It had been held every year, rain or shine, since 1921. No one remembers how the rivalry started, but that didn't keep the citizens of Guthrie from desperately wanting to win. We hadn't taken home the trophy—a coiled yard of bronze-plated rope—in over two decades.

Fern had made a garland by stitching together cornhusks that she had collected from the kitchen, which I intended to hang over the entrance. I set up the ladder and climbed up, garland and nail gun in hand.

"Looks very festive," said a calm voice. I looked down to find Elliot Danforth gazing up at me. "Need a hand?"

"Sorry if I'm keeping you from your brunch. Almost done." I nailed the garland in five spots and climbed down the ladder. When I stepped off, Elliot reached over and folded the ladder back to flat.

"I've already eaten, just out for a walk." Elliot eyed the garland. "Special occasion?"

"There's a festival coming up." I brushed away the loose strands of hair that were sticking to my face. "Corn and Tomato. You've probably seen the signs."

Elliot nodded. "'Old-Fashioned Family Fun.' And I may have noticed some decorations." He waved his arm down the street. Every business had a cornstalk or two tied to the trees near their doors, or tomato cages decorated with streamers stuck in their planters alongside the mums.

"Guthrie takes its festivals pretty seriously."

"Is that so?"

I leaned a little closer to him. He had that good smoky scent. "If you don't decorate for Corn and Tomato Festival or the Harvest Festival, or for the Mud Season Spectacular, or the Sugar on Snow Fair, you open yourself up to all sorts of speculation."

"What kind of speculation?"

I looked over my shoulder to see if anyone was approaching. The coast was clear. "One year I didn't hang twinkle lights outside the diner during the Summer Solstice celebration and word got out that it was because I was suffering from vertigo and couldn't climb a ladder."

"Someone just made that up?"

I nodded. "I still have old-timers shuffle over to offer me an arm while I'm waiting to cross the street." I didn't tell him the reason I didn't hang the lights was because when I went to the hardware store to buy replacement twinkle lightbulbs, I saw Sean and the intern kissing in the glues and adhesives aisle, and I had to flee.

I held up a string of lights that were made up of little plastic cherry tomatoes. "I better put these up inside before the festival committee comes in for lunch."

Elliot reached for the ladder. "Could I talk to you while you're working?"

I glanced at him. He looked harmless enough in his dark jeans and pressed oxford shirt. Handsome even. "I can even take a break. Come on in."

Elliot sat on one of the two free stools at the counter while I poured us both cups of coffee. A group of twentysomethings wearing "Keep Guthrie Small" T-shirts waited by the door to be seated.

"Sorry," I said, nodding my head toward them.

"I'm all for a healthy debate." By his relaxed shoulders I believed him. Elliot smiled warmly at the protestors and said good morning as they passed by on their way to their booth.

I was impressed by his open attitude and his willingness to discuss the issues. It made me want to be more like him. "So what did you want to talk about?" I asked, sliding onto the stool next to him.

"Can I ask you a couple of questions about the other night?"

"You mean the town meeting? Sure."

He nodded. "Is that usually how they go?"

I poured milk from the creamer into my cup. "You mean, do they usually devolve into chaos?"

Elliot rubbed his face with his fingers. He had pianist's hands, elegant and strong and clean. "That is what I was wondering."

"I'd love to say no, but . . . the town meeting before last ended in a heated discussion over whether the winner of this year's giant pumpkin contest had cheated because he used Miracle-Gro."

"I kind of figured that would be the answer." He carefully peeled off the cap of one creamer and poured it into his cup. "What did they decide?"

"There wasn't anything in the bylaws that said you couldn't use it. They decided to break the award into two categories next year—organic and nonorganic."

"That sounds reasonable." Elliot tapped his fingertips together as he watched the cook stir hash brows on the griddle through the window. "I know this is inappropriate to ask, and I hope you won't be offended—"

I tucked my arms into the bib of my overalls, then untucked them. "Shoot."

"I may have heard that the town councilman who mediated the meeting is your ex-husband."

"How did you hear that?"

The tips of Elliot's ears reddened.

The front door bell tinkled and Fern walked in, trailed by her two daughters. The two girls plopped into a booth and whipped out their phones.

"I'm not offended," I said, although it did make me uncomfortable to think of Elliot talking about me with people in town. "It's common knowledge. Sean is my ex."

I swiveled on the stool to face the row of booths by the windows. "Hey there," I said to Fern. "What are you doing here on your day off?"

"The girls have a favor to ask." Fern glanced over at the table and gave us an exasperated look. "Come ask Nora yourself."

Fern's daughters put their phones facedown on the table and came to stand by their mother.

"What do you say?"

"Nora, we've signed up for Girls Rock Boston this summer and we are asking area businesses for donations to help us raise funds for our travel expenses," said Joan in a nonchalant way that was the perfect imitation of her mother. Joan was only twelve. I was pretty sure Fern was in for a hell of a ride through Joan's teen years.

"And for new outfits," added Alice, the youngest. She was nine and still as soft and round as she was as a baby. Joan elbowed her in the ribs.

"And what happens at Girls Rock Boston?" I asked.

"We start a band," Joan said in a distracted way, her eyes on a table of junior high soccer players who were throwing French fries at each other.

Alice looked over her shoulder to see what had captured her sister's attention. "And we learn to write songs."

"That sounds like a worthy cause. Could I ask you to do something in return?"

The two girls looked at each other.

"Sure," said Joan.

I put my hand on Elliot's shoulder. "I'll be right back."

I popped into my office, plopped the string of lights on my desk, and grabbed my checkbook and the stack of missing dog flyers I had made. I stopped by the freezer and plucked out two ice-cream sandwiches.

When I returned to the dining room, Elliot was showing the girls a Sleater-Kinney video. "Carrie Brownstein is widely recognized as a pioneer in the Riot Grrrl movement," he said, tapping on the screen. I wrote each of the girls a check for fifty dollars while they watched.

"Could you post these around town as you are soliciting donations?" I asked as I handed each of the girls an ice-cream sandwich, a stack of flyers, and a check.

"Got any tape?" Joan asked, biting into the ice cream.

"I'll grab it," Fern said. "Okay, girls. Next stop."

"Okay," I said, sliding back onto my stool. "Where were we?"

"We were talking about your ex-husband. Here's the part that might offend you." He had a way of saying things so calmly that they sounded reasonable, even when he was telling you that they might not be. "Would you mind asking Sean to put the zoning vote on the top of the agenda for the next town meeting?"

"Even when we already decided no?"

Elliot looked sheepish. "It will give me a chance to see if the town is open to the idea at all. Even if you don't want to sell the Johnson property to HG, how the town votes will give me a chance to see how people are leaning. If they vote no, I'll take Guthrie off my list of prospects."

"And if they say yes?"

He raised his eyebrows. "Maybe you'll change your mind?"

I shot him a look.

Elliot smiled and held his hands up in surrender. "If they say yes, then I'll keep looking in the area. There are a couple of pieces of property that might work. Not as good as the Johnson land, though."

"Nothing is as good as the Johnson land," I agreed. I had caught myself a couple of times daydreaming about living in Peggy's little house. It held the same warmth and charm as my childhood home. Every time I returned to my apartment from visiting Peggy's, I found myself feeling restless and itchy, confined. "Can I be honest with you?"

"I'd expect nothing less."

"The issue not coming to a vote the other day . . . that might have been the town's way of voting without—"

"Without offending anyone. I'm familiar with the tactic." Elliot tapped his fingertips together. "Still, I'd be curious to see what happens when an actual vote occurs."

"Just curious?"

"A lot of my work is based on intuition. Let's just say I'd like to settle a hunch. But I'm afraid the conversation might . . ."

"Drift?" I offered.

He smiled. "Drift, and we'll have to wait another month before we know if the town will even consider changing the zoning. I'm afraid if that happens it will push HG in another direction."

As much as I wanted to see Peggy's land preserved, I was grateful to still have Elliot's interest. No one else had made an offer and I was starting to get nervous. There were utility bills to pay. The oven stopped working while Max was baking a cake, and we had to bring in a repairman. The quarterly property tax payment was due in September, and now that the bank had said yes, I would have to budget in making loan payments at the end of every month. I had enough in savings to get us through three, maybe four months tops as long as business at the diner kept steady. HG might have to be my emergency backup plan. "I'll mention it to him. But I'm not making any promises."

"No promises needed." He smiled at me then, and I noticed for the first time that his eyes were hazel: green and gold and brown, like autumn leaves floating on the surface of a pond. I fought the urge to snap his picture.

Elliot stood and followed me out the door and back onto the street. "So what do you do on a sunny Saturday?" he asked.

"Normally nothing too exciting—laundry, grocery shopping, chores." I shrugged. "Right now I'm headed over to see how my sister's callbacks are going."

"She mentioned something about making a movie?"

"It's called *Side Work*. It's for a film festival. I have no idea what it's about."

Elliot nodded. "Freckles has been seen several times now, by a sugarhouse on the inn's property."

"Erika mentioned it. I guess she ordered some sort of trap but it is back-ordered."

Elliot tapped a couple of small stones with his toe. "I've seen him over there myself."

"How did he look?"

"Good, actually. He's definitely eating. Coat looks shiny." He hesitated. "I've been working on a way to get closer to him, but I could use some help. Next evening you're free, would you want to come out and see?"

"To the sugarhouse?"

"He usually comes around sometime between late afternoon and dusk."

I laughed. "You've been watching him, haven't you?"

Elliot smiled. "That's my favorite time of day so I like to be outside then. Best time to see night birds. They're more active then."

"I'm free tomorrow."

He looked pleased. "Sun sets at seven thirty these days. Want to meet me at the inn around six? That will give us enough time to get set up."

I had no idea what he meant by getting set up, but I was too distracted by the fact that my pulse had doubled to care. "Yes. Okay."

Two young women, both wearing overalls and red Keds, walked by, clutching scripts.

I looked down at my own overalls.

"I'd better get over to the auditions."

"I'm headed to the hardware store. Are the auditions in that direction?"

"They're at the Guthrie Playhouse." I waved my hand up the street, toward the Guthrie Hammer and Nail. The playhouse was just a couple of doors down.

Elliot held out his arm. "In case you feel dizzy."

I hesitated for a moment. If my failing to hang twinkle lights led to gossip, what would happen if I walked arm in arm with the representative of the big-box store? I looked up at his ear tips. Bright red. I took his arm anyway.

I could hear Kit's voice while still outside under the awning of the Guthrie Playhouse. The door had been propped open.

Inside, someone had written *Side Work—Callbacks Upstairs* on a piece of poster board and propped it up on an easel. I walked up the grand curved staircase, the banister shiny from the oil of a hundred years of theater lovers' hands. Each step was rounded at the edges, soft with wear. At the top, in front of the main doors to the theater, a young woman sat behind a card table with a list and red pen.

"You must be here for the role of Cora. Name?" she asked. I didn't recognize her. Maybe one of the White cousins?

"Nora Huckleberry, I'm Kit's sister, I'm—"

"I don't see your name," she said, biting on the pen cap. "Open auditions are closed, I'm afraid. These are for—"

"I'm just here to see Kit," I said, pushing aside the thick velvet curtain that was hanging in front of the doorway.

Onstage there were two women. One was wearing a bright patterned minidress, the other overalls, a black long-sleeve T-shirt, and a pair of red Keds. I looked down at my own feet as it hit me.

"You're not going to the contra dance in a skirt that short," the woman in the overalls said.

"It's not that short." The minidress wearer stuck her legs out one at a time. "It's barely above the knee."

The other girl tucked her hands into the bib of her overalls. "But when you twirl, it's going to be around your waist. Do you want—"

"Every old farmer seeing you in your underwear?" I mumbled to myself, in unison with the actress. The argument with Kit was as clear in my memory as if it had happened last week.

I rushed down the steps to the front of the theater in the darkness, looking for Max and Kit. I found them in the third row center, leaning back with clipboards on their laps, legs propped up on the seats in front of them.

"Kit," I whispered, squatting down in the aisle, at the beginning of their row.

"Hey, Nora." Max smiled up at me and patted the seat beside him. He motioned to the two actresses on the stage. "This is the last pair before we break."

"And what about your side work?" The overalls actress held up a half-empty sugar shaker. "The other waitresses have been complaining, Kate."

"Side work. Side work! Don't you know there are more important things in the world than whether there is the same amount of Equal and Splenda packets on the tables? Don't you see? Ever since Mom died you've—"

"Kit," I said again.

"Shhhhh." Kit waved a hand in my direction but kept her attention on the actors on the stage. "This is the emotional center of the scene."

"This is—you can't do this!" I said louder than I meant to.

The women on the stage stopped mid scene. "Should we keep going?"

Kit looked over at Max.

"That was great, really great, ladies. Let's take five, then we'll pick it up when Cora picks up the sugar shaker."

Max stood and turned to the back of the room. "Paul, will you raise the houselights just a notch?"

The soft lights of the auditorium came on. Max gave a double thumbs-up.

"Kit," I said as calmly as I could muster, "you never mentioned when you said you were making a movie that you were making a movie about me."

Kit rolled her eyes. "It's not about you, Nora. Everything's not about you."

I felt my face flush. Kit, who cried when she didn't receive a gift on my twelfth birthday. Kit, who refused to fill in when the flu hit the staff and I had a fever of 101 degrees, because she was in the middle of recording a demo with her goth band. Kit, who insisted on performing an interpretive dance at Dad's funeral to "fully express her grief," accusing *me* of making everything about me.

I shoved my hands into the bib of my overalls, remembered that that was what the actress had done onstage, yanked them out, and shoved them into my pockets. "I am not *making* this about me. There is no *making* this about me—this *is* about me."

"It is about a pair of sisters," Max offered calmly. "And it's true, the deepest well we have to draw from as artists is our own experience."

"Draw from your own experience, then. Just leave me out of it."

"It's not about us. It's fiction. It's not even in the past, or the present. It's postapocalyptic!" Kit climbed over her seat and into an empty row and walked toward me.

"It's postapocalyptic, with contra dancing?" I may have yelled this.

Max threw his arm around both of our shoulders. "Nora, it's a really beautiful story, trust me. And Kit, now that I've met Nora, I can see that you did a little more than 'borrow a few details' from her. We can make edits, yes?"

Kit and I glowered at each other. If it weren't for Max, I was pretty sure this argument would have been bigger than the one we had when Kit was fifteen and ran away to live on a commune.

"We can make edits," Kit relented.

Max swatted Kit's butt with a packet of papers. "Give Nora a copy of the script."

Kit reached into her bag and pulled out a rumpled pile of papers and handed them to me.

"Think you could have it back to us by tomorrow night, Nora?" Max asked. He nodded toward the stage. "I think we found our stars. It would be great if we could start filming by the end of next week."

I took the wad of papers out of Kit's hands and patted them into a tidy pile. "I'll do it right now. Let me see if your stage manager will lend me her red pen."

The bright yellow of the Sugar Maple Inn glowed in the coppery evening light. The inn stood in a clearing high on the mountain, and from the driveway you could see the lush green of the valley below. The day's warmth was quickly being displaced by the cool air rolling off the mountain. Margaret had planted sunflowers along the side of the barn, and their heads hung heavy with seeds. A pair of downy woodpeckers hopped from plant to plant, the splash of red on the back of their necks flashy against their plump black-and-white bodies.

Elliot hadn't mentioned where we should meet, so I let myself into the inn through the main door. Sarah, the front-of-the-house manager, was breaking down a tea service in the sitting room.

"Hey, Nora," Sarah said warmly. "Just seeing you makes me crave Charlie's blueberry pancakes."

I laughed. "I'll take that as a compliment."

"You should." Sarah looked over her shoulder. "Alfred is a whiz at savory food, but he can't manage a pancake to save his life. Burnt every time. It's why we don't serve hot brunch."

I couldn't wait to share this intel with Charlie.

"You here for dinner? Dining room is booked solid tonight, but I could get you a glass of wine if you'd like, and Alfred would be happy to make you something. I could serve you in here. Sit by the fire?"

I couldn't remember the last time I had been out to dinner someplace that had cloth napkins. It sounded heavenly. "I'd love to. I'm actually meeting one of your guests—Mr. Danforth?"

"Elliot? He's a sweetheart. Let me call up to his room."

I wandered into the sitting room, admiring the eclectic way that Margaret had decorated the place. The walls were jammed with old family photographs, landscape drawings of covered bridges and the area hills, watercolor studies of local birds and plants. The Sugar Maple felt homey, but still elegant. The scent of roasting chickens and browning garlic wafted in from the kitchen. My stomach growled.

"Oh, good," Elliot said from behind me. "I forgot to ask you to wear something neutral. That's perfect."

I looked down to see what I was wearing, and wasn't surprised to find I had thrown on black jeans and a gray long-sleeve T-shirt under a thin gray fleece vest. I had twisted a green scarf around my neck at the last minute, when I heard the temperature might drop into the forties. Kit seems to have inherited all of the fashion genes in the family. I loved to look at clothes from an artistic point of view, but when it came time to dress myself, function always came before form. I pulled the zip tab of my vest a little higher. "Good. Great. Ready for action."

I followed Elliot out the front door and around the building, letting him lead the way, even though I had been on hayrides and sleigh rides between the Sugar Maple and the McCracken farm every year since we were little and knew the area well.

We walked into the little patch of crab apples. The trees were thick with fruit, and the ground beneath was verdant with green grass. Elliot pulled one of the stray apples and tossed it far back into the field. "For the deer," he said, and kept walking.

Past the crab apples and down a twisting path we came upon the sugarhouse. It looked like the Sugar Maple in miniature: a tiny yellow house with a wraparound porch with four rocking chairs, two adult-sized, two for small children, lined up in a row. I was surprised to see the lights were on.

"Mrs. Hurley offered us the use of the house while we try to catch Freckles. She said the family doesn't use it much outside of sugaring season. It's nice to have someplace to coordinate." Elliot pushed open the door and stood aside, inviting me in.

Inside, the sugarhouse looked like a sweet playhouse for children. There were Lincoln Logs stacked up on the braided rug in front of a cozy-looking couch, and the bookcases were crammed with board games. Stuffed animals were piled onto a futon in one corner. The wall by the door was covered by a blown-up map of Guthrie. Red pushpins were pressed into the spot marking the inn, as well as the locations of the White Market, the diner, and Tom Carrigan's dairy farm. There were a few yellow pins as well.

"Is this a map of Freckles sightings?"

Elliot nodded. "The red ones are known sightings, the yellow ones are reports from people who weren't quite sure. Like here." Elliot pointed to a pin stuck in one of the far edges of Guthrie, by the creemee stand over by Starlit Lake. "Someone reported they saw something with Freckles's coloring moving over by the Dumpster behind the ice-cream place." Elliot drew his finger across the map from the creemee stand down to the sugarhouse. "It strikes me as unlikely, given the distance and the fact that the only food there is the ends of ice-cream cones, but it's worth noting."

I studied the map while Elliot gathered up whatever it was he thought we needed to capture Freckles, but really I was just admiring how thorough he was about all of this. I had entertained the thought that Elliot might be feigning interest in capturing Freckles to get on my good side, but no one would go to this much trouble if he wasn't truly engaged. It said something about who he was, that he cared about Freckles's welfare even though he had never even pet the dog once.

"Come over here," Elliot said from the row of windows that looked out onto a stand of maple trees. "Let me show you what I've been working on."

I joined him at the back of the cottage. I could see a red-painted canoe tipped upside down in the yard, about halfway between the house and the beginning of the carriage trail that wound through the sugar bush and up to the McCracken tree farm.

"I've seen Freckles several times just at the edge of the forest over there," he said, pointing to the tree line. "The pastry chef at the inn has been leaving food out for him. See the bowls?" Elliot glanced over at me.

I nodded.

"Someone moved them from the porch to the yard, and he stopped eating from them. It took a week before Freckles would venture over to the bowls in the new location. He spooks easily. I didn't want to risk moving the bowls once he started eating from them again," Elliot continued. "But they were too far away from any cover for me to try to capture him with the net gun. Then I saw the canoe."

"Of course," I said, nodding as if the canoe were an obvious solution. Really, I just didn't want to interrupt him. I liked the slow way he unfolded a story, carefully as if it were a well-worn map of a place you loved that you didn't want to tear. Like it was worth taking the time to do it right.

"Every day for the past week I've moved the canoe a couple of inches toward the tree line. I've elevated it bit by bit as well. I think it's in shooting distance now. And we can fit underneath it."

"So wait, we're going to hide under the canoe?"

Elliot beamed. "We're going to hide under the canoe." Elliot grabbed a backpack by the door. When he opened it, I spied the handle of the net gun, a flashlight, and some other supplies. He pulled out two pairs of binoculars and handed them both to me. "One is for night vision," he said. "So, we are going to slowly, quietly make our way over to the canoe, and then wait. When you spot him, I'll use the net gun to catch him. Deal?"

I don't know what I had imagined we would be doing, but sitting under a tiny upside-down boat hadn't been it. Thank God I had brushed my teeth before I left the house. Was my breath okay? When was the last time I washed this fleece? "Deal," I said, waving a pair of binoculars in each hand.

We kept our bodies low and crept slowly to the back of the canoe. I watched as Elliot placed the backpack under the boat, lay on his stomach, and snaked his way underneath. I did the same with the binoculars. The inside of the canoe smelled like the deep woods, the cedar scent of the boat mingling with the tang of crushed blades of grass and the damp smell of the dirt underneath. And then, on top of that, was the smokiness of Elliot that lingered despite the fact that he was out of his business suit, wearing a pair of faded jeans and a soft-looking dark green chamois shirt from L. L. Bean. I only hoped that I didn't smell like the Miss Guthrie.

The canoe had been raised high enough that we could lean on our forearms while lying underneath. Elliot balanced the net gun on a little tripod made of twigs while I uncapped the binoculars and focused them on the dog bowls by the maple trees. We both silently looked out at the tree line for what felt like hours. I grew conscious of the space under the boat. It was as if it were shrinking.

"So how did you know Mrs. Johnson?" Elliot asked quietly.

"She was my neighbor growing up."

"You lived on that little farm next door? That's a beautiful spot. Why did you leave?"

It felt like too long and sad and complicated a story to tell while lying underneath a boat. It was too small a space to explain about my mother wasting away while we all tried to pretend she would never die, or about my father who gave up on life after she passed. Never mind Sean and me.

"We needed the money," I said finally. I figured that was a story he must hear all the time.

"I'm sorry. I could tell by the trees that were planted around the house that it was well loved."

This was the kindest response I could have imagined, and an unexpected one. "Do you still have family in Maine?" I asked, to move the conversation away from me.

"We still have a little spot up by Acadia, but years can pass between visits. It's pretty rough. It isn't winterized or anything." He looked a little embarrassed. "My parents moved down to Florida about ten years ago. Mom's arthritis is bad—she can barely walk. It's easier for them down there."

"I've never been to Florida. Do you like it?"

Elliot shook his head. "Honestly? Not really. There are some beautiful places, sure, and some extraordinary birds . . ."

"But?"

"But there are a lot of gun shops and chain restaurants."

I poked his net gun. "I'm pretty sure this isn't the only gun you own."

"These aren't the kind of gun stores that specialize in hunting rifles," Elliot said.

"And don't you develop chains?"

Elliot looked shocked. "Not chain restaurants."

"Is there a big difference between a chain restaurant and a chain store?"

"I think there is." Elliot leaned over on his side to meet my eyes. "All stores sell manufactured goods. Ninety-nine times out of a hundred, a small hardware store is selling the same factory-made nail as a store like HG. But food, what you do at the diner—"

"What Charlie does, really," I said, because honestly, if I were working the grill at the Miss Guthrie, the lines at the McDonald's in the town next door would be miles long.

"What Charlie does, and what you do—the way you know your customers, and the way you can tailor the food you make to the community you serve—a chain restaurant can't compare."

"But Burt Grant down at the Hammer and Nail does the same thing that I do. He knows all of his customers. He offers credit to farmers who need to mend their fences before their cash crops come in. He tailors what he carries in his store to the town's needs."

The sun had dropped below the trees, and the sugar bush was beginning to take on the inky blue of dusk. Elliot reached over for the night vision binoculars. He uncapped them and handed them to me. "These can take a little getting used to."

I raised the binoculars up to my eyes and peered into the woods. The world looked hyperfocused, bright and green.

"I'd never say that a store like HG doesn't have an impact on a town like Guthrie. And of course it would have a huge impact on someone like Burt Grant. But some corporations do good for a community as well."

I sighed. I didn't feel like hearing the HG pitch when my belly was wet from the damp earth. "Tell me something good, something not in your pitch. Tell me something you're proud of in your work." It was a question I had been wanting to ask him. Maybe it was easier because of the darkness.

Elliot was silent for several minutes. I played with the focus on the binoculars while he thought over my question. Through the lenses I could make out the distinct shape of a gray fox walking along the edge of the woods.

"Oh."

"Freckles?"

"No. Look," I said, handing Elliot the binoculars.

"What a beauty," he said. Elliot's bottom lip hung down a fraction, and his tongue just barely stuck out as he leaned forward to get a better view. I wished there was a little light—just enough to capture the look of pure wonder on his face, but I knew it was impossible in the darkness. "Do you see many foxes around here?"

"They were the reason I stopped trying to keep chickens," I said.

Elliot turned his face toward me, his expression still unguarded. "HG commissions local artists wherever they develop," he said quietly. "And they pay them very well to make art in their spaces. Some of the artists get to create on a scale they could never afford to on their own. HG even has a curator on staff in charge of taking care of the work, and reaching out to the communities to find out what they would like to see. I'd love to show you some of the art. That's something I'm really proud of."

I opened my mouth, about to tell him about Peggy's sculpture garden, but a part of me hesitated.

"There he is!" Elliot thrust the binoculars at me and grabbed the net gun. "Keep your eyes on him."

And there he was. Freckles, all one hundred pounds of him, paced in front of the bowls of kibble and water, stopping to sniff in the direction of the canoe, his white-striped muzzle moving in a circular motion, his white-tipped tail hanging low.

"Tell me when he reaches the bowls," Elliot said in a whisper.

Freckles took one step toward the kibble bowl, and then another.

"He's eating," I whispered into Elliot's ear.

Elliot leaned up straight onto his forearms, held the gun steady, and pulled the trigger. Freckles flinched at the sound.

The net shot across the field, opened, and snared the two speck-led bowls. Freckles had bolted a split second before. I scanned the woods—he was nowhere to be seen. Elliot scooched out from underneath the canoe and reached down to help me up. He pulled a Maglite out of the backpack he had brought with him and flashed it into the trees. The gray fox looked straight at us, blinking in the bright light, then slinked back into the woods.

"Well," Elliot said, brushing off his pants.

I peeled several wet blades of grass off of my vest. "Erika said the trap she ordered uses a pressure plate trigger to close the trapdoor. Maybe that will work."

"Maybe," said Elliot. He turned his face toward the cabin, and the light from the windows illuminated his disappointment. "Would you come in for a glass of cider? I have a bottle in the cabin."

It was dark, and I felt dirty from lying on the cold ground, and my back was a bit stiff, but I wasn't quite ready to face my little apartment and my little sister. "Okay."

Elliot handed me a glass of cider as I settled into the puffed cushions on the sofa. I took a long sip, and then another more thoughtful one. It was like no cider I had ever had. The bubbles were tiny, like champagne. It was clean tasting, like maple sap straight from the tree, and perfectly balanced, walking the finest line between dry and sweet. I hoped the bottle was full. "This is incredible."

"It's made from a variety of apple that was around during the time of Shakespeare."

"A really old apple, then," I said, and drained my glass.

Elliot laughed, and filled my glass to the rim. "Did you know that if you plant an apple tree from seed, the tree will produce fruit that tastes completely different from the apple it came from?"

"That's my sister Kit. She isn't like either of my parents."

"Or very much like you?" Elliot settled into the other end of the couch.

"At first glance. We do have some things in common. We have the same sense of humor. And we both love film—"

"Are you a filmmaker, too?"

I shook my head. "No, no. Kit is the artist in the family." I turned my attention back to the cool cider. "So how do all Red Delicious apples taste the same if you can't grow a tree from seed?" I asked, wanting to change the subject.

Elliot shuddered. "First of all, although it's technically an apple, let's take the Red Delicious out of the conversation."

"Not a fan?"

"Have you ever actually eaten a Red Delicious?"

"Of course."

Elliot shook his head. "And you weren't disgusted by it?"

I held my hands up in surrender. "They are mealy."

Elliot leaned back. "And they taste like a Yankee Candle."

I laughed. "It's true. I've never thought of that before, they taste like—"

"The idea of an apple, not an actual flavor that comes from nature."

"So, no Red Delicious. How do you make a McIntosh apple—"

"Now you're talking."

"—taste like a McIntosh apple?"

Elliot leaned back, his hands resting on his belly. "Grafting."

"I remember my dad teaching me a little about this when we were kids. That's when you tie two branches together?"

"Let me borrow your scarf."

I unwound the scarf, my neck feeling exposed when the last few inches of fabric slipped onto my lap.

"Give me your arm." Elliot reached over and placed his hand by my elbow, so that my arm was resting on his, my fingers curled into the crook of his arm. "You carefully make a long slice at the end of a fresh branch on a tree, and the end of the apple branch you want to grow, then fit them together like this." Elliot pressed his forearm to mine. He took the scarf and started to wind the fabric over our joined arms, tossing the scarf over and pulling it back, binding us together. "Then you wrap them with cloth, snug, like this."

"You're good at this," I said softly, aware of the warmth of my arm on his, and the way his hand cupped my elbow. He was leaning forward, his face close as he worked.

"I'm an Eagle Scout," he said and gave me a small smile as he tucked the end of the scarf into the fabric around my wrist. With his free hand he rubbed our bound arms, inspecting his work. "In time, the new branch will heal onto the tree, and will bear its original fruit." He said this quietly. I could feel his warm breath on my skin.

"That's really cool," I said lamely, my cheeks burning at the realization that I liked the feeling of being pressed against him, even in this small way. The binding reminded me of what I thought a marriage could be—joining yourself to a new family, and with their support, growing and blooming. "Are some trees better than others?" I asked, and a little trace of hope escaped in my question. I hadn't done a lot of blooming as a LaPlante.

Elliot thought for a moment as he slowly unraveled the scarf. "I think technically you could join any fruit tree onto another, but some trees are better suited than others. Climate, environment, the health of the tree, the soil, all of those things come into play."

I thought the same was true for couples, but I didn't say anything.

"There's a man in England who has grafted over two hundred and fifty varieties of apples onto one tree."

The last loop of fabric loosened and the scarf fell free. Elliot squeezed my elbow before letting go. My arm felt cold without his. "How do you know so much about apples, anyway?"

"It was a hobby of my father's. He collected apple varieties. He actually saved three varieties that were extinct here in the U.S."

"What are they like?"

Elliot stood, straightening his shirt. "Sour. And small. Terrible, really."

I laughed. "Good thing he saved them."

"He has a soft spot for the neglected and unlikable." Elliot took both glasses and brought them to the sink. "At the town meeting, who was the older woman with the long silver braid?"

"That's Dotty McCracken. She's Margaret's best friend. I'm sure you'll see her at the Sugar Maple if you stay a little longer."

"She mentioned an orchard here in town?" he asked over the rush of water pouring from the faucet.

"On Peggy's land. Yes, there is a small orchard. It's full of odd fruit. Berry bushes, too." I thought I heard a deep *woof* from outside. I looked out the back window, but could see only the reflection of Elliot rinsing the glasses. "She must not have kept it up—it's really overgrown."

"Would you take me there?"

He could have asked if he could see it, or for directions or a map. He could have just added it to the list of things for the surveyor to take account of. But he asked if I would take him there.

"Did you bring muck boots?"

Elliot laughed, a full, loud laugh that left him openmouthed. "You have to be the most practical woman I have ever met."

The way he said it sounded like a compliment.

"I have some sturdy, waterproof boots with me, yes."

"The ground is thick with old fruit," I said, cheeks burning, feeling dumb and pleased at the same time. "It's super slippery."

"Was there anything ripening?" Elliot's face held that hopeful look again.

"There were some tall bushes covered with shiny black berries."

He thought for a moment. Then his face brightened. "Did they have red stems?"

"Blood red. They reminded me of drawings of the vascular system."

"Elderberry," he said, and he looked as if he were forming a plan. "You're in for a treat."

Max met me on Peggy's porch on Monday afternoon, wearing one of Peggy's aprons—this time an orange chiffon with white lace. He held a matching red apron in his hands. "Put it on," Max said. I tied it around my overalls. I looked like a farmer wearing a tutu.

"Perfect!" He slapped his hands together. "Now you are prepared to learn to bake. My teacher always said it was important to dress properly for whatever you are doing—that it puts you in the right mind-set."

"Your baking teacher?"

"Meditation teacher. Guru. It's all the same." Max beamed. "Let's do this."

In Peggy's kitchen, Max had already pulled out all the ingredients. Judging from the state of the kitchen, it looked as if Max had been baking for hours. The counter was piled high with bags of flour, cartons of eggs, and softening sticks of butter. A sifter half full lay on its side, dusting the floor with confectioners sugar. Rivulets of maple syrup ran down a gray gallon jug and onto the table. But Max seemed to thrive in all the chaos. He pushed back two half-empty bottles of milk to clear a work space.

"The first step is to measure out all of your ingredients. The French call it *mise en place*—everything in its place. That way you don't get halfway into a recipe and find out you needed softened butter or that you are out of eggs." Max reached into the wood-paneled cabinet and took out four Pyrex bowls in descending sizes that were nesting together. Each bowl was white on the inside, a different primary color on the outside.

Max slid the recipe card toward me. I dutifully dipped a straight-edged metal measuring cup into a box of cake flour.

"Hold that out for me. Now watch." Max slid his finger across the top of the cup so that the flour was level. "That's it. Perfect. Now just sift that with the salt and baking powder."

I followed Max's instructions, swiping the teaspoons of leavening and salt with my finger so that they were even.

"I'm really sorry about the other day, at the auditions," Max said, handing me a pound of butter. "I hadn't realized how much Kit had pulled from your relationship when I first read the script, since I hadn't met you yet." He smiled at me sweetly.

"And now?" I asked as I poured maple syrup into a metal measuring cup.

"Not that one," he said, taking the cup of syrup out of my hands. He held up a glass measuring cup with a little spout. "This one is for liquids. Go ahead and pour it in. See how the dry cup is just a little more? Baking is all about measurement."

"Will it really make a difference?"

"It will. That's what I love about baking." Max squatted down so the maple syrup was at eye level. He poured out a little splash, then checked it again. "It invites you to slow down and pay attention." Max poured the syrup into a saucepan and turned the flame on underneath, adjusting the gas until he was satisfied. "The frosting was too thin when I tried this recipe last week. Maybe reducing the syrup will help."

"My grandmother used to do that. I remember her scolding me for trying to taste the syrup while it was still cooking down."

Max pumped his fist and mouthed *yes* to himself, happy he had guessed correctly.

"Have you read the script yet?" Max asked.

I hadn't. I had tried, after I left the sugarhouse on Sunday night, but I was only on page 3 when I realized I didn't want to know how my sister saw me. I just added a note at the top to make the older sister less depressing and angry and left it under Kit's bag of mini Snickers bars to find when she got home.

"You don't need to apologize for my sister," I said. I pretended to study the recipe card. "I know her better than anybody. I practically raised her."

"She told me," Max said. He took a pat of butter and worked it into the sides of one of the cake pans. "About you two losing your mom, and basically losing your dad at the same time."

"Dad was there," I started, but I knew this was only half true. He kept the diner barely afloat, and paid the bills, but he wasn't able to be there for Kit and me the way we needed.

"You did a good job, Nora." Max lowered the flame under the maple syrup, which was boiling away. "Kit is extraordinary. She's kind and friendly. She has this magical way of making anyone laugh at themselves, which is such a gift, you know?" Max shook his head. "She's super generous with her talents and her ideas. I've never met anyone who went so out of her way to help her friends."

I had always felt a little jealous of Kit's friends. I had Fern, and Charlie, and Sean, of course, but Kit always seemed to have a mob of people orbiting around her, as if she were the sun. And I was a piece of space debris.

"It's like she radiates goodwill," Max continued. "I feel so lucky to have her in my life. And now I'm doubly lucky because I know you. The unstoppable Huckleberry sisters!"

I laughed. "You make us sound like superheroes. Kit is extraordinary, I agree with you. But I'm pretty sure I am quite stoppable."

"That's the craziest thing I have ever heard. Here, stop saying ridiculous things and get back to work. We need two yolks," he said, handing me a carton of eggs.

I cracked an egg open, and carefully poured it back and forth from shell to shell, trying to separate the white without breaking the yolk.

"Check this out," Max said. He broke an egg and put it into his hand, fingers closed. He held the hand over the sink, cracked his fingers slightly, and let the white ooze between them. "I used to do it this way at the Zen center, when I needed gallons of yolks for the brioche." He handed me an egg. "You try it."

"But we don't need any more yolks."

"Just try it. It feels kind of good when the white gives."

I cracked the egg and let the white slide through my fingers. A perfectly plump yolk sat in my hand. "That is cool. I can't believe Charlie doesn't do it this way."

"You'll have to show him," Max said, cracking a couple more eggs and adding them to the bowl of yolks. "You're a superhero to your sister, you know."

"To Kit?"

Max laughed. "Tell me there are more of you. I'd love it if there were five more Huckleberry sisters. Six even." Max rinsed his hands under the faucet. "It means the world to her that you agreed to the loan. That you have faith in her."

I snorted. "Kit Huckleberry is not in need of my approval."

"Of course she is. You're her sister, Nora. She looks up to you."

Kit, who ran off to join a feminist burlesque dance troupe the summer she was seventeen. Kit, who made traveling to Nepal look like a trip to the White Market. Kit, who had made it through her first thirty-four years without ever having a full-time job. "I have a hard time believing she looks up to me when my life is so—it's the opposite of everything that she has ever wanted."

"I don't think you have to want the same things to admire someone. And I know she admires you. You're the reason she's a screenwriter."

"She's a screenwriter because I run the family diner?"

"She's a screenwriter because she wants to be able to see the world the way you do. It's her way of paying attention. Some people meditate, some people take walks, she writes and directs. You take photos. And she said you used to paint?"

What he didn't know was that the pictures I took were studies for future paintings, for when I started again. If I started again. "That was a long time ago."

"It'll be there when you feel like it. That's been my experience, anyway. Everything has a way of cycling back. Like baking cakes—when I left the Zen center, I didn't think I would have a chance to bake again. And look what I'm doing right now." Max dunked a spoon into the maple syrup, inspected the round back to see how thick the liquid had become, then turned off the flame. "Do you mind if I ask why you feel stoppable?"

"Because I've—stopped?"

"What do you mean?"

"It's more like I've never begun." I leaned against the kitchen counter. "Look around, Max. I'm forty-two. I've lived in Guthrie my whole life. I run my dad's dream business. I live in an apartment complex for the elderly where I can't even keep a cat due to the lease, and my marriage failed. I went from taking care of my mom, to taking care of Kit, to taking care of the diner, and then taking care of my husband, and then my father. I feel like I haven't started my life."

"And why did you do all of those things?"

Why did I take care of my sister, and my mom, and my dad? Why did anyone do anything? "Because it was the right thing to do."

"Come here for a sec. Time to make the burnt sugar." Max put a cup of sugar in a deep saucepan and turned the flame on high. "First rule of caramel—never stir the caramelizing sugar— it can form sugar crystals, which chunk up and make the caramel grainy." As the sugar began to melt around the edges, he swirled the pan. "Second rule—never walk away from caramelizing sugar. It takes forever to reach temperature, but it can turn into a smoky, burning mass in a matter of seconds." He moved me by the shoulders so I was standing in front of the pot. "Third rule—do not touch the sugar, ever. It's like napalm. It will adhere to your skin and burn. Promise me you won't touch it."

"I promise."

"Okay, then. Tell me when it starts to brown." Max unwrapped a stick of butter, pinched off pieces, and tossed them into the bowl of Peggy's stand mixer. "So what would you do if you could do anything? If your life started right now?"

"No one's ever asked me that before. I don't really know." It's not like I hadn't thought about it. I spent hours at the diner wrapping silverware in napkins dreaming about what my life would have been like if I had been an ounce like Kit. If I had had her courage and her focus. Her talent, her clarity. Her determination. But I wasn't Kit. And, being Nora, I didn't know what I would do, so I did nothing. I said none of this to Max. It was one thing to admit that I felt like I hadn't started my life. It was another thing entirely to admit I felt I never would. "It's browning."

Max walked over to the stove. "Swirl it carefully! That's it!"

He turned off the flame. "Now we have to stop it from cooking—I should have set this up first. *Mise en place*, remember." He reached into the cabinet, pulled out another bowl, and filled it with cold water. He set the caramel pan right into the water bath. It steamed and hissed angrily. He pulled it out again and set it back on the stove. "We'll have to cool it a bit before mixing it into the cake or we'll scramble the eggs." He tossed the measured cup of sugar on top of the butter and set the mixer whirling. "Did Kit tell you I went to Harvard?"

"You went to Harvard? Undergrad or graduate school?"

"Both, actually. I was a philosophy major as an undergrad, and I went to the law school."

"I'm sorry," I said, trying and failing to stifle a giggle. "I cannot imagine you as a lawyer."

"Right?" Max said as he turned off the mixer. With a plastic spatula he scraped the butter and sugar off the edges of the bowl. "I couldn't, either. My dad wanted me to be a lawyer." Max pointed the buttery spatula at me. "He was a bricklayer. His dad was, too. He wanted more for his kids." Max swiped a bit of the butter and sugar mixture with his hand and licked it off his finger. "So he worked overtime and made patios for people out in the suburbs on his days off and never took a vacation."

"That's really sweet," I said, thinking of how hard both my parents worked so that Kit and I could have a happy childhood.

"It was. It was incredibly generous of him. The problem was I hated law school. Hated everything about it. I knew I should be grateful—here I was, in a prestigious school, working with my mind, not my hands." Max held his hands out. They were bony and one of his ring fingers was bent at a funny angle. "Every day

I felt as if I were one step closer to living this life I didn't want. I tried talking to my dad about it, but he wouldn't listen. So I went to see my meditation teacher, and I explained how miserable I was, but that leaving school would break my dad's heart." Max added an egg yolk to the mixture. "You want to add these one at a time, so it emulsifies, or the whole thing kind of refuses to come together." Max stopped the mixer and handed me the spatula. "Here, scrape everything down. You can never do that enough."

I pushed the golden yellow batter down to the bottom of the bowl. It looked fluffy and pale, as if it had transcended the original ingredients and had become something new entirely.

"And you know how my teacher responded? He just shrugged his shoulders and said, 'Okay.' When I pressed him for more—I mean, none of it felt okay—he said, 'Sometimes you have to be the person that makes someone unhappy.' That was it. No big deal." Max shook his head like he was hearing this advice for the first time, his shaggy brown hair drifting into his face. "My mind was blown. It was as if someone had just given me permission to be a human being."

"I don't know exactly what you mean," I said, resifting the flour. "Aren't Buddhists supposed to not cause suffering? Or is that just doctors?"

"That's exactly it! I was trying to be *good*, but by dividing things, actions, feelings into good and bad, I was just creating more pain."

"So what happened?"

"I dropped out, and headed west. That's when I entered the Zen center."

"And was your dad upset?"

"Oh, yes. We didn't talk for several years."

"So letting your dad down *did* cause your dad more pain, right?"

"But the question is, is that wrong?" Max held his arms up over his head. The spatula in his hand dripped butter, sugar, and egg onto his arm. *"Out beyond ideas of wrongdoing and rightdoing, there is a field. I'll meet you there.* That's Rumi. He was a Sufi, not a Buddhist." Max scraped the batter off of his arm and plopped it back into the mixer. "I'm just saying, you've done a lot of *doing what you think is right*. Which is great. No judgment. But now you know what that looks like. Maybe it's time for another option." Max dipped a finger into the caramelized sugar. "Perfect. It's cool enough. Let's get this bad boy in the oven."

Chapter Six

❧

Charlie and Fern were hunched over one end of the counter. When I went to see what they were up to, I found them hot-glue gunning yellow pom-poms onto green aprons to make them look like giant ears of corn—their uniforms for the Corn and Tomato Festival.

"Did you finish the corn chowder?" I asked.

Fern held one of the aprons up to my body. "Try this on."

I popped the loop over my head and tied the back.

Charlie and Fern studied me with concerned faces. "It's not really saying *corn* to me yet," Charlie said after several moments.

Fern balled up a fist full of pom-poms and balanced it on my head. "What if we added a headpiece?"

After considering me for a moment, Charlie cut a bunch of pale yellow yarn into strips and tied them into the neck loop of my apron, so that they draped over my shoulders.

Fern clapped her hands. "Tassels. Perfect!"

Charlie had propped the door open to let the warm afternoon breeze in, so I had no warning when Sean walked in. He was wearing another new suit.

I walked him down to the end of the counter, away from Fern and Charlie. "What can I get you?"

"Coffee would be great, to go, if I could. Thanks, Nor."

I studied Sean while I poured the coffee into a Styrofoam

cup. He looked tired. A little older, even. Maybe life as a public servant was wearing him down. "Charlie made a crumb cake." It had always been Sean's favorite.

"I'll take two."

I wrapped two pieces of the cake in wax paper, put them in a to-go bag, and placed it in front of him, next to the coffee. "Everything all right?"

Sean lifted out a piece of cake and took a huge bite, crumb topping tumbling down his lapels. "This town council gig has got me working all hours. We have an emergency meeting tonight about a sudden spike in kindergarten students for next year. The schools are asking for two more teachers, but there's no room in the budget."

I counted back, and confirmed that it was exactly six years ago that we had those back-to-back blizzards that had the town trapped for a solid week. "I knew that stormy winter was going to create a baby boom."

Sean raised his coffee cup to me. "You called it."

I leaned my arms on the counter. "Speaking of your new role in the town, I have a favor to ask." These were not words that ever came out of my mouth. I especially didn't like to ask Sean for anything because he was the kind of person who would bring it up over and over again. But I had said that I would. "Listen, about the agenda for the next town meeting." I took a deep breath. "Mr. Danforth was hoping that you could move the vote on the zoning change for Peggy's land to the top of the meeting."

"Did he fill out the paperwork?"

"He did, but he was certain that some other articles were ahead of his, and he was concerned—"

"You know the rules, Nora. First come, first served. Do you have any idea what Ben Smith is going to do to me if we don't hear him out about his neighbor's pigs?"

"But, Sean, his vote got bumped after that new science teacher at the high school got everyone talking about Peggy's orchard." I said this casually, but I kept a sharp eye on Sean's nose. It twitched. He did have a thing for that ecologist. "So isn't it technically his turn?"

"I thought you didn't want to sell to HG." Sean brushed the crumbs off his jacket, and folded over the edge of the bag, as if to stop himself from eating the second piece of cake.

"I don't. But without the zoning change I won't even have the option." I reached into my apron and pulled out a check pad and a pen. I quickly scrawled the price of coffee and the two pieces of cake and handed it to him. "We haven't had any other offers. I'm going to need the money soon."

"Why do you need money?" Sean was the spender in our little family. He knew I'd have some savings to lean on.

"I took a loan to help out Kit," I said quietly as my stomach did a small flip. I had just signed the loan papers on Monday and transferred the money into Kit's account the following day. My bailing out Kit from time to time had been a sore spot in our marriage. Sean thought I didn't give him enough slack—that the slack I had to give all went to Kit. He was probably right about that. "Please, Sean. Just give him five minutes. Once the vote is in I'll at least know where I stand."

"It's not so simple." Sean leaned over the counter, so close that the yarn tied to the neck of my apron tickled his face. "Let's just say the town council has a way of fitting onto the agenda what they think should be on the agenda. *Shaping the conversation,* they call it."

"Could you just ask? Please?"

Sean took the lid off the Styrofoam cup, swirled the dregs of coffee around, and drank them down in one shot. "I'll see what I can do," he said, slapping his hand down on the counter.

I followed him to the cash register. He handed me a ten, and waved me off when I tried to give him back his change. A pity tip. From my ex-husband. Charlie raised his eyebrows but didn't ask any questions. Kit had joined them at the counter. She had already glued three rows of pom-poms onto the headband she had been wearing. Sean leaned over and kissed her on the cheek before pushing his way out the door.

"Where's Max?" I asked, realizing I hadn't seen him since we had baked the burnt sugar cake.

Kit sighed. "Driving down to New York. He left late last night. We found a set of used lights we need for sale on Craigslist. Max wanted to see them firsthand. And he's going to try out the cameras down at one of the pro shops before we put our money down."

I was grateful Max had a head on his shoulders about money. If it were up to Kit, half the loan would already be invested in a camera a friend of a friend of hers had sworn was perfect for the job.

"When will he be back?" I found myself a little anxious to be alone with Kit, which was crazy since we had spent the first part of our lives sharing a canopy bed. Max had proved to be an excellent buffer between Kit and me, and I was pretty sure he had kept more than one conversation from turning into an argument. Now it would be just the two of us.

"Tomorrow, Thursday at the latest, depending how it goes. He told me to tell you that the Grant birthday cake is in the walk-in, and that he expects you to help with the Browns' wedding anniversary cake next week."

A group of teenagers came in wearing T-shirts and shorts and flip-flops, looking like they were just back from a day at Lake Willoughby.

Phyllis the mail carrier followed them through the door. "Nice to see you two sisters together again," she said warmly. "Nora, the lawyers said I should have Peggy's mail forwarded to you, in case there's something you need for the house. I have it with me. Do you want me to drop it off here or over at your apartment?"

"Here is fine, Phyllis. I'm here more than there, anyway." I took the thick stack of mail out of her hand. Most of it was junk—back issues of the *Pennysaver,* some gardening catalogs. The utility bills I put in a separate stack, as well as notices about property taxes and the refuse and water bills from the town. Two familiar matching green envelopes, one fat, one thin, caught my eye. I pulled them out of the stack. *The Pudding Hill House,* the return address read. The nursing home where my dad had spent the last couple of years of his life. I tore one of them open. It was a bill for $8,897, addressed to Peggy.

"But Peggy wasn't in a nursing home," I said to myself. Charlie came to look over my shoulder.

"What's that?"

"I'm not sure," I said, reaching for the fatter envelope. It was a bill for $17,794 and a letter.

Dear Ms. Johnson,

Your payment for the care of Elsie Cole is overdue. We are sure this was just an oversight. If you are in need of assistance, please contact our financial services specialist, Mary Beth Swindon, as soon as possible. We know the uninterrupted care of your loved one is of the utmost importance.

Sincerely,
Sandy Pines
Accounting
The Pudding Hill House
Senior Living and Long-term Care
Guthrie, Vermont

"Fuck," said Kit.

"Seriously," I said, thinking she was reading over my shoulder, but she was looking at her phone and texting furiously.

"Who is Elsie Cole?" asked Charlie.

"I'm not sure," I said, although the name sounded familiar. I removed my phone and car keys from my overalls pocket and shoved the letters in. "I'm sure it's just a mistake." I didn't feel confident in this at all. I looked over at my little sister. "What's up with you?"

"It's the Vanagon," Kit said, her eyes fixed on the screen. "It broke down at the Massachusetts border. Max got a tow to a shop in North Adams. They think it might be the starter. Or the alternator. Or both."

"If he's waiting for it to get fixed, there's a cool art museum there," Fern said. "Tell him to check out MASS MoCA."

"Oh, yeah, Max would *love* that," Kit agreed, and started texting him the details.

"What's MASS MoCA?" I asked, but most of my attention

was on the envelope in my pocket. It seemed to get heavier by the second.

"They have space for huge installations," Charlie added. "I heard there was an exhibit once that breathed, like you were inside a lung."

"And a whole room where Sol LeWitt works are painted right on the walls." Kit showed us a mural in bold primary colors on her phone.

"And trees that are planted upside down and hanging from the sky," said Fern.

"And there are music festivals, too, in the summer. Wilco has a big party there every year," Charlie added.

Fern, Charlie, and Kit all started making plans, dreaming up road trips when the Vanagon was fixed and their time was freer. I was half listening, but my mind was swimming with the things that no one wanted to think about, the details underneath the dreams—the bills that were mounting, the cakes that needed baking, where Kit and Max would go once their movie was complete, who would buy Peggy's place, who would cover the grill and the counter if we all went away. And now this, this—I couldn't even let myself imagine what the envelope in my pocket meant for me, and for Kit.

"That sounds great," I said, not wanting to be on the outside of all the fun. Not wanting to do the right thing, like Max said. Not wanting to be the person to shoulder the burden. Not *Saint Nora*. "Sign me up. I'm in."

I changed out of my work clothes after the lunch rush on Thursday before driving out to the Pudding Hill House, even though Mary Beth Swindon came into the diner every Sunday evening with her parents for supper and knew what I looked like in my uniform. I used to change before visiting my dad every afternoon, too. I wanted to treat my visits like they were a special occasion, not something to dread. But the truth was, they were hard. Sean and I had kept dad at home for as long as we could, until he started wandering. The third time Sheriff Granby called me at the diner to let me know someone had found Dad sitting in their kitchen in the middle of the night, asking for a cup of coffee, we knew we didn't have a choice.

The Pudding Hill House was the nicest nursing home in town. They made an effort to make the dayrooms look homey, with lace doilies on the tables and table lamps with warm lightbulbs. They even put some money into the cafeteria and the food they served, even though the sense of taste was one of the first things to go in Alzheimer's patients. But at the end of the day, the Pudding Hill House was what it was—a place where people went when they couldn't be cared for at home.

"After this, let's get out of Guthrie and go have dinner somewhere new," Kit said and rolled her window down a crack. She had insisted on coming along for the ride, which surprised me. Kit seemed a little unmoored with Max away, antsy and unfocused. She stared out into the cornfields that hugged Pudding Hill, the yellowing tassels on the tips of the tall green stalks waving like streamers.

"There's a new Thai place over in Lyndonville," I said.

"Can you imagine coming to the U.S. from Thailand and ending up here?" Kit waved her hands at the rows and rows of corn.

"Well, Lyndonville is a bigger town than Guthrie. And I've never been to Thailand . . . maybe it looks similar to this. Maybe they feel right at home."

"Nora, Thailand does not look like *this*."

The way Kit said *this* made it sound like an insult. I took in the landscape: dark forest to our left, a mixture of spruce and pine trees, their trunks tall and straight, mixed in with maple, oak, and poplar. It seemed still and quiet, but I knew if I stopped the car we would hear a chorus of birds and insects and frogs. The ground would be spongy with a carpet of fallen leaves, bark, and needles. To the right was the cornfield, acres of it, soft and green. Beyond the corn, in the distance, stood the stark ridge of mountains that shaped the town. Pudding Hill was a giant hill, and every time it felt like a leap of faith to drive up the dirt road. It may not be Thailand, but I thought anyone could see the beauty of the place.

We reached the crest of the road and drove into the Pudding Hill House parking lot. I pulled into a space and turned off the car.

"It's so weird that Dad was here," Kit said, toying with the drawstring of her metallic silver hoodie.

"It was the best place for him." I unbuckled my seat belt. Kit had been in Los Angeles or New Orleans or Chicago the couple of years that Dad was in the nursing home, and had only come back for Christmas. Dad always remembered her, although he talked to her like she was a teenager still. Kit played along, which I was grateful for.

Inside, I asked the woman at the front desk where I could find Mary Beth Swindon. Kit wandered into the dayroom and sat down next to a woman who was crocheting something in variegated rainbow yarn.

"Right this way," the receptionist said, and led me to Mary Beth's office.

The office was cramped, her desk covered in insurance forms and patient files.

"Nora Huckleberry, nice to see you." Mary Beth stood and held out her hand. "How are things at the diner?"

"The same," I said. "Things are good."

"I heard your sister is in town?" She said this cautiously. Kit had dated Mary Beth's brother briefly while they were in high school, and Kit had broken his heart.

"I am," Kit said from the doorway, and squeezed into the office, taking the seat beside me. "Good to see you, MB."

"I'm sorry it's not under better circumstances. Close the door, would you?"

I reached over and shut the office door.

Mary Beth sat down and pulled out a file. The tab read *Elsie Cole*. "I talked to Jack Hickey yesterday. So, just to clarify, Peggy Johnson's will didn't include a mention of Elsie Cole?"

I shook my head. "Not that I'm aware of. The bill was the first I heard of Elsie. Do I know her, by the way? Her name is so familiar."

"She used to volunteer at the children's library," Kit said. "Don't you remember her? She was really cool. She had all of these interesting dresses, and she always wore red cowboy boots. I've always wanted a pair."

"Maybe?" I said, remembering dropping Kit off at story hour. That was back when I was still juggling high school and the diner. "Didn't she have a stand at the farmer's market?"

"That's right," Mary Beth said, "years ago. Herbs and lotions. Candles, too. A little handmade jewelry. I don't remember when she stopped." Mary Beth opened the file. "Ms. Cole has only been with us for two years. She lived over at the Victoria Hotel for a while, after she sold her place. Did you know you were neighbors?"

I had picked up a prescription or refreshed a litter box for almost every tenant at the Victoria. "No, we must not have been there at the same time."

"Since you aren't family, I wouldn't ordinarily discuss this, but I think you need to know for decision-making purposes. Ms. Cole is in the middle to late stage of Alzheimer's—some days she is with is, most days she isn't. With your own family history I know you know what that's like. She doesn't have any family that we're aware of. Ms. Johnson has always paid for her care here."

With what, cakes? I wanted to ask, but didn't. Peggy's will hadn't mentioned any money, and the only bank account we found was a small passbook savings account that she withdrew money from every month to pay her bills. Mr. Hickey had mentioned that the will was drawn years ago. Maybe her circumstances had changed? "So, tell us what this all looks like."

Kit stood up and wandered out of the room, closing the door behind her. She never liked talking about money. To her, money was a way to fund the next adventure. It was about the present, never the past or the future.

"Ms. Johnson signed a financial agreement with Pudding Hill, so technically her estate is responsible for the bills. I went ahead and inquired about the state nursing home down in Middleton— since Ms. Cole doesn't have an estate to speak of, they can help with the Medicaid paperwork—but they don't have a bed for her right now."

"What does that mean?" I asked, but I braced myself, knowing that it wasn't good news.

"She's on the waiting list. When someone . . . leaves, Elsie can be moved there. It's a perfectly decent place. I know some of the staff over there from my nursing days."

My heart sank. We were basically waiting for someone to die so Peggy's friend could be moved to the state nursing home. The private nursing homes were depressing enough.

"And until then?" I asked weakly.

"She'll stay with us. We wouldn't kick her out, of course. We're not that kind of place. But . . . there will be a lien put on Ms. Johnson's estate after ninety days of nonpayment. You understand."

I nodded. No matter what, the nursing home was going to get paid. Another lien on the estate would make it more difficult to sell. We were already thirty days late. We only had two months to get everything sorted out.

"In the meantime, we need to know if you would like for us to file a motion to appoint you the official health-care proxy. Peggy held that role."

How could I make health decisions for this person that I didn't even know? "If I choose not to?"

"Then the Pudding Hill House will ask the state to appoint guardianship, since Elsie isn't able to do it herself. Someone needs to be in place to make decisions."

"I see. Thanks, Mary Beth. I appreciate you sharing the whole picture with us."

"Of course." Mary Beth reached over and patted my hand. "It's just one thing after another, isn't it? We found out Jim's mother has to have her hip replaced on the same day our hot water heater died."

"It can feel that way," I said, smiling, even though I knew her husband's family owned the ski operation on one of the mountains, and they could pay for a hip replacement, two knee replacements, and a house reroofing without having to change their vacation plans for next summer. Something Max had said while we were baking popped into my head. *The antidote of envy is to rejoice in the good qualities of others.* I said a silent apology to Mary Beth for keeping tabs on her bank account as I let myself out, trying to think of some good qualities other people had. Charlie and Fern were always so cheery, even when we were slammed at the diner, and made work so much fun. Max was a great listener, and brought calm into every situation. Elliot was so interested in everything. Open. And kind.

"Have you seen my sister?" I asked the receptionist, turning my attention to Kit and away from the fact that Elliot Danforth was on my short list. Kit wasn't in the lobby or the dayroom. "Short, curly red hair, dressed like Stevie Nicks and one of the Disney princesses started a fashion label together?"

"Room 117," the receptionist said without looking up from her computer.

I followed the signs down the corridor, waving hello to my neighbor Pat, who worked part time at Pudding Hill as a janitor. I could hear the singsong sound of my sister's voice. I found her sitting in a cushioned chair pulled up close to a tiny, elderly woman lying in bed, covered in a mountain of blankets. Her face was made of a thousand wrinkles, like a Shar-Pei.

"This is my favorite part," Kit said, showing the woman a picture in a copy of *Us Weekly*.

"The one on the left," the woman said, pointing her finger.

Kit popped a cherry Lifesaver into her mouth, handed one to

her friend, and offered the rest of the roll to me. "What do you think, Nora? Who wore it best?"

"Could she choke on those?"

Kit rolled her eyes at me. "She doesn't remember a lot of things, but she remembers how to eat. "You're cool with the candy, right, Elsie?" Kit turned the page. "Stars—they're just like us!"

Elsie laughed and popped the cherry candy into her mouth.

I turned and went back into the corridor.

"Gotta fly," I heard Kit say. "But I'll be back."

When we both had our seat belts buckled and were back on the road headed toward Lyndonville, Kit turned to me and said, "I know what we need to do."

My shoulders dropped an inch. Maybe she would use some of the loan money to cover Elsie's expenses, at least for a couple of months, to buy us time.

"Let's get maple creemees."

It was our go-to snack whenever things were rough at home— an excuse to take a drive and treat ourselves to something sweet.

"I know just the place."

An hour later we pulled into the town of Beldon, home of the Sweet Peony Dairy Farm, which sold maple soft serve year-round in its farm stand/grocery shop.

We sat in the car looking out over the cow pasture, our hands sticky with ice cream, sucking the trapped pools of soft serve out of the little air pockets in the rim of the cake cone, not wanting to miss a drop. The Sweet Peony made the maple-iest creemee of all the Vermont dairies. We would know—Kit and I had been to them all.

Kit leaned back and sighed. "I miss these so much when I'm not in Vermont."

I never thought about the fact that I could eat a maple cree-mee every single day of my life if I wanted. It was one of the fringe benefits of never leaving home.

"Do you remember getting knocked into the mud by an over-friendly cow when you were little?"

"That happened?" Kit asked. She always liked hearing stories from when she was a baby.

"Yes, you walked off to share some of your ice cream with one of the cows and managed to climb under the fence and into the pasture. One of the cows gave you a good lick and you fell into a pretty serious patch of cow patties. Mom was horrified, but Dad thought it was funny." I grinned over at her. "You had to ride home in just a pair of pull-ups."

"How old was I?"

"You must have been around three," I said, wiping my hands off with a napkin.

"So it was before she got sick."

Kit had been six when Mom was diagnosed with an aggres-sive form of breast cancer. Mom had to have both breasts re-moved, followed by chemotherapy and radiation. She was just gaining a bit of strength back when she found out the cancer had already returned.

"Yeah, a few years before."

"What if Mom hadn't had cancer?"

The *What If* game rarely took such a serious tone. I looked over at Kit. When had those crow's-feet formed by her eyes? When had she become an adult?

"And what if Dad hadn't started drinking?" I asked in response.

"Maybe you would have gone to art school in New York City."

I tried to picture myself in a small apartment, surrounded by people and concrete. "It's hard to imagine. We'd both be different people if things hadn't happened the way they did, I guess."

"Yeah." Kit leaned back in her seat. "I can't say there's anything I would want to change, exactly. I mean, I've had a lot of adventures. It's just . . . I don't really have any memories from when Mom wasn't sick."

"You were still pretty little," I said, although I didn't know if that was a comfort.

"Yeah. I just wish—I don't know. It's, like, my whole memory of being mothered is through this filter of her having cancer. I think that's why I haven't had kids."

I remembered. It felt like every day Mom was saying good-bye.

"Do you want kids?" I asked. I hadn't ever thought of Kit having children. She never seemed to slow down enough to consider it, but of course she must have.

"I didn't think I wanted them." She glanced over at me. "I had a scare six months ago. With Max. When I found out that I wasn't pregnant, I was disappointed, which was a huge surprise— to me and Max both. Max was thrilled, of course, when I told him how I was feeling. He's dying to be a dad."

"Do you think you and Max . . . ?" Sean and I had tried for years. I could get pregnant easily enough, but my body wasn't able to hold on to a baby for long. After the tenth miscarriage we stopped trying. The funny thing was, when I went back on the Pill, I found myself feeling relieved—content, even. As if a silent question had been answered.

Kit licked her fingertips, then rubbed at them with the tiny square paper napkin. "I don't feel ready."

"I'm pretty sure it's one of those things you can only get ready for by doing it."

"Yeah." Kit rolled down her window and stuck her whole arm out. "I know you're right. But my brain is always saying *Just this last project* or *One last big trip* . . . I think part of my hesitation about having kids is that my feelings about being a mom are wrapped up with all the bad feelings about our mom not being there. But I'm afraid I'm going to wake up one day and realize it's too late."

"I'm sorry you never got a chance to be mothered by her. She was a good mom." What I really wanted to say was *I'm sorry I couldn't be the mom you needed.* I didn't realize how much mothering Kit needed until she was up and gone. I took for granted the thirteen years I had of Mom and Dad just being regular Mom and Dad. I had had a bucolic Vermont childhood—sledding and ice-skating in the winter, swimming in the summer. Girl Scouts and 4-H and sleepover parties. Getting grounded for cutting school during kidding season so I could see the baby goats being born. Helping Mom with her garden and Dad with the diner. Kit had missed all of that. Instead she had teenage me and grief-stricken Dad trying to cobble together a life without Mom, who we had relied on for everything.

"You'd be a great mom," I said truthfully.

"Really?" Kit leaned her back against the headrest and turned to me. "You don't think I'm too much of a mess?"

"Well, you are a bit of a mess, but I think you could be a mess with kids." This was the truth. Kit was a lot of things—impulsive, a bit careless at times, unpredictable—but she was passionate about her work and dedicated to it. "You'd be a fun mom. And your kid will always have me when they want some regularity in their life."

"They could come up in summers," Kit said.

"And for the holidays." I kind of liked the idea of being an auntie, having little sprouts around without having to actually do the birthing and raising on my own. "You know, Mom and Dad were pretty fun before she got sick."

"Really?"

"Not that Mom wasn't strict. If my bed wasn't made, or if I left a plate in the sink without rinsing it, she would lecture me for hours on end."

"Just like you," Kit said, laughing.

"I don't lecture."

"Kit, what are you doing with all of that money? Now, I want you to keep a ledger showing all of your expenditures—"

"That's just sound thinking—you'll thank me come tax time."

"Nora, I haven't filed taxes since—"

I held up my hand as if I were trying to stop traffic. "Please, don't tell me. That way I can't incriminate you in court. But seriously, Mom was pretty fun when she wasn't trying to wrangle Dad and me. She had the best stash of dress-up clothes and costume jewelry. She was big on crafts. In the summer she would make huge watercolors on bedsheets tacked up to the old barn. She taught me how to throw pots and how to crochet. The blanket on the back of the couch Mom and I made together."

"I always thought it was Dad who was the creative one and Mom who was the taskmaster."

"No, Dad was the dreamier of the two, but I would say Mom

was actually the more creative one. She could figure out a way to solve any problem."

"I wish I had known that side of her."

"She had a sense of urgency when she got sick. I think she didn't want to leave anything undone." Out in the field, a farmhand raked hay into a long, wooden feed tray. The cows ambled toward it. "Can you imagine, knowing you might leave two kids in Dad's hands?"

Kit laughed. "She was right about that. He was not prepared to be a single dad. So how did he deal with all of Mom's lecturing and bossing around?"

"I think he was grateful for it. That's the thing. I think he fell in love with Mom in part because he knew he needed somebody to hold on to the end of the kite while he was floating among the clouds."

"Dad needed tethering?"

"Sometimes. I mean, it was Mom who worked the cash register. You know if it had been Dad he wouldn't have charged anyone."

"Remember that time he bought the homeless guy breakfast without telling him who paid for it?" Kit asked. We had been on vacation with Dad in Maine. A man had come into the restaurant we were eating in asking for money. The hostess wanted to throw him out, but Dad quietly told her to get the man anything he wanted and to put it on his tab.

"That was classic Dad."

"I don't need a tether," Kit said, sucking on the end of one of her braids. It was as if she were answering a question she had asked herself. "Every decision I have ever made has been about not being tied down."

"You don't have to be tied down to be connected to someone, though, Kit. Think of it like the mint plants in Mom's garden. They were all connected, but they spread and sprouted up wherever they wanted to."

Kit was silent for a few minutes. Finally she asked, "Did you like being married?"

She had me there. Every year with Sean had felt a little heavier. "Sean and I were not a good example of a healthy, balanced relationship."

"But how do you know?"

"What a healthy relationship is? I'd start by not entering into it at the age of fourteen."

"How do you know you've found someone that will let you be like mint?"

"We're talking about Max, right? He's full of joy, Kitty. I can't picture him trying to hold you back."

"That's what he keeps saying." Kit shoved a huge piece of the maple fudge she had bought for Max into her mouth and focused on chewing.

"Has he asked you to—?"

"No, no. He hasn't asked me anything. But he's always, like, trying to make plans. You know. For the future."

A deep belly laugh rose up and out. "God forbid."

"You know what I'm saying. I don't want to get myself so tied down, so in a rut that I'm like a root-bound plant—"

"In a too-small pot," I said to the windshield. "Like me."

"Nora, you know I don't mean it like that." But her face was full of apology.

"I know," I said, and turned the key in the ignition. "I didn't want to end up root-bound, either."

When we arrived back at my apartment, Max was sitting on the living room floor surrounded by cardboard boxes, a spiral-ringed notebook propped up on his bent knees, typing figures into my mom's old calculator.

"Hey, baby," he said, smiling up at Kit.

Kit leaned down, balancing herself on his knees and kissed him. "It's good to see your face," she said sweetly.

"This old thing," Max said, rubbing his palms across his stubbly cheeks. "Hey, Nora," he called and waved as I stepped over several boxes to reach the kitchenette. "Did you take a stab at another burnt sugar cake?"

"On my own? Never!" I said, and reached for a bottle of wine. "No one's come looking for it, anyway. "

"Tomorrow's Friday. You never know. I'll throw a couple in the oven tomorrow morning just in case."

Kit moved from box to box, squealing at tripods and cooing at soft boxes to diffuse the lights.

"If you take everything out, we'll just have to repack it before we haul it over to Peggy's," Max said calmly as he watched Kit take out roll after roll of thick black tape and put them on the floor.

I looked at all the boxes. "It's not a problem, but why did you bring everything up here, anyway? Wouldn't it have made more sense to leave it in the Vanagon and drive it straight to Peggy's?"

Max ran a hand through his hair. It looked like he hadn't seen a shower since he had left Guthrie three days ago. "That's the thing. The Vanagon is still down in Massachusetts."

Kit stopped rifling through a box of cables. "What?"

"I left you a message. The transmission blew. It's a total

rebuild, and it's going to take the guy some time to gather all the parts." Max stretched his legs out and shook them one at a time. "I didn't have Peggy's street address, but I had this one on my phone, so I had to have everything shipped here."

Kit eyed the calculator. "How much?"

"With the parts and the labor, almost ten grand."

"Shit." Kit sat down beside Max and leaned against him.

"I know. I thought about scrapping it, but it's been our home. It didn't make sense to just get rid of it."

"You did the right thing," Kit said, rubbing Max's forearm. "The Vanagon has plenty of adventures left in it."

"That's what the mechanic said. He was impressed with the body, and the state of the engine."

I wanted to ask how they were going to pay for it, but I knew the answer. Fifty thousand dollars. That meant they were down 20 percent of their budget. How could they be so calm?

Max kept his eyes on Kit. "The camera from Craigslist was crap, but the guys over at B and H had a great price on a used one. It's just one model before the one we hoped for."

"That will work," Kit said. I admired how positive she sounded.

"They gave us a break on the lighting kits, too, and all the cables."

"Did you get the mics?"

"Are you still going to be able to make the movie?" I asked. I didn't need to hear the full inventory. I needed to hear that I hadn't leveraged the diner for nothing.

"We'll have to cut back on some stuff. Like craft services."

"Maybe you could help us out there, Nora? Would you order sandwich stuff at cost, and let us use the kitchen at the diner to make food for the crew?" Kit asked.

"Of course," I said.

"We're not going to be able to hire the assistant director of photography like we had hoped."

Kit leaned over and kissed him. "It will all be fine. Better than fine. Sometimes the most creative thinking comes out of need. Remember that time when the airlines lost all the costumes for that music video?"

"And we re-created them all out of stuff from the dollar store!" Max reached over and scooped her up so that she was sitting on his lap. "You are an inspiration—you know that, right?"

I tossed my car keys at them. "Why don't you get all of this stuff over to Peggy's and pick up a couple of movies at the library on the way home. I'll make the popcorn."

"No butter," Kit and Max said at the same time.

"No butter for you guys." I would be making a buttery bowl all for myself.

CHAPTER SEVEN

B reakfast had been busier than usual on Friday, keeping me from hanging up the red, yellow, and green crepe-paper garlands I had scored at the party store. A mix of regulars, tourists, and summer people, most of whom were flanked by their children and grandchildren, were getting an early start to their Labor Day weekend. The highlight of the weekend was tomorrow's Corn and Tomato Festival; after that, it would be time to head back to their autumn and winter lives in the city. By noon almost all of the tables were filled, and a line started to form outside. In the middle of the lunch rush Charlie came out of the kitchen, dragged a chair over to the front door, and climbed up and removed the bell above the door, to the applause of everyone sitting at the counter.

Elliot walked in with a man I didn't recognize. I wished that I could chat with him, but I was in the middle of filling water glasses for a large table full of tourists in town for the festival. I watched as Fern grabbed a couple of menus and led them toward the back. Elliot smiled at me and waved as he passed, glancing over his shoulder to look at me one last time before he disappeared into the back dining room.

"Excuse me, miss? The water?"

I looked down at the glass. It was filled to the brim and water was spilling over onto the Formica.

"Sorry about that," I said, swiftly pulling a clean side towel from my apron and wiping down the table. "Your waitress will be right over."

The diner buzzed until long past two. Fern and I collapsed into one of the booths after the last customer had paid his check. Charlie brought us both large glasses full of icy Diet Coke with wedges of lime.

"Now that was a lunch shift," Fern said, pulling out singles from her stuffed apron pockets. "I could use a couple of shifts like that a week."

I looked at the sales report from the cash register. "You and me both. I wish Guthrie had a festival every week."

Burt Grant walked in, posters under his arm, and asked the young waitress working the counter for a cup of coffee to go.

"Hey, Burt," Fern called. "Did you get all the tents set up?"

He came over, coffee in hand. "Yup. We're ready to go. How about you all? I hope you'll save me a cider donut to eat after we drag Rowan into the mud."

Fern laughed and patted the seat next to her. Burt slid in, placing the posters down on the table.

"What have you got there?" she asked. "Are they for the festival? We need a better slogan than "Old-Fashioned Family Fun.""

Burt looked up at me shyly before flipping one of the posters over.

Keep Guthrie Small!
Against changing the zoning laws
that would make it possible for large corporations
to develop land in Guthrie?

Stop by the Hammer and Nail and sign the petition.
Every signature counts!

"Give me one," I said, holding out my hand. "I'll hang it in the window."

"You will?" Burt asked, incredulous.

"Of course," I said, taking the poster and sliding out of the booth. "I have to run a quick errand," I said to Fern. "Make the high school girls do all the resets when they come in. I'll be back later."

I stepped out of the sticky heat of the afternoon and into the cool, softly lit, beige-colored everything of the Pudding Hill House, my life savings in the form of a cashier's check weighing down my purse as if I were carrying a sack of baking potatoes. Mary Beth Swindon met me in the hall in front of her office.

"Great to see you, Nora. Come on in."

After she closed the office door and settled back into her ergonomic office chair, I handed her the envelope. "The health-care proxy forms are in there as well. Did you need anything else?"

Mary Beth opened the envelope, smoothed out the forms, and put the check aside. "Are you sure about this, Nora? I know this is a lot of money for you—it's a lot of money for anybody. And Ms. Cole isn't exactly your responsibility."

The check represented the $3,000 I kept in cash in my freezer, the $5,000 I had in my personal checking account, and the $9,794 of the $12,000 I kept in the Miss Guthrie account for the never-ending little emergencies at the diner. It made me queasy just to think about it. "It feels like the right thing to do— what Peggy would have wanted."

"You're a good person, Nora. But we already know that."

I sighed. When had I developed the reputation for being so good? All I did was run the diner. It made me want to go shoplift something.

"My husband mentioned you were thinking of selling to that HG?"

I braced myself for the lecture. Every day since word got out, I had received e-mails, phone calls, and visits at the diner from folks wanting to share their opinion on whether or not to sell to HG. Notes were left on the backs of Miss Guthrie guest checks, sometimes without a tip. I was even stopped in the feminine hygiene aisle of the White Market by a Christmas tree farmer. I couldn't go anywhere without the citizens of Guthrie giving me speeches about the importance of growth or about the sanctity of the small town.

"We did receive an offer from them, pending the town vote to change the zoning of Peggy's land." I didn't want to give Mary Beth my opinion; if she spread the word I was against the sale to HG, other potential buyers might not be in a hurry to come forward.

"You do what you need to do. Between you and me, it would be nice to be able to buy laundry detergent by the case without having to drive all the way to Littleton." Mary Beth looked over the forms. "I'll submit these to the state this afternoon. I'm sure they'll approve you as health-care proxy—they always prefer that someone in the community makes these kind of decisions."

I stood. "Thanks, Mary Beth. I'll let myself out."

I walked down the hallway toward the front door. Instead of the calming sounds of smooth jazz that were usually piped in the reception area, I heard the thump of someone playing the bongos, and the unmistakable sound of Max's deep voice.

"Ommmmmmmmmmmmmmmmmmmmmmmm."

I peeked in the dayroom. Kit was sitting cross-legged on a cushion on the floor, hands resting on her knees, palms open, her hair twisted up in a yellow chiffon scarf trimmed with little silver mirrors that caught all the light and sprinkled it across the faces of the residents. Max was beside her in his usual white T-shirt and jeans, his head down, hitting the drums with his fingers and palms. They both had their eyes closed.

"*Om na-mah Shi-va-ya. Om na-mah Shi-va-ya,*" Max sang.

"*Om na-mah Shi-va-ya. Om na-mah Shi-va-ya,*" Kit answered, her voice round and sweet. "Everybody join in when you feel ready."

The room was packed with residents, some in wheelchairs, others resting on the love seats and chairs. A few of the aides and the head nurse leaned against the wall, clapping the beat.

"*Shivaaya namaha. Shivaaya namah om.*"

Kit stood, grabbing a large purple velvet bag by her side. She smiled and waved at me. She walked from resident to resident, handing out maracas and little wooden egg-shaped shakers that sounded like they were filled with rice, and something gold and glinty. When she got to me, she took my hands in hers and slipped black elastic bands attached to little brass cymbals onto my middle fingers and thumbs.

"Perfect," she said, moving on to her next victim. "There's no wrong way to do this, friends," she called, demonstrating how to use a castanet. "Make a joyful noise!"

I tapped my cymbals together. They made a flat sound like

change being tossed into the cash register drawer. I felt a dry hand on my arm. When I looked down, a man with wisps of white hair on his head was smiling up at me with pearly false teeth. "Pull right back up after you strike the cymbal, sweetie. That's how you get the nice ring." He moved his finger and thumb away from each other, sort of the opposite way a lobster moves its claws. I tried to mimic the motion. The cymbals chimed loud and bright.

"Oh," I said, surprised. "How did you know?"

The man gave me a thumbs-up. "Used to play percussion with the Boston Symphony. They work the same way as the big ones."

Max picked up the pace each time he began the chant again. By the third or fourth time, the dayroom was a riot of sound. Some of the elderly residents were playing instruments, others were singing responses to Max's call. Others were just tapping their fingers on the arms of their chairs. Everyone looked happy. Kit danced around the room, chiming her own set of finger cymbals at the end of each line.

Max ended the chant with a freestyle solo on the bongos. With a whoop he stood up, wiping the sweat off his face with the hem of his T-shirt, flashing the starlets of the 1940s to an appreciative crowd. Max put his hands together as if in prayer and bowed to the room.

"I bow to you, dear friends. I bow to myself. I bow to Shiva, who knows all of our true selves."

The residents clapped. A few shook their maracas and egg shakers. Max beamed at all of them, bowed one more time, then grabbed a glass pitcher from a small table at the front of the room. "Does anybody need some water? Raise a hand. Shiva doesn't want you getting dehydrated."

Max poured small cups of water, helping the aides with a few of the people whose hands were too shaky to bring the cup up to their lips. Kit collected the instruments, pausing to talk with each of the residents, laughing and chatting as if they were all her dear friends.

"Wasn't that fun?" Kit asked, holding her hands over her head and playing the cymbals in fast triplets, as if she had learned from an expert belly dancer.

"What was it exactly?" I asked.

"Kirtan. It's the practice of Bhakti, the yoga of devotion."

I looked at the men and women who were shuffling out of the room, all of them as pale as the top of Hunger Mountain in February. This pocket of Vermont wasn't known for its large Hindu population. "But aren't they probably mostly Christian?"

"We could be singing *God, God, God*. It's all the same," Max said. He picked up Kit from behind and spun her around in a circle. "Kirtan always makes me feel like dancing."

Kit shrieked until Max put her back down on the ground. I slipped the cymbals from my fingers, immediately missing the weight of them, and wished I had chimed them one last time, but I handed them back to Kit.

"So what are you doing here?" Kit asked as she walked over to where her little red video camera was set up and pressed a button to turn it off.

"I was going to ask you the same thing."

"Max and I came by to drop off some library books for Elsie. I've been bringing her books I remember her recommending to me as a kid. They seem to give her a little spark."

"While we were checking in, we heard that the chair yoga teacher bailed for today, so we offered to fill in," Max said, as if this were the obvious choice. Apparently they traveled with an extensive collection of percussion instruments. "What about you?"

"Oh," I said, not wanting to talk about the money. "I was just dropping off some paperwork. What does that song mean, anyway?"

Max threw his hands up in the air. "Shiva, you beautiful destroyer, come on down and wipe away all of my illusions so that I may see the truth."

"Be careful what you wish for," I heard Kit mutter, but Max had danced his way to the other side of the room, out of earshot. "You should go peek in on Elsie. Say hello. We had a good chat earlier today. She started telling me something about living in New York, but we were interrupted by a nurse and she lost the thread. Did you know she lived in New York?"

"No." I didn't know anything about Elsie, other than that Peggy cared enough for her to pay for her health.

Kit slung the velvet bag over her shoulder. "Grab those cushions, Max. I bet we can get all the lights set up tonight and be ready to start filming tomorrow after the tug-of-war."

"Ready to roll," Max said, balancing the cushion on his head. He played a few beats on the bongo. "And armed for action."

After helping one of the aides put the dayroom back in order, I walked down the hallway to room 117. Elsie was in bed, snoring quietly, a cotton blanket pulled up to her chin despite the warmth of the room. I sat beside her bed and tentatively reached over and took her hand. It felt delicate, like a newborn rabbit. "Hey there, Elsie," I said in a whisper. "How are you today?"

Elsie opened her eyes briefly. The hand I wasn't holding moved under her blanket. After a few moments, she seemed to find what she was looking for. She pulled her hand back out. In it was a stuffed fox doll. She let it rest on her belly, and closed her eyes again.

"Did you want to show this to me?" I asked, reaching for the fox.

It was fashioned out of scraps of sweaters—Fair Isle sweaters, judging from the zigzags and diamonds in the patterns. The body was sewn and felted, then stuffed with something soft, like cotton. His eyes, nose, and mouth had been embroidered on. His expression looked like he had just raided a henhouse. It was the perfect gift for Elsie—sturdy enough, with no sharp edges. But I could tell by the mark making, the pointed shape of the ears, the curl of the tail, that it was made by the same hand as the sculptures in the woods. It was a thoughtful gift, made with love and attention, every stitch placed with precision, as if someone would notice. I rubbed the little fox's snout.

I tucked the fox back under one of Elsie's hands so she would find it right away when she woke up and wondered where she was. I hoped the fox would make her feel like she was home.

At ten o'clock the morning of the Corn and Tomato Festival I walked from my apartment to the village green and made a beeline for the corn tent, easy to spot from a distance thanks to the steam billowing up from under the flap. It was never too early for corn. A couple of teenage boys, long hair flowing from under baseball caps, poked at the fire underneath two large kettles of boiling salt water while their mother, one of the farmers from the east side of town, dropped in husked ears of white and yellow corn by the armful. Her daughter was fishing the ears out with tongs and placing them into red-and-white-checkered cardboard boats she had lined up on the table. They disappeared as quickly as she put them out. I grabbed two ears, brushed them down with melted butter, and sprinkled them with a heavy dose of sea salt, and made my way over to the Miss Guthrie table, where Charlie and Fern were setting up the coffee urns and cider donuts for after the tug-of-war contest.

Charlie's pal Alfred was over by the table, holding two paper plates piled with tomato slices. The plates were soaking up the juice and threatened to collapse at any moment.

"You can't be serious," Charlie said, popping a slice of purplish red tomato in his mouth. "The Mortgage Lifter has good flavor, but it has nothing on the Brandywine."

Alfred held up a dark pink wedge and shoved it toward Charlie. "Try it again. It's sweet. It's complex. You can roast it. Have you ever tried roasting a Brandywine?"

I handed Fern an ear of corn. "How long have they been at it?"

Fern checked her watch. "Only about fifteen minutes. I'm sure we have at least another half hour of debate to look forward to."

"Hope you like the consistency of a canned, stewed tomato," said Alfred. "That's all I'm saying."

I sat down on one of the white plastic chairs behind the table and bit into my ear of corn. Warm butter greased my lips as the salty-sweet kernels burst in my mouth. "Damn," I said, leaning back. "It's been a good year for corn."

"Right?" Fern handed me a napkin, then took a seat next to me. "I've already had three ears, but I want to go back for more."

"Let's take turns," I offered. "That way we won't look too greedy."

We waved hello at a pair of volunteer firemen as they dragged the heavy black hose over to where the tug-of-war took place every year, by the soccer field. When they reached the spot, they signaled to the men on the truck to turn on the water. Water sprayed fast and heavy onto the grass, flooding a small section. Even though it took all spring for the grass to grow back, this was the tradition. They say the first tug-of-war happened during a nor'easter. Now if it's been dry, the town makes a muddy patch for the losers to slip into.

"I might take a walk through the festival before we get too busy," I said to Fern. "Want to come with me?"

Fern gazed over at the firemen and sighed in appreciation. "No, I think I'd better stay here and hold down the fort."

I followed Fern's gaze. Two of the firemen were stomping their booted feet in the wet grass to make sure the surface was sufficiently muddy. I chuckled, wondering which one of them would wind up in the back of Fern's car tonight. "I'll bring you more corn on my way back."

The festival tents were set up on the two sidewalks that ran the length of the green, with the lawn and the gazebo in the center. On the grass, children were lining up for the potato sack race.

"Hey, Nora," a voice called out from under one of the tents. I ducked inside and found Maude Finley, the head librarian, sitting behind a card table guarding a cashbox.

I looked over at the tables stacked high with hardcovers and paperbacks. "Looks like you have a great selection this year."

She tilted her sharp chin once. "Used-book store over in Barton just closed. They donated their stock for our sale. Here." Maude bent down, disappearing underneath the tablecloth.

She brought up a tall stack of books. "Thought you might enjoy these," she said, patting the covers. One was a book about diner history, one a collection of Rothko paintings. There were a couple of copies of *Modern Farmer* magazine, both of which featured dairy goats on the cover, a biography of Frank O'Hara, and a copy of the famous Hitchcock-Truffaut interviews. Maude had been paying attention to my library habits over the years.

"You're so thoughtful," I said, taking out my wallet. "I'll take them all."

Maude waved her hand at me. "Let's trade for a hot breakfast." She looked over both shoulders before slipping a book on top of the pile. It was the latest steamy bestseller, the one that had been banned in four countries. "Take this one, too," she said, leaning over the table. "I read it in one sitting."

Maude put the books in a discreet brown grocery bag from White's, and offered to keep the bag under the table until after the festival.

I made my way past the face-painting tent, where Sarah was turning a young boy into a sunflower, cut through the cornhusk-doll-making station, and managed to avoid getting covered in tomato pulp when I sprinted by the bull's-eye game, where kids tried to hit the center of the target with an overripe tomato. Finally, I reached the tasting tents. Tables were set up along the length of four tents and covered in vinyl tablecloths. On them sat paper plate after paper plate, hundreds of them, each piled high with wedges of heirloom tomatoes, their names written on the plates in Sharpie. A young woman handed me a sheet of paper that listed all the varieties. "So you can keep track of what you liked," she said proudly. I bet it was her idea.

"Good to see you out from behind that counter," a voice rumbled. I turned to see the worn face of Sheriff Granby.

"Nice to see you out of your uniform," I said, smiling. "They actually give you a day off?"

Granby chuckled and cuffed my shoulder. "You're one to talk. Besides, they have to give me the day off." Granby held up his arms, Rocky-style. "If I were on the job, I couldn't help take back the golden rope."

I laughed, handing him a toothpick and a paper plate. "Careful of your back, now. You don't want a repeat of last year." I gazed down at the rows of tomatoes, bright reds, glowing orange, dark purple, and every shade of yellow imaginable.

"Are you looking for something in particular?" a smooth voice asked. When I turned, I found Elliot Danforth right behind me, a speared piece of red-and-green-striped tomato in his hand. He offered it to me without explanation.

I popped it into my mouth and chewed. "It's so sweet. What is it?"

Elliot leaned over to read the plate. "It's called Chocolate Stripe." He pierced another sample with a fresh toothpick. "I don't really get the chocolate," he said thoughtfully, "but its sweetness is earthy."

"Like beets," I offered, feeling a wave of shyness creep in. The last time I saw Elliot had been at the sugarhouse. The sensation of our arms banded together flooded my thoughts, and I felt my cheeks flush.

"Exactly," he said, and smiled at me with such warmth that I had to look away.

"Attention, everyone." A friendly voice crackled over the loud-

speaker that was attached to the edge of the tent. I squinted at the gazebo. It looked like Jonathan Doyle, one of the town doctors, had taken on the role of emcee for the festival this year. *"Some of you have been asking about the goat parade. It was scheduled for noon."* He scanned the festival grounds from end to end. *"But I'm not seeing any goats lined up. All goats, please report to the gazebo."*

"A goat parade?" Elliot asked.

"The 4-H kids have it every year, to show off the animals they've raised."

"We can't miss that," he said. "Shall we head over and grab a good spot to watch?"

I tossed my plate and toothpick into a nearby trash can. "I'd be happy to."

When we reached the gazebo, we found Livvy and Martin McCracken tuning up their banjo and fiddle. Livvy's hair was the color of the Pink Bumblebee tomatoes that Tom Carrigan grew in his garden just for this event. The McCrackens' youngest crawled around the stage at their feet, while their four-year-old daughter, Maggie, chased their Irish wolfhound, Salty, around the pavilion.

"No goats," I said, waving my hand around.

"No goats. But it looks like there may be some music."

Martin McCracken leaned into the mic. "Dr. Doyle asked us to start playing while he tries to locate the goat parade." He pressed his fiddle to his chest and counted to three, and the pair launched into one of the waltzes that were usually reserved for the end of the contra dances. Several of the older couples got up from their lawn chairs and picnic tables and started to dance.

"Have you seen Freckles lately?" I asked as we watched.

"I have." Elliot pulled out his phone. "I managed to get a couple of shots of him the other evening before it grew too dark." He leaned close to me, so close that our shoulders were touching, and swiped through a couple of images of trees before he reached the ones of Freckles. "There he is."

Freckles stood in the yard in front of the sugarhouse, his tail high, staring into the maple trees.

"He looks happy," I said.

"He does."

A text message from HG flashed across the screen. Elliot turned the phone off and slipped it back into his pocket. He glanced over at the couples waltzing on the lawn. "Some people are dancing."

"They are," I said, feeling a little self-conscious.

"Do you like dancing?"

"I haven't danced in a long time." Twenty-two years long, since my wedding night.

"Ms. Huckleberry, would you like to dance? With me?"

I felt my eyes widen a fraction. We were in the middle of the town green, in the center of the Corn and Tomato Festival, where everyone in Guthrie was currently eating corn or tomatoes or both. "I'm not very good," I stammered.

"Neither am I," he said and offered me his arm.

I looped my hand through and rested it on his forearm. Elliot led me a few steps forward, where the other couples had made a makeshift dance floor. He placed his right hand on my back, his left hand in my right. I rested my free hand on his shoulder. We took a few awkward steps, fumbling like middle-school kids at their first formal.

"It's easier if we're a little closer," he said quietly, and gently circled my waist, pulling me to him. I let my arm move from his shoulder to his back. Our cheeks touched briefly, and I felt his shoulders relax. "That's it," he said into my ear, as we waltzed on the grass.

Frank and Bonnie Fraser waltzed by. Bonnie met my eye and gave me a thumbs-up. I grinned shyly and felt relieved when Elliot turned me in a different direction.

"All right folks, we're really ready now." Jonathan Doyle's voice broke in over the music. *"Just a change of route. The goat parade is going to start over by the corn tent and walk by the gazebo. Here they come now!"*

Elliot and I stopped waltzing, but his arm lingered around my waist for a moment. We both turned to face the gazebo just in time to see seven dairy goats with bells attached to their collars and ribbons woven into their tails run by, herded by seven children dressed all in white. I looked down the field, but there were no more goats to be found.

"Well, it was a short goat parade."

A few of the dancers laughed.

"If the parents of the 4-H club could help remove the goats from the tomato tent, it would be most appreciated. Tug-of-war starts in thirty minutes. Get those hands chalked up. And remember, the folks at the Black Bear Tavern tent are offering free pints to anyone with rope burn. See Mrs. Doyle in First Aid before you start drinking. Go Guthrie!"

A cheer rose from across the green.

"I should head back. Fern might need help finishing with the setup."

"I'll walk with you, if you don't mind."

I led him straight to the steaming tent. "I hope you've had some corn," I said, grabbing ears for me and Fern.

"I'm afraid my hands will get too slippery and I'll cause the team to lose."

"You're tugging?"

It was then that I noticed Elliot wasn't wearing his usual business casual. He was dressed in faded jeans and a worn gray Red Sox sweatshirt that made him look younger. He even had sneakers on.

Elliot nodded. "We used to play tug-of-war as a training tool when I rowed crew in college. That was a long time ago," he added. "But I'm excited to give it a try."

"If we lose, it won't be your fault," I said, licking butter off the side of my hand. Kit and Max were at the Miss Guthrie table when we arrived, both wearing skinny black jeans and long-sleeve black T-shirts that read "KILL ROWAN" in sparkly silver puff paint.

"Don't you think the sparkles kind of soften the message?" I asked Kit.

Kit bit into an ear of sweet corn. Butter dripped down her chin. We were related after all.

"I can't think of a single occasion where a little sparkle didn't improve things," Kit said and took another bite.

"Are you both joining in?" I asked, tying the pom-pommed apron around my waist. Weak ankles kept me out of the competition. If I couldn't stand, I couldn't work.

"I am, absolutely." Max rubbed his hands together. "I love the primal aggression of the whole thing." He took a big bite of corn, as if he were tearing flesh off a mutton leg, and tossed the cob into the rosebushes behind him.

Kit held up her red video camera. "And I'm going to capture it all on film, so we can all replay Max getting dragged into a mud puddle over and over again."

Fern came over and placed a yellow pom-pommed tiara on my head, and another one on her own. The pom-poms came to a point on the top. Kit held up her camera to my face and took a fast series of shots. I glanced over at Elliot, who laughed out loud.

"You've outdone yourself," Charlie said to Fern, who beamed with pride.

From across the field, the town manager arrived with several kids from the Guthrie football team, who were carrying the rope.

"It won't be long now," I said. Max grabbed Kit's hand. They took off running across the field.

Fern sliced up a couple of burnt sugar cakes that Max had made on Friday before he and Kit tried to turn the residents of Pudding Hill into devotional yogis, and placed the slices on little plastic plates. When Guthrie lost, everyone would be wet and cold and in need of warm coffee and something sweet to cheer them up. It had been Max's idea to make the cakes. He thought that maybe someone might recognize the taste and solve the mystery cake order.

"Pullers, five-minute warning," Martin McCracken said into the microphone. He kissed Livvy on the cheek, put his fiddle into its case, and hopped off the gazebo steps.

A battle cry rose from the participants as they made their way to the muddy grass.

"That's my call," Elliot said. "Wish me luck."

On the muddy lawn, a crowd of people gathered at the field's edge. The spectators were mostly from Guthrie, but the infamous Rowan varsity high school football team had arrived all together, a pile of boys as thick and tall as oak trunks. They stood at the corner of the field, arms crossed, trying to look tough.

Elliot waved to me before joining the team.

Fern and I elbowed our way into the crowd of spectators. The rules of the tug-of-war were best of three games. Kids ten to thirteen went first, lining up in order of size. Then came the high school team, and finally, the adults. Both men and women were encouraged to play. Phyllis, our mail carrier, was the adult team anchor.

The kids' match ended as it always did, with all the kids diving into the massive mud puddle in the center, but not before team Rowan took the first point. The high school teams were evenly matched. The Rowan varsity football team may have had girth, but the wiry track kids of Guthrie had the footwork. A deep roar rose from the crowd when the first football player's feet were sucked into the muddy edge of the puddle. By the end, all of their white football uniforms were covered in mud.

"It's tied up," Fern said to me, gripping my arm, her eyes searching the crowd.

"Who are you looking for?" I scanned the Guthrie adults, who were passing a bag of chalk down the line. "Is there something you aren't telling me?"

"I may or may not have gone on a date with one of the volunteer firemen. But I'm not ready to say which one." Fern held up her hands. "I don't want to jinx it."

"I'll give you two weeks," I said, pretending to check out the crowd of men in their Guthrie Fire Department T-shirts, but fixing my eyes on Elliot. He had taken off his sweatshirt. Underneath he was wearing a striped cotton shirt that was a little tight around his biceps. I felt my cheeks flush, and turned my attention to finding Max and my little sister. "And then I'm going to take you to the Black Bear and get you drunk until you spill all the details."

"Deal." Fern held her pinkie out to me.

"Everyone take your places. This is for the win," the town manager called. He had taken over whistle duty since his gallbladder surgery.

I was surprised to find that the town had given Elliot the front position. It might have been because he was one of the shortest members of the team. But he was agile.

"On your mark. Get ready. Pull!" The town manager blew the whistle. The members of both teams leaned back, so that they were almost perpendicular to the ground.

"Pull harder," I heard Max cry from the middle of the line.

The loggers in the back of the line dug their feet into the ground and yanked the rope with all of their strength, pulling the members of the Rowan team maybe an inch toward the puddle.

"Keep tugging!" Fern and I screamed along with the whole town of Guthrie.

The loggers took hold of the inch of rope they'd gained and

pulled. Elliot worked his feet quickly. He had excellent balance, like a dancer, and seemed to be able to adjust with every twist of the rope.

"Go Guthrie!" the crowd shouted. Hands clapped a rhythm in unison. The sound thundered across the field.

Out beyond the tug-of-war, at the edge of the adjacent soccer field, a flash of black caught my eye.

The Rowan team leaned farther back, gaining back the inch they had lost. The crowd gasped as Elliot slid toward the mud puddle, his feet scrambling, as if he were running backward. It looked as if he had no traction at all.

"You can do it, Guthrie," Fern cried. The loggers in back pulled harder, digging their heels into the earth.

From off in the distance, I heard the rumble of barking. I rested my hands on Fern's shoulders and stood on my toes. Out beyond the game was a shiny black dog, the white of his muddy feet barely visible, hackles up, body low, barking his head off at the players.

"Oh, my God, that's Freckles," I said to Fern.

"Freckles!" someone in the crowd shouted.

Freckles ran back and forth, from one edge of the crowd to the other, as if he wanted to herd the whole town.

Elliot turned his head toward the barking. The Rowan team pulled him to the very edge of the mud. He had to twist his body to keep from slipping in.

"Keep pulling," I yelled.

"Someone control that dog," one of the spectators from Rowan yelled. The town of Rowan hadn't joined the Front Porch Forum.

"Now," shouted one of the loggers. They gave one last great

heave, and the first puller of the Rowan team skidded into the mud, and then the next, sliding and collapsing on top of each other in a great big pig pile.

The crowd roared. The Guthrie teammates leaned into each other, their arms too weak to embrace.

I looked for Elliot, but he was nowhere to be seen. I pushed my way into the mess of players, my sneakers sucking the wet grass and the mud that lay beneath, slipping past spectators until I found him. He was on his knees in the middle of the soccer field, his hand outstretched. Freckles was just a couple of yards away, leaning low in a puppy bow, but his tail was tight between his legs, and he was growling, uncertain.

"It's okay," Elliot said in a gentle voice. "It's okay, boy."

Freckles backed up slowly a few steps at a time, whining a little. I kneeled beside Elliot, the muck seeping into the legs of my jeans, keeping my gaze down, as Erika had instructed. "Hey, Freckles," I said, in a singsong way.

Freckles pricked his ears up, but just for a moment. He turned quickly, then disappeared behind a line of rosebushes that hugged the town green.

Elliot leaned forward and lay facedown on the grass, his arms limp at his side. "He was right there."

"I know," I said, stretching out to lie on my back beside him. "But he was scared. There was no way we were going to get him now, with all this chaos." I looked over at the crowd. The spectators had lifted the tug-of-war champs off the ground and were carrying them toward the tomato tents, where heirloom Bloody Marys were being served, under the yearly temporary suspension of the laws against open-air drinking.

"I just want him to come home."

There was something about the way Elliot said *home* that surprised me. As if home—Freckles's home and his—were a place not too far from here. I felt my heart fill with hope.

"Me, too."

From across the green, the rosebushes rustled. A couple of rabbits flew out of the bushes and leapt across the grass in great strides. Freckles came tearing out behind them, tail high, his stride as long and reaching as the rabbits'. He didn't look stressed. He looked happy. Free.

I rolled over onto my side and looked at Elliot. His face was turned toward me, his cheek pressed against the grass, eyes closed. I thought for a moment he might be sleeping, but his eyes opened, and he returned my gaze.

"I'm free tomorrow." Some part of me had made a decision I hadn't been aware I was debating. "If you want to see the orchard."

Elliot rolled over onto his back, his shirt a mess of mud and grass stains. "I'd like that," he said to the sky. "Very much."

We met just after sunrise at Peggy's place. Elliot stood before my car with two Styrofoam cups of coffee from the gas station.

"This was the only place open, other than the diner, but I thought you might like a change of coffee."

I had told Fern that I needed a day to get caught up on paperwork, which wasn't a lie, exactly. I was planning on spending the afternoon filing invoices and putting together the dry goods order. Still, I was glad an early morning Elliot hadn't shown up at the diner and told anyone about our walk. I didn't want to have to face Charlie's and Fern's relentless teasing on my next shift.

I took a sip of the coffee. Milk, no sugar. Had he remembered from before? I hadn't noticed that he was paying attention. "This is secretly my favorite coffee in town," I said, holding up the cup. "Don't tell anyone."

It was a cold morning. You would never have known that the forecast said it would reach eighty-five degrees in town. The air held an undeniable taste of autumn. A breathtaking show of vermilion reds and persimmon orange would soon blanket the mountains. The morning fog lingered, making Peggy's yard look soft in the early light. "The grass is still wet," I said absently, and glanced over at him. He looked dapper in a cranberry fleece jacket that made his hazel eyes sparkle, dark jeans, and a pair of well-worn brown leather hiking boots. I had found myself dressing more carefully than I normally would to go for a walk, and wore my favorite green cardigan—the one that Charlie said made my eyes look like Grade B maple syrup—and had braided my hair in two neat ropes. I felt nervous to be out with Elliot and excited, but mostly nervous. "Ready?"

Elliot held up his coffee cup. "I have everything I need. Lead the way."

I led Elliot through the white picket fence and into Peggy's yard, then around the east side of the house. The tall grasses that had originally hidden the trailhead were well tamped down. The sun hadn't quite reached the woods, but the birds were wide awake. As we walked crows cawed warnings to each other of our arrival. Soft light filtered through the thin branches of a stand of pines. I had walked down this path dozens of times by myself, but it felt different with Elliot. He looked at home in the woods, walking carefully, stopping every so often to inspect a hole in the ground. "Hornets," he said, pointing to a mound off the path. I stopped and took a picture with my phone. I liked the thoughtful way he looked at everything. And I liked that he didn't need to fill in all the quiet with words, and he didn't seem to mind that I didn't, either. I had always thought that mornings were a time to take things in, so you would have something to savor later. Elliot reached over to rub a smooth bare patch on an otherwise knobby-barked evergreen. "Deer scratching its antlers, probably. Too low for a moose." I pressed my palm against the bare trunk to feel its cool, smooth texture.

"We're getting close," I said, noticing a couple of tiny golden apples on the ground that some animal must have carried and then forgotten. Soon the musty, dank scent of ferment filled my nostrils. "Can you smell that?" I asked.

"I can," Elliot said, quickening his step, looking up. "Extraordinary." Elliot circled the tree, inspecting the rough gray trunk, reaching up to pull a leaf off a low-hanging branch. He picked an old, blackened fruit off the ground, held it up to his nose, and breathed it in.

"Medlars," he said by way of explanation, as he let the old piece of fruit slip from his fingers.

"What are medlars, exactly?" I asked.

"You haven't eaten one?" Elliot picked a rusty-colored fruit off a branch. "They're a member of the rose family. See how they look like a rose hip?" He traced a finger lightly around the dry, pointy tentacles that hung off the bottom. "They can't be eaten in this state. You have to pick them and basically let them ripen to the point of decay."

"That sounds kind of terrible," I said.

"You wait until they're brown and wrinkled and squishy to the touch." Elliot closed his eyes. "And then they're heavenly. Like fresh apple butter. So smooth you need a spoon to eat them." He picked up a fruit and tossed it into the woods. "They are a bit unusual. I think the process is why they aren't too popular."

"People like things fresh and young," I said, thinking about the intern.

Elliot looked at me carefully. "I don't know. Some of the best things in life take time to ripen." He pulled on several of the branches, lifting up the leaves and turning them over to inspect underneath. He knocked on the trunk. "So what other treasures are you hiding in these woods?"

He had no idea. But he would spot the yellow warblers in a moment or two. When I had invited him to see the orchard, I knew I would be sharing the sculptures with him. There was no way to see the orchard without the warblers leading you deeper into the forest. I wanted him to see them. And to know if he saw the beauty in them. I had to admit I was also excited to explore further. With Elliot, I could go deeper into the woods without fear of getting lost. "Many, many treasures," I said, walking ahead of him farther into the orchard. "Keep looking up."

Elliot walked us off the path. He identified a quince tree, two unusual varieties of pear, several heirloom apples, a shaggy, ground cherry plant that grew low across the forest floor, and an overgrown elderberry bush that was heavy with clusters of dark blackish red berries. He picked a handful, and extended his hand to me. I took a couple and popped them in my mouth. The taste of sour blackberry pricked my tongue. I chewed quickly and swallowed like they were medicine, too shy to spit them out.

"Delicious," I said, scrunching my face up in pain.

Elliot laughed and popped a couple of the berries in his mouth. "They're tart, but when they're cooked into a pie or jam they taste like honey and wildflowers." He offered me another berry.

"I think I'll wait until I can try the cooked version," I said.

"It was definitely planted as an orchard," Elliot said as we circled back to the medlar trees. "By a collector, I'd say—it's a marvelous selection of fruits. You don't remember anyone harvesting the orchard when you were a kid? It really is overgrown. It doesn't look as if anyone has cared for it in . . ."

He stopped short when he spotted the first glint of yellow wing in the trees.

"What is that?" He pointed his hand up toward the branches. I didn't have to look up to know he had seen one of the warblers.

I had been admiring the way his fingertips were stained with elderberry juice, and had taken out my phone, trying to find a subtle way to snap a picture of his berry-stained lips. He looked over at me, his face full of questions, his mouth open in childlike awe.

"Keep looking."

I snapped about a hundred pictures of Elliot as he discovered the warblers. He kept looking up at them, and then over to me, but he didn't say a word.

"Follow them," I said. "They're leading the way."

The sun had burned off the haze of morning, and the bright light glinted off the yellow tin wings and bodies. Elliot picked up the pace, and I walked quickly behind him, unbuttoning my sweater in the rising heat. Summer had claimed victory over the push of autumn for another day.

"Oh, my goodness," Elliot said quietly, his voice full of awe. I smiled up at him. The Moxie horse stood proud, forever paused in mid gallop. It gleamed bright in the morning sun. Peggy had placed him in exactly the right place. Impressive on his own, standing in the clearing he looked even more majestic.

"Did you?" he asked, his expression questioning.

"No, no, not me. I found them when I was looking for Freckles, right after Peggy died."

"It's magnificent." He walked up to the horse, running his palm over the long flank, then brushing back the horse's mane with his long fingers. He rubbed its muzzle as if it were a real horse. "Them?"

"There are more," I said. "I think I've only found a few. I've been wanting to explore more, but . . ." I looked over at him shyly. "I thought maybe the two of us could walk farther in, if you don't have anywhere to be."

"I'd be delighted," he said.

I showed him the crystal egret, and the soda-can doe, all the way to the pair of computer keyboard letter sheep, quietly grazing in a patch of moss. "This is as far as I've gotten. I don't have a great sense of direction," I admitted. "I've been a little nervous about getting lost in the woods."

Elliot looked up at the sun and checked his watch. "I've got a compass on my phone, and we've got plenty of sunlight." He tilted his head to the right, beyond the sheep. "Let's go see what we find."

We walked awhile without talking, each of us focused on

searching, hoping to catch a glimpse of something the artist
made. To the right was a small stream. We could hear the water
trickle over stones in the places where it bubbled to the surface.
It offered us a direction, a path to follow.

"So what do you know about these sculptures?"

"Not much. I assume they're Peggy's. She has a barn full of
collected materials."

"Did you know she was an artist?"

"That's the thing. I had no idea. She never mentioned it. I've
never seen anything like these sculptures at the county fair craft
competition, or the holiday art sale." I shrugged. "She was just
Peggy the cake lady. I never would have guessed."

"I love that about people," Elliot said, holding a branch back
for me to walk by.

"What's that?"

"Their passions. Their surprises. I've never met anyone who
didn't have a little obsession." Elliot looked over at me, his face
open. "I thought I might have stumbled on yours by now, but I'm
not sure that I have. Maybe photography?"

"I like to take pictures," I said. "But I wouldn't call it my
passion."

"What else?"

"I haven't really had a lot of time to do much," I said. "I
don't—mostly the diner keeps me busy."

Elliot looked at me sideways. "So, just Nora the diner lady."

"Yup," I said. "Nora the diner lady. That's me."

"And you like being Nora the diner lady?"

"No one has ever asked me that before."

"Really? I'm surprised to hear that."

I shrugged. "I guess people just assume that I do. I grew up in the diner—it's a family business. It wasn't my life's dream, exactly—but it's been my life."

"Do you dream about doing something else?"

"Not exactly. I mean, I don't know what other job I would like to do, but . . . do you really want to know?"

"I do."

I took a deep breath. "Okay. I dream about having a little herd of dairy goats. A big garden." I held my arms out wide. "Really big. An herb bed and rows of vegetables. Berry bushes and a cutting garden made to bloom every week of the growing season. Enough space for a dog or two to roam. A kitchen large enough to put up vegetables, a cozy spot with a fireplace for reading on winter afternoons, and a big sunny room with wood floors just for painting."

"So you are an artist, then."

I ignored him and kept talking. I hadn't spoken any of these dreams out loud, and telling them to the trees felt like they might somehow come true. "The room would have to be big enough for large canvases. Big enough so that I could have the space to sit across from whatever I am working on and just look at it for a while. Seeing takes time." I shrugged, tucking my vision safely back inside me. "Not a grand life."

"It sounds like a grand life." Elliot eyed me carefully.

"It sounds like Peggy's," I said with a laugh. Until that moment I hadn't really realized how happy Peggy must have been.

Ahead of us, the sun seemed to burn a little brighter. "Look," I said, pointing, "I think there's a clearing over to the right."

We walked carefully, Elliot forging the way, warning of

wobbly rocks and tree roots in the path. The stream beside us had grown wider, the ground beside it damp and spongy. At the edge of the clearing, knee-deep in the water, was a life-sized moose made of stretched-out wire coat hangers, as if someone had drawn him in three dimensions. The moose was leaning against a tree, head down for a drink of water. When I reached out to touch it, one of the antlers splashed into the water. I quickly grabbed it before it could float downstream.

"Oh," I heard Elliot gasp. "Nora, come here." I followed him into the clearing. Before us was a pond the size of a tennis court, the water dark and cool looking, dotted with bright white water lilies. Someone had carefully cleaned the banks of the pond, and pillowy clumps of moss had grown around the edges. The banks were dotted with flat pieces of rock, and it was free of the usual branches and debris. All around the pond, and in and among the trees, were sculptures. Some were figurative, like the animals that we had found before. A family of turtles made of oyster shells sunned themselves on a rock by the water. On the edge of the tree line, peony bushes with broken-china blossoms were in full bloom. Patches of Queen Anne's lace made from real lace doilies waved in the soft breeze. A porcupine made entirely of flat-headed tin thumbtacks posed beneath. Some of the trees were wearing Victorian-style nightgowns sewn from orange, netted clementine bags. Wisteria made of clumps of costume-glass beads swung from the branches of another tree. Other sculptures were more abstract—made from materials wild-crafted from where they were—and were less preserved. An arrangement of ombré mosses were put together in a way that played with color and light. Next to it, a twisting labyrinth of fieldstones led back into the woods. Far across the field, there were giant shapes made of woven twigs that looked so light I wouldn't have been surprised if one drifted up and floated away. Everywhere you looked there was a surprise to be found. It was a handmade Eden.

I turned to find Elliot removing his fleece and pulling off the T-shirt he was wearing underneath. There were soft wisps of dark hair across his chest, which surprised me, then I found myself surprised at being surprised, not knowing that I had been thinking of his chest at all. When I realized I was staring at him, I felt blood rush to my cheeks. "Um, what are you doing?"

"Doesn't the water look good?"

"But it's not hot out."

Elliot looked up at the sky. The sun was burning bright, and in the clearing it was sticky and growing warm.

"We found a magic swimming hole. You can't not swim in a magic swimming hole. It's bad luck."

When Elliot reached for the top button of his pants, I quickly focused my gaze on the ground and didn't look up again until I heard the soft splash of water and a long sigh. When I peeked I found Elliot neck-deep in the dark water. "How is it?"

"Cold, and probably full of leeches. Maybe five feet deep. Come on in."

I pulled off my sweater and the soft knit shirt I had on underneath it, but left my tank top on. Elliot had the decency to swim away from me as I kicked out of my hiking boots and pulled off my jeans. I was wearing my most grandmotherly pair of underwear. Good for coverage, I thought, but not great for anything else. I slid into the water before I could think anymore.

The water was cool, but soft against my skin. The pond had a wonderful green scent to it, and the bottom felt squishy from decades of decaying leaves, as if it held all of the seasons at once.

"I haven't been in a good swimming hole since I was a kid," Elliot said, treading water beside me.

"I haven't, either," I admitted. "Fern and I get over to Lake Willoughby from time to time, but it's always crowded. I never knew this was here."

"It's funny how that is—how you think you know a place, but there are still so many hidden surprises."

"Just like people," I said, thinking of his earlier comment.

Elliot smiled. "Exactly like people."

"What about you?"

"Do I know any hidden places? I haven't been here all that long—Guthrie is one big hidden surprise to me. I have come to know the sugar bush behind the inn pretty well, though. There are a lot of owls."

I laughed. "No, I mean, what's your hidden place? What you dream of. Or are you just Elliot the HG guy?"

Elliot floated on his back for a moment, looking up at the cloudless September sky. "I have a lot of dreams, actually. But I'm a lot like you. Work seems to be the thing that I actually do most of the time."

"Do you enjoy it?"

"I like scouting for locations. That's the best part. It's like a puzzle, trying to match the needs of the company with the needs of the community, and the possibility of the land." Elliot reached over to one of the white water lilies and brushed the petals with his fingers. "I like meeting the people in the towns."

"And if you could have a do-over, right now, what would you do?"

"I don't know what that looks like, exactly. Something outside. Something that is connected to the land, that would allow me to stay in one place." He leaned back into the water and floated. I was relieved to find he had kept on his boxer shorts. "And I write some. I guess sometimes I dream about doing something with that." He looked over at me and smiled. "Does that make me more than just Elliot the HG guy? Because I really don't want to be just Elliot the HG guy."

He was an artist, too. I don't know what I was expecting him to say, but this felt like a surprise. "You're a writer?"

Elliot laughed. "I don't know if I'd go that far."

"Fiction? Essays? Nature guides?" I could picture him being good at any of those things.

Elliot's ears burned. He nodded. "Mostly essays, about ecology, and the way all things are connected. If I'm being honest here, I should tell you I'm trying to write a novel. It's terrible."

"That's amazing," I said. I loved books as much as I loved movies.

"You wouldn't say that if you read it. But it gives me something to do at night in the hotel rooms." Elliot dove into the water, swam to the edge, then he did a slow backstroke to where I was treading water, trying not to let my feet hit the silty-soft bottom.

"You don't feel like . . . I don't know. Like it's too late to start something new?" I asked. "I don't mean to say you're old."

Elliot laughed. "I'll tell you mine if you tell me yours."

"Forty-two," I said, watching his face for a reaction.

"Why, you're just a kid. I turned fifty a couple of weeks ago."

He had been in Guthrie for at least a month. "What did you do to celebrate?"

"I spent it with a lovely, kind woman."

"Oh." The water felt a little colder all of a sudden, and I found myself wishing I was dry and warm and alone in my apartment.

"Under a canoe."

Realization dawned. "You should have told me!"

"I didn't want to make a big deal about it."

"But it was your fiftieth. It was a special day."

"It was," Elliot said softly.

I gathered up a little courage. "Can I ask you something that might sound a little rude?"

Elliot laughed. "I'm all ears."

It took everything I had to keep a straight face. "Don't you feel . . . I don't know of a better way to say this. When you are working on your novel, do you ever feel . . . nervous? To start something new?" I dunked my head under the water, afraid to look at his face. When I came up, he smiled warmly at me.

"Have you ever heard of a century tree?"

"The white oak that Peggy crashed into was over a hundred years old. But I've never heard that expression."

"I saw the scars on that tree. I truly am sorry about your friend Peggy. I really loved the little time I spent with her. She was a sweet old duck."

"She really was."

"And those cakes. Every time we met she would insist that we sit down and have a cup of tea and a slice of cake before negotiating. She served this one with maple frosting—"

"The burnt sugar cake!" Elliot hadn't been in town long enough to be the standing order, but it made me happy to know he had tasted the cake.

"Yes, that's the one."

"She didn't mention who she had baked it for, by chance?"

"I assumed she just made it for guests."

"I'm going to ask you for a cake-related favor in a couple of days." I wanted to know how Max's and my burnt sugar cake stood up next to Peggy's.

"Anytime." Elliot swam a little closer to me, the ripples he made in the water brushing against my skin. "My mom grew up in the Southwest. She used to tell us stories about growing up in the desert. One time both of my brothers ended up on the same whiffle ball team. It was a town thing, you had to try out. I was short for my age and couldn't hit a beach ball with a bat, never mind a little whiffle ball."

"They're hard to hit," I said, my tiptoes touching the pulpy bottom of the pond.

"So that first night my brothers were at practice, my mom told me the story of the century tree. Mom was raised by her grandfather and lived in the house he grew up in. They had a century tree in their yard. Her grandfather told her that the tree only bloomed once every hundred years, and that he had never seen it bloom."

"What do the blooms look like? Is there any chance they would miss it blooming?" Maybe the flowers were small, or the same color as the plant, and would go unnoticed.

"I asked the same question. So one day, my mom went out into the yard and noticed something different. The century tree had a stalk growing out of it. Every day it would grow. Six inches, a foot, two feet." Elliot slowly stood until he was standing tall, the water only to his chest, his arms outstretched to the sky. "All the way up to twenty-seven feet, and thicker every day. From the stalk sprouted branches, and from the branches bloomed clumps of great green flowers with yellow stamens."

"That sounds incredible," I said, enjoying how the story lit up his face. Of course he was a writer.

"So, being eight, I asked my mom what a cactus plant had to do with my not being able to play whiffle ball with my brothers. And she said that people were just like century trees. You never know when they will bloom, but when they do, it's always an extraordinary sight to behold."

The story reminded me of my own mother, and the tales she would spin as I was drifting off to sleep. "She sounds like a wonderful woman."

"She is. You should meet her. You two would like each other."

I smiled shyly at him. "So you don't think you've bloomed yet?"

"Definitely not yet." Elliot dove back into the water.

My fingers were pruney, and the sun felt hot on my neck and inviting. I paddled to the shore and leaned my back against one of the rocks next to the family of turtles. I stretched my arms and grasped on to the rocks, letting my legs float in front of me in the water. I watched Elliot swim, his pale chest a shimmering bright light in the dark water. He moved like an eel or a fish, effortlessly, as if he were a part of the ecosystem. After a few laps, Elliot paddled over to where I was resting.

"This is an exceptional place," he said. His voice held a trace of longing, and it felt more like he was talking to himself than to me.

"All of this work," I said, petting one of the turtles, admiring the way Peggy had captured the stretch of the neck, the pleasure the turtle must feel in the sun. "I wonder why she never shared it with anyone."

"Maybe she did," Elliot said. "Or maybe she kept it private, just for herself. Either way, it means a lot that you shared it with me. I'm honored."

Elliot treaded water just an arm's length away, facing me. His lips were open slightly, his dark, wet hair glistened in the now-hot sun. I had never noticed the freckles that dotted his nose and cheeks, or the way his eyes crinkled at the edges when he looked happy, like now. He floated a little closer. There was just the leaf of a lily pad separating us. Elliot's expression was soft, open.

"Nora," he said, and his voice held a question I was afraid to answer. I let go of the rocks, took a deep breath, and dropped down into the water until my hair was floating like snakes around me, and stayed there until my lungs felt like they were going to burst.

When we reached the steps of Peggy's front porch, I told Elliot I was heading back to the diner. My underclothes were still wet beneath my jeans and shirt. Elliot had gallantly let me use his fleece jacket as a towel before I attempted to pull my jeans over my damp legs. We'd had a cheerful walk back through the woods, Elliot telling stories about his childhood in Maine, the trouble he used to get in with his brothers. In the orchard he'd told me the names of some of the fruit trees. He'd picked a goldeny green apple called a Roxbury Russet and said it was the oldest apple variety grown in the United States. It was crunchy, sweet, and tart, and tasted bright like a clear morning. In the woods, it had been easy to be with him. But by the time Peggy's house had come into view, my usual shyness had flooded back. I waved good-bye from the porch and pushed my way into Peggy's house with no intention of sticking around.

Peggy's foyer was a tangle of black cables. The living room was crowded with lights set up on stands. The cables ran up the stairs and into the rooms beyond. The kitchen felt hot. Two carrot sheet cakes sat on cooling racks on the counter, and when I pressed my palm gently to the top of one it was still warm. I must have just missed Max and Kit. I wondered what they thought when they saw Elliot's little car next to mine in front of the house.

I walked from room to room, wanting to give Elliot enough distance so I wouldn't be trailing him in my car. Upstairs, Peggy's room was the only one not littered with film equipment. I lay down on her bed, careful to keep my dusty hiking boots off of her hens-and-chicks quilt. She kept the house so tidy, so spare. I studied the photographs that were hanging on the wall across from me. They were all in black and white, and looked as if they had been on the wall back when this room was Peggy's parents', or even her grandparents'. There was a small girl in some of the family photographs that I thought must be Peggy, but I couldn't be sure. But there were no pictures beyond Peggy's childhood to give a hint of the life she lived outside of her family.

I woke up to the sound of my sister's voice, and for a disorienting moment I thought we were back in our childhood home across the way. But then Max's enthusiastic voice came up the stairs clear as a bell. Still more voices—the actresses in Kit's film. I got up, crept down the back stairs, which led straight to the kitchen, and slipped through the door that connected the house with the barn. I didn't want to get enlisted by my sister to hold a microphone or to do hair and makeup.

The barn door was open, the space light, and a warm breeze filtered in, making the wood shavings scent smell even sweeter. I sat down on a metal stool and spun around, looking at all the piles of raw material. Something colorful caught my eye. In the corner were large spools of old braided telephone wire. Red and white wires twisted together like candy canes. Yellow and green twists that reminded me of pea vines in the garden. I pulled out a long piece of royal blue and lifeguard orange wire and cut it. It bent easily and held its shape. I wrapped it around my arm, then pulled my arm free, admiring the tube the wire made. I twisted and untwisted the wire until I found a shape that I liked. It looked a little like a Viking boat, full and deep in the middle, with the sides high and pointed. Soon I was weaving in other wires, creating patterns of color. I lost myself in the materials, playing with the textures and layering color. I didn't look up until the late afternoon sun had set low enough to beam its way into the barn, lighting the yellow-painted pegboard ablaze with its raking light. I glanced at my watch—it was past five o'clock. I had been there for hours. I kept working until the piece felt finished. When it was done, I held it up, turning it around, viewing it from all angles. I wasn't sure what it was, but it felt as if it held some truth about myself that I didn't yet have words to describe. I slid the sculpture onto the top shelf of the workbench, hung the wire cutters in their designated spot on the pegboard, and slipped out of the barn, closing the door behind me.

❦

CHAPTER EIGHT

Max leaned back against the kitchen counter, clad in a pair of skinny black jeans and a black T-shirt, holding his favorite apron in his hand.

"Today is the day when the teacher becomes the student, Grasshopper," Max said, bowing. He then walked behind me and wrapped the apron around my waist. "Burnt sugar cake. Maple icing. Go." Max sat down at the kitchen table and leaned his chair back so that his combat-booted feet were airborne.

"Aren't you going to help?" I asked, feeling a little lost. I was expecting Max and I to bake the cake the way we did the last time, elbow-to-elbow.

"Nope. I have to take off my baking hat and put on my cinematographer hat. I'm handing the icing spatula to you."

"But—"

"No 'but,'" Max said. "Bake."

"I don't know why we are making this cake anyway. No one has called or stopped by, asking for it, ever."

Max leaned forward, then sprung out of the chair, which landed squarely on the floor with a loud thud. "Because tomorrow is Friday, and somewhere out there is a beautiful soul of a human being who loves burnt sugar cake so much they ordered one to be made every week—*every week*—and when the magical day comes when they discover that someone has taken up the mantle of Peggy the cake lady, and that their lives will be cakeless no more, we will be ready for them. With a fresh, rich, maple-frosted burnt sugar cake."

"Fair enough."

"All right, what comes first?" he asked.

"*Mise en place*," I said, reaching for the measuring cup.

"Yes. *Mise en place*. Perfect. Now get to work. Show me what you know. I have to be behind the camera to do light checks in two hours."

I made a pot of Irish breakfast tea once the cake was in the oven. Max poured the tea while I filled the cow-shaped creamer with milk.

I nodded my head toward the door that led to the rest of the house. "So how's the film coming?"

Max ran his hands through his hair, making it stand on end. "More slowly than I'd like. Your sister has been caught up in volunteering at the Pudding Hill House."

"Again?" I had thought Max and Kit's chanting event had been a one-off.

"Yeah. Chanting turned into a yoga class, which led to an authentic movement class, which led to an expressive dance workshop." Max tried to sound weary, but a smile threatened the edges of his mouth. "I can't complain, though, right? *All the suffering that is in the world arises from wishing ourselves to be happy. All the happiness there is in the world arises from wishing others to be happy.* That's this old Buddhist dude's way of saying you should always think about other people. Like Kit—she's making the world a better place. Plus, she's really good with the elderly people."

"Kit's really good with all the people," I said, stirring sugar into my tea.

"Truth."

"She's always been like that," I said. "She always got the most tips, even when she botched all of her orders."

"Kit worked in the diner?"

"Only when we were desperate. She was always running off to band practice or dance class. She's never been one to stay with things."

Max looked for a moment like a dog whose owner had just left the house with suitcase in hand. "That's what worries me."

"What do you mean?" I got up to spin the cakes around so that they would bake evenly. Peggy's oven had a hot spot.

"Kit is always on to the next thing. But I'd like to—I'd like to be the thing that she keeps doing." Max put his head down on the kitchen table. "I didn't mean that in a dirty way."

I poked his arm with the end of a wooden spoon. "You want to marry my little sister?"

Max's head moved and he made a little moaning sound. "If it's all right with you."

I laughed and sat back down. "Of course it's all right with me. It's Kit you have to ask."

Max lifted his head, but hid his face in his hands. "I'm pretty sure just asking her is going to freak her out and make her leave."

"You must know she adores you," I said, patting his arm with the spoon.

"She also adores the dairy farmer, Charlie at the diner—"

"You know he's gay, right?"

Max shrugged as if to say *Does that really matter?* "The guy down at the recycling center, your ex-husband—"

"They are like brother and sister," I said.

"All the old men at the Pudding Hill House—"

"*Old men.*"

"All of the loggers at the tug-of-war, the film society guy, the hot male nurse at the Pudding Hill House—"

He had me there. We all adored the hot male nurse at the Pudding Hill House.

"—Donkeys, maple creemees, clogging—"

"Okay, now you are just being silly."

"But you get my point—she loves, like, everything. Makes it a little hard to know where I fall on the What Kit Huckleberry Loves spectrum."

"It's just her way of making sure she feels loved, I think."

"What do you mean?"

"When we were kids—she doesn't have many memories of our family just being a regular family, before Mom got sick. And after she died, Dad really turned in on himself. He didn't have a lot to offer. And I was so—" Overwhelmed? Busy? Resentful?

"She always says how you took care of her. She really loves you, Nora."

I squeezed his hand. "I know. But I also know I didn't—couldn't—give her everything that she needed. So she turned to her friends. I think she's always been searching for what was missing at home. The attention. The affection. The lightness."

What I didn't say was that there were times, too, when I really needed her and couldn't pin her down. My heart ached a bit for Max. My little sister wasn't the easiest person to love sometimes. Neither of us were.

"Yeah." Max walked over to the counter and started sifting confectioners sugar for the frosting. "Any thoughts on convincing her that my love is enough?"

"Maybe if you could find a way to make it her idea?" I said, knowing it was terrible advice. It had worked when she was a teenager.

Max laughed. "I'm not sure how I could pull that one off, but I'll think about it."

The kitchen timer dinged. Max and I went over to the oven. I put on the quilted oven mitts and pulled the cake toward me. Max gently touched the top. "It's springing back," he said.

I handed him a wooden skewer. He slipped it into the center of the cake and pulled it out quickly. It was clean.

I gently set the Bundt pan on a cooling rack.

Max leaned over and inhaled deeply. He held out his hands to me. "Ladies and gentlemen, a cake baker has been born. Let me introduce you to Nora—the—cake—lady!"

Max waved his hands over his head like Kermit the Frog and made the sound of a crowd roaring.

I curtsied to Max and waved a stiff, queenly wave to my imaginary audience.

"Master the maple icing and a simple buttercream for layer cakes and you are ready to roll."

I spent all morning Friday from after the breakfast rush through lunch in my office going over the new health insurance plans my broker had sent. I ate my way through a whole bag of ruffled potato chips trying to choose the best plan that we could afford.

"Nora, the most fashionable person that has ever stepped into the Northeast Kingdom is here to see you," Charlie said, poking his head in. He had just had his beard trimmed and was looking more gentleman farmer and less angry duck hunter. I wondered if he had met someone over at the Bear Cub.

Fern's head appeared over his shoulder. "It's like she just stepped off the set of *Project Runway*. Come quick, before she realizes she has the wrong person and place."

I closed my laptop. Who on earth? Maybe it was an art student from the college who was working on a documentary project on small-town diners? That had happened before. I stood, brushing off the potato chip crumbs that had gathered in the bib of my overalls, and then patted my hair to remember what it had looked like that morning when I left the house. Two scruffy buns. Well, since she didn't have an appointment, she couldn't expect much. I made my way through the kitchen. Charlie waved me forward, as if I were keeping the queen waiting, then arched his neck out the window so he could watch.

A tall, thin woman with a platinum pixie cut was standing at the end of the counter, paging through a copy of the *Pennysaver*. She was wearing a pale blue dress that seemed to float around her, defying the laws of physics. A large necklace that looked like it was made of silver pussy-willow buds hung around her neck. She looked like a modern fairy godmother.

"Ms. Huckleberry?" she asked when she saw me gaping at her. Fern wiped the already-clean table across from us with a rag.

I held out my hand. "Nora, please. How can I help you?"

The woman smiled, a big genuine smile that made her eyes crinkle. "I'm Sonya Bellwether. I work for the HG Corporation." Sonya dug into her giant leather handbag and produced a business card, which she handed to me. "I was in town interviewing artists for a possible installation at the new HG location here in the Northeast Kingdom. Elliot Danforth mentioned you."

"I'm not an artist," I said quickly.

"No, no. I'm sorry, I'm not being clear." She took a tissue out of her purse and blew her nose. "Sorry. Allergies. I've been like this since I got up here."

"The ragweed has taken over." I handed her a stack of paper napkins. "Can I get you something?"

Sonya slid onto a stool. "Coffee. Black, please. The Benadryl is going to put me in a coma."

I poured her a cup of coffee and stayed behind the counter.

"Elliot mentioned that you have a sculpture garden on your land, and that you might need some advice about conservation. I have a master's in art restoration."

I looked over my shoulder to see if Fern or Charlie had heard what she said, but Fern was busy taking orders from a large group from the Garden Club who were peppering her with special dietary requests. Charlie's head was no longer in the window. I felt a pang of guilt for keeping the sculptures a secret, and another pang of something else—jealousy? Disappointment? At the fact that Elliot had told someone else about them. Someone who was beautiful and elegant and sophisticated in a way that I never would be. I hadn't explicitly said that the sculptures were a secret, but I thought he had understood that they were special, not to be shared. Certainly not with this mysterious woman who could afford clothes that float.

"I do have a sculpture garden," I said, because I did, and I wasn't a fan of lying, even to strangers. "But I can't afford to pay you. I'm sure Mr. Danforth told you we aren't selling to HG." And I was barely keeping the diner running as it was. Leaf-peeping season couldn't start soon enough. I made a mental note to call the Realtor and ask if there had been any new interest in

Peggy's property. One of the sheep farmers had said he might like to have some of the farmland for grazing, but I hadn't heard anything in a while.

Sonya flashed a pearly smile that advertised thousands of dollars in dental work. "No charge. I'm on HG's expenses right now. And Elliot just made the work sound so extraordinary. I'd love to see it, and help if I can."

"How long are you in town for? I don't know when I can get away."

"Just until tomorrow morning. But I don't want to be a bother. Elliot said he would show me around this afternoon, with your permission, of course."

Would he try to impress her with his extensive knowledge of rare apple varieties? Would she take her physics-defying dress off and skinny-dip with him at the swimming hole? My cheeks burned, and a wave of anger at my own foolishness washed over me. That day in the woods I had felt a connection, and a spark of something more. But that had been almost a week ago, and he hadn't been in the diner since. It must not have been mutual. I took a quick glance at Sonya. Here was a woman who was more Elliot's speed. I could see them together at some elegant, candlelit restaurant, or at the theater, or at a dinner party on the Vineyard. She probably had panties to match all of her bras. "Of course. You'll need to wear better shoes," I said lamely. She had on a pair of cream patent-leather flats that probably cost more than my rent.

Sonya laughed. "Elliot said you were charming. It was wonderful to meet you."

"You, too," I said. "Thanks."

I was pretty sure I had just thanked her for spending a roman-tic afternoon walking around my secret garden with the first man I have been drawn to since Sean. I hurried back into my office and shut the door before Charlie and Fern could grill me about who Sonya was and what she wanted. I wasn't in the mood to hide my disappointment.

I didn't feel like going back to my empty apartment after work. Thoughts of Sonya and Elliot flooded my imagination and I needed distraction. Besides, the apartment had become the film office of Kit and Max, packed with scripts and costumes, cables and tripods, even an occasional filmmaker friend in town to help shoot a difficult scene—anything that was in the way at Peggy's had been dumped in my living room, to the point where it was difficult to walk. I couldn't bear to be there.

I drove around the back roads for a while, taking in the early signs of color. Little patches of leaves the colors of butternut squash and sunflower petals popped against the expanse of green. I breathed a sigh of relief. We took in a solid 25 percent of our yearly profits between the end of September and the end of October. If we had a good season, that meant I could keep the diner—and Elsie—going until I could find a buyer for Peggy's place. If we didn't . . . I couldn't even let myself think about it. "Mom must be rolling in her grave," I muttered to myself. *Freedom is low overhead*, she always said.

I traveled the length of Pudding Hill Road. The corn had been plowed down, spent for the season. In the neighboring field was a pumpkin patch, the green lawn dotted with bright orange pumpkins, their plump bodies still attached to curling vines. As

I turned down Hunger Mountain, the paved road turned to dirt, dry and dusty from lack of rain. There was a big SUV parked in front of our old house. The summer people.

I pulled into Peggy's drive, breathing a sigh of relief that Elliot's car was not in sight. Peggy's Shasta daisies and black-eyed Susans had grown tall and bushy and were threatening to take over the whole raised bed. The sunflowers were just naked stalks, the heads long since pulled apart by winter-gathering squirrels.

"And cut," Max said from the living room. I slipped into the kitchen without saying hello, not wanting to interrupt.

The burnt sugar cake stood on the counter, untouched. Max walked in, large headphones hung around his neck.

"Hey there," Max said, leaning down to kiss my cheek.

"No one picked that up, I see." I pointed to the cake.

"Nope. Not yet." Max looked at the clock over the stove. "I guess it's late enough to call it a day. Want a slice? Savor the success of your first solo bake?"

I laughed. "I haven't eaten since breakfast. I better hold out for some protein." From the other room I could hear two female voices, neither one my sister's. "Is Kit in there?"

Max shook his head. "Nope. She's over at the nursing home."

"Again?"

"She's teaching a workshop—storytelling, I think."

I took a seat at the kitchen table. "Has she been here at all?"

Max sat next to me. "Yeah, she was here for the shoot last night, actually, and we got some more shooting in this morning. I'm just redoing a few of the scenes we felt needed a little work." His words were positive, but he sounded exhausted and a little disappointed.

"Everything all right? You want me to talk to her?" I asked.

Max laughed. "Nah. We're due for a sit-down." He rubbed his eyes with the heels of his hands. "The deadline is starting to feel like a black bear riding piggyback on my shoulders. We need to finish shooting if we're going to have any hope of being ready in time for postproduction."

"Did you find someone to help you with the edits?"

"She didn't tell you?"

"Tell me what?" The only thing Kit had told me last night before I went to bed was that we were out of tequila and limes.

Max sighed. "An old film school buddy of mine offered to help us edit it at his studio for cheap. He had a last-minute cancellation. He's even got his sound guy lined up."

"Where is he located?"

"Brooklyn."

"And when can he take you?"

"We're due on September twenty-first."

In two weeks.

Kit and Max were leaving. Of course they were. I had known that their stay was temporary. When did my sister ever stay anywhere? But I had grown accustomed to their showing up at the diner late every morning for breakfast, to Max and Charlie philosophizing about the state of the world while my sister entertained the customers at the counter with a story or a song or a reenactment of a scene from a Meryl Streep movie. I would miss the late nights talking in the living room. Baking with Max. Eating a second bowl of popcorn with Kit while binge-watching Alfred Hitchcock movies. Listening to Max serenade Kit from the bedroom while she was taking a shower. Talking to Kit about growing up, and Mom and Dad. The little apartment, despite it being a total wreck, felt like a home for the first time since I had moved in.

"You'll miss peak color," I said, trying to keep my voice steady.

Max wrapped his arm around my shoulder and squeezed hard. "We'll be back soon, I promise. We'll come for Christmas."

"All right," I said, slapping my hands against my thighs. I stood and picked up the cake. "Mind if I take this with me?"

"Your first solo cake? Take it! I want you to eat the whole thing with your hands! Spread it all over your face like it's your first birthday."

"I can't guarantee there will be any smearing, but I promise I'll eat at least one piece."

"You better," Max said, and put his headphones back on before disappearing into the next room.

When I poked my head in the sunroom, I found Kit standing by the door, her small video camera attached to a skinny tripod, filming a man in a wheelchair who was speaking to the crowded room.

"I had no idea she was Elizabeth Taylor, I swear," the man said, and the audience members gasped in unison. "It wasn't until my sister bought one of those movie magazines with her allowance. There was a whole article about Ms. Taylor and her tour of Vermont. I couldn't believe my eyes. She looked real different without all that makeup. Prettier, if you ask me."

Kit pressed a button on the camera and rested the tripod on her shoulder. "Good thing Richard Burton didn't catch wind of your shenanigans. Fabulous story, Mr. Shelburn. Let's give Harry a round of applause."

Harry bowed. One of the nurse's aides combed his hair into place with her fingers when he was vertical again.

"Shouldn't you be at Peggy's, working on *Side Work*?" I shifted the cake box from one arm to the other.

"Max has it under control," Kit said, fussing with the tripod legs until they reached the length she was looking for. "All right, who's next? Janice, would you share that story about the time you hiked the Long Trail? You were the first woman to hike it solo, right?"

"The first one on record. I'm sure there were others before me," Janice said, reaching for the microphone.

I pressed on. "Don't you think Max might have some questions—for the *director*? Since you are on such a tight deadline?"

Kit turned to me. "Did he say something to you?"

"Max? No, of course not," I lied. I had been telling Kit little untruths my whole life—it was part of the job of being the oldest. I liked to think of it more as editing, but sometimes lying was necessary for the greater good. It's what big sisters did to protect their younger siblings. This time, of course, I was actually protecting Max. I didn't want to give her any ammunition against him if she was looking for some. When Kit came back to Guthrie next, whenever that would be, I hoped that Max would still be with her.

Kit adjusted the camera one more time. "He's been acting weird all week. Like a squirrel."

I laughed, picturing Max with a mouthful of sunflower seeds. "What do you mean?"

"He keeps, like, darting toward me, like he has something urgent to say, then when I get two feet from him he skitters away. It's stressing me out."

Janice tapped on the mic. "Is this thing on?"

Kit pressed record. "Go for it, Janice. Start with when you made the decision to do the hike. What did your family think?"

I brought the cake over to the receptionist's desk. "Is there someplace where I could leave this for the staff?"

The receptionist led me to a small break room the nurses and aides used when she noticed the cake box.

"Oh, I hope that's what I think it is," she said when I opened the lid. She rustled through the cupboards, and set out paper plates and plastic forks.

I stopped fussing with the box and turned to face her. "What do you think it is?" I said carefully.

"Each week Peggy used to bring a burnt sugar cake for Elsie. It made her eyes light up every time." She elbowed me in the side. "Made ours light up, too. I hope yours is as good as Peggy's!"

Friday—LC—bsc/mi.

"I hope so, too," I said, sliding the cake out of the box. Of course the cake was for Elsie. Peggy loved this woman enough to pay for her care—of course she would show her love in the way she knew best, with cake. "Can I bring her a slice?"

The receptionist poked her head out of the break room and looked down the hall. "The nutritionist frowns on treats, but most of us here think these folks deserve whatever happiness they can get. If anyone asks any questions, would you mind leaving my name out of it?" She smiled, cut herself a thick wedge, and covered it with a paper napkin. "It smells delicious."

I cut a dainty piece of the cake, gathered a fork and several napkins, and made my way down to Elsie's room. She was sitting up in bed, a yellow sweater draped over her shoulders. Her gaze fell on the cake.

"Is she here?" Elsie asked, her voice excited. She looked about the room.

"No, it's just me. I brought you a slice of cake."

"I know who made that cake, Missy, thank you very much." I hadn't seen Elsie this animated before. Most days she looked so frail. Today she looked formidable.

I pulled a chair up to her bed and gave her the plate. She clutched the fork with a shaky hand. I reached over to help, but with her other hand she waved me away.

Elsie managed to get a bite of cake into her mouth. Frosting coated her lips. "It's my favorite. Peggy always remembers. She brings so much sweetness to my life." Her face softened then, as if she were deep in memory.

After offering Elsie a napkin, I eased the fork out of her hand, took up a small bit of cake, and held it to her lips. She relented and opened her mouth.

"She's got herself locked up in that kitchen of hers, hasn't she? She can never turn anyone down when they need a cake. I swear, she's busier now than she was back when she was working full time at the bank."

"Elsie, how long have you and Peggy known each other?"

Elsie gave me a warm smile. "Oh, we've known each other for lifetimes." Elsie chewed thoughtfully. "She was the first person to make me feel welcome. I came here for solitude, you know. It was my choice. But I never realized how truly difficult it is to be alone." Tears formed in Elsie's eyes. "The loneliness. I didn't think I could make it. It was unbearable. But then I met her."

I took her papery hand in mine and squeezed. "Can I bring you some water, Elsie?" I asked. Elsie shook her head. I reached over and wiped a little bit of frosting from the corner of her lip. Elsie leaned back, her hand pushing the cake plate away.

When I turned to put the cake plate on the table, I saw that Kit had slipped into the room.

"Peggy is your friend?" she asked quietly.

Elsie closed her eyes. Her soft gray hair had come loose from its clip and lay splayed across the pillow.

"Oh, she inspires me. I hadn't made anything in decades, but for her I want to create a whole new world just to see her delight in it."

"She's your muse," Kit said.

"She is my everything."

⁕

Guthrie Front Porch Forum
Nor'easter Watch
User: ToG

We just received a report from the National Weather Service. There is a possible nor'easter forming over Georgia. If the current models are correct, it could hit the Guthrie area at the end of this week. I know we are in need of rain, but if we get a good hit, the ground will have a hard time absorbing the water. That could mean flooding. Hopefully the almanac is right about the fall foliage and the National Weather Service is wrong about this storm. We'll keep you updated.

Hayrides Are Back
User: LivvyR-MC

The hayrides are back! Starting the weekend of September 30, bring your family on a hayride through the sugar bush between the McCracken farm and the Sugar Maple Inn. Hop on at either location. Pumpkin cookies and sweet rolls along with hot cider, tea, and coffee will be served at the inn. Pick your own pumpkin at the McCracken farm. Saturdays and Sundays, 10–3, until the leaves have passed. A special Haunted Hayride will be held on Halloween night—details soon!

Fall Color Maps
User: LeafPeeper

The Old Farmer's Almanac has not let us down—it's looking to be a fantastic year for color! We are already seeing some color in the higher elevations, close to the border. It's going to be an early one, folks, I can feel it in my bones. I've set up an interactive color map on my website so tourists can find the most up-to-date foliage. Link down below. Advertisement opportunities are still available. E-mail or call for prices. I'm also running the state foliage hotline this year, so while you are driving those back roads, remember to fill me in on what you are seeing. Thank you for your support—your personal foliage reports help support the entire community by drawing in those tourist dollars. Here's to a successful leaf-peeping season!

—Annie W. www.peepvermont.com, e-mail annie @peepvermont.com

Haunted House Volunteers Needed
User: GuthrieHouse

The Haunted House at the historic Dewey House is looking for volunteers to do hair and makeup the week leading up to Halloween. We especially need someone who can do sugar-free fake blood, as several of this year's zombies are diabetic.

Town Meeting This Week
User: ToG

There will be a town meeting held on Wednesday, September 13, at 6 p.m., at the town hall.

Refreshments provided by Girl Scout Troop 235. Please bring small bills.

To be discussed:

Article 1: Pigs—Ben Smith has filed a formal complaint against the Sweet Pea Farm, stating that the farm has moved its manure pile too close to the Smith property.

Article 2: Say No to HG petition—the Keep Guthrie Small coalition will present their petition and signature collection to the town.

Article 3: Zoning—HG Corporation has asked about the possibility of rezoning the land owned by Nora Huckleberry LaPlante and Katherine Huckleberry, formally the property of Peggy Johnson. A vote will be taken.

Looks like it's going to be another doozy of a meeting. Bring a folding chair or two if you could.

Freckles Update
User: GuthriePD/DW

Freckles has been spotted several times in the trap I set up, happily eating the meat donated by the Haskell farm— thanks again, Haskell family. I'm going to engage the trigger to work now. Next time Freckles enters the cage and steps on the pressure plate, it will cause the door to close, trapping him in. Hopefully Freckles will take the bait (ha ha) before the hayrides begin.

User: LivvyR-MC

Sorry about the hayrides—really hope we don't scare Freckles away with the horses!

User: GuthriePD/DW

No worries, Livvy. We all look forward to the McCracken hayrides!

User: GotMilk

My wife went into labor after one of those hayrides :) She was three weeks overdue.

 I caught a glimpse of Freckles this morning—looked like he had a bit of a limp. Can anyone confirm?

User: GuthriePD/DW

Yes, Tom, I saw him limping, too. Hopefully we will have him back safely soon and can get him to the vet. I'm guessing the limp won't be the only issue. He has a ton of burrs stuck in the curly hair of his flanks. He's going to need a lot of love.

User: GotMilk

Speaking of which, whose home is he going to go to when we do catch him?

User: MissGuthrieDiner

I'll take him.

User: ElliotD

I'll take him.

User: TheVictoriaHotel

A friendly reminder that there is a strict No Pets policy for all residents of the Victoria Hotel.

User: GuthriePD/DW

Let's worry about that when Freckles is safe and sound.—Erika

CHAPTER NINE

❧

Charlie walked into the dining room after his shift smelling like musk and sandalwood. He was wearing a pair of dark-washed jeans and a close-fitting red plaid shirt that more than hinted that he liked to spend his free time over at the gym in St. J.

Fern whistled a catcall. "Let me guess—you're working at the Bear Cub tonight?" She squeezed his bicep. "Good lord, is that guy from Burlington coming?"

Charlie laughed, running his fingers through his beard. "Maybe. It is karaoke night. He occasionally comes for that. He does a pretty good Rufus Wainwright. You should come."

"On a Tuesday night? What do I look like, a twenty-two-year-old?"

Charlie snorted. "It being Tuesday never stopped you before."

"Do they have any of the old country songs, or is it all Taylor Swift?"

"Hank Williams, Merle Haggard, and Johnny Cash, of course."

"Loretta Lynn?" Fern had been asked on more than a dozen dates after she sang her version of "Don't Come Home a Drinkin'."

Charlie rolled his eyes at Fern. "Help me out here, Nora."

I plopped myself down next to Charlie on one of the counter stools, ready for my late lunch/early dinner of grilled cheese and

French fries. The bread was a perfect buttery golden brown. I took a bite and sighed. Charlie was a cheese snob. He had banished American cheese from the diner several years before and had come up with a blend of artisanal cheeses that he refused to divulge. He had to make little packages of cheese for the night crew so they could fill the dinner orders.

"You should totally go, Ferny," I said. "I hear Charlie makes an excellent margarita."

"He uses my secret recipe," Fern said.

I had figured out a long time ago that Fern's secret recipe was to double the tequila.

The bell above the door chimed and Max and Kit came in carrying the movie camera, a laptop, and several stand lights. Heavy black cables roped up their arms. Kit slid the camera and laptop onto one of the Formica tables and dumped the rest of their equipment in an empty booth. "Hey, sis," she said, sliding onto the stool next to me. "Did you tell them about Elsie?"

I shot Kit a look. I didn't think it was right to gossip about Elsie and Peggy. They had chosen to keep their private lives private.

"Elsie Cole?" Fern asked. She had an excellent memory for names. "Whatever happened to her?"

"Did you know her at all?" I asked, spooning sugar into my cup of tea.

"Not really. She used to volunteer for story hour over at the library. Nice lady. Kept to herself." Fern brought over a little pitcher of milk and placed it in front of me. "Is she still alive?"

"She's living in the Pudding Hill House," Kit said. "We think she and Peggy were in love."

"Peggy the cake lady was a lesbian?" Fern asked. "It's true she never did marry."

"We don't know anything for sure," I said weakly, but it was no use. When Kit was in the mood to tell a story, there was no stopping her.

"She said Peggy was her muse," Kit said, as if this explained everything.

Max leaned down and kissed Kit. "You're my muse."

Kit beamed up at him. "And you're mine. Was Elsie an artist of some sort?" she asked Fern.

Fern shrugged. "Not that I can remember. Did you know her, Charlie?"

Charlie raised his eyebrows. "You do realize that not all gay people know each other. There isn't some secret clubhouse."

Fern laughed. "Unless you're talking about the Bear Cub. I meant from your childhood."

"I wasn't much of a reader," Charlie said, taking a large sip of his Diet Coke.

"What's the big deal, anyway?" asked Max. "Isn't Vermont the most liberal state in the country? Didn't you all have civil unions before anyone else?"

"We did, but there was a lot of backlash," I explained. "For a while there were giant black TAKE BACK VERMONT signs hanging on every other barn."

Charlie flinched. "My parents had one of those signs."

Kit got up and leaned against Charlie, hugging him from behind. "Damn, you smell good." She snuggled closer.

A gong rang out. Max pulled his phone out of his back pocket and glanced at it. "Hey, babe," he said. "The Vanagon is ready to roll."

Kit reached for the phone. "That's the best news! Now we know how we're getting to New York."

"You guys are leaving?" Charlie turned on his stool and held out his arms.

Kitty fell into Charlie's embrace. "Yup. Time to get back to the city. We have an editor and sound guy waiting for us."

"We scored a pretty sweet house-sitting gig, too," Max added. "Right across the street from our favorite latke place in the whole world."

"Latkes," Kit sang, as if latkes were all you needed for happiness.

"If you wanted latkes, all you had to do was ask," Charlie said, sounding a little offended.

"I'm sure yours are divine." Kit scooted out of Charlie's arms and leaned her head on my shoulder. "Nora, my sweetest, most favorite sister?" She reached for my grilled cheese.

I slapped her hand away. "What do you need?" Kit never had told me she was leaving. Max must have let her know that I knew. It stung that she treated leaving like it was no big deal to her.

"Could we borrow your car to go pick up the Vanagon?" Max said. "It would just be a couple of nights."

"Why so long?" I wasn't prepared to give up any of the days I had left with them.

"Max was asked to do some work on a short," Kit said.

"They just wanted me to shoot some landscape stuff."

"Max has perfected the art of the long shot. You know, like all of those cool landscapes in the beginning of *Down by Law*."

"Jarmusch is the master of doing much with little," Max said with a sigh. "If our movie could be a tenth as cool as *Down by Law*—"

"It *will* be as cool as *Down by Law*. Cooler." Kit slung her arm across my shoulders and gave me a sideways hug before she moved over to Max, leaning her body across his back like a sloth moving from tree to tree.

"When do you want to leave?"

Kit bent her head so she and Max could look at each other.

"What do you think?" Max asked.

"We're not doing anything now." Kit turned to me. "Now?"

The chime over the door rang and Elliot Danforth walked in, dressed in his work outfit—pressed khakis, crisp dress shirt, tasseled loafers. He looked handsome.

"Hello, everyone," Elliot said warmly. "Okay if I join you?"

Charlie patted the stool next to him. "Have a seat. I'd offer to make you supper, but I have to leave in a minute to go to my other job. You could come with me. You like karaoke?"

The Burlington guy had put Charlie in a good mood. It was fun to see him flirt.

"And you'll be back when?" I asked Kit.

She slid down off of Max's shoulders. "By Friday afternoon at the latest."

I reached for my purse behind the counter and fished for my car keys. "It's all gassed up. I just had the oil changed. The hatchback sticks a little, so be sure to slam it shut, and make sure it's locked—"

"Okay, Mom," Kit mumbled.

"Thanks, Nora. We really appreciate it." Max leaned in and kissed me on the cheek. "We'll get her back to you in one piece."

Kit grabbed her purse and slung it over her shoulder, blowing kisses to everyone at the counter.

"Farewell, my lovelies. Eat some kettle corn for me tomorrow night!"

"What about all this stuff?' I called as they were halfway out the door. Their laptop, camera, and the rest of the abandoned movie equipment still cluttered one of the booths. "Why do you have all of this with you anyway?"

Kit spun around. "We were shooting exterior shots all day. One of our crew guys was late to his night job, so we had him drop us off here. Would you take it home for us?"

"Without a car?" I said, grabbing the giant light on the tripod. "Help me get this stuff into my office before you go."

I leaned the light into a corner of the tiny office. The umbrella diffuser flopped over like an overripe sunflower. Kit trailed behind me with the movie camera in her arms. She plopped it on my desk, on top of a pile of overdue invoices. Max came in with the laptop. "What about this?"

I waved a hand. "Anywhere you can find space."

Kit and Max slipped out of the office. My attention was focused on an invoice stamped thirty days overdue. I needed to get some money over to Tom Carrigan soon or we were going to be a diner without eggs.

Someone knocked lightly on the doorframe. Elliot stood in the door, holding a tangle of black cords.

"Hi," he said, stepping into the room. "Where do you want these?"

I looked around. There wasn't an empty inch of space. The dark room was already small on its own, but with Elliot inside, it felt smaller, intimate. His cologne wafted over to me. I pictured being in other small, dark rooms with him and felt my face flush at the thought. "Just toss them on the ground there. Anywhere is fine."

Elliot carefully placed the coil of wires down, then put his hands in his pockets. He looked around the cramped room. I followed his gaze, trying to see the office for the first time. There were no windows. Tacked up on the walls were yellowing family snapshots my mom and dad had stuck up over the years—Polaroids of Kit and me at Lake Willoughby, a picture of Mom and Dad in front of the diner on opening day, looking impossibly young. Mom was wearing a short Marimekko print dress, Dad a pair of faded jeans and the type of white uniform shirt that snapped up the front, the kind usually worn by the dishwashers. That was back when he worked the line. There was a photo of me holding baby Kit in my lap, and one of Mom holding baby me. The first dollar we made was framed on the wall, along with our licenses from the state. A promotional calendar from a meat salesman was tacked up, too, with reminders to call the Dumpster service and the air vent cleaning person.

"So this is the Miss Guthrie central?

"This is it. Sorry it's such a mess. I don't usually have guests."

"I like it. It's a nice surprise."

I laughed. "How so? Have the other diner offices you've visited been super organized?"

Elliot rocked back and forth on his heels. "No. But you're usually so—in control of things. It's nice to see that you make a mess here and there."

"You have no idea," I said. "I haven't seen you in a while. How've you been?" I tried to make this sound breezy, like I hadn't spent all of my free time thinking about him unzipping Sonya's light blue dress and watching it float to the floor.

"Busy. I've been to every town in the Northeast Kingdom. They had me down in the Barton area, scoping out options."

"Any luck?"

"Not so far," he said, but he didn't sound upset about it. "Still hoping someone might change their mind."

I laughed. "You are persistent."

"I tend to go after what I think is the right match."

I searched his face, looking for a double meaning, but he just looked like his pleasant self.

"Are you coming tomorrow night?"

For a moment I wasn't sure what he meant. "I'm sorry?"

"To the town meeting? If you need a ride, I could pick you up."

"I live right in town," I said, and immediately regretted it. It would have been nice to ride in his little car. I pictured us going for a drive down one of the back roads afterward. I could show him the road to the fairgrounds that was awash in golden beech leaves, so bright they looked like flakes of the sun.

"That's right," he said. "But you'll be there?"

"I wouldn't miss it."

Elliot smiled and rocked back and forth one more time. "I'll see you there, then."

"Okay." I picked up one of the invoices then, not sure what to do with my face, which I was sure showed every ounce of my excitement that he was here, in my office, asking if he would see me tomorrow night.

"Okay," he said, and lingered in the doorway just a second longer before he turned to leave. Kit appeared a couple of minutes later with the last of the cables. She pushed the pile of kitchenware catalogs aside and sat down on the edge of my desk. "So big-box guy was back here for a while. I didn't want to interrupt. What were you guys talking about?"

I waved my hand. "Nothing, really. He was just being helpful."

"That was nice of him." Kit looked at me for a long moment. "You know, in order to be helpful, you have to be around."

"Yes, I know."

"And according to Fern, he has been around—to be helpful—an awful lot, don't you think?"

"He doesn't have that much to do. He lives at the inn."

"Nora, my dear, sweet sister. I'd bet my share of the Johnson land that that man is interested in you."

"Kit—"

Kit held up her hand. "Hush. I've been wanting to say this to you for a while now. As much as I love Sean, I think it's time for you to get out there. Date a little. Move on."

"I know all of that," I said, pretending to be engrossed in *Diner Uniforms and More.*

"It's not like Sean took a lot of time before he—"

"I know." I said this more sharply than I meant to. I tossed the catalog into the trash. "It's not about Sean. I just—I'm not like you."

Kit leaned back and shook her hair, as if she were Rita Hayworth. "We can't all be like me. But that doesn't mean that you can't get busy with the developer."

"I can't."

"Why not?"

"I feel like I don't know how to—look, everything I know about dating and men I learned with Sean. When I was fourteen. I haven't—I don't know what I'm doing. And I feel like an idiot around him, and I—"

"Him, Sean?"

"Him, big-box guy. Elliot."

"So you do like him!" Kit clapped her hands together. "I knew it. This is awesome."

"Yes. I mean, no. I don't know! He's handsome—"

Kit nodded. "I can see it."

"—and nice, and thoughtful, and quiet, which is a great difference from Sean. And he seems to care about things."

"Things like . . . ?"

"I don't know. Birds."

Kit arched her eyebrows. "And?"

"Trees. Fruit? His family."

"Those are good things to care about." Kit leaned down so she could meet my eyes. "Now, I need to ask you something important. Have you shown him any encouragement?"

I leaned my head against the desk. "Maybe?"

"That means no."

"How would you know?"

"Nor, you can be a little . . . taciturn."

"I'm not taciturn."

"Have you ever noticed that all the guys that come in here are a little nervous around you?"

"Nonsense," I said, but an image of one of the delivery guys sputtering an apology for being a half hour late the other day sprang to mind.

"I bet there are at least three or four regulars who would love to ask you out—"

"No way."

Kit counted on her fingers. "Mohawk potter guy, hot microbrew guy, ridiculous cowboy hat, world's palest mushroom forager—"

"I don't think world's palest mushroom forager has the strength to stay up past eight."

"Not my point. My point is that you never act like you are

open to anything. Men need a little encouragement. Everyone does. I practically had to jump out of a cake to get Max to ask me out. No one likes rejection. How is Elliot supposed to know that you like him if you don't give him a hint?"

"I'm just not . . . a fancy art curator with a floating dress."

"Huh?"

"I'm terrible at flirting. I don't have an arsenal of fascinating stories to tell. I don't know how to be anyone but who I am, do you know what I mean?"

Kit shook her head. "Why would you have to be anyone else? You're Nora Huckleberry, diner goddess. Finder of lost dogs and caretaker of mysterious old women. Fixer of everything. Eccentric photographer of discarded food. You are basically the kindest person I know, and you've got that nineties grunge look going on. Everyone adores you. Why wouldn't Elliot?"

"I'm your sister. You have to adore me."

"Being your sister doesn't mean I have to adore you. But it does mean I need to tell you what I'm sure Charlie and Fern have been dying to say to you for a while. It's time, honey. Take a chance. Have a little fun. Enjoy something—or someone. Try doing something for the hell of it and see what happens."

"That's what Max said."

Kit smiled. "Well, Max is super wise. You know what else Max would say?"

"What?"

Kit stood and made herself as tall as possible. "There is no path to happiness. Happiness is the path."

"Does he ever drive you crazy with all the inspiration?"

Kit sighed. "All the time. Sometimes I just want to shake him until he says something sarcastic. I think that's why he loves me—I provide the snark." I was sure Kit brought a lot more than snark to Max's life. "But the even more annoying thing is that he's almost always right. It's been my experience that happiness does come from going toward all the things you love."

"Are you happy?" I asked her.

Kit thought for a long moment. "I really am," she said. "Now it's your turn. What's the thing you want to go toward?"

I thought of the picture I had taken a few days before of the lone piece of bread pudding in that large aluminum pan. "I have this idea for a series of paintings," I admitted. "Of last pieces of things."

"You are a total weirdo. I love it. Do you want me to pick up paints and a couple of canvases when we go get the car?"

"If you have time." Paint, canvases, brushes, and turpentine. Some sketch pads and charcoal, too. "I'll text you a list of what I need." I covered my face with my hands. "You really think Elliot might be interested?"

Kit got up and put her arm around my shoulder. "Nora. Why wouldn't he be? You are a beautiful, strong, creative woman. No one makes me laugh harder than you. And no one is more compassionate. And I don't see big-box guy pushing to get out of Guthrie, even after you foolishly turned down his bazillion-dollar, once-in-a-lifetime offer to buy the Johnson land. If anything he's been dragging his heels. I'm betting that's because of you."

I wriggled out of Kit's embrace but turned and gave her a quick hug. "You really think I'm beautiful?" I asked, piling my hair on top of my head and pouting my lips, giving her my best *Project Runway* model.

"Don't push your luck. Now, while I'm gone I want you to buy something other than overalls to wear to the town meeting."

I rode my bicycle out to Peggy's after work the next day, enjoying the slow ride up Pudding Hill. It smelled like fall—dried leaves, browning pine needles warming in the sun, freshly mown hay. I spent the afternoon swathed in bright orange, stapling NO TRESPASSING signs to trees along Peggy's property line. Bow-and-arrow season was about to begin. The mornings at the diner had already picked up with men coming into town early to stock up on firewood and food for their lodges, eager to try a new rifle, taking their teenage kids on their first hunt. I wouldn't be surprised if a few hunters took it upon themselves to take a chance on Peggy's land, knowing it was unattended, and I was worried someone would mistake the fringe of Freckles's tail for that of a white-tailed deer. I couldn't cover all the land by foot, but I wanted to clearly mark the areas around the orchard and garden, to discourage anyone from getting too close.

Fern came over to my apartment at five with a six-pack of IPA, which we drank while I showed her outfits I was thinking of wearing and Fern said *no way* to each of them. She ended up digging through the clothes my sister had left in piles behind the couch, and convinced me to put on a pair of Kit's jeans, which fit like leggings. I paired them with a fuzzy, dark red mohair sweater that my mom had knitted for herself. Fern thought it was too boxy, but I pointed out that the weather forecast had said a storm was headed our way, and reminded her of how chilly the town hall would be—the town never turned the heat on until after Halloween, actual weather be damned. Sexy would have to wait until June.

Fern and I arrived at the town hall early, while the high school kids were still setting up the gray folding chairs. We headed straight for the kettle corn line. Fern elbowed me in the side when I asked the scout for a single bag.

"Buy Elliot a bag and bring it over to him."

"He's here already?" I asked, ducking my head down.

"Up front, talking to Mrs. Fairbanks. It's perfect. You'll bring him the world's best snack and save him from having to talk about the Seed Savers' Club at the same time."

"What if he doesn't like popcorn?"

Fern gave me a squinty-eyed look. "Not the point, Nora."

"Fine." I handed the scout an extra dollar, and stuffed a third into the coffee can that had been decorated with construction paper. *Scholarship fund* was written in glitter paint around it.

Fern nudged me toward the stage, then took a seat in the back row. I walked down the aisle, feeling as if all eyes were on me.

My next-door neighbor Pat stepped into the aisle. "Hello there, Nora."

"Hey, Pat. Is your refrigerator still making that weird sound?"

"No, no. Your fix did the job."

Elliot was nodding in response to whatever Mrs. Fairbanks was saying, hand to chin, looking thoughtful. I felt my pulse quicken.

"I have something for you," Pat said, handing me an envelope.

"You didn't have to do that, Pat," I said absently. Elliot was smiling at Mrs. Fairbanks, but his expression looked strained. "You know I'm happy to help anytime I can."

Pat closed his hands around mine so that the envelope was secure in my hand. "I wanted you to have it. I have more. I think you might be interested."

Elliot looked over at me from across the hall. When our eyes met, he smiled wide and waved.

I folded the envelope and stuffed it into my purse. "You are the sweetest, Pat. Thanks." I gave his arm a squeeze before making my way to the front of the hall.

By the time I joined Elliot and Mrs. Fairbanks my cheeks were burning. I immediately regretted having worn red.

"Hello, Nora," Elliot said softly.

"Nora, we heard your sister has been doing some volunteer work over at the Pudding Hill House. Nice to see Katherine has the Huckleberry generosity you and your parents have always shown."

"She has been," I said. "She and her boyfriend, Max. Have you met him?"

"Not in person, but my friends over at Pudding Hill all adore him. One of them said he has tattoos of forties starlets all over his chest and back. Imagine that!"

I tried to think of what kind of class Max could have been teaching that gave him the opportunity to take his shirt off. "Some from the thirties, too," was all I could think to say.

"Can't forget Garbo," Mrs. Fairbanks said in approval. She looked over at the check-in table. "I'm neglecting my official duties. If you'll excuse me."

"Hi," I said shyly, looking at Elliot. He had on a purple-and-white-checked shirt that made his eyes greener. I handed him the bag of kettle corn. "I should warn you, once you start you can't stop."

"Thanks." He popped a few kernels into his mouth. "What's in this?"

"No one knows. We don't want to know. We just want those little scouts to keep making it."

We both stood in front of the stage, crunching. I started to become horribly aware of every kernel in my teeth. I felt as if a spotlight were on me, and the whole room could hear me chewing. I was suddenly desperate for a glass of water.

"Will you sit with me?" He moved his camel wool coat off of one of the folding chairs. I slipped out of the raincoat I was wearing and draped it over the back of one of the chairs.

As I sat down, my arm brushed his.

"This is nice." Elliot's hand reached out and touched my arm. He stroked it lightly, just around the wrist. I held my breath, not moving my body. I stared at his hand on my arm. His touch felt warm, his hand strong. The bag of popcorn slipped from my fingers and hit the floor.

Elliot seemed to wake up from a dream. "I'm sorry," he said. "Your sweater—it looks so soft, I wanted to see—"

"Mohair," I whispered. "From angora goats."

Elliot leaned in a little closer. He took the sleeve between his fingertips, rubbing it gently, as if studying the craftsmanship of the weave. The back of his thumb brushed my skin. "Did you knit this?" he asked, his head close.

I swallowed and shook my head. "My mom did. But the wool is from goats I raised. I helped spin and dye the fibers."

"It's lovely," he said, so close I could feel his breath on my ear.

"Thanks," I said, as if he were some knitting enthusiast I had met in line at the farmer's market. Really what I wanted was for him to reach up higher, to feel the sweater's softness from the inside out.

The pop and squeal of a microphone pierced the room. I suddenly became aware of the din of voices talking and laughing, the crunching, the squeak of the metal chairs. Elliot and I were only an inch apart. I leaned over and picked the popcorn bag off the floor. When I glanced at Elliot, his lips turned up in a slight smile. He focused on the stage, where the town manager was patting his jacket and pants pockets in search of his reading glasses.

Elliot kept his gaze on the stage, but leaned his head toward mine. "Nora, can I take you—"

"Here we are," the town manager said. "We've got some important announcements to make before I turn the meeting over to Councilman LaPlante."

Sean waved at the crowd from a seat on the stage. I hadn't even noticed him come in. He looked different tonight. The suit was gone, replaced by a dress shirt under some kind of high-tech-looking fleece vest. His dress shoes had been swapped out for a pair of expensive-looking hiking boots. I glanced down both front rows—Sean's girlfriend was nowhere to be found. I glanced back at Elliot. He smiled shyly at me in a way that made my stomach flip.

"Last report from the weather service was the storm has been downgraded. That means no serious winds, but we're still expecting heavy rainfall starting—"

As if on cue, the hall echoed with the clatter of rain driving into the long windowpanes. The audience erupted in laughter.

"—right about now, I guess. That's good news for the foliage season—no strong winds means hopefully the leaves will stay on the trees where they belong. Our friends over at the forestry service have predicted that we will be at peak color Columbus Day weekend and into the week following. I know many of us are counting on those tourist dollars. If everyone could take some time in the days leading up to that weekend to give their businesses a little spruce—"

My cell phone made a loud ping. The town manager glared down at me for a moment before continuing his plea for tidiness. I dug around in my purse, then sheepishly pulled it out to turn off the ringer. There was a text message from Max.

> **Forgot to tell you—the lady from the nursing home ordered a 10" burnt sugar cake! Said ours was just as good as Peggy's—even better. Couldn't say no. Pickup at diner, Thursday, 8 a.m. Me & K won't be back until Friday. You're on your own, kid. Just emailed you the recipe. You can do it! GO NORA THE CAKE LADY. ;)**

Thursday 8:00 A.M. was the following morning. I was going to have to bake the cake that night.

"—change your window boxes, sweep the sidewalk out in front—anything you can do to give Guthrie a little extra shine. We want to encourage people to come back, and to tell their friends. Should be a good weekend for the hunters as well. Might be a good idea for the hospitality businesses to bring on extra staff." The manager shuffled some papers. "Margaret Hurley from the Sugar Maple Inn tells me that the Harvest Festival dinner has sold out. If anyone has tickets that they can't use, she would be happy to offer a refund—she has a waiting list of hopeful diners. And let's see here. I think that's it." The town manager looked over the audience. "Time to get down to business. Councilman LaPlante?"

Sean walked across the stage and took the mic. "Thanks, Mr. Manager. All right, folks. I know you are all anxious to get home and get ready for the influx of tourists coming our way, but let's give our full attention to the matters at hand. First up—article one. Ben Smith has filed a complaint against John Hammond, owner of Sweet Pea Farm, stating that the farm has moved its manure pile too close to the Smith property. Mr. Smith, you have the floor."

Ben Smith walked up the steps slowly, leaning heavily on a cane. Sean met him over by the steps with a chair.

"Don't have much to say. John Hammond has been a good neighbor. But that manure pile is stinking up my whole house. Can't even enjoy a cup of coffee on my own front porch. The missus has started drying the laundry indoors. There are bedsheets hanging in the living room."

Mr. Smith handed Sean the mic and sat down.

"Okay. Mr. Hammond, would you like to respond?"

John Hammond was one of those enthusiastic new farmers who had moved to Vermont after getting his agriculture degree. He handed the toddler on his lap over to his wife, who already had a newborn in her arms.

"It isn't that we moved the pile," John explained when he reached the stage. "It's that we had to add another pile. Three actually. We added four sows this season, and we just haven't been able to keep up with—"

"Production?" Sean offered. He was always pretty good at smoothing things over.

John sighed. "Yes." He leaned over and addressed Mr. Smith directly. "We haven't been able to sit outside, either. I'm sorry."

Oona Avery, the new science teacher at the high school, stood up. "May I offer a solution?"

Sean beamed down at her for a brief moment. It took everything I had not to whip around and gesture to Fern. Sean took the mic. "Mr. Smith, Mr. Hammond, what do you think?"

"I'm all ears," said John Hammond.

"What do you have to say, young lady?" Ben Smith said.

Oona made her way to the mic in the center aisle. "There is no shortage of vegetable farmers in the area. Why not set up a co-operative manure exchange?"

"How does that work, Oona?" Sean asked. I had a sneaking suspicion he had already heard all about this over a candlelit dinner.

"It wouldn't cost a thing. We would just need to set up a website. Animal farmers with excessive waste can list what they have available, and the vegetable farmers can come pick it up. It would be like Craigslist, for manure. It's win-win."

Sean smiled as if she had just discovered the cure for cancer. "Let me get a show of hands from the vegetable farmers in the room. Would you be willing to shovel some crap to get free manure?"

Dozens of hands shot up.

"Mr. Smith? Mr. Hammond?"

"Sounds great to me," John Hammond said, as his face visibly relaxed.

"Mr. Smith?"

Mr. Smith scratched his ankle with the heel of his cane. "The missus might want some of the compost for her flower beds in the spring."

"Ms. Avery, are you willing to set up the website?"

"It would be my pleasure."

"Sounds like we have an agreement. Thank you, gentlemen, and special thanks to you, Ms. Avery. These kind of creative initiatives are what make a town like Guthrie thrive."

I could feel Fern rolling her eyes from the back of the hall.

John Hammond walked over to Ben Smith, and extended his arm to help him out of the chair.

"Okay, next up we have article two—Say No to HG petition—the Keep Guthrie Small coalition will present their petition and signature collection to the town. Come on up, Burt."

Burt Grant stepped onto the stage, papers in hand. He looked thinner than the last time he was at the diner, and the dark circles under his eyes gave him a raccoonish stare.

"The Keep Guthrie Small coalition has collected more than four hundred signatures, all verified, from Guthrie citizens who oppose changing the zoning laws in Guthrie to allow a large corporation such as HG to build within our community. Let it be a part of the official record—we want to keep Guthrie small. Small businesses, small community, small taxes. It's like what Sean just said—what makes us great is our ability to band together. Don't let some corporate giant come in and tell us what we need and want. It's only a matter of time before it starts making demands of us, not the other way around. Thank you." Burt handed the pages of the petition to Sean, but as he walked off the stage he looked defeated. No one applauded him off the stage. I turned around. More than half the chairs were still empty. Maybe it was the threat of the nor'easter—the farmers probably hadn't heard about the downgrade. A big storm meant a lot of work, harvesting pumpkins in case of flooding, mending weak areas of fences, and making sure the doors to the animal stalls were tight and secure. Checking the backup generators that would keep milk and cheese supplies safe and fresh. No matter what had kept the normally civic-minded citizens of Guthrie away from the town meeting, it didn't seem as if the bulk of the Keep Guthrie Small coalition had shown up to vote.

"Thanks so much, Burt," Sean said, turning the pages of the petition. "That's a lot of work right there. Let this petition be a part of the permanent record." Sean handed the pages to Mrs. Fairbanks, who was in charge of those sorts of things.

"Last on the agenda tonight, article three. Zoning—HG Corporation has asked about the possibility of rezoning the land owned by Nora Huckleberry LaPlante and Katherine Huckleberry, formerly the property of Peggy Johnson, for commercial use. HG made its case at the last town meeting, and I know there has been much discussion of the issue in both the *Coventry County Record* and the *Guthrie Independent*. Is there anyone who has something to add to the discussion before we take a vote? No one? All right. Should the town of Guthrie rezone the Huckleberry property for commercial use? Those in favor, say aye."

"Aye," said a good portion of the crowd. Elliot glanced over both his shoulders. He looked pleased.

"And those opposed to a change in zoning, say nay."

"Nay," said what sounded like the exact same number of people.

Elliot leaned over to me. "Now what happens?"

"This has never happened before that I can remember."

Sean looked like he didn't know what happened next, either. He stepped away from the mic. The town manager and Mrs. Fairbanks joined Sean on the stage, and the three of them talked quietly.

After a few long moments, Sean stepped up to the mic. "It's too close to call, folks. We're going to have to go to a show of hands. Troop 235, would a couple of you serve as assistant counters? I need one to count ayes and one to count nays. Come on up here, girls."

Two girls in green sashes marched boldly up the aisle, as if they had been training for this moment their whole lives. The brown-haired girl stood by Mrs. Fairbanks, and the redhead with the freckles went over to the town manager.

"Those in favor, say aye and hold up your hand."

"Aye," said Elliot, his hand waving.

"You're not even a resident," I said, pulling his arm down.

"You got a count, sweetie?" Sean said, squatting down to meet the scout at eye level. The girl nodded, her face serious. "Mrs. Fairbanks, you are both in agreement? Great. Those opposed? Say nay and hold up your hand."

"Nay," I said, my arm straight up in the air.

"Are you really opposed?" Elliot asked, looking a little hurt.

"You've known that all along. Besides, now our votes cancel each other out."

"Scout? Mr. Manager?" Sean handed the two teams pieces of paper. "Write down your counts and give them to me."

The two scouts sat on the floor, taking their time to form their numbers neatly. Each folded her paper in half and handed it to Sean.

"Votes in favor of changing the zoning of the Huckleberry land: 53. Votes opposed: 49. The Huckleberry land will be re-zoned to allow for commercial development. Town meeting is officially adjourned. Be safe, everybody."

Elliot Danforth stood up and draped his coat over his arm. I did the same. He cocked his head toward one of the doors that led behind the stage. I followed him, thinking he must have parked his car in the back lot.

When we were safely out of view, Elliot tossed his coat to the floor. He wrapped his arms around me, lifting me off the ground. "Yes," he said, spinning me from side to side before putting me down.

When my feet hit the floor his arms were still around my waist, and he was holding me lightly to him. I breathed in his peat fire and woolly scent. "This doesn't change anything, you know," I said, not wanting to break the spell, but needing to be clear.

"It does for me. Even if you don't sell to HG, it shows the company I'm good at my job. And it will make it easier for you to sell the land, no matter who you sell it to. That sounds like a win for both of us."

I smiled up at him. "To me, too."

"Celebrate with me. What are you doing tonight?"

"I have to go bake a cake." I have never felt so frustrated by a baked good in my entire life.

"Tomorrow night, then. Let me take you out. We could drive

over to Montpelier. I heard there are some nice restaurants over there." Elliot placed his hands gently on my upper arms and squeezed. "To be clear, I'm asking you out on a date. Will you go on a date with me, Ms. Huckleberry?"

"Okay," I said softy. "Yes. I'd like that."

Elliot lingered for a moment, his hands sliding gently down my arms, until he was holding both of my hands in his. He leaned toward me then, pressing his lips to the sensitive spot between my cheek and my ear.

A door that led to the front hall opened, and the muffled laughter of the teenage boys hired to clean up after the meeting filtered into the room. Elliot leaned his forehead into mine before letting go of my hands.

"I'll pick you up at seven," he said quietly. It sounded like a promise.

I ducked out one of the side doors and walked briskly down the sidewalk, holding the hood of my raincoat to keep it from flying off, avoiding anyone I knew. I wanted to linger in the moment, to remember the feeling of Elliot's hands in mine, and not get caught up in a conversation about my plans for the Johnson place.

I let myself into the diner through the back door and turned on the lights in the kitchen. Without a car it would be too difficult to get to Peggy's to bake the cake. And I was sure we had all the ingredients and a Bundt pan at the diner.

I sifted the flour and leavening while I played the short clip of Elliot's hand stroking my arm over and over in my mind. His touch was gentle, but not tentative. The soft feeling of his breath on my cheek, sweet and minty. The way the tip of his nose lightly skimmed the shell of my ear. The smoky scent of him. I liked the way he took his time. As I turned on a low flame under a pot of sugar I found myself wondering if he took his time at other things.

I was acting like a teenager, I mused, but that didn't stop my silly grin from growing a little wider. I tossed chunks of butter into the bowl of the stand mixer, covered them with sugar, and turned the machine on. It began to whirl. When was the last time I had felt desire? Sex with Sean had become like most things in our marriage, a habit, something that we did occasionally because we were supposed to, like going to church on the major holidays. I hadn't felt a true longing for Sean since we were in high school, and even then it felt more like escaping into something, disappearing, a break from all the pressures I was facing. When had I stopped seeing myself as a woman who wanted, who had dreams and ambitions and longings of her own? All of that changed when Elliot took his shirt off at the pond in the woods. What else had I stopped myself from wanting without even realizing it?

Kit had said to go toward what I love. But I wasn't even sure what that was. All I knew in that moment was that I wanted to paint. And I wanted to have someone look at me the way Max looked at Kit, as if he were a wanderer and she was home. And I wanted to know what it felt like to have Elliot Danforth's hands on my skin, beyond my wrist.

My cell phone buzzed to life on the counter. *Elliot Danforth* popped up on my screen, as if I had conjured him out of thin air. A wave of heat washed over my body. If he had been in front of me in that moment, and not on the phone, I would have pushed him into the corner booth and climbed on top of him. I switched off the mixer, pressed answer, and held the phone up to my ear.

"Nora," Elliot said breathlessly, and for a moment I thought he might be feeling the same way. "It's Freckles. He's shown up on the game camera we set up by the sugarhouse. He's in the cage."

"You caught him?" My mind scrambled, trying to switch gears. "He's in the trap?"

"Yes." He sounded elated. "Yes, I think we did. He's there, and the trapdoor is closed. He's pacing back and forth. He looks soaked to the bone, the poor guy. I called Erika. She's gone to pick up temporary fencing to put up around the trap so he doesn't bolt as soon as we open the door. Can you come?"

"My sister has my car," I said. "I'm at the diner."

"I'll be there in ten minutes," he said.

I grabbed my raincoat and keys, flicked off the lights in the kitchen, and locked the door behind me, ready to see what would happen next.

"The image was shadowy—the camera is set up pretty far from the trap. And the rain has fogged the lens up. But it's Freckles, that much I know for sure."

It was cozy in Elliot's little two-seater. He had the seat warmers on, and it felt as if I were sitting on someone's lap. The car raced up the dirt road toward the Sugar Maple, kicking up the water that had gathered in the ruts. It looked as if we were driving through a tunnel. The road was pitch dark, the rain beating down through the canopy of tree branches above us. Elliot reached over and squeezed my hand.

"I just can't wait to get ahold of him," he said, sounding like a little kid. "He's been out there for so long."

"Erika said it might take some time before he's comfortable with people again," I said carefully, not wanting him to be disappointed. I was bracing myself at the same time. I had read that it could take months, even years, for a dog to switch back from survival mode. Some never recovered. There were stories of dogs coming back to their old selves right away. But I worried that without Peggy, Freckles's chances were low.

"I had a dog that went feral after a hunting accident. I was around nine or ten. We never caught him. Every so often I thought I would catch a glimpse of him in the woods, but I was probably just seeing what I wanted to see. It would still happen years after he would have died of old age." He glanced over at me. "Even if Freckles doesn't come around, I'll just be happy to see him safe. How about you?"

"I want to do right by Peggy," I said, thinking about her and Elsie. "She left us everything. It was so generous of her. Making sure Freckles is safe is what she would have wanted. "

"I'm sure she would be grateful to you."

"It's funny. I thought I knew what her life was like, but I barely knew her at all. I had made all of these assumptions—but her life was much bigger than I imagined. She had a great love. And she was an artist—at least I think she might have been. At the very least she inspired one. It may have been her partner who made the sculptures, or they made them together, I'm not sure. But now I look at her flower gardens and taste her cakes and I can see what a creative person she was."

"It sounds like a good life," Elliot said softly. "And a meaningful one. Better than most."

"Do you think so?"

The Sugar Maple appeared before us. Elliot pulled around the building and into the back parking lot, the one nearest the crab apple trees. Erika's town truck was nowhere to be seen.

"I do," Elliot said. "There is a lot to be said for being a part of a community, and for taking care of the people in it any way that you can. And if you can do that, and make time to make something of your own . . ."

It was something my mom would have said. She would have loved Elliot. *Capable*, she would have said to me when we were in the kitchen doing dishes. That was one of her highest compliments. Along with *thoughtful* and *kind*. She would have said these things, too. She'd have teased him about his ears and put him to work replacing lightbulbs in the diner or weeding in the garden as soon as he arrived. At supper she would have peppered him with questions about birds and fruit trees and his childhood in Maine, and she would always have served his favorite dessert, no matter who else came to the table.

The windshield was blurry with rain. Elliot turned the headlights off. In front of us was complete darkness.

"Peggy's love, Elsie, is in a nursing home. I think it's why she was going to sell her land to HG. To pay for Elsie's care."

"Who is taking care of her now?"

I watched the rain rush down in thick rivulets.

"Wait. Have you been—?"

I nodded. "I've been paying the nursing home bills, and visiting Elsie—"

"And that's why you're selling the property. I always wondered why you weren't going to keep it for yourself."

"If it were just me, I might have tried. But half of it is my sister's. I can't afford to buy her out. There are liens against it, which you know. And back taxes. And Kit needed the money. All of that was already the case when we found out about Elsie."

Elliot blew out a long breath. "You take care of everyone, don't you?"

"Not everyone." Not myself, anyway.

"What are you going to do?"

I kept my gaze trained on the darkness in front of us. "Honestly, I don't know. I haven't received any other offers on the land. I'm almost out of money. The nursing home will be patient, up to a point, but I took out a loan . . . I'm sorry. I don't mean to burden you. This isn't your concern."

Elliot reached over and took my hand in his and ran his thumb over my knuckles.

"If I were a different man, I'd ask you if you were reconsidering my offer."

"I'm glad you aren't a different man." I stole a glance at him. When our eyes met, he squeezed my hand. I felt my pulse quicken, but I held his gaze. "And the answer would still be no, I don't think HG is good for the town."

"You want to know something?"

"What is it?"

"I don't think so, either."

"You aren't a very good deal maker, are you?" I laughed. "I thought a corporate developer was supposed to swoop in on the vulnerable seller and offer less than market value right about now."

He smiled. "Well. A person could argue that a good deal isn't just about money. It's about making a decision that benefits everyone."

"Is that HG's philosophy or just yours?"

"Let's just say they give me a certain amount of latitude to do the job, as long as I meet their quarterly goals."

Elliot looked in his rearview mirror. The rain was falling harder, fat drops pounding against the windshield and roof. "I wonder what's holding Erika up. Could she have come in a different way?"

The only other way into the sugar bush was the carriage path that connected the Sugar Maple to the McCracken farm, but you couldn't take a car down that way.

"No, this is it. Shall we go up and see Freckles? I hate to think of him nervous in that trap. And what if it's in a low area?" Freckles had been through enough without having to fear drowning.

Elliot leaned over and popped open the glove compartment, retrieving two flashlights. "Let's go make sure he's okay."

We walked slowly through the crab apple trees, the path impossibly slick with wet grass and mud. Elliot held out a hand and I took it. His hand was warm, his grip reassuring. We kept our flashlights trained to the ground. The wind picked up, blowing the rain into our faces, making it difficult to raise my head. Elliot walked confidently into the darkness. "I've taken this walk every day since I arrived," he called over his shoulder, guiding me around a tree stump hidden under a patch of tall grass.

There were no cheery lights on in the sugarhouse.

"The trap is just a short way up the carriage path." Elliot held out his arm. I slipped my arm into his. "This way."

Elliot called to Freckles when we were still a few yards away. "Hey, boy. We're here. It's okay." He aimed the beam of light at the corner of the woods. There it was, a sturdy wood frame covered in a thin chicken wire. At the base, the wire had been pulled out of the frame, exposing a ragged edge. We reached the trap. There was black fur caught in the raw ends of the wires.

"You're kidding me." Elliot squatted down, his fingers on the wire. "It looks like he gnawed his way out."

"Poor guy," I said, thinking of the time one of my goats chewed some wire fencing a blackberry bush had grown around—her mouth had needed eight stitches, and I had to give her antibiotics for weeks.

Elliot sat down on the wet ground, defeated. I sat down next to him.

"It would be nice if something were simple, wouldn't it?" I said.

Elliot pressed his palms into his eyes. "Yes, it really would."

I reached into my raincoat pocket and took out a clean wad of paper napkins from the diner. I handed half the stack to Elliot. He wiped at his face.

"Maybe he hasn't gone too far in the rain. Let's go farther up the path."

"I'm afraid even if we found him, we wouldn't be able to grab him. It would just be like all the other times. We need him contained."

Elliot's cell phone lit up in his jacket pocket, illuminating his face.

"Sorry about that. The main office is in California. I get calls at all hours." He plucked it out to turn it off, glancing at the screen first. "Oh." Elliot stood up. "We have to go."

"What is it? Was that Erika? Did she find him?" Maybe

someone had been able to catch Freckles because he was injured? It was a long shot, but I was ready to grasp at straws.

"Does Erika volunteer with the fire department?"

"All of the members of the force do. What's going on?" I scrambled to my feet and leaned over to read the text on his cell phone.

"It's the diner," he said, his voice barely reaching me over the sound of the rain. I was already running.

CHAPTER TEN

✦

A s you can see, the fire started here in the kitchen," the fire inspector said, pointing to the greasy black stripe that went up the wall behind the range. "Whatever started it seems to have fallen to the floor, and the fire spread from there." The wooden floors were original. I remember my father sanding and waxing the floor by hand. Knowing my dad, he had probably been more interested in using the most authentic floor stain, and not the one that was flame retardant. "Thankfully your gas setup was up-to-date and it shut itself off. Otherwise you could have been looking at a total loss."

The county fire inspector couldn't get over to the diner until Friday afternoon, after the nor'easter had passed. The kitchen was a blackened, sopping mess. The sprinkler system had done its best to control the fire, but had steeped the floor with water. After the system had been turned off, water from the storm had poured in through the roof and the broken windows. The firefighters had had to break the glass door and several windows in front to get in, and there were bits of broken glass covering the tables and benches out front. The electricity had gone out. A month's worth of hamburger patties and Boston cream pies were melting in the freezer.

I'd run the whole way to the parking lot after seeing Erika's text, falling twice in the wet mud, not realizing that I didn't have my car until I reached Elliot's. He'd been close behind me, and had driven me to the diner. By the time we'd arrived, the flames had been put out, but the head of the volunteer fire department wouldn't let me in until the next morning, when the fire inspector had made sure it was safe. I'd stood outside in the rain until Erika, who was concerned I was in shock, had gently pulled me away. She'd insisted on coming home with me to make sure I followed her instructions. Elliot had made me a cup of tea while Erika had helped me change into warm, dry clothes. They'd both sat with me until Fern came over, her kids in tow, to spend the night.

The fire inspector continued. "The building inspector has to come in. You know Doug, don't you? And your insurance guy. Have you called your insurance company?"

I nodded.

"Doug will have the final word about the structure, and of course it depends on your contractor, but I would say you are looking at three, maybe four months until you are back up and running."

"Three months?" In three months it would be the New Year. No leaf-peeping rush. No family breakfasts over the Thanksgiving weekend. No ice cream and pie for the kids after they went Christmas shopping with their moms. Three months of no work for Charlie and Fern and the rest of the staff. Three months of loan payments to make.

"Maybe four. Doug will have a better idea. Things will go faster once he says the building is sound." The inspector carefully walked over to the stove and kicked the charred remains of a saucepan. "Pretty sure this was the culprit. Went up fast. Do you know what it was?"

I nodded but couldn't make myself say the two words out loud.

Burnt. Sugar.

———————

Max and Kit were waiting for me in the apartment when I returned home from my meeting with the fire inspector. Fern must have called them. Kit wrapped herself around me while Max stood behind us, petting my shoulder.

"Are you okay? How is the diner? Is it fixable?" Kit asked in a rush.

I felt like I couldn't catch my breath. I extracted myself from Kit's embrace and sat down in the chair, needing some space.

"It isn't a total loss, but it's going to be months. I'm waiting to hear from the insurance agent. I'm pretty sure we're covered." Were we covered? I had just kept renewing the insurance my dad had set up years ago. Surely a restaurant must have insurance against fire. My heart pounded an extra beat.

"Do you know what happened?" Max asked. He and Kit had settled into the couch.

"You were right—I should have done my *mise en place*. I was distracted while making the burnt sugar cake, then I got a call about Freckles." I buried my face in my hands. "I thought I had turned the burner off. But now I can't remember."

"Why don't you come to New York with Max and me?"

My already-queasy stomach roiled at the mention of Kit and Max's New York trip, and acid crept up the back of my throat.

"It will be perfect, right, Max?" Kit said, grabbing his hand. "We were just talking about how sad we felt leaving you. We'd love to have you come with us. When is the last time you've had a vacation? This is, like, the perfect opportunity for you to get away for a while."

"Kit, I—"

"And you can take in all the museums while we edit during the day. The place we are staying at is pretty close to the Whitney. The library has passes. It won't even be that expensive."

"Kit—"

"You'd have to sleep on the couch, though. It's only a one-bedroom, but you've always said you wished you had adventures like—"

Max put an arm around Kit's shoulder. "I think your sister is trying to tell you something. What is it, Nora?"

"I didn't have my car. And the equipment was heavy. I decided to just leave it—"

Kit froze. She looked all around the living room, her head whipping back and forth. "It's not—"

"The laptop, the camera, the lights you left—they were all in my office. On the floor of my office. I don't think—" The scorch mark on the floor had led into my office. I hadn't looked in, not wanting to see the melted family photos.

"Om namah Shivaya," Max said quietly.

"Are you sure?" Kit stood and paced around the room. "You never would have left everything at work. Maybe you put the laptop in your safe? Most of the movie is on there. Or maybe the camera? You wouldn't have just left the camera—"

"There were the sprinklers, too, Kit. And the water from the hoses. And it was raining. There was water everywhere."

"Oh, my God. All of that work. The festival. We won't make the deadline, there's no way." Kit's words came out louder and faster as she talked. Watching her circle the couch made me feel even sicker. "We'll never have another opportunity like this. This was it."

"Kit, come sit down," Max said quietly, but I knew my sister. There was no calming her.

"I might as well quit now. My career as a director is over."

"I'm so sorry, Kit, I really am."

Kit sat down heavily on the couch. "I've lost everything."

"*You've* lost everything?" the words came out of my mouth before I had even finished thinking them. Kit reared back, as if I had slapped her. "Kit, the diner was all I had."

"I wish you could hear yourself, Nora. Can you really not see it?"

"What on earth are you talking about?" My mind flooded with all the times Kit had done what she wanted, all the things she wasn't afraid to ask for, all the risks she took.

"Honey, look around. You have everything. You always have. You have the diner. A place in the community. You're surrounded by friends. You've had a husband, and his family. You had Mom's love—"

"Mom loved you. You must know that."

"I know Mom loved me, but did she need me? Same with Dad. God, he looked to you for everything. Do you have any idea what it was like for me? You guys were like a team. I was always on the outside. Anything I have in my life now I've had to create for myself."

Her words ripped off the scab of a wound I thought had healed long ago. "I don't see what's so great about being needed. I've sacrificed everything I can to give people what they needed, including you. You had me. Doesn't that mean anything to you?"

Kit sank down onto the couch and rubbed her face with her hands. "Don't you think your resentment about being stuck taking care of me came through? Nora, you seriously have the worst poker face. Why did you think I kept so busy? And left as soon as I could?"

"Because you had the choice," I spat. "I didn't."

"Well, you have it now." Kit slapped her hands against her thighs. "No more diner," she said with a bitter laugh. "No more family to worry about. Go ahead and sell to HG. Pay off the bills. You're free, Nora. Let me know how great that feels."

Kit pulled her boots on and grabbed her coat. "Come on, Max," she said over her shoulder as she thundered out of the room.

Max lingered for a moment, then pulled on his jacket. He leaned down and kissed my cheek. "I'm really sorry about the diner."

"I'm really sorry about the movie," I said, barely able to choke the words out.

Max placed a hand on my shoulder and squeezed. "I know. She knows, too."

I drove for hours, around the town, down the highway, and on the back roads into Guthrie, my head spinning. Kit was right—I did have a choice now. Once we settled Peggy's estate, I would be free to do anything I wanted. But the only thing that I seemed to want to do was to stand behind the counter of the Miss Guthrie, pour coffee, and listen to the old men in the early morning talk about what they thought of the Little League team this year. The contractor Sean had recommended sent me over an estimate, as did the company who would desmoke the diner and clean up all the grease and soot. Insurance would cover most of

it, but anything cosmetic—like replacing the embossed aluminum backsplash that had melted in the heat—would have to
come out of my own pocket. And there was Elsie, of course.
Why hadn't I just followed Peggy's plan to sell all along? I am
sure she had weighed the decision as carefully as I had, and realized this was the only option.

The parking lot to the Sugar Maple Inn was full, so I parked
in the back, where Elliot and I had been just a few nights before.
I let myself in through the green door. The foyer and sitting
room were packed with men and women in sharp clothing,
drinks in hand.

I caught the eye of Sarah, the front-of-the-house manager.
She smiled at me from across the room and waved me over.

"Hey, Nora. We're all heartbroken about the diner. Is there
anything we can do?"

I looked across the crowded room. "Do you have any extra
work for Fern and Charlie?"

Sarah smiled. "I desperately need an extra server through the
holidays. I bet Alfred and Livvy could use a hand in the kitchen,
too. I'll talk to Margaret tomorrow morning and have her give
you a call."

A little wave of relief washed over me. "I'd be grateful."

Sarah poured champagne into a dozen glasses that were set
up on a tarnished silver tray. "I should get these out. Was that
what brought you here tonight? Charlie and Fern?"

"I was looking for Elliot Danforth," I said, feeling my cheeks
flush.

"He's in room 8, second floor. Go on up—he's in. I just saw
him."

"Thanks, Sarah."

I slinked my way through the crowd, conscious that my overalls and sneakers weren't exactly party attire, and for a moment wondered who all of these people were. They didn't look like the average leaf peepers.

I knocked quickly on room 8. Elliot came to the door in a faded Bates T-shirt and a pair of sweatpants. I almost didn't recognize him.

"Hi," he said, stepping aside to let me in the room. "Are you okay? Did you get my texts?"

Elliot had texted me several times since the fire but I had been too overwhelmed to answer him.

"I did, I'm sorry. It's been a rough couple of days."

Elliot slipped his feet into a pair of running shoes. "Can I get you something to drink? There is no room service, but I could run down. The chef showed me where they keep a stash of bourbon."

"No, thank you. I can't stay long." I did a quick scan of the room and sat in a chair next to a small desk. "I'm here to talk about the Johnson land. I'm ready to sell."

"Oh, Nora." Elliot pushed aside a folded pile of laundry and sat down on the bed. "What made you change your mind?"

"I have no other choice. It was what Peggy was going to do. I don't know why I thought I could come up with a better solution." I pushed the hair out of my eyes. "I need to move forward. Which means I need to wrap up the things in the past."

I had thought Elliot would be happy. It was what he had been sent here for. Instead he looked as if he had lost his childhood dog all over again.

"What is it?"

Elliot tapped his fingers together. "I already gave them my assessment. That I didn't think the community was a good match."

"You did what?"

"I agreed with you. I think HG would have a negative impact on the town."

"Couldn't you call them back? They liked the location, right?" My mind was spinning. Without HG, I had no options.

"I had a teleconference this morning. They had come to the same conclusion out there. They just started working with a new analyst, and the numbers came out weak."

"What does that mean?"

"They've decided to pull out of the Northeast Kingdom altogether."

"Oh," I said. "Oh."

That's when I noticed the suitcase.

"You're leaving."

"They're sending me to Tennessee," he said softly.

I nodded, looking around the room. The nightstand and the top of the dresser were bare. "When?"

"In the morning."

"Oh."

It struck me in that moment that my entire life had been one loss after the other—my mom, my dad, my sister, my husband, the house. Even my little herd of goats. And now this. It was just the loss of a beginning, but it was more than my heart could handle.

"I thought, maybe we—"

"I did, too."

My heart started to speed up, trying to get ahead of the tears that threatened to spill before I could make it back to my car. "I mean, I thought you, I mean we—I—"

"I did. I do." Elliot moved down to the edge of the bed and reached for my hand. "If I had any idea this was going to happen, that I was going to be leaving so soon, I wouldn't have—I don't know." Elliot turned away from me, but his grip on my hand grew stronger. "I'm so sorry."

I stood up quickly. His hand dropped into his lap. "Me, too," I said, not knowing exactly what I was sorry for. I felt sorry for everything. I walked out the door before he could try to start saying good-bye.

When I returned to the apartment, the stacks of screenplays, the Indian-print bag overflowing with scarves and embroidered tunics and vintage dresses were all gone, though the sweet honeysuckle scent of my sister still lingered in the room. I walked straight into my bedroom without turning on any lights, closed the door, and crawled into my bed.

I didn't leave my apartment for six days. Max texted from the road. He said that they had picked up their equipment from the diner, and a tech guru friend from the city was trying to dig deep into the hard drive to retrieve the movie files, but it wasn't looking hopeful. Kit was fine, he assured me, getting sunnier every day. He didn't mention whether the camera was reparable and I didn't ask.

The evening of day three Charlie and Fern showed up with the makings of Fern's margaritas and Charlie's portable karaoke machine. We got drunk and ate nachos and sang old Patsy Cline songs, which did make me feel better in the moment, but a little worse the next day. I was relieved to hear that the Sugar Maple had hired them both part time, and Charlie had hooked Fern up with a few shifts as a barback at the Bear Cub, which she said was so much fun I was going to have to offer her a raise to lure her back to the diner when it was up and running.

On day six I listened to all the voice mails I had been avoiding. Elliot had called several times, but left only one message, saying he would be in touch when he completed his project in Tennessee. Both the cleaning company and the contractor had questions, and the insurance guy needed me to sign some paperwork. Since my fax machine was melted into a bookcase in the office, I made a plan to meet him at the diner the next day.

I went in through the front door. The broken windows had been boarded up and the shards of glass had been swept away. The air still reeked of acrid smoke, and was dank, like forgotten towels left to fester in a heap. I ran my hand across the counter, relieved to see that the sparkly boomerang pattern wasn't stained. The Naugahyde stools and benches were covered in soot but looked cleanable. The old Dr Pepper clock had been hosed off the wall. One of the workers had placed it faceup on the counter, but the domed glass cover was cracked in several places.

A ragged hole remained where the old range had stood, dark and absent like a missing tooth. Wires and pipes were carefully marked, ready for their replacements. The walls and ceiling had been power washed, but the floor was still black and ashy—it would need to be completely replaced.

The smokiness mixed with the scent of industrial cleaner was making me dizzy. I went to open the back door and found a letter taped to the window from the outside.

Dear Nora,

So you'll always have a bit of the orchard, no matter who you sell it to. My dad said it's not the best time of year to do this, so it might take a season or two for the tree to bear fruit, but I think the best things are worth waiting for. I hope you do, too.

E

I looked out the screen door. Over by the picnic table, the little McIntosh tree my dad had planted was covered in what looked like white ribbons. I pushed my way out the door to have a closer look. Elliot had grafted eight varieties of fruit onto the tree, each carefully wrapped in thin strips of white fabric. One of the branches had a russet fruit dangling from it, the tentacle-like edges prickly to the touch. "A medlar," I said to myself. At the sound of those words, the fruit dropped to the ground with a heavy thud, and with it went all of my defenses. I sat on the table, my feet on the bench, cradling the fruit in my cupped hands, and let the tears come. I cried for my mom, who suffered for so long, and for my dad, who couldn't live with the loss. I cried for Kit for never having had true parents, and for all the ways I had failed her. I cried for my marriage, and for the years that I had gone through the motions, which hadn't been fair to Sean. For all the miscarriages. For the diner. For Peggy and for

Elsie, who both lost the one they loved. And I cried for myself, for all the years I had lost wishing for something to be different, and for all the wasted time not seeing what I had.

A twig snapped in the woods. I heard a rustling in the leaves. And then the bench shifted slightly. Nails scratched against the wood, and I felt the hot, sweet breath of a dog on my neck. A wet tongue raked across my cheek.

I looked up slowly. Freckles stood on the table, panting, his long pink tongue hanging out of the side of his mouth. He turned, and for a moment I feared he would jump off the table and bolt into the woods, but instead he turned around, and around, and around, before lying down next to me, his body flush with my thighs. Freckles laid his muzzle on my leg, snuggling in, and sighed heavily. I stroked the white stripe that ran between his eyes. When I rubbed around his velvety black ears, he moaned and leaned into me. When I stopped petting him for a moment, he pressed his head into my palm. I smoothed the soft, short fur on his muzzle, and under his chin, following the strong lines of bone. Freckles closed his eyes and licked his lips. I dug my fingers into his ruff, scruffing his neck, then smoothing down the fur along his back. He was a little thin, his tail and legs were covered in burrs, but his coat still looked shiny.

We sat there for what felt like hours, me crying and petting Freckles, working out the occasional burr, him sleeping heavily for what may have been the first time since Peggy had passed.

"All right, sweetie," I said softly, wrapping my arm around his chest and pulling him a little closer. "Let's see if we can get you home."

CHAPTER ELEVEN

Guthrie Front Porch Forum

Freckles Update—FRECKLES IS HOME

User: GuthriePD/DW

We here at the dog warden's office are pleased as punch to announce that after almost two months on the run, Freckles the Border collie has been found, and is safe, happy, and healthy. Thanks to everyone who pitched in: To the Haskell farm, which donated fresh meat for the trap, and everyone who left out kibble and water. The vet says he actually gained five pounds! To Burt Grant and everyone down at the Hammer and Nail for help with the construction of the trap. To Tom Carrigan for the use of his game cameras, and to the McCrackens and Margaret Hurley for letting us set up the trap on their land. And of course to everyone here on the forum who sent in tips. You made me proud.—Erika

Wanted: Small, dog-friendly apartment

User: MissGuthrieDiner

Hi, everyone. I'm looking for a small, affordable, dog-friendly apartment to rent. Extra bonus if it's sunny and has hardwood floors! Happy to consider any options, but dog friendly is nonnegotiable. If you know of a place, please leave a message for Nora at the Miss Guthrie Diner. 802-228-0424. (We're not open yet, but I check messages every day.)

Emergency Fund-raiser for the Miss Guthrie Diner
User: CouncilmanSean

I know everyone is missing the pancakes and corned beef hash down at the Miss Guthrie as much as I am—now is your chance to help. A fund-raiser will be held at the grange hall on Friday, October 20. We scheduled it to happen after peak color so all could attend. Both the Hungry Mountaineers and the Beagles are going to play all of your favorite dance and Eagles tunes. There will be a bake sale and silent auction. And yes, Troop 235 is making kettle corn. All proceeds go to the Miss Guthrie Emergency Fund. Dotty McCracken and Margaret Hurley will be handling all bake sale donations. If you have something you'd like to donate to the silent auction, contact Mrs. Fairbanks over at town hall. Help us show Nora Huckleberry how much the Miss Guthrie means to all of us. Any questions, shoot me an e-mail: slaplante@guthrievt.gov.

Call for Volunteers: The Pudding Hill House
User: PuddingHill

We have lost a couple of lively volunteers, and the residents of the Pudding Hill House deeply miss the creativity and fun they brought to our afternoons. Do you have a talent you'd like to share? Or a flair for leading discussions about current events or the latest bestseller? Or perhaps you are an expert at meditation or movement therapy? Come enrich your life and the lives of this vivacious group of seniors by becoming a volunteer at the Pudding Hill House. Please call M–F. Ask for Mary Beth.

The doors to the grange hall were wide open, and a warm yellow light spilled onto the wooden steps. I sat in my car and watched the activity inside, overwhelmed at the number of people who had come out to help me get the diner up and running. A part of me wanted to stay in the car and watch from afar all night, but Freckles started whining from the backseat, leaning over and relentlessly licking my neck and ears until I gave in and turned off the ignition.

Freckles hadn't left my side since the day he appeared at the diner. He was constantly underfoot, a half step in front of me, swinging his head around to make sure I was following him, even if it was just from the kitchen to the living room. He leaned against my thigh when I was decorating a cake, and he came in very handy when I dropped lumps of frosting or a bit of cake trimming on the ground. I carried the thick nylon leash with me, and attached it to Freckles's harness as a precaution, but really, I was lucky if I could even pee without the company of a one-hundred-pound herding dog. It was like having a giant, furry toddler.

"Go on in, Ms. Huckleberry," said the high school girls who were collecting donations at the door. The diner had sponsored their trip to the state cheer dancing semifinals two years before.

"Nora," Fern called from a table near the entrance. Both she and Charlie were dressed in their Miss Guthrie uniforms. Charlie had set up three George Foreman grills and was cooking up cheeseburgers, while Fern served sodas, passed out condiments, and collected donations for the food. Judging by the bulging pockets of her apron, it looked like people were being generous. Either that or everyone was paying in singles, which wouldn't be that unusual. As we approached the table, Charlie tossed Freckles a bun, which he wolfed down in one bite.

"It's so cheery to see you both back in action," I said.

"It's good to be back in action." Fern threw her arm over my shoulder. "It's fun over at the Sugar Maple—"

"But it's a little stuffy," Charlie said, handing a burger to one of the Beagles. Next to him, a tall, clean-cut man in a Miss Guthrie T-shirt with an apron tied around his waist handed Charlie a slice of cheese.

"Ignore him," Fern said. "He just hates being ordered around by Alfred."

"He's a tyrant," Charlie said, shaking his head.

"You don't like him because he makes a better omelet than you do," said the helper.

Charlie held his spatula up to the man. "Careful, those are fighting words."

Fern took Freckles's leash so I could shake off my coat. The room was packed with people, and had grown as hot as the kitchen in August. I tossed my coat behind the table.

"Amazing turnout, right?" she asked, handing back Freckles's lead. "We'll be open in no time."

"It's overwhelming."

Martin and Livvy McCracken were playing a jaunty fiddle

and banjo tune, with Tom Carrigan backing them up on the piano. Several couples were dancing in front of the stage. The line in front of Troop 235's kettle corn table was at least twenty deep, even though they were selling the bags for ten dollars a pop. Along the back wall Dotty McCracken and Margaret Hurley, along with this year's Mrs. Coventry County, were manning a long table that was crowded with baked goods.

I leaned closer to Fern. "Did Charlie hire someone when I wasn't looking?"

We glanced over our shoulders at the two men, who were giggling behind the counter.

"That's the karaoke guy from Burlington."

"Karaoke guy?" I asked, stealing another glance.

Fern nodded. "He's a sweetheart. They're sickening together. You'll adore him."

"Hey there, ladies," a warm voice said. I turned around to find Mary Beth from the Pudding Hill House. "Nora, do you have a minute?"

I glanced at Fern. She squeezed my arm and turned back to her duties at the burger table. "Let's go to the coatroom—it might be quieter there."

We closed the coatroom door behind us. The scent of mothballs and wet wool was dizzying.

"I'm sorry to bother you during this celebration, but I just got word this afternoon that there is a bed available for Elsie over at the nursing home down in Middleton. Should I start the paperwork?"

I should have felt relief, but instead my heart felt heavy. "Do I need to make the decision right away?"

Mary Beth looked at me with sympathy. "The beds get filled

so fast." She hesitated. "I don't usually offer my opinion when it comes to this sort of thing . . ." Mary Beth stood a little taller. "You've shown Elsie such kindness, Nora. But she isn't your responsibility. She'll get good care over in Middleton. I'd just hate to see—I'd hate to see you get dragged down by something like this."

I reached out and gave Mary Beth a hug. "Thanks, Mary Beth. I really appreciate it. Do you think we could wait until Monday? I'm signed up to lead a sculpture workshop over at the Pudding Hill House then. I can come early."

Mary Beth looked relieved. "They won't fill the bed over the weekend anyway. There's paperwork to be done. Monday is fine."

We opened the door and stepped out into a crowd that had gathered in the front hall. "It must feel good to see all these people come out for you."

"It really does," I said, and I meant it with my whole heart.

"Your parents would be proud to see how much you mean to everyone."

I followed a group of teenagers back into the grange hall, and made my way over to take a look at the bake sale table. There must have been one hundred plates. Tea breads and coffee rings, stack cakes and fruitcakes. Platters and platters of cookies of every stripe. There were crumb pies and double-crust pies, and pies covered in whipped cream and meringue. I found Erika with a Baggie full of buttercrunch toffee in her hand, over by Margaret Hurley, who was handling the cashbox.

"There's my boy," Erika said, leaning down to scratch Freckles behind the ears. He jumped up on her and placed his two front paws on her shoulders.

"Freckles," I said, giving him a tug on the harness.

"Oh, I don't mind," Erika said. "He's looking great, Nora."

"I brought him down to the groomer in Littleton to get all the burrs out."

"He's like a new dog. Mind if I take him for a walk around the parking lot? I could use a breath of fresh air."

I handed Erika the leash. "Be my guest."

"Don't worry. I won't run off with him," she said. It was good to know I had a backup in case I couldn't find an apartment that would accept dogs. We had been staying at Peggy's.

"There you are," a gruff voice said. "What did you think about that news article? Surprising, right?"

I turned around to find my neighbor Pat. His white hair was standing on end, and he looked a little like those troll dolls we had as kids. "I'm so sorry, Pat," I said. "I didn't get around to reading it." The residents of the Victoria were always sending me coupons they had clipped from the *Pennysaver* that they thought I might need, or stories from *Parade* magazine about some diner in Wisconsin.

"It's just one of many. She left boxes and boxes in her storage unit in the basement when they moved her over to Pudding Hill. Full of this sort of thing. Like that little bird I left you. Peggy said she would come get them, but you know how she always had her hands full."

Realization washed over me. "Wait. You left the little bird? Made of twist ties?"

Pat nodded. "There must be eight dozen of them. They'd look good on a Christmas tree. You could wire 'em straight onto the tree. Do you still decorate for Christmas? I've found since my wife died I've lost interest. Too much work."

I fished through my giant handbag, looking for the letter he had given me weeks before, at the last town meeting. My fingertips caught the edge of a piece of paper at the bottom of my purse.

The envelope looked worn. My name in Pat's shaking handwriting had been smudged. I tore open the flap. Inside was a faded newspaper article. I unfolded it carefully, trying not to tear it in two.

ART STAR DISAPPEARS AFTER MUSEUM RETROSPECTIVE OPENING. POLICE HAVE NO LEADS.

I flipped the article to face him. "Elsie?" I asked Pat. He nodded, and took a bite of a large molasses cookie.

Critically lauded sculptor Elspeth Coleridge, recipient of the MacArthur Genius Grant, has not been seen since the opening of her one-woman retrospective at the Museum of Modern Art. Attendees reported that Ms. Coleridge had appeared agitated and left the event early. Art consultant Franklin O'Connor, who runs Ms. Coleridge's business affairs, said that there appeared to be a few items missing from her apartment, among them a pair of dark red cowboy boots that she had possessed for over forty years and "wouldn't go anywhere without." Mr. O'Connor has filed a missing persons report with the New York City Police Department. Police say they have no leads.

"She was famous?"

Pat shrugged. "Looks like it. I remember when she first came to town. She was a real recluse. Didn't even come out for the Harvest Festival."

"I never saw her at the diner," I offered.

"They were going to toss all those old boxes once her apartment was rented out. That's your unit, you know."

I shook my head. "I didn't know."

"Seemed a shame to have some whippersnapper toss all of those old memories, so I took them. You can have all the boxes, if you like. I figure they're more yours than anybody else's. Stop on by. And if you could come tomorrow morning, would you mind bringing a stepladder and a couple of lightbulbs?"

I folded the article back up and placed it carefully in its envelope. "Sure thing."

Sean walked across the stage then, and tapped the mic. The Hungry Mountaineers stepped offstage and made a beeline for the Miss Guthrie table.

"Hey, folks, sorry to interrupt. Thank you all for coming out tonight to help support my oldest friend, Nora Huckleberry, and the Miss Guthrie Diner."

The crowd burst into applause. Margaret Hurley came to stand beside me, and patted my shoulder in support. "Just smile and wave," she said in my ear. "You'll have time to cry later when you have some privacy."

I obediently smiled and waved at the crowd.

"That's a good girl," she said.

"Now, before the Beagles start their set, I wanted to say a few words. Nora could have sold the Johnson land to that big-box store for a good chunk of money, but she didn't because she had all of you, and Guthrie, in mind. Nora loves our little town, and she shows it every day through her kindness and generosity at the diner."

"Nora," yelled Frank Fraser. He and his wife, Bonnie, brought both sets of parents in for breakfast every Saturday morning.

"Not many of you know this, but Nora has been struggling with a lot more than just the fire at the Miss Guthrie. She needs to tie up some unfinished business of Peggy Johnson's. Now I know none of us have the funds to buy the entire Johnson place, but I think if everyone in this room chipped in and took on an acre or two, we could make this happen. That way we would be keeping Guthrie small," Sean nodded to Burt Grant, who tipped his hat in response, "while helping out a friend. Oona, would you come on up here?"

Oona, the new science teacher, climbed up on the stage, holding a large-scale map of Peggy Johnson's property. She propped it up on a wooden easel that Sean had set up. It showed the farm and land broken down into small parcels. One of the lots was colored in red.

Sean continued. "So I am happy to announce that the town of Guthrie has authorized the purchase of two acres of land, to be used for the newly formed Manure Compost Project, which will be run by Oona Avery."

The crowd applauded, and Oona took a small bow. She leaned over into Sean's mic, their heads touching briefly for a moment. "We should have the compost sites set up within a few weeks, once the sale has gone through. Farmers, if you have manure to donate or are looking for manure, shoot me an e-mail. We'll have a website up with more information soon."

"Thanks, Oona," Sean said, smiling at her as she walked off the stage. "Now, as you can see, we chose a spot far away from any houses, so the smell won't be a problem. So what I want to ask you is, do you need a little bit more land? Is there a crop you'd like to grow but you have no space? Do your cows need more grass to graze on? Who here could commit to making an offer on a small piece of the Johnson property?"

The young farmer John Hammond raised his hand. "My wife has been wanting to start a pick-your-own-flower garden, but we didn't think anyone would want to come to our farm because of the pigs. We would take a couple of acres."

Sean wrote down the farmer's name on the map. "We'll work out the details about who gets which parcels when we find out who needs what. Now, who's next?"

Tom Carrigan raised his hand. "We just added dairy goats, and we can't keep up with their appetites. We could use an acre or two to plant clover."

Lewis, a logger who came in every day for breakfast, called out, "I don't need land, but I'd be interested in doing some selective cutting in the old-growth forest. We wouldn't have to clear-cut."

"Perfect. That's the kind of thinking we need. Who else?"

Acre by acre, farmers and loggers and community garden groups made offers on the Johnson property. By the end, more than half of the farmland was spoken for, and hunting rights and logging rights were on the table.

Sean beamed at the audience. He was joined by Amy, the Realtor who had been showing the property.

"And we've just had an offer from a conservation group that

wants to preserve the orchard and the woods surrounding it," Amy said into the mic.

Dotty McCracken gave a whoop, and the whole town laughed and clapped their hands.

"This is all pending the Huckleberry sisters' approval, of course," Amy said. "I'll meet with them to discuss the details. In the meantime, if you have expressed an interest tonight, come see me at the check-in table by the coatroom so I can take down your contact information."

"All right, folks. Now it's time to let your hair down—here are the Beagles!"

Tom Carrigan flicked on his amplifier, and the band, which had filed onto the stage as Sean talked, broke into a jaunty blue-grass version of "One of These Nights."

Sean wove his way through the crowd until he reached me. He looked uncertain for a moment. I wrapped my arms around him and squeezed tightly.

"Was that okay? You can say no to any of it. But it's a start."

"It is more than a start. It was brilliant," I said, breathing in his wood-chip scent. "Thank you for arranging all this."

"Anything for you, Nora. You know that, right? We'll always be family."

I rested my head on his chest for just a moment, and then pulled out of his embrace. "So, the science teacher, huh?"

Sean shrugged. "The intern was a little young."

I punched him in the arm. "You think?"

Fern came over to us and offered me her plastic water bottle. "We ran out of burgers. Shift drink?"

I laughed. "Not tonight. I have to get up early and help a neighbor with a few chores."

There were fourteen cardboard boxes in all. One was filled with gallery notices and beautiful glossy postcards of Elsie's larger works and site-specific installations. Another held copies of catalogs from various shows, leading up to her retrospective. There was one box of newspaper clippings. Some were reviews—one called her work "a refreshing meditation on the idea of impermanence." Others were about her disappearance. She had followed the story in the newspaper. I imagined she must have had the *New York Times* delivered—it wasn't carried at the White Market or at the gas station. After I did a bit of Googling, I found a long piece about her work and disappearance that had run just a couple of years before in *Vanity Fair.*

The other boxes held treasures from her life here in Vermont. Well-read children's books that were stained and dog-eared. Sketchbooks filled with drawings, with plans for the sculptures in Peggy's woods. And one was filled with love letters. Even though they lived only a few miles apart, they sent each other the most marvelous letters, filled with sketches and poems and made-up stories. A photograph had slipped out of one of the envelopes. It was a Polaroid of Peggy and Elsie that they had taken of themselves, leaning into each other, their hair slick with pond water, the trees with the clementine-net Victorian dresses dancing behind them. And in another box was a pair of well-worn cowboy boots the color of the oxblood stools in the Miss Guthrie. I pulled them on. They fit perfectly.

It took most of the afternoon, but I finally found the crumpled business card in the pocket of one of my work aprons. *Sonya Bellwether. HG Corporation. Art Curator.*

"Ms. Bellwether? I don't know if you'll remember me. I own

the Miss Guthrie Diner, up in Guthrie, Vermont. That's right, Elliot's friend." I took a deep breath. "I've discovered something about the sculptures, and, well, I thought you might be able to help."

The back of the Subaru was stuffed to the ceiling with bags of wine corks and pipe cleaners, bits of old ribbon and lace and spools—soft things that wouldn't bite into the seniors' delicate skin. I left just enough room for Freckles to sit in the backseat. I drove carefully up Pudding Hill Road, unable to see out the back, until we reached the nursing home.

One of the volunteers met me at the back door, and I left her to unload the car. Freckles and I slipped inside and headed straight for Elsie's room.

Elsie was sitting up in her bed, listening to the radio. I knocked lightly on the door.

"Elsie, I have a surprise for you."

Freckles took a tentative step into the room. The nursing home smelled like disinfectant, a little too much like the animal hospital, I imagined, and the waxed floors were difficult to walk on.

"Freckles!" Elsie cried out.

Freckles barked, then sniffed, then flew across the room and onto Elsie's bed, and began to lick every inch of Elsie's face, his tail wagging furiously, knocking a water glass and a vase of mums off her bedside table.

"Come on, you sweet old boy," Elsie crooned, her delicate hands wrapping around Freckles's ruff.

Freckles turned around and around in circles on her bed, his tail whipping Elsie's face. She giggled like a schoolgirl.

"There's a good dog," she said, her hands stroking his thick black fur. Freckles leaned his whole body against hers and sighed.

An attendant came in searching for the source of the crashing sound. He looked at Freckles on the bed and shook his head.

"He's a certified therapy dog," I lied. "His vest is in the car." I fished a twenty out of my pocket and handed it to him. "Could you keep an eye on these two for a few minutes? I have a meeting with Mary Beth."

Mary Beth waved me into her office, cradling the telephone between her head and her shoulder. *Just one minute*, she mouthed, and returned to her conversation.

I pulled out the printouts of the e-mails I had received from Sonya Bellwether. She had put me in touch with the head of a nonprofit devoted to caring for elderly visual artists, as well as Elsie's manager, Franklin O'Connor, who continued to oversee her business dealings. They explained that there had been a lot of interest in Elsie's work lately—several of her pieces had recently been sold at auction for more than double the expected price—and that the sculptures in the woods were potentially worth a lot of money. They set in motion a plan to collect and auction off the sculptures. All proceeds would go into a trust that would pay for Elsie's care, along with the money that Mr. O'Connor had safely invested over the years. It was all very hush-hush—no one wanted the press to catch wind of the fact that Elsie had been found before the sculptures were secured. We were concerned for Elsie's privacy at the Pudding Hill House. And I certainly didn't want to be bothered with a bunch of newspeople and art seekers trampling all over Peggy's land.

Franklin O'Connor called me late one night to confess he had hoped this had been Elsie's fate. "She always wanted to live a simple life. She detested New York, even though it loved her. When I noticed that her boots were missing, I knew not to worry. I knew she was off living her dream."

"Sorry about that," Mary Beth said, putting the phone back in its cradle. "I have the state paperwork right here."

"No need," I said, handing her the e-mails. "Tell them to give the bed to the next person. Elsie can stay right here where she belongs."

When I returned to her room, Freckles and Elsie were both asleep in the bed, and the attendant was napping in a chair. They all looked so peaceful that I decided to leave them be, and quietly closed the door behind me. I made my way down the hall to the dayroom to set up the materials for my sculpture class. My Keds squeaked on the newly waxed floor.

"Hang the screen from the top of the easel. That's right. You're an angel. Perfect."

I squeaked to a halt. That was Kit's voice.

In the back of the dayroom, a large screen was hanging crookedly on a black metal stand. A pair of hot-pink legs hopped behind the screen. Max was in the back of the room, stacking books underneath a projector that was attached to a new laptop.

"Someone turn off the lights," he called.

I stepped into the room and flicked the light switch off. Max adjusted the focus of the projector. "Excellent. We're in business."

"Excuse me, but I'm pretty sure this is the room I've been assigned for my sculpture class."

"Nora!" Kit ducked under the screen and ran toward me,

tackling me in the stomach. We flew back, landing hard on one of the sofas. "We're back!"

Max leaned down and kissed my forehead. "Good to see you, cake lady."

Kit rolled over and sat beside me on the couch. Max took the seat on my other side.

"We really missed you," Kit began.

"And we're sorry we took off," Max added.

"I would have done the same thing." I reached for both of their hands.

"No, you wouldn't have," Kit said. "You would have stayed and taken care of everything."

Max reached into his pants pocket. "We sold some of the lights and cables."

"And we got the deposit back from the editor and sound guys."

"They were really cool about it," said Max.

"And we hadn't spent *all* of the money," Kit said shyly. "Max, give it to her."

Max handed me a wad of cash. "It's almost seven grand."

"That you are carrying around in cash," I said, horrified. "You could have been mugged."

Kit and Max both laughed. "Who is going to mug us, droopy suspenders guy?"

"When you were on the road."

"Oh, Nora. The world isn't full of people out to get you, I swear." Kit reached over, took Max's hand with the money, and pushed it toward me. "Now take it. I was going to just give it to Mary Beth, but I thought you might need it to make a loan payment, or—"

"Keep it," I said, pushing Max's hand back. There would be

plenty of time to explain everything later. "Now, what's all of this?"

"It's our new movie," Kit said, leaping off the couch and hopping around the dayroom like a sparrow in a patch of breadcrumbs.

"But you couldn't—it's not *Side Work*, is it?" I would never be able to forgive myself for ruining their film, and their chance to show at the Premiere Festival.

"Nah," Max said. "Even the nerdiest of tech guys couldn't grab it off the hard drive."

"But this is even better, Nora. We can't wait for you to see it. It's called *White Oaks of the Northeast Kingdom*."

Max punched a few keys on the laptop. "Check it out."

Kit flopped back down next to me on the couch and leaned her head against my shoulder. The first image was of Dotty Mc-Cracken and Margaret Hurley.

"Guthrie wasn't such a big town, the way it is now," Dotty said, looking at Margaret.

"And girls weren't allowed out with boys by themselves, not like kids today."

"So we'd go out in groups," Dotty explained. "I'd tell my parents I was going to the fair with Margaret."

"And I'd tell mine I would be with Dotty."

"Which wasn't a lie."

Margaret shook her head. "We respected our parents."

"But we still liked to have a little fun."

Margaret went on to tell the story of the first time she was ever kissed, on top of the Ferris wheel at the Coventry County Fair.

The next person on the screen was my neighbor Pat. He told a story about the year a nor'easter hit Guthrie during mud season, and how the town flooded so bad the only way to get help was by rowboat.

"This one's my favorite," said Max.

June, one of the Pudding Hill House residents, began to speak. "All of the able-bodied men were off at war. So the women stepped up. We ran the tavern and the market. One of my sisters took over her husband's butchery. Everyone said her cuts were cleaner. We tilled the land and grew our own crops, and still found time to knit sweaters for the boys overseas when we heard they were freezing. No one wanted to say this out loud at the time, but it was hard when the men came back. We had learned something about ourselves. We were strong on our own. It was hard to put that knowledge aside."

Frame after frame, the wrinkled faces of the oldest residents of Guthrie told stories about the town, how it was made, how much it was loved, how it was home.

The last image of the film was of Elsie. She was in a chair in the sitting room, a bright yellow cardigan buttoned up to her neck. She had a serene look on her face. Kit could always bring out the best in everyone.

"I knew the minute I pulled into town. There wasn't much there, just a post office and a general store, the tavern. That funny chime of the bell on the town hall. The people were kind, and the landscape was an inspiration. I thought I might have found the right place, and then I knew I had."

"When you met Peggy," Kit's voice offered.

"When I met Peggy." Elsie smiled. "What a spirit. That woman is a force of nature. You know the first thing she did when we met? She baked me a cake. Burnt sugar cake—have you ever tasted a cake like that? One bite of that cake, and I knew I had found where I belong."

The film ended, and the room went dark. I rubbed my eyes with the sleeve of my sweater. Max flicked on a light. Kit was perched on the edge of the couch, like a bird of prey. "What do you think?"

"It's beautiful, Kit. It truly is."

Kit let out a whoop, and pulled me up off the couch and into her embrace.

"The festival accepted it. We just heard today. They said they loved the grainy look, and the *Our Town* feel."

"Kit pitched it as a modern-day *Our Town*."

"We have a few more interviews we'd like to shoot."

"Does that mean you're staying?" My voice may have gone up several octaves, and tears threatened to spill down my face. In public.

"Do you mind?" Max stood behind Kit. He put both of his hands on Kit's shoulders.

"Of course I don't mind," I said, wiping at my face with my shirtsleeve. "This is still your home."

"About that." Kit looked up at Max. "We wanted to ask you. When we finally sell the land, what if we held on to Peggy's house?"

"I've got so much to tell you. We have offers on about half of the acreage. If you agree, and the offers come through, it would be enough to settle her estate, and then some. Maybe if we use whatever's left to pay off part of the Miss Guthrie loan, the bank might lower the payments." I watched as relief poured over Kit's and Max's faces. "But," I said carefully, "not selling the house would mean there wouldn't be a nest egg for either of us."

"A home is like a nest," Max said.

"And what we really would love is a home base for us to come back to," Kit said softly.

"For when we are in between projects," Max said.

"And for the holidays. Can we get a live tree? Like we used to?" Kit had always picked out the largest, fullest tree on the McCracken lot. On more than one occasion we had to saw the top right off to fit it in the house. Mom always said angels were overrated.

"I want to go on the sleigh ride through the McCracken farm that I've been hearing about."

"And sugaring season. We can come home for the Mud Season Spectacular!"

"Both of you?" I asked, looking up at Max with raised eyebrows.

Max raised his eyebrows back at me and patted the pocket of the shiny black vest he was wearing over a Metallica T-shirt. The pocket bulged out a little. I hoped she would say yes. "If that's cool with you," Max said.

And just like that, I had a family again. People to take care of. I wouldn't have it any other way.

CHAPTER TWELVE

❧

Three months later

The painting of the half-eaten jelly donut fit perfectly between the windows that lined the Worcester dining car. I had restored the diner almost to its original glory, but I took a few liberties. The Formica counter and the oxblood benches and stools I kept, of course. But I got rid of Mom's checked curtains and let the light pour into the dining room. The Dr Pepper clock was replaced by a large stainless steel one with a bright white face and stark black numbers. I took down all the generic New England prints of covered bridges and tree-lined dirt roads and hung up the paintings I had made while I waited for the renovation to be completed. The real changes happened in the kitchen, where I redid the floors with fireproof material and a larger convection oven. That way I would have a place to bake cakes without having to listen to Charlie complain about lack of oven space whenever I had baking to do.

I was rehanging the HOMEMADE DESSERTS sign—baking cakes wasn't so hard; I thought I might take a stab at making a few pies, maybe a bread pudding—when the little bell over the front door tinkled.

"I'm sorry, we aren't quite open yet," I said over my shoulder. "Just waiting for our final inspections. Hopefully by next week."

"That's too bad," said a calm, steady voice. "Can you recommend a place to get coffee? I'm new in town."

I turned slowly around. Elliot was sitting at my diner counter. He rested his arms on the Formica, leaning forward. He looked eager. His ears were bright red.

"New in town?" I asked, my hands shaking.

Elliot smiled up at me. "I just moved in. My nonprofit bought the orchard on the old Johnson property. I'm the new orchardist."

I turned and walked over to the coffee station where I had just brewed a pot of decaf for myself, unable to suppress the grin that threatened to take over my face. I poured coffee into two thick Miss Guthrie cups, and topped them both with cream. I carried the coffees around to the other side of the counter and slid onto the stool beside him.

"That means we're neighbors," I said, swiveling in my seat to face him. When he did the same, our knees pressed against one another. "I live in the little house by the orchard." I held out my hand. "Nora Huckleberry."

Elliot took my hand in his. It felt warm, strong. Capable. "Nice to meet you, Nora Huckleberry. Elliot Danforth."

"Good to meet you, Elliot Danforth." I raised my coffee cup. "Welcome to Guthrie."

Burnt Sugar Cake with Maple Icing

❧

INGREDIENTS

For the syrup

    ½ cup sugar

    ½ cup boiling water

For the cake

    3 cups all-purpose flour

    1½ teaspoons baking powder

    ¾ teaspoon baking soda

    ½ teaspoon salt

    9 ounces unsalted butter, at room
       temperature

    1 cup sugar

    ½ cup light brown sugar

    3 eggs

    2 teaspoons pure vanilla extract

    1 cup sour cream

    ½ cup burnt sugar syrup

For the maple icing

    ¼ cup unsalted butter, at room temperature

    ¼ teaspoon salt

    2 cups confectioners sugar

    1 teaspoon pure vanilla extract

¼ cup maple syrup

2 tablespoons heavy cream

To make the syrup

A quick note: Remember Max's rules for working with sugar syrup—never walk away from it, and never touch it. Caramelizing sugar is an extremely hot process. Please use caution.

Place the sugar evenly in a pan and turn the burner on high (a cast-iron skillet is great for this). Let the sugar melt. You don't want to stir the sugar—it will form sugar crystals and clump up—but you can gently move the pan to swirl it. The sugar will dissolve, then start to turn light brown. While the sugar is cooking, boil the water. When the sugar has turned to a golden amber color and is smoking a bit, take it off the heat. Very carefully drizzle in the boiling water. It will sputter when you do this—make sure you are wearing long sleeves. Return the pan to the heat once all of the water has been added, and stir until combined. Set aside to cool.

To make the cake

In a medium-sized bowl, sift together the flour, baking powder, baking soda, and salt. Set aside. In the bowl of a stand mixer (or using a hand mixer), cream together the butter, sugar, and light brown sugar until it is light and fluffy. Add the eggs one at a time. Add the vanilla extract. In a separate small bowl, mix together the sour cream and a ½ cup of burnt sugar syrup. You will have extra syrup. Save it—it's delicious in coffee!

Add ⅓ of the flour mixture to the butter, sugar, and eggs, mixing just until the flour is incorporated, then add ⅓ of the sour cream/burnt sugar syrup mixture. Repeat until you have a uniform cake batter, taking care not to overmix. Scoop the batter into a well-greased 10–12 cup Bundt pan.

Bake at 350°F until the top springs back when you press it and a cake tester comes out clean, about 1 hour.

Let cool completely before unmolding and icing.

To make the icing

In the bowl of a stand mixer, beat together the butter, salt, and confectioners sugar. Add the vanilla extract and maple syrup. Add the heavy cream one tablespoon at a time, until the icing is a nice, spreadable consistency.

Place the cake on a platter. Using an offset spatula, spread the icing over the top of the cake.

Acknowledgments

❧

With boundless appreciation, I would like to thank the following people who made this book possible:

My fierce, fearless, and funny agent, Alexandra Machinist—thank you for all of your work, advice, and friendship. Thanks to Hillary Jacobson, Christina Lin, and everyone at ICM. And to Sophie Baker at Curtis Brown—thank you for finding homes for my books across the sea.

My editor Pamela Dorman and assistant editor Jeramie Orton—thank you for your thoughtful, insightful editing, and for all the work you have done to bring this book out into the world. I am so proud to be a part of Pamela Dorman Books.

Thanks to the whole team at Viking Penguin, including Brian Tart, Andrea Schulz, Lindsay Prevette, Kate Stark, Allison Carney, Mary Stone, Jessica Fitzpatrick, Roseanne Serra, Sandra Chiu, Megan Gerrity, Cassandra Garruzzo, Megan Sullivan, and the whole sales team at Penguin Random House. Special thanks to copy editor Jane Cavolina, who paid such close attention to every detail, down to the number of eggs cracked.

Heaps of thanks to Karl Kruger, sales rep extraordinaire, wonderful book champion, and most excellent brunch partner—the best part of publishing a book is the friends you make along the way.

I am filled to the brim with gratitude for Kate Racculia and Erika Swyler, who are the best author-mentor-friends a writer could ask for. Thank you so much for all of your advice and guidance.

Thanks and appreciation to J. Ryan Stradal, Beth Harbison, Erica Bauermeister, Ellen Airgood, Natasha Solomons, Brenda Bowen, Mameve Medwed, and Juliette Fay for your generosity.

I have been so lucky to have the support and friendship of two fantastic book lovers—thank you to Pamela Klinger-Horn and Robin Kall Homonoff for everything that you do for authors. I am so happy to know you both.

Thanks to all the indie booksellers, librarians, and book bloggers who recommended my first novel to readers. I am so grateful.

And to the readers—thanks so much for the notes, the e-mails, and the reviews—you have made my dreams come true. With extra special thanks to Mike McCarthy, reader-turned-friend, for all of your cheer. I hope every author has a reader like you.

To chefs Luc Robert and Charlie Binda, and to the whole staff at the Union Club of Boston, thank you for making it possible for me to have both a pastry chef life and a writing life.

Screenwriter, filmmaker, and old friend Jim Picariello answered my indie filmmaking questions. Thank you for sharing your knowledge and joy.

Thank you to all of my dear writing friends, especially Cathy Elcik, Jennifer S. Brown, Susan Bernhard, Chris O'Connor, and Lissa Franz, who all thought I could write another book. Thank you for cheering me on.

And thank you to Carter Winstanley for telling me that developers in novels are always made to be the bad guys. As soon as you said this, I knew how the book would end.

To the Albritton family—Bill, June, and Brit—thank you for all of your encouragement.

If you met Carol Rizzo, she probably tried to sell you a copy of my first book. Thank you for everything, Mom. I love you.

To my extraordinary sisters, Brenda Miller-Holmes and Lisa Cataldo—the kindest, strongest, most creative, big-hearted people I know—I am so proud to be your little sister.

To my dad, the late Douglas P. Miller, who dreamed of having a little breakfast-and-lunch place, thank you for all of those meals at all of those diners. Everything I write is in some way inspired by you.

And most of all, thanks and love and gratitude to my Elizabeth Albritton, who was right beside me, helping me at every stage of the process of making this book, from first spark to the final pages. You make my writing, and my life, better in every way.